THE CURLEW'S CRY

Other Novels by Mildred Walker
Available in Bison Book Editions

FIREWEED

WINTER WHEAT

MILDRED WALKER

THE CURLEW'S CRY

Introduction to the Bison Book Edition by
Mary Clearman Blew

University of Nebraska Press
Lincoln and London

First Bison Book printing: 1994
Most recent printing indicated by the last digit below:
10   9   8   7   6   5   4   3   2   1

Library of Congress Cataloging-in-Publication Data
Walker, Mildred, 1905–
The curlew's cry / Mildred Walker; introduction to the Bison Book
edition by Mary Clearman Blew.
p.   cm.
ISBN 0-8032-9757-2 (pbk.)
1. Women ranchers—Montana—Fiction. 2. Dude ranchers—
Montana—Fiction. 3. Ranch life—Montana—Fiction. I. Title.
PS3545.A524C87   1994   93-43768
813'.52—dc20   CIP

Reprinted by arrangement with Mildred Walker Schemm.

∞

October 5, 1954

INTRODUCTION

By Mary Clearman Blew

I was fifteen years old when I found a newish copy of *The Curlew's Cry*, by Mildred Walker, on the shelves of the old Carnegie library in Lewistown, Montana. Today a copy of that same mottled hardcover edition, which I ordered this summer through interlibrary loan, lies on my desk. Its corners are frayed and its pages as soft as dust, and it reminds me of my younger self who checked it out and carried it home with her usual armload of historical novels and discovered that it spoke to her in a way none of her previous reading had ever done.

The Curlew's Cry is about a smalltown Montana girl who graduates from high school in the fictional town of Brandon Rapids, Montana, in 1905, leaves home briefly for a short, sad marriage to a wealthy man in the East, and returns to Brandon Rapids to live out her life. Pamela Lacey is bright, evasive, lonely, brought up in the openness of the West, fiercely loyal to her heritage, and yet full of doubts about that heritage as it seems to stifle her ambitions. For me at fifteen, Pamela was an older fictional self with whom I could identify. She was also an assurance that the real place where I lived and my struggles with its landscape and ideals, with my half-understood conflicts and hopes, were valid topics for a writer.

This summer I reread *The Curlew's Cry* with the sensation of double vision that many readers experience when they return to old favorites. Pamela Lacey is still Pamela, bright, evasive, and lonely, and I am still her partisan; but, while I can clearly remember my indignation at age fifteen at the conclusion of the novel, I am no longer certain that Mildred Walker allows Pamela less from life than Pamela can claim. I am struck by Walker's understated wisdom and humor, and I am startled at how she anticipates the themes of myth and the past, independence and community, freedom and restriction, which many western writers and historians are exploring today.

The questionable glory of the pioneer past, for example. Walker suggests that it was already a cliché in 1905:

> The teacher was weary with Pioneer Day before it started. There was one every year; the chances were there always would be one as long as she taught in Montana. Each year she asked for suggestions from the class and each year they gave the same worn-out ideas for the float that would represent Room 21. The same worn-out themes: Crossing the Plains, the Road Agents, the Vigilantes, the Gold Strike, the Shooting of Rattlesnake Jake. These Western children were more conscious of their pioneer past than New England children were of the Pilgrim Fathers. (p. 9)

Worse than a cliché is the past as obsession. Harmless old Mr. Sewall in the Brandon Rapids hardware store, for example, devotes most of his time to keeping the records of the Montana Pioneer Society, which detail a history of a mere fifty years but saddle the children with an impossible and self-contradictory ideal of the past. The teen-aged Pamela, typing his speeches for him, comes to know by heart sentences like

> We must realize that the pioneers who braved the hardships and dangers of this then unknown territory are the aristocracy of this great state and the roll of their names is a proud roll. They were guided by a dream . . . perhaps a dream of gold, a dream of peace after the inferno of civil war, of greater opportunity for their children, but a dream! (p. 93)

An obsession with the past is no longer harmless when it distorts the present. Pamela adores her father, an old-style Montana cattleman who seems to her a model of the strength and daring that settled the frontier. But when Charlie Lacey is ousted from his position as ranch manager by his eastern partners when he secretly borrows money against the company, Pamela begins to see her father's risk-taking as foolish and his settle-with-a-handshake code as naive. The very qualities that settled the frontier are a liability in a modern business climate.

Torn between loyalty to her father and disgust at his flaws, overly sensitive to implied criticism from friends, Pamela quarrels with Wrenn, her high school sweetheart, and loses him to her classmate Rose. From this point, Pamela not only must resolve her feelings about the West and its myths, represented by her father and his ranch hands, and the East and its pretensions, represented by her mother and by handsome Alan (nicknamed "the lady cowboy" by the ranch hands), but she also must come to terms with imperfection before she can find a place for herself.

Alan offers Pamela marriage and an affluent life in the East, but she can tolerate neither his condescension nor his finicky manners. Certain only that she belongs in the West, she allows Alan to divorce her, returns to Brandon Rapids and converts the old home place into a successful dude ranch, rescuing her parents from penury but in the process alienating her father and the ranch hands, who cannot abide the glossy surface of the new venture.

Admired but unloved, Pamela finds herself more and more alone. She discovers she has fallen out of love, indeed become disenchanted, with her lost sweetheart. She rejects a chance of remarriage to a pompous young man who is willing to overlook her status as a divorcee for the sake of her bank account. As a single woman who does not subscribe to traditional women's activities—socials and clubs and gossip—she is out of place in Brandon Rapids.

And yet a place for herself is difficult and painful for Pamela to establish. Not even the ranch offers her a secure haven. Ruby, the tough ranch cook whose pithy advice has guided Pamela to womanhood, continually points out that she is not a man and never really can head up a cattle outfit. The best she can achieve—the dude operation—is a pandering of her heritage and a fraudulent reflection of the real thing.

I remember at this point becoming angry with Mildred Walker's plot line. What is Pam supposed to do? She has had the guts to leave a stifling marriage and live on her own, supporting her parents as well as herself, and then she is punished for her courage by being made brittle and shallow. Where did Ruby get off, I wanted to know, turning up her nose at the dude ranch and walking away from Pam? Where did Charlie Lacey get off, leaving Pam alone on the ranch so he could hang around the bar in the Western Hotel and drink and reminisce about the glory days? And Pam herself, agonizing over her failures as she tries to write her mother's obituary—why does Pam have to carry such a burden of guilt and loss? Pam muses:

> How did that heritage of the Pioneers help the sons and daughters? It taught them how to live when life was exciting, not when one day followed another . . . how to live when you had found your lover, who loved you, not how to make your life rich and full and sweet when you were that awkward person known as a spinster. . . . Mr. Sewall had willed her the hardware store because he felt she would carry on the myth, and what had she done? Helped explode it by making a dude ranch out of the N Lazy Y. (p. 344)

In 1987 Mildred Walker read an essay of mine in which I argued that, in her three Montana novels, she looks thoughtfully at the conventions which thwart her heroines and assesses the penalties they are likely to pay for walking their own way. She appreciated my thoughtful reading of her novels, she wrote to me, but she thought I had missed the main thrust of *The Curlew's Cry*.

I had written:

> In *The Curlew's Cry* (1955), Walker explicitly identifies male and female territories with West and East. Pamela Lacy is first seen arguing for space for women on the Class of 1905's traditional high school Pioneer Days parade float. "Does it have to be divided?" Wrenn asked. "Couldn't it be the women weeping over at one side and hiding their eyes?" Instinctively they all looked at Pamela. She clasped her long fingers tightly together on the desk and lifted her chin in a little gesture of decision. "They wouldn't go to the hanging. They'd be sitting home waiting for someone to come and tell them it was over," she said sadly (p. 12). When the float appears, it depicts not only the predictable Vigilante hanging, but also an interior scene where women weep under a banner labeled HELPLESS HEARTS HURT MOST. Wrenn's question—"Does it have to be divided?"—and Pamela's answer sum-

marize the questions and answers about men's and women's territories provided by the rest of the novel.

Mildred Walker did not intend to stress the West, in *The Curlew's Cry*, as a man's brutal world in which women have no place, or to characterize men and women as separate human beings who are basically opposed to each other's worlds. "The concept of the Wilderness grew and grew for me as I wrote, and kept changing," she wrote to me after she read my essay. "In *Curlew's Cry* it meant loneliness, being unloved and finally loving no man. I wanted to get a certain atmosphere into that novel so I wrote these paragraphs, that I'm taking the liberty of enclosing, to keep it before me."

Her paragraphs follow:

"Women in the early West often heard the curlew's cry. . . . in the lonely places where the wind blows the prairie grass and weights it with the dust. Cry of the curlew . . . or cry of the loneliness those women feared . . . sharp as the edge of a green grass blade, piercing the stillness like a woman-scream, freezing the blood with an instant of fear, and making the blood contract [crossed out] congeal.

But once the towns were built out west, and tied together by twin lines of steel, women lived on streets, with neighbors, and counted themselves safe from the curlew's lonely cry. They filled their lives with love and hate, and talk and busyness. . . . as women always, everywhere.

Yet out beyond the Western towns, where the prairie grass still grows, and down by the river's edge, the curlews walk stiff-legged, long billed, and curious. And a woman still may hear that cry, that harsh curlee-li-li flung back on the wind from the bird's swift flight down the sky . . . sharp as the edge of a green grass blade, piercing the stillness like a woman-scream, lingering on the brain longer than the wire-thin whistle of the midnight train."

In a handwritten note at the bottom of the page, Mildred Walker adds, "Do curlews fly? I'm not quite sure. I'm enclosing this just to show the feeling which I aim [for] in this novel."

Now, as I reread *The Curlew's Cry*, I am struck, of course, by the

recurring theme of loneliness. But I am also struck by Pam's am-
bivalence about Brandon Rapids and the ranch. Homesick, she
leaves Alan and a comfortable life in the East to return to Montana, but she can't find her bearings as a single woman in the
West. Sometimes she perceives her family ties as a trap, as when
her mother's heart attack keeps her from the adventure of going
to France during World War I as an ambulance driver, or when
her father asks her for a loan that she can barely afford to give
him.

Does Pam love the N Lazy Y ranch? Without hesitating, she
uses a small inheritance to pay off her father's mortgage.
"'Wrenn advised me to invest the money, and I'm not sure he
isn't right, but I wouldn't like to see that ranch go out of the family,' Pamela said. It was better than saying as she had to Wrenn, 'I
love that ranch.' He had probably told that to Rose, and Rose
had pitied her because she had no husband to love (p. 302)."

I think perhaps Pam finally is incapable of loving wholly. Her
feelings for Wrenn are mixed until she loses him, and then she
mainly feels wrath at Rose for what she sees as her friend's be-
trayal. And Pam constantly feels torn and reacts defensively
when she sees the weaknesses of her mother and father. She cannot accept imperfection. She instantly drops the most interesting of her later suitors, a labor organizer from Butte, when she
sees him drunk. Eventually she perceives even Wrenn as weak.
And Pam fears weakness; her father's, Alan's, Wrenn's, and finally her own.

The weakness in the men in Pam's life has a direct correlation
to the pioneer spirit. The autonomy and independence cherished by the mythmakers are the ruin of her father when he
comes up against a modern banking system.

Although Rose's mother, an independent woman herself,
points out to Pam that she must gamble if she is to succeed with
the dude ranch, Pam worries that her father's gambler's instinct
will be the ruin of her, too.

So what kind of a life is possible for a young woman who has
come of age on the last vestige of the frontier and who has absorbed its values along with its harsh physical demands? Can
such a young woman ever accept the constraints of a traditional

female role? Can she assume fully a male role? If not, what space is left for her, and what air can she breathe? What will she do for friends, companionship? Can she ever love a man? Rose's mother tells her, "It is very great pleasure to be independent and know you do it yourself (p. 303)." But Madame Guinard is a widow who must have loved her husband passionately, for she told Rose years ago that real love was "ecstacy."

What hope, finally, for a single woman?

> A shadow fell dark across Rose's face as a bird swooped down to the river's edge, cutting the stillness with its shrill curli-li-li. . . .
>
> Rose sat up. "What's that?"
>
> "Nothing but an old curlew bird," Pam said. "Curlews always make that sound. Ruby says it's the loneliest sound she knows."
>
> "It scared me," Rose said promptly.
>
> "Not when you know what it is. At least, I'm not afraid of it," Pamela answered. (p. 134)

As it turns out, Pam will need the courage to face life on her own. Her life will seem set on a lonely course, caught as she is between the shadow of the past and the prospects of a bland future. But Pam finally will face loneliness head on, when, at the conclusion of the novel, she turns to a surprising source for a measure of balance and satisfaction in her middle years.

When I was fifteen, I thought Mildred Walker was punishing Pam for her strength, that the conclusion of the novel was forcing Pam to settle for a foregone conclusion. But I now believe that Mildred Walker has allowed Pamela to draw strength from the land and, in her maturity, to reach a level of forgiveness and tolerance that may even allow her to love. I am very glad that the University of Nebraska Press, in this new edition of *The Curlew's Cry*, will make available to a new generation of readers a portrait of a remarkable woman coming of age in Montana in the first half of the twentieth century and living with the tensions of western mythology and her own nature in a way that anticipates so much contemporary writing in the West. Pamela Lacey is still Pamela, and I am still her partisan.

PART ONE

1905-1907

" 'We are young;
Oh, leave us now, and let us grow:' "
—Edwin Arlington Robinson,
Cassandra

CHAPTER 1

1905

The teacher was weary with Pioneer Day before it started. There was one every year; the chances were there always would be one as long as she taught in Montana. Each year she asked for suggestions from the class and each year they gave the same worn-out ideas for the float that would represent Room 21. The same worn-out themes: Crossing the Plains, the Road Agents, the Vigilantes, the Gold Strike, the Shooting of Rattlesnake Jake. These Western children were more conscious of their pioneer past than New England children were of the Pilgrim Fathers.

She wrote the titles on the blackboard so that they could vote on them, and tried to remember that these subjects were fresh and exciting to the children even though they bored her. The Vigilantes won the vote. The boys applauded so loudly she had to hold up her hand for silence.

"Can I hold the rope?" one of the boys asked, and loud laughter filled the room. They always staged the float the same way, as a hanging.

A slender arm was raised in the back of the room.

"Yes, Pamela?"

"Why don't we divide the wagon and have the hanging at one end and at the other end have some women sitting waiting and looking sad?" There was a clear enunciation about Pamela Lacey's voice that made it stand out.

"Naw, we don't want any women in on this," Bill Kossuth declared.

The color rose in Pamela's face and flooded the high forehead to the pompadour of fair hair. "But it just happens that they were in it, Bill Kossuth, and they have their own way of taking things. Besides, it would be different. You have to have something different if you want to win a prize." She sat down.

Hands flailed the air. Some of the pupils talked aloud without bothering to raise their hands.

"You need the whole wagon to do it right. You oughta have one of those pioneer courts at one end and a tree . . ."

"Sure, you gotta have a big tree to look like anything!"

"Class, we won't get anywhere if you're all going to talk at once," Miss Ferris said sternly. "Yes, Wrenn?"

Wrenn Morley stood to speak. As son of one of the town's lawyers he had a feeling for authority.

"I think Pamela's idea about having the woman's side of it would be different, and we don't need the court to give the idea of a trial." A murmur of disagreement began but Wrenn raised his voice. "Besides, it would be fairer!"

There was a quick short laugh from the back of the room. Even as Miss Ferris nodded approval at Wrenn she saw that Pamela Lacey was twisting the end of her hair and her face was flushed. A boy leaned over and poked Wrenn in the ribs and the girl beside Pamela whispered something to her. A titter ran over the room.

"I think we've had enough discussion. The idea of trying to show the women's part in the early days is a very good one. All those in favor raise their hands. Those opposed."

The opposition emphasized their feeling with stamping feet, but there were three more girls in the senior high-school class of 1905 than boys.

"Since it was your idea, Pamela, I will appoint you chairman of the girls' end of the float and . . ." Miss Ferris glanced quickly over the room trying to pick fairly . . . "Rose Guinard will work with you, and Alice Reed and Mary Marsten. You can get to-

[10]

gether with the boys' committee and I'll appoint Bill Kossuth chairman, and to work with him, Wrenn Morley, John Donaldson and Sam Heccla." As Miss Ferris was fond of saying to other teachers, her class was a perfect melting pot; all the different sections of the town's population were represented, the Finns and Southern Europeans brought in by the smelter, the Irish and Canadians, the old vigilante aristocracy, from both New England and the South, and she made a point of mingling them whenever she could.

The committee met after school, the boys sitting on the desks rather than in the seats: Bill Kossuth was a little uncomfortable as chairman.

"Any of you fellows got ideas about where we could get a tree for the hanging?" he asked, ignoring the girls.

"We gotta have it high enough so the road agents' feet are off the ground," John Donaldson insisted. "There's plenty of trees we could get, but making 'em stand up in the wagon that's the hard part."

"I suppose there has to be a hanging," Wrenn Morley said slowly.

"Wrenn, we'd have to have a hanging," Alice Reed said. She was short and plump and looked too gentle for such a statement. Sam and John nodded. The hangings of the vigilantes were symbols of early-day justice; as familiar to them as the sign of the cross. They had all seen the gnarled old cottonwood down by the river where more than one desperate holdup man had been hanged. They had picnicked under it and made jokes about it; the boys had pretended to be hanging from it, but more than one of them had shivered a little passing it alone at dusk on a winter's afternoon.

"Some road agents were hung from a beam in that store in Virginia City," Wrenn suggested.

"No," Pamela Lacey said. "A tree is more dreadful." She looked away from them to the window but none of the young trees planted by ordinance of the city fathers reached the second story of the new brick high school.

[11]

"Why don't we let the boys figure that part out? I've got to go to a music lesson at four-thirty," Mary Marsten said. "Let's us fix up our half of the float."

"Does it have to be divided?" Wrenn asked. "Couldn't it be the women weeping over at one side and hiding their eyes?"

Instinctively they all looked at Pamela. She clasped her long fingers tightly together on the desk and lifted her chin in a little gesture of decision. "They wouldn't go to the hanging. They'd be sitting home waiting for someone to come and tell them it was over," she said sadly.

Rose Guinard twisted one black curl as she listened. Her big dark eyes studied Pamela's face. She was adoring that light straight hair and the narrow nose which contrasted so sharply with her own round nose.

Bill Kossuth scratched his ear. "Are they the wives of the road agents or of the vigilantes or what?"

Pamela hesitated only an instant. "Probably of the road agents, but it doesn't make any difference, Bill. They're worried and they hate killings and all they can do is sit and wait."

Bill didn't see. His face showed his disgust. "Then we oughta leave 'em home and not have 'em on the float. They'll just spoil it."

"The class voted, Bill. We can't go back on that," Wrenn said, but it didn't seem like such a good idea to him now either.

"We could fix a wall with logs on one side and wall paper and lace curtains on the other for the inside of the house," Mary Marsten said.

"If we can get one of the lumber wagons we'd have a lot of room," Sam Heccla offered. "My Pa could loan us one."

"And we'll all wear old-fashioned dresses. I guess everyone has something she can wear," Pamela said as the girls went down the stairs.

"I haven't," Rose said. "My mother's got a dress from France I could wear, with a lace cap . . ."

Pamela looked at her as though she had never seen her before.

[12]

She saw her in some foreign dress like pictures in the geography book. Rose had only lived here two years. Last year she had been a new pupil. She wouldn't know anything about all this. "You can come home with me and find something. We've got lots of old clothes in the attic," she said.

"So've we, trunks of 'em." Alice smiled a superior little smile at Pamela. "We've got my grandmother's going-away suit she wore coming up the Missouri." She slipped her arm around Pamela's waist at the door. "Wrenn Morley said he thought we should have the women on the float just because of you, Pam."

"He certainly did not," Pamela answered. "He said it because it was fair," but under her eyelashes she glanced across at the boys' walk where Wrenn was waiting. She was sorry that Rose was coming with her. Wrenn often walked home with her. He came along now and took her books.

"What do you think we ought to have for signs?" he asked.

"Oh, we could have *Pioneer Justice* on your side and *The Woman's Part* on ours. Whenever you think of something write it down and I will, too, and the rest of the committee can," she added for Rose's benefit; "and then we can choose. Do you want to come and try those clothes on today, Rose? There's no hurry," Pamela said as they turned north from Main Street.

"Sure. It don't make any difference," Rose said, noticing with pleasure the way Wrenn Morley moved over to walk on the outside of the street like a real gentleman. She was glad she had worn her best corset cover today if she was going to try on clothes at Pamela Lacey's. She blew at the cotton fluff that floated in front of her face. "Look at that, it must come from those cottonwood trees down by the river!"

"They travel miles," Wrenn explained in a lordly masculine way. "That's the way new trees get planted."

Rose laughed so loudly she startled Pamela and Wrenn. "Not many got planted, then! I never saw a place so bare of trees unless you call those little things trees." She jerked her head at the bare saplings planted at regular intervals along the street.

"Some day these will be great big trees," Wrenn said.

They came to the Morleys' house before Pamela's, but usually Wrenn walked on home with her. Today he stopped in front of his own steps.

"Good-by, Wrenn," Pamela said quickly, echoed by Rose. She glanced up at the front of the house and waved to Mrs. Morley who was watching them from the curved windows in the turret at the corner of the second story. Two rows of colored glass panes, red and blue, bordered the window and threw a purplish light on Mrs. Morley's cheek and hand and shirtwaist.

Rose wondered what it was like inside that curved window. She wished Wrenn would ask them in.

"I'll see you after supper, maybe, Pam," Wrenn said.

"Good, because I'm going out to the ranch with Papa to-morrow."

"You forgot her books," Rose giggled.

"Here," Wrenn said and a flush mounted up under his hair that was only a shade darker than Pamela's. "Good-by, Rose," he added politely. He wasn't prepared for the sudden flashing smile Rose turned on him. He had hardly noticed her in school before.

"He's about the politest boy in the class," Rose said.

Pamela smiled, accepting the compliment calmly as a verification of her own feeling about something that belonged to her. "He is going to be a lawyer," she added. "They have to be polite."

There were three vacant lots next to the Morleys' house and you could see way across to the mountains beyond the town. The prairie grass that had been yellow all winter had paled to white, but new green was pushing from the deep-matted roots of the virgin sod. The spring wind rattled the empty milkweed pods and bent the faded grass against the ground.

"I'd like to build me a house here," Rose said. "Of red brick with stone trim and a big porch. Then I'd be neighbors with you and Wrenn Morley."

[14]

Pamela scowled at such a thought. "I hope nobody ever builds on these lots."

"I don't see why," Rose said. "There's plenty of vacant lots beyond this one, nothing but vacant lots."

CHAPTER 2

The Lacey house had an Eastern look to its long narrow windows and spindled balcony but there was a Western indifference in the sparse and scraggly shrubs against the porch and the thin dryness of what should have been a lawn but was only grass. In fifteen years' time the wind and sun had scoured most of the paint off the clapboards on the western side of the house but the north side was still decently covered with white paint. The brass knob of the door was polished and heavy lace curtains hung stiffly at the plate-glass windows. The wind blowing across the empty prairie could roll tumbleweed right up the front walk and lodge it securely in the corner by the steps, it could seed thistles in the front yard and sift dust from the flower beds underneath the windows but that was as far as it could go. The heavy draperies and carpets, the very house itself, shut out the atmosphere of the crude new West.

"Come on in," Pamela said, pushing open the door.

The front hall seemed dark after the thin white light of the spring day, and very still after the wind. Portiered doorways led into the library on one side and the dining room on the other and the only direct light came through the lace-curtained windows of the front door. A high chest of drawers faced them and a wide gold-framed mirror hung above it.

Rose's bright eyes moved quickly around the hall. There was no lace or crocheted runner on the chest of drawers. At home above the millinery shop, every surface was always covered by a doily. Only a marble clock stood on the top. There was a big fern on a high table by the hatrack and a scalloped dish beside the plant held two calling cards.

"The clothes are all up in the attic," Pamela said, starting up the stairs. "You can leave your books on the hatrack."

They went faster than Rose wished, past a room with a four-poster bed and a room with a brass bed and a bathroom with a long claw-foot bathtub. The stairs to the third floor were not carpeted and led to an unfinished chamber, but the front window was as well curtained as those on the lower floors. Rose hurried across the room and knelt by the window that came within a few inches of the floor. She had looked up at this window from the street many times and thought it must open into a handsome bedroom. It was really a kind of sham, like the skirt that made her mother's chamber chair look like any other. The street was different from up here. The spindly little trees showed a green that you didn't see when you were beside them.

Pamela threw back a trunk lid and pulled out clothes recklessly.

"These are about the oldest. That brown mohair dress my grandmother wore on the covered wagon. Here, try this one."

Rose stepped out of her own dress conscious for a moment of her well-rounded bosom beside Pamela's flat chest. She retied the lavender ribbon that ran through the embroidery on the top of her corset cover.

Pamela asked suddenly, "How old are you?"

"Seventeen."

"I'm sixteen," Pamela said.

The dress Pamela gave her smelled old and the silk felt papery thin.

"That's too tight," Pamela pronounced. "Maybe you could fasten it with safety pins and wear a shawl. Here, this looks bigger."

"Oh, let me try the red one," Rose said, seizing on a red silk with a satin stripe. She had to hold the red silk dress together in front and draw in her breath in order to fasten the belt but her cheeks grew red from her exertions and she burst out laughing.

Rose was pretty, Pamela thought, almost with surprise that anybody so . . . so different could seem to her actually pretty. Her teeth were little and as shining as the whites of her eyes, but mostly, it was the way she threw her head back when she laughed.

"I'd starve myself, but I don't suppose I'd be thin enough in time for the float," Rose said. "Why don't you make this over for yourself, Pam? I would. Look at all the material there is!"

"Oh no. My grandfather brought this dress to my grandmother the first time he went back east. It came up the Missouri by boat."

"It's good yet, though."

"But it's historic, Rose! Don't you see?" Rose was the first person she had ever met who wasn't impressed by pioneer things. But Rose was trying on another dress.

"There's more material in this one. My mother could let it out and put it back just as it was afterward. You must save all your old clothes and furniture and things," she said, looking around the attic.

Pamela laughed. "I guess we do."

"Pamela!" a voice called. It sounded a little cross. Rose stepped swiftly out of the black silk and put her own dress back on. Pamela went to the stairway. "We're up here."

"What on earth are you doing upstairs? Mamie said she thought she heard you come in."

Rose laid the other dresses back in the trunk. The black one she folded neatly over her arm. Maybe Mrs. Lacey would mind her borrowing the dress. She watched Pamela to see if she was scared; she didn't seem to be.

"We have to get some costumes for the float on Pioneer Day. We'll be right down."

Rose followed Pamela down the stairs. She had seen Mrs. Lacey before in the millinery shop and thought she was very fashionable, but she wasn't today. Her face was hot looking and there was a smutch of flour on her cheek.

"Pamela, did you forget that the gentlemen from the cattle company are coming tonight?"

Rose was so close behind Pamela that she could feel her catch her breath.

"Oh goodness! And Mr. Randell and Mr. Crawford will be here . . . oh, Mother, this is Rose Guinard. She came home with me to get a costume."

"How do you do, Rose," Mrs. Lacey said in a very friendly way, but she added, "What dress did you take?" Rose held it out hoping Pamela wouldn't say anything about her having to fix the waist because she had a feeling that Mrs. Lacey wouldn't like it. "It's a lovely dress," she said, not so much because she thought so as because it would please Mrs. Lacey.

"Yes, it is," Mrs. Lacey said, much as Pamela had agreed to Rose's praise of Wrenn. "Be very careful of it, won't you? Sometimes I think I ought to give these old clothes to a museum, they're so historic. Both Mr. Lacey's father and my father were here in the early days, you know.

"Pamela, I've been waiting for you to come so you could run over to Cora Morley's for me and get five tall-stemmed goblets. She has them all packed. I need them right away." She took out one of her combs and catching back the loose locks around her face fastened them in more securely with the comb. "Come out through the back way, girls, Mamie just washed the porch."

Pamela looked at the dining table with pleasure. She was glad Rose could see it. The table was set with the best damask cloth that fell in shining stiff folds almost to the floor. In between occasions she forgot how elegant the best silver was and that the butter knives did look like Turkish scimitars with their notched blades. The silver candlesticks were on the table, and the fern from the taboret in the parlor had been used as centerpiece. The late sun glanced off the cut-glass rest for the carving set.

"Oh," Rose said. "You're having a banquet."

"The cattle company men are coming from the East. We always have them to dinner," Pamela explained. She hoped Mama would let her sit next to Mr. Randell; he was the nicest.

How had she forgotten anything so exciting? Then she remembered it was the meeting about the float.

Meringues were spread out on a blue towel in the pantry, like pieces of white cloud. The best dinner plates were piled there, too, and the silver gravy dish.

"Hello, Mamie, this is Rose Guinard," Pamela said as they pushed open the door into the kitchen.

"Pleased to meet you," Mamie said. She was cutting cabbage for coleslaw and didn't stop.

"How do you do," Rose said politely, wondering if Mamie were full-time help or just for dinner.

"Hurry right back, Pamela, because they'll be here on the six o'clock train."

"Is Papa back from the ranch?"

"No, and I don't understand why he doesn't come. It makes me so nervous I could fly!" Rose stared at her, seeing the bright spots in her cheeks, her hair slipping down in back, her hands gesturing as she talked. She wondered what Mr. Lacey was like, and what Mrs. Lacey would say if he didn't come!

Outside the house the street seemed calm and cool after the busy kitchen. "I'll walk over to Morleys' with you," Rose offered. She was loath to leave so much excitement. Anyway, she and Pamela Lacey were friends now. Then her curiosity forced its way into a question. "Does Mrs. Morley have your glasses?"

"No, we always borrow back and forth for company," Pamela explained. "Wrenn's mother always borrows our six-yard tablecloth. Her father and my grandfather came out the same year." Rose pondered that. How funny; Pamela meant came west, as though that made them relatives.

"See you tomorrow," Pamela said when they came to the Morleys'. Rose was sorry because she would have liked to go in with Pamela, but something in her tone of voice made it too difficult to say so. After a few steps she turned around and watched Pamela. She was so straight and thin and her black stockings were so tight over her legs. She had the clearest blue eyes with dark lashes. It was no wonder Wrenn Morley was sweet on her. Pamela Lacey was just the way she would like to look herself, except for the straight hair. Rose touched her own wiry curls. Pamela was running up the Morleys' walk. Her heavy blond hair, tied with a black ribbon, bobbed out from her back. She reached around and held it with one hand. Rose could hear her feet on the wooden steps of the Morleys' porch.

CHAPTER **3**

Every room in the house was lighted. A fire burned in the grate in the parlor. In her father's den the big roll-top desk was dusted and bare except for the blotter and the big piece of copper ore from the Butte mines and the cigar box that was made of saddle leather. The dining room waited in all its glory. The company gentlemen were late, and so was Papa. Pamela sat at the piano playing. The parlor shade was up so she could see when the hack stopped in front of the house and, she fondly hoped, be seen. She held her wrists a little straighter and tipped her head as she played.

"I do wish your father would get back from the ranch in time to go for them," her mother said, appearing in the doorway.

Pamela's wrists dropped against the keys as she looked at her mother. She was beautiful to Pamela. Her dark hair was gathered up in wide waves to the crown of puffs on top and a comb with pearls shone against it. She wore her pearl earrings tonight, and the coral brooch surrounded by pearls that had been her mother's before she ever came to Montana fastened the lace at the neck of her black velvet dress. Pamela wished that she were dark like her mother.

"I suppose that wretched train has broken down again, and if it has I don't know how your father will get here!"

There was something exaggerated in the tone of alarm in her

voice that made Pamela feel her mother was acting. "Oh, Papa will get here someway, Mama. You know he always does."

"Yes, he'll come in late and go on as though it were nothing at all to hold dinner for two hours!" A little smile almost showed around her mouth and Pamela realized suddenly that her mother *liked* Papa to be that way. Then the little smile was gone and Mama was back in her regular voice. "We'll just have to explain to them and let them see what life is like for a rancher. In the East, you know, Pamela, people are very correct about dinner hours. When we were entertained at the Randells' and the Crawfords' two years ago, everyone dressed for dinner."

Pamela had heard this before until she could tell it herself.

"And they had a library with paneled walls and bookcases to the ceiling. . . . It was so good to be in a really civilized place!" Maybelle Lacey sighed a little, and catching sight of her image in the glass door of the secretary patted her hair into place.

When her mother talked about the East or "civilization" it gave Pamela the same feeling she had when she tried to decide between a soda or a sundae at the BonTon, a torn sort of feeling. "The East" and "civilization" were where they had come from, although her mother had been born out here in Virginia City and her father had been only three when he came west, but still she felt disloyal to the West when her mother talked that way about it. When her mother talked about the great trees that you could put your arms around back east she wanted to put her hand around the little slips of trees along the sidewalk here so they would feel she loved them.

"Pamela, go out and tell Mamie not to forget to put the roasted almonds in the silver bonbon dish."

So she was out in the kitchen when the doorbell rang and the gentlemen couldn't see her through the window. She could hear them talking as she came through the swinging door of the pantry. She straightened the big bow at the back of her neck and went on into the parlor.

"There's the young lady!" Mr. Randell said, coming to shake hands with her. Mr. Crawford said, "How do you do, my dear," and Mr. Bell bowed as though she were a grown woman. They were different from the men here, even from Wrenn's father who never wore Western hats. She tried to think why it was, and, stealing quiet glances at them while her mother was talking, her eyes settled on Mr. Bell's shoe that was black and more pointed than any of her father's shoes, except his riding boots, and this was not in the least like a riding boot.

Mr. Bell had never been west although he was one of the original members of the cattle company. He said the usual things about the trip out and the country that people from the East always said, and Pamela could see him being charmed by Mama.

"You are not a native Montanan, yourself, are you, Mrs. Lacey?"

"Oh, yes indeed," Maybelle Lacey answered. "I was born when the state was a territory and my father was a Vigilante." She had a way of sitting very straight and lifting her head ever so little, like a noble statue. "Of course, my people were Eastern, from Virginia, and I know the East, but I'm a Montanan."

The way Mr. Bell said, "Is that so?" made it a compliment. It spurred her on to a more dramatic statement.

"I suppose I have too much pioneer blood to be contented back east any more."

"And do you still ride horseback with your father?" Mr. Randell asked Pamela as though aware that she had been sitting very still.

"Yes," Pamela said briefly because she was still confused in her mind by Mama's changing so. She wondered which Mama *really* liked best, the East or the West.

"I'd like to get my boy out here this summer. He needs a little of this sort of life." Mr. Randell looked at Pamela very directly as though he enjoyed the thought of his boy and Pamela riding across the prairie. "I wanted to get him out here a few years ago when he was still in his teens, but his mother didn't want him so far away."

"Is he in school, Mr. Randell?" Pamela asked.

[22]

"Yes, he's in his third year at Harvard. Let's see, he's twenty-two."

Before she could ask another question, she heard her father's voice saying "whoa!" "There's Papa, Mr. Randell. He must have driven all the way in from the ranch!"

Charlie Lacey seemed to burst open the door and his gladness at seeing everyone took away from the unreal feeling Pamela had had listening to her mother. He wore his ranch clothes and his heavy boots were muddy along the soles. None of the company gentlemen were as tall as he and they looked pale beside him. His skin never lost the heavy sunburn it got each summer, or else the wind burned it in winter. He was the only one of the men who didn't have at least a mustache.

"Well, when I found how late the train was going to be, I took the buckboard and drove in. I'll take you out to the ranch tomorrow morning in it, if you don't mind a little jolting. Thirty-five miles is quite a little jog."

The men glanced at each other and laughed. Pamela couldn't think how they would look sitting up in the buckboard and jolting over the ruts. The white cord around Mr. Crawford's vest would get dirty and out at the ranch Slim and Jack and the others would look at them as though they were "crazy Easterners" and poke sly fun at them. "This man thinks nothing of riding horseback in the rain twenty, thirty miles, and then lying down with his saddle blanket over him and his head on his saddle for the night," Mr. Randell told Mr. Bell.

"We were pleased with the report of the roundup, Charlie. That's getting back to the old days," Mr. Bell said.

"It's a long ways from that," Charlie said, "but it could have been worse. If you'll excuse me a minute I'll call the livery stable to come and get the team so they'll be ready in the morning if we need them!"

Pamela noticed when he came back that Papa had washed his hands and face and combed out the ridged mark that his Stetson had made in his hair. And he had changed his heavy shirt and vest to a white shirt and coat.

Now the men looked more at her father than her mother. At the table, Mama wasn't really listening, anyway. After they had commented on the roast beef and said there was never such beef in all of Buffalo, they were busy asking Papa questions. Mama's eyes were watching the way Mamie served, or noticing that Papa hadn't used his salad fork. He had explained so many times that living at the ranch and eating with the boys made it hard to change completely around and use unnecessary utensils when he happened to be home, but Mama didn't think that was any excuse. Why didn't Mama *listen* to what they were saying instead of being so busy watching everything?

". . . so I said, all right, we'll run a fence along the south forty and we'll cart hay out there and feed 'em through the winter. The boys were plenty mad. They went on about how they didn't count on being farmers, but . . ." Charlie Lacey shrugged and smiled his easy smile. "I said to them, let me ask you one thing: What are we in business for? To raise cattle that'll bring the top price at the Chicago market, and what it takes to do it is beside the point." Her father's voice was always quiet. He only yelled out at the ranch.

Mr. Randell nodded his head. Mr. Bell made a little sign of approval in his throat. She could see how smart they thought Papa was. They were the company and owned part of the spread, but it always seemed as though her father really owned it all.

"Pamela!"

She caught her mother's eye. "Pamela, don't lean forward so; sit back." Mama's eyes and mouth moved together in an expression that said, "You and I are ladies and must keep our minds on certain things." Pamela sat up straighter but she turned her eyes back to her father. She had missed what he said and now they were all laughing. Her mother smiled a little late, just in time to meet the gentlemen's eyes when they glanced over at her. She didn't really know what they had been laughing at either, Pamela could tell.

Dinner was over too soon and her father and the gentlemen all went into the study to smoke their cigars and talk. Mama hummed as she lifted the centerpiece off and Pamela helped her fold the best linen tablecloth. Mama was always happy after a party dinner.

"They really are a pleasure to have, such fine, cultured gentlemen, only I do wish your father would go east to report on the business instead of their always coming out here. Pamela, come and see the beautiful hothouse fruits they brought in the refrigerator on their train."

The basket was handsome with its great yellow bow. Purple-red and green grapes hung in heavy clusters from the handle over the apples and pears and grapefruit. A pineapple balanced one end, its stiff green spines sticking out like an ornament on a hat.

"What's that?" Pamela touched the cerise-red fruit lying next to the pineapple.

"Oh, that's a pomegranate," Maybelle Lacey said in the same tone of voice that she always used when she talked about the East. And in that instant it became The East to Pamela. She picked a grape and popped it in her mouth. The skin was tough and a little sour. There was hardly any taste at all.

"Don't pick at it that way; you'll spoil the looks. I wonder if the back porch is cool enough for it tonight?"

As Pamela went through the hall she could hear the men talking and she wished she could go in and listen. Papa's voice carried above the others.

"I don't suppose the cattle business is *safe*. Since the end of the open range days it's always something of a gamble." The way he said "safe" made it seem something no one would want.

"But, Charlie, we can be reasonably sure . . ." she heard the precise voice of Mr. Bell insisting. She hadn't cared for him. He was "with the railroad" Mama had said, raising her eyebrows to show that that meant something. Mr. Randell was much nicer. He owned a brass foundry in Buffalo that was somehow connected with the copper business out here.

"Why, I remember when the lightning started a fire way up in the Cypress Hills . . ." Papa was saying. "Destroyed all the grass for more than a hundred miles . . ." She couldn't hear all the words, but she knew about that time, anyway.

"If you've never seen a prairie fire . . ." Of course they hadn't, but she had. She wandered into the parlor and played the first few bars of "Juanita"; that was easy because it didn't have any flats or sharps. Perhaps the music would float into the den and one of the men, maybe Mr. Randell, would raise his hand and say, "Listen! Who is playing?" And then he might come out and say, "My dear, you have a very delicate touch!"

But the sound of their voices went on without interruption. She could hear Mama putting the best silver away in the sideboard, wrapping it up in its flannel cases. Pamela sat idle on the piano stool. She wondered what Mr. Randell's son would be like if he did come west next summer. Of course, he was awfully old, and a college man. But Wrenn would be in college next year, too.

CHAPTER 4

The parade for Pioneer Day was late in starting. One of the boys on the Rattlesnake Jake float fired off a blank cartridge and frightened the horses of the Covered Wagon float and the Pioneer Mother sitting on the seat holding the reins screamed and let them slide out of her hands. The Vigilantes float was fifth in the procession, and came behind New Frontiers. It was divided in two by a wall that was papered on one side and had bark on the other. The front end of the float was the interior. It was a little crowded with the four girls sitting there. One bowed figure in black taffeta knelt on the floor with her head hidden in her arms. Her shoulders heaved with her sobs that could be heard from one side of the street to the other. A figure with powdered hair patted the heaving shoulders, wiping at her own eyes from time to time. Another woman sat rocking, her Bible open on her knees. The fourth sat erect in a chair facing the horses' tails. Her hands were knotted in her lap.

"I wouldn't weep," Pamela had said yesterday when they rehearsed. "I know I wouldn't, if my husband was really guilty. I'd hate him for doing it or, if I loved him enough, I'd hate them for hanging him."

A sign in slightly crooked letters on their side of the wall proclaimed to onlookers that HELPLESS HEARTS HURT MOST. The hanging tree was a triumph of engineering. Bill Kossuth had found a dead cottonwood tree down along the river and bolted it to the floor of the dray. It reared a good three feet above the top of the partition. One road agent dangled realistically from the rope by the simple device of having his feet rest on a stool covered with black tarlatan. One culprit waited with his hands tied behind him. Two men wore guns and grim expressions. Another stood by in frock coat and stovepipe hat.

"What are you, Wrenn?" Rose had asked when the tableau was arranged.

"I'm a vigilante," he told her, "like Sam." But there was a difference. There was less gusto in his stance, more gravity of manner. He didn't tell Rose that Pamela had said, "You ought to look as though you hate what you're doing."

Rose was more interested in the present and future than the past. "I can just see you as a lawyer, Wrenn."

Wrenn was rather pleased and had difficulty resuming his sad demeanor.

The sign on the exterior read: JUSTICE WINS OUT. Cheers and the quick uneven clapping of hands from the spectators on the sidewalk made them all assume their roles more dramatically. Rose's sobs grew louder. Alice bent more tenderly over her, patting her shoulder. Mary wept into her handkerchief and Pamela stared unseeingly above the horses' tails. Wrenn's brow darkened as he watched the hanging. The waiting culprit cringed and the hanging man dropped his jaw wider open. Only when Mr. Watts, the barber, said audibly, "Where do you suppose those kids got that tree?" Bill Kossuth forgot that he was to hang next and grinned broadly.

Pamela clasped her hands more tightly in the lap of the red taffeta that had been too snug for Rose. She looked across the wide swaying backs of the horses at the float ahead where a scout held his hand to his eyes and scanned the distance.

Suppose it *were* her husband and he had held up the stage-coach and killed innocent people and then been caught. How would she feel? What if she had suspected right along, for surely you'd know what your husband was doing. But she would never marry anyone who could do a thing like that. She would marry someone like Wrenn, of course, and he would be on the side of right and justice. But suppose, just suppose, and now her husband were hanging and she was left out here in a new raw country, with a child, maybe.

Clapping crackled forth sharply from the group in front of Madame Guinard's millinery establishment, where Mrs. Morley and Mrs. Lacey and Mrs. Cheavers sat to watch the parade. Madame Guinard, seeing them standing there, had brought out chairs. She herself stood in the doorway, a plump figure in a black dress with white starched collar and black cambric protectors over her sleeves. Her black hair was combed in a stiff pompadour and she wore jet earrings that matched her eyes. A gold watch hung from her waist.

"Maybelle, Pamela looks like your mother with her hair like that and that old red dress, doesn't she?" Cora Morley exclaimed.

"She looks as though she had lost her last friend!" Mrs. Lacey laughed.

"And my daughter, Rose, just listen to her sobbing her heart out!" Madame Guinard held up her plump ringed hands.

"Look at Wrenn's arms hanging down out of those sleeves! He's going to be tall like my side," Cora Morley said with her eyes on her son.

None of the occupants of the float showed any sign of recognizing their parents. Pamela was too deep in her own imaginings. She would wait till they cut her husband down from the tree, or she would do it herself and see him decently buried, and put up a marker in spite of the shame and then she would leave this town and go far away. She looked back and met Wrenn Morley's eyes but her own showed no recognition. Wrenn smiled but she looked away, after all, he had helped to hang her husband. Riding down Main Street she felt herself alone. Let people pity her, or scorn her, it made no difference to her.

"Are you going home to change before the picnic, Pam?" Mary had grown tired of weeping into her handkerchief.

"I guess so," Pamela answered, still in her role of newly made widow.

They had to assemble in the auditorium at the high school after the parade. The boys in side whiskers and beards and strange costumes and the girls rustling long skirts along the halls. Mr. Sewall made a speech about keeping alive the memory of the brave days of the past, "On this Pioneer Day let us not forget how much we owe the pioneers of the West." When he came to give out the prizes even the rustling of the girls' skirts was stilled.

Float 12, the Lonely Fur Trader, won first prize. The Pioneer School won second. Pamela sat waiting to hear the prize awarded for the most original float. If it was theirs she would be the one to go up to receive it, or maybe they'd ask a boy to go up, too, because the float had been divided and then Wrenn would go up to the platform with her.

But the prize was awarded to the Saturday Night Bath.

"How could they!" Rose whispered. "That was nothing but somebody sitting in a washtub in front of a stove."

"I thought Pamela Lacey's idea was crazy right from the start," Sam Gillette muttered so Pamela could hear it.

Room 21 sang "America" without enthusiasm and went to their home room for dismissal. It wasn't her fault—anybody else could have suggested something if they had an idea—any more than it was her fault that her husband was a road agent, Pamela told herself, but she felt responsible.

"I don't care what they say, I thought it was the best float,"

[29]

Rose said, twining her arm around Pamela as they went down the steps. Indian maidens and braves, prospectors and fur traders and the man who drove the golden spike to join the railroad separated at various street corners to be seen no more until next Pioneer Day.

"Bill Kossuth is going to get the tree off the wagon and then most of the class can ride in that out to Harpers' woods," Wrenn told the girls. "Hurry and get your clothes changed if you're going to." Rose and Pamela lifted their hoop skirts and ran up the board walk to the Lacey home.

The woods fringed the Missouri River and spread a thin shade of new green leaves. Gray-boled cottonwoods grew giant high and the squat box elders twisted shyly beside them, spring decorated with red-tipped tassels. The grass was green under the trees.

They climbed down from the big wagon, over the sides and the end. The boys still wore their sideburns and beards and their grandfathers' clothes but the girls had changed back to their own persons and dresses.

"Maybe we should have asked Miss Ferris to come, but it wouldn't be as much fun," Alice said. "My mother thinks she is going to be here."

"Mine, too," Mary Tooms giggled. "But I should hope we are old enough to go on a picnic by ourselves!"

They left their baskets of food on the old plank table and lingered there, uncertain as to what to do next, feeling vaguely that it was an occasion, something they were going to remember, Pioneer Day picnic, senior year 1905 . . . well then?

"Anybody want to play ball?" Bill Kossuth suggested, pulling a ball and mitt out of some place.

"If the boys are going to play ball they won't get through till dark," Rose pouted.

"I suppose you'd rather play post office!" Ginnie Blair twisted her mouth as she said it.

"What a horrid thing to say, Ginnie!" Pamela flew to Rose's defense. "Come on, Rose, let's walk along the river."

The sound of the boys yelling and the ball on leather came down to them on the shore. Young willows whispered together in groups and old maimed willows stretched their stubby limbs out over the river as though begging for youth. There had not been enough sun this spring to warm the sand so it was still slate-colored and held, imprinted like a gigantic pie crust, the tracks of curlews' feet. The water was blue and moved gently along the shore making an eddy around the branch of willow that touched it.

"Yoo-hoo, yoo-hoo . . ." the girls called after them.

"Oh, now they'll all come with us," Rose said. She and Pamela started to run along the shore, catching their skirts on the rough weeds, and hanging on to roots or bushes where the bank sheared down to the river. When they came to an old cottonwood tree that spread its roots out to make a sheltered seat they stopped. The wash of the river against the shore sounded like approaching voices at first. Rose squeezed Pamela's arm. As Pamela turned toward her, she saw a strange thing: a tiny hole in the lobe of each of Rose's ears. "Why, you have your ears pierced!" she said, forgetting to whisper.

Rose nodded. "It was done when I was a baby. I've got some beautiful earrings I'm going to wear when I'm old enough, they're coral with real solid gold around them."

"They must be pretty," Pamela conceded.

"Pamela, who do you like best in our class . . . male?"

"Wrenn Morley," Pamela answered promptly. "I guess because I've always known him. Who do you?"

Rose hesitated; her brown eyes lost their shining and became like brown velvet that showed nothing behind them. "I guess I like Wrenn Morley best, too. . . ." Her eyes were on Pamela's face, ready to disclaim this liking if it seemed annoying to her. She had not been her mother's daughter and heard her placating customers in the millinery shop without learning some protective wiles. But Pamela was combing the end of her hair with one of

[31]

her side combs, then she retied the big bow. The sun through the new leaves of the cottonwood made a shadowy pattern on her face. She was all greeny-gold.

"If I ask you something will you tell the truth?" Rose asked.

"Of course," Pamela said promptly.

"Have you ever been kissed by a boy?"

"Nope." Pamela emphasized her answer with a vehement shake of her head.

"Oh, my goodness, not ever?"

"I said no," Pamela said.

"Are you going to get married . . . I mean soon after school?"

"Why, I don't know." She said it as she did when somebody asked what she got in algebra, for of course she did know, pretty well. She knew she would get married, too.

"I don't know whether I will or not," Rose said, resting her rounded chin on her fist and looking away from Pamela at the river. "When you're married they can touch you, any time they want."

Pamela frowned. "Who can?"

"Your husband, of course."

The thought was unpleasant, but not entirely clear. Pamela sat silent, wishing she hadn't come off down here with Rose, but held here, not able to run back.

"But my mother says, if you love him, it's ecstasy." She stated it calmly, like an answer in history.

Ecstasy! The word was strange, not one that people used. She had never heard anyone say it before. It was a delicious word. She thought of Madame Guinard's black beady eyes, her curly hair that waved back into a pompadour. Madame Guinard's husband was dead. Ecstasy! She liked the sound of it.

"Oh, I might," Rose said archly, dropping her head back against her shoulders. "Can you and me be best friends, or is Alice your best friend?"

"I hadn't thought about it. I think it's silly to have a best friend. Come on, let's go back."

The other girls were sitting on the bank when they came

around the bend of the shore. The boys had moved one of the old wooden tables over and were collected around it, the bolder among them talking to the girls, the shier occupied with carving initials in the planks. Three of the boys still played catch.

There was a faint hostility in the air as Pamela and Rose came up.

"Well, did you go to China all by your lonesomes?" Mary Tooms called out.

"We just went down the shore a ways," Pamela answered coolly. "We thought you would have the food all laid out."

"Let's go swimming first!" Bill Kossuth suggested and there was a sudden burst of laughter from the boys. One of them said something in an undertone and the laugh rose again, but with a different note this time that separated the girls from the boys, making the girls draw together, taking in Pamela and Rose. Then Pamela lifted her head a little and there was a defiant note in her voice that made the words more than they seemed.

"I might wade," she said. "If anyone else would."

"Take off your shoes and stockings and walk right out? Pamela Lacey, you know your mother wouldn't let you!"

"I would, though!" She didn't know herself whether she would or not. She wanted to do something none of the rest of them would do, something to show the boys who thought they were so smart. . . . They were looking at her, waiting to see. Mary Marsten giggled. The boys in their camp murmured something, and again that laugh.

Almost against her will, still believing that somebody would stop her, Pamela began unbuttoning her shoes. She reached up under her petticoats and unfastened her garters, not looking at anyone now. She rolled her stockings down off her feet. Her ankles looked indecently naked, she buried her toes in the cold grass. Stockings were awful things, dangling in your hand with the place where the garters fastened showing at the top. She rolled them into a discreet ball and hid it in one shoe. Then she walked past them all down to the shore.

"Wait, Pam, I'll come too," Rose cried. She peeled off her

shoes and stockings and hurried after her. "It's going to be terrible cold," she whispered when she came up to her. "None of the boys darst to come!"

"I don't care!" Pamela said. She was cross with Rose for coming.

"Don't drown, Pam!" one of the girls called.

Pamela walked out into the water holding on to a branch of a half-dead willow tree. It was cold, but she wouldn't say so. She held her skirts up with the other hand. Rose put one toe in and shrieked.

"It's really warmer than the air," Pamela lied for the benefit of those on the shore. She took another step and let the water rise halfway up to her knee, but with the next step the river bottom dropped off and the water came above the edge of her skirt. She clung to the tree and walked back out. Rose turned as quickly.

"There, I did it!" she said to the group on the bank. "Come on out, Rose." Her skirts dripped coldly around her legs as she climbed back up the bank.

"Here, I'll wring your skirt out," Amy Wentworth offered. "You showed your leg way up above your knee!" she whispered to Pamela.

"What if I did," Pamela answered crossly. She felt a little silly now. The sand stuck to her feet and she couldn't get it all off with her handkerchief so she put her stockings on anyway. "Stand in front of me while I fasten my garters," she told Amy. Rose was putting on her shoes and stockings in the middle of a group of girls. Pamela walked toward the table. She was cold and her feet felt horrid. The other girls moved over to the table and began laying out the food. Then Rose was beside her taking deviled eggs out of a box. Rose had gone in the water, too, but Rose didn't count, really. She was too different. Even her deviled eggs were different; the yellow centers had dark rings around them and dark pieces of something in them.

"What did you put in your eggs, Rose?" she asked.

"Fish. That makes them extra good."

"Oh!" But who ever heard of fish in deviled eggs! She felt Amy and Alice looking at them too, and smiling in a superior sort of way.

Alice called out to the boys the way she often heard her mother address her father, "Say, are you going to unwrap your own food or do you want us to do it for you?"

Pamela felt better. Now she was back in the camp, calling over to the boys, not apart. "Oh, they haven't the strength!" she said.

"We thought you'd do it for us!" Bill answered, but they were coming now, self-consciously, straggling toward the girls. "How'd the water feel?" Bill asked her, grinning, standing close beside her. He touched her arm. "Gee, you're as cold as an iceberg. I bet you catch cold."

Pamela jerked away. "Stop it!" She moved away from him around the table and said to Alice in an undertone, "He's fresh."

"What can you expect!" Alice answered. "Parading around with your skirt up to your knees! Here, Fred, here's your potato salad!" She turned abruptly away from Pamela.

Pamela flushed. She stood by the table, looking down at the wide space between the rough boards. Why didn't Wrenn come over? Then she heard Rose asking Wrenn if he wanted a dill pickle. "I'm fixing a plate for you, you're so slow," Rose told him shamelessly.

Pamela felt cross. It was the fault of Pioneer Day. You couldn't be on a float and act out a hanging and then stop all of a sudden and be yourself. Wrenn Morley acted as though he had forgotten all about Pioneer Day, as though he was as shocked as someone's grandmother because she'd gone in the river and got her skirt wet. Pamela took one sandwich, one pickle, and one deviled egg and arranged them elegantly on her plate. She sat down beside Alice and pulled her damp skirts well down over her ankles. Rose Guinard was sitting beside Wrenn, urging him to eat as though he were a baby. It was disgusting.

[35]

"Try one," Rose said. "They're French pastry; I've got a whole box of them. My mother made them."

They were pretty with crinkled crust and a dab of jelly and a dab of whipped cream, very small and different from the large sour cream cookies or oatmeal hermits or ginger cookies most of them had brought.

"No thank you," Alice said when Rose passed her box around. The delectable little morsels were laid out on a lace paper doily which made them look much more appetizing than a clean dish towel.

"No thank you," Pamela said although she did want one.

"That Rose Guinard shouldn't be in on Pioneer Day, she's a foreigner, really," Alice murmured.

Coolness seemed to rise out of the river while the sky was still light. It inched up the bank like a tide. Bill Kossuth hitched the horses and the girls began packing their baskets. Only one piece of Maybelle's orange sponge was eaten and Pamela held the rest up in the air.

"Who wants a piece or I'll throw it out?"

"Let me throw it," Bill Kossuth yelled. He threw it in a high arc so it cleared the bank and fell with a splash in the river.

"Here, throw my pie," Alice said.

It was great sport. They threw the pickles one by one and someone hurled a quart of lemonade.

"We won't have to take anything back home," Alice said. "The fish will have a good meal." The paper plates floated slowly down the river and the quart jar bobbed for a time.

Dusk came slowly as they rode home. Wrenn sat beside Pamela at the end of the wagon but they sang as they rode so they had no need to talk. A woman came to a lighted doorway in a ranch house and stood watching them. Pamela waved and the woman waved back. They passed the barn below the house and the smell of pigs and cows came to them. The boys shouted and the girls held their noses and called to Bill to drive fast. But just as the road dipped out of sight of the ranch house Pamela glanced back and saw the woman still looking after them. There was something so sad about her standing there . . . Why was it? Pamela forgot to sing, wondering about it.

The sadness seemed to come out of the cool dusk and wrap around her. And all the songs they sang sounded sad. Room 21 would never ride out to Harpers' woods again and have a picnic . . . never again, never again creaked the wheels. No, it wasn't that. She didn't care about Room 21. The sadness was not around her, it was in her, caught from the woman in the doorway.

"Pam . . ." Wrenn said, under cover of "Maxwelton's Braes Are Bonnie." "Don't be mad, Pam."

"I'm not, Wrenn. Really, I'm not." All the time he was sitting with Rose and eating Rose's French pastry he had known how she felt. He hadn't thought her going into the water was just to show off, either . . . though maybe it was in a way. Her voice rose happily with the others, putting off sadness.

As they came up from the river road the streets of the town lay in front of them, like aisles. Only Main Street was lighted by regular arc lights, but Diamond Avenue was bedizened by the brightness inside the windows of the saloons, where the doors stood open to the street; Diamond Avenue where you never went alone.

They could drop off without stopping the wagon. Sam Heccla got off at the first crossing. His father had built his house there before there was much of a town. Rose jumped down in front of her mother's millinery shop. Bill pulled the horses up and made a brave show trotting down the street until they came to the corner where the Morleys lived. Then for a block Pamela rode alone in the back of the wagon. The horses no longer trotted but walked as though they were tired, too.

Mr. Cheavers was spading up the dirt in front of his porch. Their own house was dark except for a light at the top of the stairs. Papa was out at the ranch, Pamela remembered.

"You'll miss Pioneer Day," she had told him.

"I don't need to see Pioneer Day, Pam. Our people were the pioneers out here."

[37]

She slid off the end and went slowly up the walk. The house always felt empty when her father was away, even tonight when Mama yoo-hooed from the sewing room upstairs as soon as she opened the door.

CHAPTER 5

There were not so many secret places in town as at the ranch that Pamela took for her own, but there were a few. There was the high bank above the river where the swallows had their bee-hive nests, and the wooden supports of the bridge that you could climb out on and look down into the greeny-dark ripple of the water, while drays and wagons thundered over your head. But the best place of all was the iron fire escape that hung airily against the brick side of the Opera House, dangling its last flight within reach of the ground. It was made romantic by its height, its scary look and the delicious knowledge that it clung to that building where actors played and singers sang and even Pavlova had once danced. Beside the skeleton stairway the late June sun had sketched a second flight in delicate outline and set the purple shadow of a second door at the top, next to the wooden one that opened into the "peanut gallery" of the Opera House.

Pamela sat on the top landing, one book under her as cushion, one open on her knees, and her skirts tucked tightly around her ankles, blissfully suspended above the street and the whole town of Brandon Rapids, Montana. The sun-warmed bricks kept off the fickle spring air that blew now cold, now warm, and their rosy reflection softened the lines of the angular young creature perched there. No one passing on the street below looked up so high, and no one had happened to glance across from the library opposite. Pamela read undisturbed.

"*It was many and many a year ago,*
In a kingdom by the sea,
That a maiden there lived whom you may know
By the name of Annabel Lee . . ."

The words fitted the rhythm of the horses' hoofs clopping past below her. Then a bicycle scraped to a stop on the wooden walk and the whole fire escape was violently shaken.

"I thought you'd be up there!" Wrenn Morley called up to her. "Your mother said you were at the library and you weren't in there."

Pamela looked down at him from her celestial height, still half in her poem. "Stop rattling it!"

Wrenn swung himself up on the landing, looking gigantic against the sky until he crouched down beside her. "I wondered if you'd listen to my valedictory speech. I got it done this afternoon, about ten minutes ago."

Pamela chewed the inside of her cheek and nodded. "Tonight, right after supper." Then her eyes went back to the page in front of her.

"Say, it's five o'clock now; come on!"

Pamela kept her finger in the place as she went down ahead of him, taking pains to make the loudest possible noise on the iron steps. Wrenn jumped from the lowest landing.

"What are you reading?" he asked.

Pamela opened her book and rested it on the handle bars of the bicycle so Wrenn could look for himself.

"Poetry! What for?"

"'Cause I want to."

Wrenn read aloud from the page as they walked, emphasizing the sing-song of the rhyme.

"*It was many and many a year ago,*
In a kingdom by the sea,
That a maiden there lived whom you may know
By the name of Annabel Lee;

[39]

And this maiden she lived with no other thought
Than to love . . ."

He broke off, but Pamela went on . . .

"*. . . and be loved by me.*
'I was a child and she was a child,
In this kingdom by the sea,
But we loved with a love that was more than love . . .'"

Her voice made the most of "more." Wrenn's eyes centered on the rings of his bicycle handle and the color rose under the soft blond down on his cheek.

"I and my Annabel Lee . . ." The vibrations of the word love reached Pamela's ear belatedly and she broke off.

"What happened to 'em?" Wrenn asked.

"The gods envied them for their love. Listen:" She was back again in the story.

"*And this was the reason that, long ago*
In this kingdom by the sea,
A wind blew out of a cloud, chilling
My beautiful Annabel Lee;
So that her highborn kinsmen came
And bore her away from me,
To shut her up in a sepulcher
In this kingdom by the sea."

"The highborn kinsmen are angels of death, you know."

"It sounds sort of silly to me," Wrenn said, trying to see how close to the edge of the board walk he could guide his wheel. "I mean that part about the highborn kinsmen."

"Oh, it does, Mr. Morley! I'm sorry I took your time to read it to you."

"Well, it would be better to say she died of pneumonia or whatever she did die of."

"Wouldn't that be poetic! Highborn kinsmen make death mysterious, don't you see?"

[40]

"It is anyway," Wrenn said, polishing one end of his handle bar with the palm of his hand. Pamela's eyes moved ahead down the street where the houses came to an end. She closed the green poetry book. Of a sudden the empty prairie beyond the end of the street became strange. The sky hid the unknown.

"Saturday when I was fishing I got a little trout, not any bigger than your little finger, and, just like I always do, I took it off my hook to throw it back in. Maybe you won't believe it, but it was about the prettiest thing you'd ever want to see; all silvery and arching up so I had to hold it tight while I got the hook out. And then, all at once, I could see the life going out of it, right in my hand. It looked more like tin than silver, and the skin got dry; I hated the feeling of it on my hand. I threw it back in the water, but it was dead. It came to the top instead of darting under a rock or something. I felt terrible."

Pamela swallowed. "I know," she said in a small voice.

Wrenn managed an embarrassed laugh. "I guess you'll think I'm crazy to feel bad about a dead fish, or even to tell you about it."

"Of course I don't." How artificial "highborn kinsmen" seemed beside the poor little trout floating on top of the water. She wanted to put out her hand and touch Wrenn's sleeve. The wanting ached up her arm. She wanted to look at him but she couldn't lift her eyes above the railing of the Cheavers' porch that they were passing. One of the spindles was broken, she noticed.

"I wouldn't tell anybody else anything like that," Wrenn said.

Now she could look away from the Cheavers' house to Wrenn; at his ear and his hair curling around it up to his forehead. Wrenn turned his head suddenly and their eyes met and fled away again.

"I wouldn't have made a very good vigilante, I guess," he said.

"Why yes you would, Wrenn. That would be taking a life for a reason."

She would like to have explained a bit more, but Wrenn said, "Do you know what you're going to do next year?"

"Mama wants me to go east to school, but Papa says to see what kind of a year he has. Mr. Sewall told Mama I could work in his office, keeping the Pioneer records."

Wrenn made a face. "I can't see you working in an office. That would be dull as dust."

For no reason at all they laughed and Pamela tossed her head back and one of her side combs fell out. Wrenn ran his wheel over it before he saw it. He picked up the pieces and held them on the palm of his hand. "You don't want them any more, do you?"

Pamela's color deepened and ran up to her temples. "No, throw them away."

"I might like to keep them. Here, you take half and I'll keep half."

"Silly, that one half won't do me much good," but she slipped it into her hair. Wrenn walked all the way home with her but Mrs. Lacey was out on the porch so he only stopped to say good evening and whirled back down the street.

"Let's go in Papa's study," Pamela said, when Wrenn came. "You can sit at the desk."

"Maybe you'll think it's awful," Wrenn began. "I haven't looked at it since I finished this afternoon." Color came up in his face like a girl's. The green shaded student lamp made a cap of shade just above his forehead, tilted a little to the side, and left the rest of his face more clearly exposed. He looked thin in the barrel armchair that Charlie Lacey filled so well.

Pamela settled herself in the big leather chair across from the desk.

"I know it's good," she said, looking over at the copper ore instead of at Wrenn's face that seemed almost too clear under the light.

He looked down at his pages and then up again. "I chose loyalty for the subject. Miss Ferris wanted me to talk on what the new high school means to our city but everybody knows that and there isn't so much to say anyway. I thought I'd talk about loyalty to your country, to your state, to your friends, and to yourself."

"That sounds wonderful," Pamela said. "But don't tell about it, begin." She could see Wrenn swallow.

"In the beginning our country was not the strong united nation it is today . . ." His voice didn't sound natural. "It did not become a nation respected by other nations with a place in the world . . . or would you say in the sun?" he stopped to ask.

"Sun," Pamela said at once. Wrenn leaned over the desk to make the change.

". . . until all these settlements of people were united by a common loyalty." His voice was higher and he read faster than he spoke. "By this I do not mean that all people in the new country at once gave up their differences, for they did not. . . ."

The sounds from outside deepened the quiet of the study: the hum of the streetcar two blocks over, the clink of a horse's shoe against a stone, the lilac bush blown against the window by the rising wind. Pamela nested her cold hands in her neck for warmth. She uncrossed her knees but without letting her skirts make any sound.

"There is much to be said for the attitude that cries, in the words of that great patriot, Stephen Decatur, 'Our country! may she always be right; but our country, right or wrong!' " Wrenn's eyes flashed as he looked over at Pamela. Pamela's eyes burned bluer listening. It wasn't so much what he said, she thought, because mostly that was quotations strung together; it was the way he said it, and the way he looked, like Patrick Henry or Cicero.

Wrenn cleared his throat, "Some people in this state of ours are so interested in money that they will sell the land and valuable mineral deposits of our state to people in other states, letting other sections of the country rule our state. This is not loyal to those who come to live here and share the fate of the state . . ."

Pamela wondered if having the cattle company gentlemen in

the East was wrong, but decided not since her father was here to run it.

"Maybe it's getting pretty long," Wrenn said with a question in his voice.

"Oh no, it seems very short to me," Pamela said.

"We all know what loyalty in one's friends means. Owen Meredith has said,

> 'Out of all best things upon earth, I hold
> That a faithful friend is the best.' "

That was the kind of friends she and Wrenn were, Pamela thought, moving her hands down to her lap, never taking her eyes from Wrenn's face.

"But a man can neither be true to his country, his state, nor his friends unless he be true to himself.

> 'This above all, to thine own self be true,
> And it must follow, as the night the day,
> Thou can'st not then be false to any man.' "

"I knew you were going to quote that," Pamela said. Wrenn frowned and went on.

"But a man must sometimes ask himself what is truth to one-self? We who stand at the gate of life today need only to look at this beautiful new temple of learning to be reminded . . ."

"Oh, I don't like that," Pamela said.

"Let me finish, will you? There's only half a sentence!—and then we shall know wherein our loyalty lies." His voice seemed to peter out. He was looking down at his pages.

"It's good Wrenn, all but the last part, about the gate of life and the temple of learning."

"I ought to say something about the new building. I thought everyone would like that."

Wrenn was angry. She looked over his head at the picture of the ranch on the wall behind him. King Butte showed in the background, squat and bold, shaped like some old tomb. She had to say what she thought; it *was* silly. "But you don't really

[44]

mean it. You know you're not going to look at the red brick high-school building all your life and then know what is right and wrong."

"It'll remind you when you do look!" Wrenn insisted. "How do you think you'll tell?"

"Well, anybody knows what's honest and what's dishonest and what's good and what's bad, silly!" She stopped and then went on again. "And you try to be loyal to the good." Sudden embarrassment overwhelmed her. She had been so sure of what she was saying a minute ago. Now she wasn't. Words were like Wrenn's fish, going dead and meaningless in your hands. Wrenn was crossing out the whole last page with heavy angry strokes.

"Don't, Wrenn!" She rushed across to the desk and grabbed his pencil out of his hand. "It's so good; you only need to change the very last paragraph. It's a wonderful subject. I was so thrilled I could hardly sit still over there."

Wrenn was mollified. "How would you change it then? I worked on it all day."

Pamela leaned over the desk. She read softly, "We who stand at the gate of life today . . ." She was aware of Wrenn's face so close to her's and drew back a little, her own face coloring, but she must make him see.

"Loyalty to yourself is doing what you know is right even if it means . . ." she tried to think of dire consequences . . . "telling the truth about your friend or . . ."

"Loyalty isn't an easy subject," Wrenn triumphed, no longer angry. "I could say all this and then end with that quotation if you think it would be better?"

Pamela's eyes warmed. "That would be much better, Wrenn."

"And then can I leave in about the high school?"

"That's not so bad if it isn't the grand conclusion, only I'd rather look at the mountains or the sky than the front of the high school, and don't call the high school a temple of learning, it sounds too silly, in Montana, anyway."

Wrenn sat back with a grin. "Now I've got to learn it all!"

[45]

Mr. Randell did get his son out to the ranch that summer and the ranch was a different place with Alan Randell there. After a while, Pamela felt it was not so pleasant. Alan didn't care for the ranch. He had agreed to come only because his father had promised him he could go to Europe the next summer.

Pamela had liked him that first night at home. He was not so tall as Wrenn, or her father, but tall enough, and thin and dark and awfully polite; not blasé as Alice Reed said Eastern boys were.

"You can see he has breeding," Mama murmured as she decorated the strawberry shortcake with whipped cream and Pamela waited to carry it in to the table. "Such lovely manners, and don't you love that Eastern way of talking, Pamela!"

"I don't know; it sounds put on," Pamela said, taking a strawberry from one of the plates.

Alan sprang to push Mama's chair in at the table. He would have pushed hers in, but she slid in too quickly. Pamela did admire the easy way he talked about Buffalo and college and his trip out, but couldn't he tell when Papa was stringing him?

"Yessir, I'm going to sign you up as a regular hand; bed and grub and seventy-five dollars a month," Papa said. Alan looked startled. "Course, you'll get a few blisters before you're broke in," Papa went on.

"Mr. Lacey is a great hand to joke," Mama explained to Alan.

"Why no, I'm not joking, Maybelle. That's what I understand Mr. Randell sent him out here for, to learn the ranch business."

Alan pushed his hair back from his forehead and his face flushed. "Well, not exactly. You see, I intend to go into our family business, after college, in the brassworks. In the management end, I mean," he explained.

Pamela was torn between wanting to show Alan off to Alice and Mary, maybe even to Rose Guinard, and her eagerness to show the ranch to Alan. Mama wanted them to stay in town until the next week end. "You know, Pam, so we can entertain a little for him." But Papa was leaving at five the next morning and in the end Pam decided she and Alan would go with him.

"You'll love it out there, Alan," she told him. "It's lots different from town." But the next morning at four when he came down to the early breakfast he looked so uncomfortable she had a moment's doubt. And he got a little train sick on the trip out to King Butte. Papa had found someone he knew to talk with and they were smoking strong cigars that smelled up the whole car. Pamela felt sorry for Alan. "Come on out and stand on the platform where you can get some air," she told him and led the way. He hung on to the iron railing but the swaying seemed to make him feel worse. "Look up at the sky, Alan; that's what I do when I feel car sick."

He shook his head. "That doesn't help any. I think I'd rather just sit still in the train," he said and went back in. They sat quietly the rest of the way. It was funny; he seemed so much younger to Pamela than he had last night.

After they reached King Butte, of course, they still had the five-mile trip in the buckboard to the ranch, so Alan had a chance to get over his train sickness before he met Ruby and Slim, the foreman and his wife, and the boys, but he was still a little pale.

"He's nice isn't he, Ruby? He's going to be here all summer," Pamela said after Alan had gone down to the corral with Slim. What Ruby thought about anybody was important to Pamela.

"Puts me in mind of one of them damned English sons used to be on the ranch out of Miles City," Ruby said with a sniff that twisted her nose violently to one side. "I hope Charlie don't count on gettin' much work out of him."

No woman Pamela knew was like Ruby. "A broom with an apron and a shawl tied on her," Slim called her because she was so thin and straight and her face and neck and hands and arms were the color of a wooden broom handle. Her hair was no color at all and brushed back into a tight knot. You never could remember the color of her eyes except when she was mad and then they were glaring light yellow and white. But you could count on Ruby; she didn't change from one side to the other, the way Mama did.

The boys were quick to pick on Alan, asking each other who that lady cowboy was and being extra polite to him. At first Pamela took his part, although the boys included her in their teasing, but then, they had always teased her. She was used to it.

"Why, Pam, I thought you was my girl," Slim would say, looking up at her with his long tanned face that was finely checked, like prairie mud dried out by the hot sun. Then he would roll a cigarette and shake his head as he said sadly, "That sure hurts my feelings to have you bring another sweetheart in here, a damned Eastern one at that!" and laughter would spread down the long table at the cookhouse, and Alan would be red in the face.

Alan usually started out with the boys in the morning, haying or mending fence, but, as Slim said, he couldn't seem to get the hang of things. By afternoon, he was tired out and ready to sit on the sagging porch of the old ranch house and read or write letters. Nobody ordered him to do anything, just left him alone, and that was worst of all to Pamela. Pretty soon the boys wouldn't even bother to kid him.

She took great pains to teach him to ride, but after three weeks he still sat stiffly on his horse and held on to the horn if the horse broke into a gallop. It was best to ride off from the hitching pole by the corral as though they were going to ride for hours and, instead, go some place and just sit and talk. She liked to hear about college and friends of Alan's, but she wondered if he stopped thinking about home for a bit if he might not get to like it here.

Today they sat by a thicket of willows near the river. Alan took off his hat and wiped his hot forehead. "If I were home I'd be going swimming at the club and it would be cool."

"Too bad you aren't home," she said.

"It's so hot and dusty and I guess I'm not used to it. Aren't you hot with that leather skirt?"

Pamela shook her head. "Anybody expects to be hot in summer. If you really want to be hot you should be down at the corral where they're shoeing horses. I thought Slim said you were going to help?"

"He was just making fun of me; he knows I'm no help. I'm tired of being made fun of all the time."

"The boys don't mean anything by it, Alan. It's just their way. If they didn't like you, they wouldn't bother."

Alan lay back on the grass and shaded his face with his hat.

"Are we going to town tomorrow?" he asked.

"I am, but I didn't know you were. I'm only going because of Mama."

"If you go, I'm not going to stay out here. You're the only good thing about the ranch."

She thought about that. He didn't even say it as though it were a compliment. She didn't suppose she was much like those girls he talked about in Boston; she wouldn't want to be, so she ignored the remark.

"There isn't much to do at home; only porch parties and croquet and riding out to the trolley park, and I have to help Mama."

"Well, it's better than this," Alan muttered. "And I like talking to your mother."

Pamela told Charlie that evening about Alan's going back to town with her, but he pooh-poohed the idea. "What does anyone want with town in summer? Nothing but ladies sitting in rocking chairs fanning themselves."

"Alan!" He called across the yard to Alan who was waiting with the boys for the dinner bell.

"Don't, Papa," Pamela begged, but Charlie paid no attention.

"How would you like to ride with Slim and me tomorrow up on the reservation?"

"All right, I guess," Alan said. Pamela saw Gus poke Slim in the ribs with his elbow, but she was relieved that Alan hadn't said no.

"We'll put Pam on the train for town and then go on," Charlie said. "Maybe you can buy some Indian stuff to take back to college next year."

When he first came, Alan had been given his choice of sleeping in the bunkhouse or on the porch of the ranch house. He chose the latter. Charlie had his bedroom just off the sitting room, and Slim and Ruby had the other bedroom. When Pamela came out in winter she slept on the couch in the sitting room, but in summer she had a cot on one side of the porch that ran around three sides of the log house. Alan had his cot on the other side. Mrs. Lacey had remonstrated a little about this arrangement, but Charlie quieted her with, "Don't be a fussy old maid, Maybelle. Slim and I are there every evening and Ruby's there besides."

But when, like tonight, they weren't there, Pamela and Alan could talk from their cots around the corner. The night cool came up from the fields by the river and down from the rimrock above the ranch house so you could hardly remember how hot it had been just three hours ago.

"Hear the owl, Alan?" Pamela called, leaning on her elbow to hear better.

"Yes. I can't sleep."

"Who wants to!"

There were more sounds than the owl's hoot. Two horses were tied to the hitching pole and now and then they shook their bridles or stamped in the dirt. A calf bawled, and from somewhere in the soft night-dark came the sound of men's voices. Pamela lay back and let all the sounds run into one.

And the smells: the river smell of marshy water and wild onion braided with the scent of wild mint. Tonight the wind was in the east and the smell of the horses came up to her. And closer, as close as the rotted window sill by her head, was the old log smell of the ranch house that Papa called the shack. And the funny smell of the blankets Ruby kept in an old trunk with moth balls half the year. How could Alan not like it here? She loved it.

She didn't want to go back to town even for a week. It was so easy being with Ruby. Ruby made her feel . . . well, like a woman, not just a schoolgirl any more. Tonight, Ruby had said right out loud when the men were busy talking, "Let's you and me take a walk, Pam." When she had started for the lantern, Ruby said, "We don't need a lantern, for gosh sakes. What do you suppose the Indian squaws did?"

Ruby knew all sorts of things. The most she had ever learned about the stars was sitting in the outhouse with the door wide open and Ruby standing out there in the dark pointing out stars to her. "Look over there toward the sand hills now, Punk. See that blue star? Outhouse is the best place in the world for studying stars; didn't you know that?" They didn't always walk as far as the outhouse, or even to the windbreak. "Damn men ain't got a corner on the whole earth, as I know of," Ruby had said. Pamela was glad Mama couldn't hear her; Mama would be shocked. Or Alan . . . heavens!

"Did you tell your father I was going back to town with you tomorrow?"

Pamela sat up. Alan's voice was so close to her. He had come around from his side of the porch and was sitting against the post just beyond her bed, smoking a cigarette.

"Yes, but Papa couldn't understand your wanting to go to town when you could be out here."

"Your father can't understand anybody but a cowboy."

"And I don't suppose you have any use for a cowboy."

"A cowboy is all right out here roping cattle or something but I'd hate to see him try to get along in Buffalo. You ought to come east sometime and see what it's like."

"Maybe I will if I go away to school next year. Good night. I'm going to sleep." Pamela thumped her pillow and turned violently in bed, then she lay still, trying to suggest by her breathing that she was already asleep. After a while she heard Alan's bare feet on the squeaking boards of the porch. She was still awake when Slim and her father came and a smell of tobacco and the corral gave the night air new substance. Pamela put back the quilt to go and tell her father that Alan really was leaving so he could talk to him. Papa could talk anyone into feeling all right again, even Mama. But wouldn't she rather have Alan leave? He spoiled the ranch for her. She lay back again.

Slim and Charlie didn't go right to bed as they usually did. Most times Papa undressed and lay down on the old iron bed in his room without lighting a lamp. She had heard him so often she knew all the sounds: his boots on the floor, then his heavy gold watch being wound and laid on the dresser, and a soft sound of clothes falling on a chair. Sometimes he whistled as he undressed, very low and sweet, one of those songs he wouldn't sing for her, but she learned the tune anyway. Then the creak of the springs as he got into bed.

A wide band of light streamed suddenly out through the sitting-room window across her pillow. She could hear the moths flopping against the chimney and Slim spitting into the brown cuspidor under the table. Mama would be sickened if she heard him, but he was awfully good at it.

"God damn it, Charlie, you can't help the drought!" Slim said. "Everybody's range's dry, even up to the edge of the mountains. They gotta expect that. You've made 'em good money, now they'll have to put their hands in their pockets for a couple of seasons."

They were silent so long Pamela wondered what had happened. Then a chair made an angry creak as though it were jerked up to the table and her father said, "They don't, though. They weren't any too happy about last year's showing. I wish to hell you and I could buy 'em all out, Slim."

Pamela knew who "they" were. They were always the gentlemen of the cattle company who owned two-thirds of the ranch and the cattle. Alan was part of them because Mr. Randell was his father.

"Well, Moore knows you gotta wait out your bad luck. He'll

renew your note if you need it and he won't send someone out to count heads neither. You ain't got nothing to worry about, Charlie," Slim said.

Pamela was thankful that Alan's bed was on the other side of the porch where he couldn't hear Papa or Slim.

The jerkwater train that connected the ranch with town in a reluctant fashion, since it came only within five dusty miles of the ranch, was delayed by a hotbox. Slim got the word from the stationmaster at Durstan and came back with it at breakfast.

"So you can have another ride, Pam. It won't be to Durstan before two o'clock," Slim said as she and Alan came in for breakfast.

"An' the lady cowboy better take off'n his city clothes so he won't get 'em dirty," Ruby called out in her louder-than-man's voice and pointed at Alan with her pancake lifter.

Alan blushed and sat down. He had put on the gray flannel suit he arrived in, a white shirt and tie, and his black shoes. But he looked different from the way he had when he came three weeks ago. The July sun at the ranch had burned his skin, and his hair had grown down to the top of his collar. The front lock that he kept pushing back as he talked had grown too so there was more reason for doing it. A grasshopper had feasted on the sleeve of the city suit and left a jagged place that looked like an exaggerated moth hole.

Pamela wore a dress this morning instead of her divided skirt and shirtwaist. It was wrinkled from lying in the suitcase all the time she had been at the ranch, but it was clean. The sun had bleached a lock of her hair until it seemed lighter than her skin.

Charlie Lacey sat at the head of the table, Slim at the foot. Jake and Bill and Ruby on one side, Albert, the sixty-year-old chore boy, and Gus and Alan and Pamela on the other.

"I don't see why your father eats with his hired men," Alan had said the first day, and Pamela had explained firmly: "That's the way you do on a ranch. Besides they're as good as you are."

Charlie Lacey looked at Alan's clothes. Instead of any comment he turned his head toward the kitchen. "You got any more of those hot cakes, Ruby?"

"I ain't never run out yet that you know of, have I Charlie?" Ruby snorted as she brought in a hot stack of cakes.

Ruby had cooked at the N Lazy Y ranch for fifteen years. She liked best to cook on the roundup. Making bread in a Dutch oven on the range had ten times the zig to it that making it in any old kitchen had, but in between the spring and fall round-ups she cooked here. Slim was a good man except when he was drunk and that only happened two or three times a year. When it did Ruby slammed around the kitchen and didn't talk much. If the binge lasted too long she "took steps." The boys didn't exactly like her but they had a certain dogged respect for her, and she could milk a cow so they had cream in their coffee which they didn't have at most ranches.

Slim wiped the syrup from his sandy mustache with the back of his hand and one eyebrow raised like a cocked hat over his blue eye.

"You're not pulling out for good are you, lady cowboy?"

Pamela saw Alan clamp his lips tight together. He helped himself to another hot cake, then he looked over at Charlie Lacey.

"Yes, I am."

Charlie looked back at him. "That's up to you," he said quietly.

"Well now, I'm sure sorry. Just when I thought you was about broke in . . ." Slim began, gently for him, if Alan could have caught the note in his voice.

"Shut up, Slim," Charlie Lacey said, but he couldn't keep Slim from twisting his face in a way that made Jake and Bill snicker.

Alan pushed back his plate with the uneaten hot cakes. He looked at Slim. "I don't care for any more of your joking and I have no intention of becoming a cowboy." His thin-soled shoes made only a small sound crossing the floor, then the screen door banged. The boys were embarrassed and looked at their plates.

"Gol darn it . . ." Slim began.

"I told you before, Slim, to shut up. You pushed him too far," Charlie Lacey said.

"I'll go after him, Papa," Pamela said.

"No, I'll go." Charlie Lacey took his hat from the elk's antlers that hung above the door and went out. Jake whistled when the old man was out of hearing. Ruby took Alan's plate with the pile of hot cakes uneaten. Her face showed no expression; it never did in tense moments, so the boys didn't mind her around when they told stories.

"You going to miss your boy friend, Pam?" Slim asked, his face innocent enough except for the corners of his mouth and deep concern in his voice.

"No," Pamela said. "But you didn't need to keep at him." Her face was as stern as Charlie Lacey's.

She went on back to the ranch house and packed her suitcase, adding to her clothes the flat red rock she had found along the creek, and the arrowhead she had meant to give Alan when he left because he never did find any. She put the blankets from her bed and Alan's in the old trunk and made a bundle of the sheets that Mama had sent out "because he's not used to ranch ways." Then she went to wait for her father and Alan.

After an hour or more Charlie Lacey came back. "I couldn't find him anywhere and he didn't answer when I yelled. Where on earth do you think he went, Pam?" Charlie took off his hat, smoothed his hair back, and put his hat on again.

"Maybe down by the river, did you look there?"

"Not very far. You see if you can find him and tell him I want to pay him his wages before he goes. It's a good thing the train's held up or he'd miss it for sure."

Pamela started, then her father called her back. "Pam, what's the matter with him? He's old enough to be a man but he acts like a spoiled kid."

"He doesn't like it out here, and Slim and the boys . . ."

"I know that," Charlie Lacey interrupted impatiently. "But everyone else gets his share of joking. The boys weren't so hard on him. I should think he'd feel pretty lucky to be out here." Charlie pulled at the lobe of his ear.

The uncomfortable thought that had been in her mind all

morning pushed its way into words. "Papa, will it matter, I mean, will Mr. Randell be mad at you because of Alan?"

When Papa looked straight at you his eyes were like certain brown pebbles in the river, Pamela thought. They were brown but little glinty gold sparks shone in them. "Pamela, I don't worry about people getting mad at me. Life's too short. I imagine Randell'll be disappointed in the boy, but he's probably been disappointed before." Then he smiled at her. "Maybe a daughter's the best bet after all."

Since last night, an uneasy feeling had stayed in her mind, but now it was gone. Her father could handle anything. She never needed to worry when he was there. That was the way Slim and the boys felt about him, too. She could tell from the way they asked him about things.

She felt proud as she climbed down the other side of the corral fence, instead of going through the gate, and got her own bridle. Socks was a wily one and she had to walk around the corral after him a few times before she caught him. She pulled herself up on his back without a saddle but once on him she spread her gingham skirt out sedately on either side so it came well below her knees. Socks wasn't hers; Socks was the jingle horse that Gus used to get in the others, but Pamela rode most of the horses on the place.

She turned out across the field toward the creek where they were yesterday. Socks had to drink and while he stopped she called. Then she saw the mark of Alan's city shoes in the wet gravel of the bank. He couldn't be far. He was just mad and wouldn't answer even though he could hear her.

"You'll miss your old train if you don't come," she called to the bare field and the rocky outcroppings that rose above the house. She put Socks to a gallop up the steep hill and came out on the flat rock where they sometimes sat. It was hot up here, already.

Then she heard the sound that made Socks's ears cock forward, a strange strangled kind of sobbing. Pamela slid off the horse and let her reins hang loose. The sound came from the rocks above.

[56]

"Alan!" she scrambled up through the scratchy wild rose bushes that grew into a thicket. Alan lay stretched out on the ground holding his arm.

"Alan, what happened?"

"A rattlesnake . . ." He could hardly talk he was so scared. "I'm going to die, Pam."

She bent over him and saw the fang marks on his arm. "Alan, listen, I'll get Socks and we'll ride back to the ranch. Papa'll know what to do."

"I'm going to die," he blubbered, rolling back and forth on the ground, beating his feet into the dirt. Pamela looked back down to the ranch buildings. From here they seemed a long way off. She knelt down beside him and felt in his pockets until she found his knife, the one he had bought along with his boots and Western hat the day they came out to the ranch. This was what you did. Slim had told her over and over, but she hadn't ever seen anyone do it.

She laid his arm out flat. It was already swelling. She took the belt from her waist and wound it tight above the fang marks and tied it in a hard knot. When she held the penknife over the skin she caught her lip between her teeth. "It's all foolishness that a girl can't stick a chicken in the throat; men are twice as squeamish as women any day," Ruby always said.

What if she made the cuts wrong? If he bled to death? Her hand shook until she got the point of the knife against the skin. She made the cut, two little marks, crosswise, like an X in ticktacktoe, just under the fang marks.

She paid no attention to Alan's moans but she lay down on the ground beside him and put her mouth against the cut. "You suck for all you're worth, see," Slim had told her, "and spit the bloody stuff out."

How long? How did you know when it was enough? Her throat shut down tight so she wouldn't swallow any of the juice. If you swallowed it, would you die, too? She spat into the ground and sucked again, hard, so she could feel her cheeks pull in. Alan lay still.

"Alan!" He was alive; she could see his coat move up and down, but he must have fainted. She knelt above him, not knowing whether to go for help or keep on sucking out poison. The hot, heartless sun glared down at them. A grasshopper close to the rock sounded like a rattler and she looked sharply along the rocks and grass. She pushed back Alan's long forelock. His forehead was cold and damp in spite of the sun. She began to suck again at the puckered X she had cut in his arm. Maybe she wasn't doing any good!

She stumbled on her skirt as she got to her feet and ran across the field where Socks was placidly cropping thistles. Tying the reins around his neck she slapped him hard on the flank so he jumped sideways and stood looking at her.

"Go home, Socks! Go on!" she cried out and digging a handful of dry clay out of the ground with her fingernails she flung it hard at his head so the horse started off at a businesslike trot toward the corral. Slim would know something was wrong. Then she knelt by Alan and began sucking again, until her mouth was full of blood, and spat it out.

"Don't die, Alan," she whispered once. "You don't have to stay here. You don't have to come west ever again." Her cotton dress stuck to her back and her hair was wet on her forehead.

"You suck for all you're worth, see . . ." What if Slim and Papa were away and nobody noticed that Socks had come home without a rider! When it came time to go to the train they'd look for them, but maybe that would be too late.

It seemed a long time before she heard Ruby calling her name in her hoarse shout that Slim called her hog-calling voice. Pamela stood up and called back but she knew they didn't hear her because then Slim started calling. She ran a little way up on the rocks where she could see them and called and waved. They saw her now. Slim and Papa were going toward the corral to get their horses. She went back to Alan and sucked so hard she sounded like a pig.

They knew as soon as they saw her what had happened. "How long ago was he bit?" Papa asked.

"I don't know. He was lying here when I found him. Did I do it right?"

"You bet you did, honey," Slim said. "You did just right. Charlie, you lift him up to me and I'll carry him down."

Slim held Alan across his saddle in front of him. Papa's horse was too lively to let them ride double so he walked down with her.

"We'll give him a little whisky and get him on that train into town and we'll wire ahead to Doc Nugent so he can meet the train . . ." Papa said, but Pamela could feel that he was frightened. He was walking so fast she could hardly keep up with him. "I wouldn't wonder if you hadn't saved the boy's life." He laid his hand heavily on her shoulder.

She swallowed suddenly to keep from crying. She was glad but she felt sick at the same time, and trembly, and she couldn't get the horrid taste of Alan's warm blood out of her mouth. She broke away when they came by the ranch house and ran over to the pump to wash her face and hands with cold water. But something was wrong with the pump and only a little warm water trickled out and the water in the pail was too warm to drink. She went into the house into Papa's room and lay down on his bed for a minute so Ruby wouldn't see her and think she was a baby.

On the slow train ride back to town Alan lay on a bed made of two seats turned together and covered with a white sheet. He was unconscious again, even after the drink of whisky. Papa sat beside him. His face was so grave that Pamela didn't dare talk to him. There were only two other passengers and they sat up in front of the car, talking in low voices to the conductor. The trip to town took two hours; a man on horseback could make better time. Pamela looked out the dusty window at the endless dry fields and brown hills. The mountains they could see at the ranch were left behind so the hot blue sky rested its full weight on the ground. It was a relief when they got to town and the station and the new courthouse and the farmers' bank building and all the houses seemed to prop it up and keep it where a sky belonged and the trees along Prospect Avenue made a little green against the glare.

Dr. Nugent wanted to take Alan to the hospital but Charlie Lacey had him taken to their own house to the spare bedroom with the brass bed, next to their room. Maybelle Lacey met them at the door with a white, frightened face.

"Charlie, how terrible! His father will never forgive us."

"Now, Maybelle, lots of people have been bit by rattlesnakes and got over it. We'll need dinner here, so you better get Mamie in to help." His voice was brisk.

"I wish I knew a lot that had been bit by rattlesnakes and got over it, Charlie," Dr. Nugent said as Mrs. Lacey went out to the kitchen. "He's swelling up like a balloon."

"Well, this boy will, Ransom. Pamela got there in time." Charlie Lacey's voice allowed no doubt.

In spite of the fact that Pamela had been with him first and maybe saved his life, Mama and Mamie brushed her aside now. Alan's room was kept so quiet and dark she couldn't even look in at him. Mama whispered that he was still unconscious.

When he did come to, he would like it, Pamela thought, in the spare room with roses on the wallpaper and the woodwork painted white and a carpet the color of green grass from wall to wall. If he did come to . . . Pamela sat down on the bottom stair.

She hadn't really wanted to come in from the ranch in the middle of summer, but now that she was here the cool shaded house seemed a refuge. She felt the softness of the carpets as truly as though she were walking barefoot on them, and where there was no carpet, in Papa's study, she could feel the polish under her feet like coolness, rising right up in her ankles. The splintery board floors at the ranch always felt hot.

The log house at the ranch was all on one floor, with rooms opening out of each other. When she came back home she felt airy-fairy climbing the stairs up to the narrow hall that ran like a street in front of the bedroom doors. She could hardly remember the heat and the grasshoppers back there on the rimrock and the fear of rattlesnakes under the rocks. Here the vine-shaded front porch had the mystery of a grotto and Mama's rubber plant on the tall table in the corner of the hall was a strange dark jungle green after the dusty gray sagebrush at the ranch.

Mrs. Lacey hurried upstairs, a hot water bottle in each arm. "Pamela, don't sit there in those dirty clothes. Go draw a bath and get cleaned up. I believe you'd like to go around in ranch duds all the time. After this I hope your father will realize that you've no business running around that ranch like a wild Indian."

Dr. Nugent's buggy stood in front of the house all night. The news of the Eastern boy being bit by a rattlesnake spread over the town and neighbors brought in food so Mrs. Lacey could keep her mind on the patient. There was a piece in the paper about it and Pamela Lacey's sucking out the poison. Mr. Randell's secretary wired that Mr. and Mrs. Randell were in Europe and Charlie Lacey felt even more responsible for the boy. Dr. Nugent said he was a little mite better; he might make it, by golly!

Since school closed Rose Guinard hadn't seen anything of Pamela Lacey. She was helping her mother in the millinery shop, but after the item in the paper, she teased her mother into making some of the little French pastry tarts to take to the Laceys. Her mother, who had sold Mrs. Lacey a purple velvet hat with an ostrich plume the winter before, agreed.

"Why, yes, Rose, tonight after the shop closes and you can go up with them tomorrow." She looked at her daughter with a quizzical black eye.

Rose was glad to get out of the shop for the afternoon. She liked selling hats to the women who came in, trying different ones on to see how they looked! She liked making flowers out of bits of silk, dyeing a plain white chicken feather to match a straw, but she missed seeing girls her own age. And she hadn't seen Wrenn Morley since commencement, when he wrote on her program: "Good luck to a very pretty girl, Wrenn Morley."

Rose was afraid he had written the same thing on several other girls' programs but she didn't look to see. He had almost forgotten to ask her to write on his until she reminded him and she had looked quickly to see if Pamela Lacey had written on it, but she hadn't. She wrote, "Never forget your true friend, Rose Guinard." Wrenn had read it as she handed it back.

"Well, say, thanks, I've got one true friend, anyway," he said, smiling at her, but he didn't really mean anything by it.

She turned over at Pleasant Street so she could go by the Morleys' house. Mrs. Morley came into the shop and didn't know that one of the girls from the Brown House came to buy hats and Mr. Morley paid for them! Mrs. Guinard was cross when Rose said anything about it. "When you're in the trade, you have to know those things but you never let on you know," she said, her mouth full of pins.

From way down the street, Rose saw Wrenn mowing the lawn. The Morleys had an iron fence around their lawn and the mower made a metallic sound each time it hit the fence. When he saw Rose, Wrenn stopped and leaned on the handle of the mower.

"Hello!"

"Hello!" Rose came over to the fence. "I'm on my way up to Pam's to take some pastry. Mother thought it might come in handy. There's lots. Have one."

"Thanks. They look good." The little tart was tiny in his long hand. "I guess they're pretty worried about that boy," Wrenn said. "If he lives, it'll be because of Pam."

"I know. She was wonderful," Rose said. "I wouldn't have known what to do."

"I guess I wouldn't either," Wrenn admitted, slowly.

"Why don't you walk up there with me," Rose suggested. "I feel sort of funny going alone." She didn't. Rose would never have any fear about going any place where there were people, but she knew that Wrenn would like to go and see Pam, and she would like walking up the street with him.

"He's in that room," Wrenn said when they came to the

Laceys' house and they both looked up at the corner room, awed by the drawn shades.

"D'you suppose he's dead?" Rose whispered.

"They had the shades down yesterday and he was still living, but his side and face were swollen." Then as though he knew Rose was wondering how he knew so much, he added, "Mother came to see Mrs. Lacey and I go by on my bicycle when I go up to do the Carsons' yard."

"Let's go around to the back," Rose suggested, remembering the day she and Pamela had gone this way.

Some woman was there in the kitchen and took the box of tarts from Rose. "I'll call Pamela," she said, "but don't you make any noise."

Three steps and a narrow board walk ran out to the alley and Rose and Wrenn sat on the steps.

"Did you ever catch sight of your nose when you were talking?" Rose asked suddenly. "Honestly, it's the most embarrassing thing! Close one eye and see."

Wrenn laughed and tried it. They were both laughing when Pamela came out. After Pamela had thanked Rose and Rose had said they couldn't stay and Wrenn had explained that he was mowing the lawn when Rose came by, they sat silent, the girls on the steps, Wrenn on the grass in front of them.

"You were brave, Pam," Rose said.

"No, I'd heard Slim say what to do, only I was afraid he'd die while I was doing it. He looked terrible. Wrenn, it wasn't like the poem at all; it was more like your trout."

Wrenn looked up quickly. His eyes warmed, but he didn't say anything. Rose wondered what they were talking about.

"What's he like?" Rose asked.

"Very Eastern," Pamela said. "He doesn't like it out here."

"He won't have any reason to now, I guess." Wrenn felt embarrassed at Pam's mentioning that about the trout, but pleased, too. He wished Rose weren't there so they could talk more.

"Maybe Pam is a reason," Rose said.

"No," Pamela said quickly. "But I'm glad he's getting better.

[63]

He sits up in bed now and I'm teaching him to play cribbage."

Pamela watched Rose and Wrenn going down the street together. When they came to the corner they turned and waved and she waved back. She wondered about what Rose had said. If Alan would want to come back here because of her. But she didn't think so; he hated it too much. She didn't care, only he had been nice the other day when she took his tray up to him and nobody was there. He had held the corner of the tray so she couldn't go and said, "You saved my life, Pam. You might have died yourself."

"Oh no. I spit the stuff right out." She had to admit it, though it didn't sound noble.

"I'll never forget what you did, Pam," he had said, and his brown eyes were dark and soft.

It was a strange feeling to know you had saved somebody's life. You seemed like a different person even to yourself; a person you weren't quite comfortable with. You couldn't think about it when you were with somebody for fear it would show, but it was in your mind. Only, saving Alan's life made a bond between them and she wasn't sure that she liked that. When he first came she had thought he was very good looking and so grown up, but out at the ranch he had seemed too pale and weak and . . . Eastern, maybe. Not grown up at all. Besides, she would never like . . . love . . . no, like was better . . . anybody but Wrenn Morley.

CHAPTER 7

Rose was in the millinery shop when Pamela and Mrs. Lacey opened the door. She wore black silk sleeve protectors and a black apron and her hair was pinned up on her head so she looked quite different from the way she used to look at school, but she had the same smile that involved her red mouth, white shining teeth, her bright dark eyes, and even the little black curls above her forehead. But Mrs. Lacey was not interested in Rose except to nod briefly. As soon as the doorbell had ceased to vibrate along its coiled spring she went to the point.

"I'd like to see your mother, please."

Madame Guinard could keep track of customers in the shop from behind the curtains that partitioned off the work space, and for more important ones she bustled forth, or for those ladies who went by their first names, whose bills were paid by gentlemen of the town. Then she sent Rose back to sew or steam with a briskness that meant "I'll handle this." She came forth now with a smile that was as bright as her daughter's but didn't penetrate as far into her dark eyes.

"Good morning, ladies." There was a bowing note in her voice of which Rose was instantly, unpleasantly aware. "And what can I do for you?"

"Well," Mrs. Lacey took the chair which Madame Guinard moved a little forward for her. "Pamela is going east, and she needs a traveling hat, something in blue to wear with a dress we've had made of this material. . . ."

"You are! Oh, Pamela," Rose broke in. "Aren't you late for school?"

"I'm not going to school. I'm just going for a visit. I'll be back in December."

Madame Guinard had the sample of serge between her thumb and fingers, approving it, nodding her head. The material was too hard and thin to her way of thinking, but that was none of her affair. "Rose, bring that blue plush."

"I thought a velvet," Mrs. Lacey countered.

Madame Guinard pursed her lips, her jet sharp eyes considered. She took a length of the material Rose brought and held it back of Pamela's head, against her light hair. Pamela looked at Rose and smiled.

"Pamela will be going a good many places, naturally. . . ." The pause suggested concerts, teas, a fashionable Eastern church.

"I thought velvet would fit more occasions. . . ." Mrs. Lacey's voice often mingled both stubborn firmness and indecision, as did her mind.

"But velvet is not quite so youthful." Madame Guinard's quick plump fingers took the piece of plush between them and made it as delicate as lace.

"I like the furry look," Pamela said in the face of her mother's doubt.

That was all Madame Guinard needed. There was a flourish of triumph in her voice. "Sit down a moment, my dear." She was a stage director as she took a wooden block from the window sill and removed the hat it supported. The block had come from Paris and been her claim to superiority in the milliner's shop in New York City where she had worked before she met Claude Guinard and came west. From her pocket she whisked a tape measure and laid it around Pamela's head, then around the head block. In the base of the block was a handle that as it turned separated the wooden sphere by a narrow crack into two halves. "There!" She gathered the plush around the head block, pinning in pleats, turning back a piece for brim.

"Now, that will give us some idea . . ." The piece of plush became so much a hat that the gray wooden block seemed to take on the features of a human face. "I made a hat for Mrs. Reed's daughter to wear east to school . . . of felt," Madame Guinard said. "I couldn't get the plush then."

"I guess you'll see Wrenn when you're back east," Rose said to Pamela under cover of their mothers' talk.

"No, I'm just going to Buffalo to visit the Randells."

"That boy's family?"

"Yes, but he's in school, of course."

"I guess he'll get home while you're there!" Rose winked.

Pamela lifted her head a little. "I don't imagine so," she said and turned her attention to the hat growing under Madame Guinard's fingers.

"Now try it!"

The hat fitted unbelievably on her head. The darker blue shade deepened the color of Pamela's eyes. Mrs. Lacey tipped her head on one side to study the effect. The feminine moment waited in silence. Mrs. Lacey saw her as she would look to Mrs. Randell; Rose considered her through "that boy's" eyes. Pamela looking in the mirror caught a glimpse of herself "in the East."

"What would you trim it with?" Maybelle Lacey questioned tentatively.

Madame Guinard opened one of the deep drawers under the counter and brought out a bolt of American beauty ribbon and unrolled it recklessly so that it looped itself in satin splendor on the floor. One end became a bow across the back of the blue hat.

Pamela, watching in the mirror, caught her breath. "That's just right, Mama."

Madame Guinard had already begun pinning the bow in place.

"Have a good time," Rose said as they left. From above the gathered curtains that barred the showcase from the shop she watched the Laceys go down the street.

"Isn't Pam beautiful?" she asked with admiration that was genuine and only lightly touched with envy. Madame Guinard caught the envy and made her voice brusque.

"I wouldn't say beautiful, but she has more style than the mother, and she knows her own mind."

Charlie Lacey sat in one of the barrel-backed chairs in front of the window of the Western Hotel, smoking a cigar. He had come into town three hours before, but he had not yet gone home. The house in the middle of the day was too full of women's doings. By suppertime it was all right, and a man could expect the peace of his study to be uninterrupted. But, as a matter of fact, the house in town seemed, as it did in legal deed, to belong to Maybelle; the old place on the ranch was his. There wasn't a thing out there that wasn't meant for comfort. Nothing was ever missing because it had gone to be cleaned or reupholstered. Ruby wasn't too good a housekeeper, but he didn't mind an ash tray filled to overflowing and a smoked lamp-chimney or a little heap of dead moths on the oilcloth-covered table, nor a bed that was left as you crawled out of it. Ruby always had coffee on the stove and a good meal coming up, and you could take a drink without anyone to say, "Not too much, Charlie!" He had things on his mind today, and he couldn't hear himself think with Maybelle talking to him. She was in such a flutter over this invitation from the Randells she couldn't talk of anything else. It was a good idea to let Pam go east just now, but not for the reasons Maybelle thought it was. Maybelle thought the Randell boy had taken a shine to Pam. If he had, so much the worse. He hadn't thought much of him at the ranch last summer.

He might have to tell Randell that he needed a good-sized loan to see him through the winter if he was going to pay the boys and buy that piece of land that joined the Rocky Mountain Cattle Company's holdings, as they'd talked of doing last spring. He had thought then that he might have the money, but . . . well, he didn't. It hadn't been a good summer . . . too dry. He couldn't help that. Randell would take it all right, particularly when he felt so grateful for bringing his son through, but he'd have to call a meeting, and Crawford would hedge, and Henry Bell would put his fingers together and talk about "the investment" and whether it was safe.

Charlie Lacey took off his hat because his forehead felt hot and then put it back on his head. It was better to make the loan from a local banker as he'd done before and say nothing about it. You couldn't explain to an Easterner how things worked out here. He got up from the chair and brushed the cigar ashes from his flannel shirt.

"How're you, Charlie?" Ben Walters called out to him. Ben had a sheep ranch over on the Birdtail.

"Well, Charlie, it's good to see you in town." Ned Morley stopped to shake hands.

Ned Morley committed no Westernisms in his dress or manner and with his tan box coat, well-brushed derby, stiff white collar, and brief case, he might have been practicing law in the East.

[68]

"I just met Maybelle and Pamela," Ned said. "Pamela is excited about her trip east."

"Yes," Charlie agreed, and in that instant he decided to ask J.B. for the loan. No use getting Randell and the rest of them worked up about something he could handle by himself, on his own name if necessary. He had a drink with Ned at the bar, keeping a lookout for J.B. Ned leaned toward him and said in his dry, confidential manner, "We've drawn up the papers for the town-site company and are selling lots faster than we ever expected to. If you want those lots you've always talked about, you better buy them now, Charlie. Those of us who were born here ought not to sit by and see the newcomers buying up the land."

"You're right about that, Ned, but just at the moment . . . until I sell some cattle, I'm pretty well tied up."

"Well, you think it over. If you decide to buy in, better do it in the next month or so. Hope you stay in town long enough to get the sagebrush out of your hair." Ned smiled.

"J.B. been in?" Charlie asked Hank, the bartender.

"Not yet, but he will be," he told him and started to bring Charlie another drink.

"I'll pass this one," Charlie said and stood leaning his weight against the bar. He didn't drink much at the ranch, but it was like a holiday to be in town at noon. Besides, he was here to do business today. He could go on over to the bank, but he'd wait a little first. There was something restful about it here in the bar at the Western; the dark polished mahogany had a kind of elegance after the plastered-over interior of the log ranch house, and there was even something rather fine about the bottles of rye and Scotch and bourbon gleaming in the electric light, even without tasting them. Coming in here was one of the best things about coming into town.

He was talking with Bert Hines when J.B. came in. J.B. saw Charlie at once. People were apt to see Charlie Lacey in any room. He stood six feet two and the clothes he wore and the color of his skin brought the open spaces from the other side of King Butte into the room.

J.B. was president of the bank that bore his name on the window, and he looked like a banker and a town man. He wore a dark gray Prince Albert coat over gray striped trousers, with a vest buttoned up like a strait jacket and an immaculate stiff white collar with a black satin tie ornamented by a discreet gold stickpin. The elegance of his apparel gave the ranchers who deposited their savings in his bank a fine feeling of adeqate resources. J.B. liked to sit at his big oak desk and hear about cattle and the condition of the grass and how much snow there was in the mountains from some wind-burned rancher who had come in to ask for a loan, or pay one. He believed in the country, and he was willing to back anyone who shared his belief, if he could, but he didn't want to bump out in a buckboard to see it for himself. Name any ranch in the country, and he could put his manicured finger on its place on one of his maps inside of a few seconds. Those maps, hanging on his walls, were his books, and he could spend hours on end looking at them. He was too fat to ride a horse, though he knew a good one when he saw it and had a pair of matched Morgan carriage horses, but he kept Jim Tracy to drive them for his wife. He was content to walk down to the bank in the morning, across to the hotel at noon, and home again after banking hours; but from that small area he had done more to build the state than most men. He could tell a doer from a dreamer and smell out dishonesty with a drawing in of his slightly bulbous nose without asking a single leading question.

His wife Lucy matched J.B. in rotundity, but she was a good four inches taller, blue-eyed, red-haired, a woman to intimidate a weaker man. She had an ear and a tongue for gossip with which she entertained J.B. at meals, but he hardly listened, made no comment and never told her anything. The story went that he had met her on his way west in a lunchroom in North Dakota. No one asked. He built the big brick house with a tower

[70]

on Prospect and Fourth, but he entertained at the hotel when he had visitors from the East. The Moores had no children.

J.B. and Charlie were old friends. "Now there's the real Montana article," J.B. often told Easterners who visited him. "Keen as they come, strong enough to lift a yearling or a wagon out of the mud, and yet gentle as a woman and easygoing as a piece of good leather. His people were the pioneers, the real ones out here, not the riffraff that came out because they didn't have anything to lose back home; the ones that set up justice and saw to it that it worked. Charlie was three years old when his folks came to Virginia City, and he's grown up with the country. Why, he'd give his friend the shirt off his back," he always ended.

"Does he have any education?" a friend of J.B.'s once asked.

J.B.'s eyes narrowed. "What is education? Tell me that. If it's understanding how to get along with people and knowing his business, an' being honest and kind, yes. Oh, he went back east to a boys' school for two years; then his father died, and he had to come back and help his mother, and by that time they owned a few acres with some cattle, and Charlie had to grow up overnight. Now there isn't a man this side of the Divide who knows more about cattle. Some Easterners with money came out here looking for an investment in cattle, and when they formed a company, they got Charlie to go in with them and run it.

"Or take Ned Morley, if you want a contrast; yet he's a Montana pioneer product, too. Ned's the straightest lawyer in the state, the smartest, too . . ." and J.B. was off. He liked to exhibit his Montana friends to Easterners as some men show off specimens of native ore.

He came over beside Charlie at the bar. "What brings you into this soot-infested metropolis?"

"You," Charlie answered.

J.B. ordered his drink, or rather the bartender saw him come in and already had his favorite Old Taylor in his hand with the shot glass. J.B. nodded and let his weight bear on his left elbow that rested on the bar. Over his glass his eyes studied the painting that some cowboy artist had put there to pay his bill. He never got tired of the details: the cattle sketched in the back, the men on horseback, the branding fire, and the man in the foreground roping a steer. But the rope from the rider's gloved hand ran straight around the steer's neck without wrapping around the horn, and the horse wasn't braced for the pull. Instead of pulling tight, the rope had slipped under the horse's forefoot. J.B. had discussed the painting before with Charlie.

"What do you figure's going to happen there, Charlie?"

And Charlie had looked with disgust and said, "The damn fool hasn't even taken his dellys. See that rope going under the horse's leg? That horse is going to come down, and the cowboy's going to be killed. He couldn't ride for me." But the imminence of disaster fascinated J.B., and he studied it a little longer with the same concentration he gave the blond nude with the golden hair and the flowers girdling her waist above the bar in the Maverick Saloon down the street.

"Well, Charlie, what's on your mind?" he asked when he had finished his study. Charlie set down his glass.

"I need some money."

"You've got cattle that are worth all you want to borrow, haven't you?"

"I've got the cattle, but they're thin. They didn't come out of the summer well enough to sell now. If I keep 'em over another year, and have a good grass crop, I'll make out all right, particularly if prices go up a bit, which they're due to."

"Makes sense to me. How much do you figure you need?"

"I'd like fifty thousand, J.B." He looked straight at him.

"All right, Charlie." J.B. brought a pencil out of his vest pocket and some papers out of his coat pocket. "Here, this'll do." He turned the envelope over and wrote laboriously on the back of it, pronouncing the words as he wrote them:

Oct. 5, 1905

On or before Oct. 4, 1906, I promise to pay J. B. Moore bank 50,000 dollars with interest at 8%.

[72]

He pushed the envelope toward Charlie. "Put the Rocky Mountain Cattle Company and your John Henry underneath it, and you can write checks on the bank."

Charlie wrote in pencil. He gave his name the large C and L that ended in a flourish. J.B. stuffed the envelope back in his pocket.

"We might have another drink on that, J.B.," Charlie said.

"Nope. One at noon's my limit. Hank knows that, and he won't give me any more." The bartender beamed above his mustache. "That's right, Mr. Moore."

"Thank you, J.B.," Charlie said as they came to the door of the hotel.

"Don't thank me. It's good business, that's all." Then he took his way back to the stone bank building at the corner of Main and Sunset, and Charlie Lacey walked a block in the other direction till he came to the place where he had left his horse and buggy. He picked up the iron weight and untied his reins. The buggy tipped sideways as he stepped in.

Why had he worried? J.B. would always back him. J.B. understood how you had to work in the cattle game. If he went into details with Bell and Randell, they'd be ready to sell out tomorrow. They'd hop on the train and come out here and go over the books and drive out to the ranch and ask the same questions over and over. It was just as Slim said, J.B. didn't send someone out to count every last calf before he made the loan either. Well, bless their little careful souls, they wouldn't have to know anything about this transaction till the cattle were sold and the money in the bank. Scared of their lives, they were, though they ought to trust him by this time; he'd run the business for them out here fifteen years next April, and he'd had loans before from J.B. that they didn't know anything about.

He wasn't often in town in the middle of the afternoon, and today he had a chance to look at it. The little cottonwoods along Prospect had grown enough so their yellow leaves made quite a scattering on the street. He had a notion to drive out south of town and take a look at the prairie land that Ned thought they ought to buy up. It was funny when you stopped to think about it, that there were just three streets of big frame houses and then prairie, with Stevens' big mansion out on the hill west of town and Langs' brick three-story house out on the hill to the south, like tent stakes to hold the town on the ground. Some folks liked moving into a town and living right next door to their neighbor, but some didn't. Some wanted their own hill and a chance to see a ways. He would have liked to build over to the west where he could see the mountain range, but Maybelle always wanted to be in town, on Prospect Avenue, where the wind didn't blow quite so hard, and she felt she was living in a "civilized town" and Pam could have friends. It was a good thing that Maybelle couldn't see Pam sitting listening to Slim and Ruby and the boys yarn!

He let the horse eat so he could get a good look. Prettiest part of town, with a view way off to the Sage Hills. There was snow on them already. Some folks hated to see the snow come; Maybelle always did, but he sort of liked it. He wouldn't mind seeing the snow about three feet deep for a few days till a little moisture leaked down into the dry ground and a man could get the smell of dust out of his nose. His eyes came back from the far view to the ground. Dry as old buffalo chips, but even so, he could see the bunch grass and bluejoint and buffalo grass . . . awful good grazing. Of course, what Ned was talking about was home sites, counting on the town running way out here, houses and streets. The town was growing all the time; no reason why it shouldn't, if enough folks wanted to live in the West. He guessed he better buy a little land while he could, say forty acres or so, something like that. Maybe they could sell their house in town some day and build out here so they'd have a clear view of the mountains without going up to the attic to see them. No reason why he couldn't write a check for it right now. J.B. said the money was there for him to draw on.

Charlie Lacey took off his hat, flapped it against his knee to shake out the dust and put it on again. He drove into town at a good clip. He would stay overnight, but tomorrow he'd get right back. He needed to pay the boys up and let them go to town for a few days.

The horse turned into the alley back of Prospect Avenue and stopped by the barn of its own accord. Charlie Lacey always drove with a light hand on the reins.

CHAPTER **8**

"It will be such an opportunity!" Maybelle Lacey had said when the letter came from the Randells inviting Pamela to visit them. "You'll get more out of it than you would going east to school with Alice."

"But I'm only going to stay three weeks, Mama."

"I know, but it will make all the difference in the world. You think now that this is the only place where you want to live but you'll find out that there are other places that you want to see before you settle down out here." Maybelle Lacey frowned as she said it. She had that tone of voice that usually preceded reminiscences and Pamela edged away, afraid she would get started on the last time she went back east. It was interesting, but she had heard it before; all of it.

It was not surprising that everything about the trip east, from the swinging green curtains of the Pullman berths to the Randells' house at the top of a terrace, with an iron deer standing under a big tree . . . *Beech, it is, Pamela, the most beautiful tree there is, I think. And beeches don't grow in the West, you know!* . . . everything was familiar to her, everything but the Randells themselves.

When Mrs. Randell met her at the station her eyes filled with tears and she said, "My dear, we can never thank you enough." Mrs. Randell was a small woman with a creamy white skin and dark soft eyes. She wore a black fur coat and a black hat and a black ribbon around her neck over her net yoke almost as though Alan had died.

And Mr. Randell took her hand in both of his and said, "Pamela, we realize that we might not have a son except for your bravery and quick thinking." She could think of nothing to say so she smiled. The Randells' carriage was waiting in a long line in front of the station and it was raining so that the horses, carriages, street, and the coachmen's hats all looked polished, and the street lights, hundreds of them, blurred in the dusk like yellow blossoms that were starting to wilt. *It rains a great deal in the East, Pamela, you will have to have an umbrella.*

"How is Alan?" Pamela asked with relief at thinking of something to say.

"He's very fine," Mr. Randell said. "In spite of his being so sick, the summer out west did him a world of good. He will be home for Thanksgiving so you'll see him." *And stay till after Thanksgiving with us,* Mrs. Randell's invitation had read.

The horses' hoofs made a sharp clop-clopping sound on the paved street. Wouldn't it keep you awake at night? At home the sound of horses' hoofs was dulled by the dirt roads. There were two little glass vases in the corners of the carriage, holding small yellow flowers, but these blossoms were distinct and fresh inside where it was dry.

"We haven't had any snow yet," Pamela said in answer to Mr. Randell's question and realized that he was disappointed.

"Why, I thought it was so terribly cold out there and you had so much snow!" Mrs. Randell said.

"How's the condition of the range?" Mr. Randell asked.

"It's been a very dry summer. That's what brought the rattlers out." *If Randell asks about the grass, tell him how dry it's been, Pamela.* Already, the old straw grass around the ranch that showed the dust right through in patches seemed far away; here it smelled wet. *The moist climate will do wonders for your poor dry skin. It always does for mine,* Mama had said.

Pamela followed Mrs. Randell up the dark oak staircase, past the landing with the stained-glass window and up another half-flight to the upstairs hall that was square and as large as the sitting room at the ranch. Her room was bigger than the rooms at home and furnished with gray painted furniture that matched the woodwork. There was a fireplace in her bedroom and on the mantel stood a figurine of a goose girl in the softest shades of blue and gray. Pamela laid her handbag on a chair and went over to it. "How lovely!" she said, stroking the back of the fat gray goose.

"Don't touch it, dear," Mrs. Randell said quickly. "That's made in Denmark and very valuable."

Pamela drew her hand back quickly. The goose's back had only looked soft; it wasn't really, just cold china. Above the mantel hung a mirror and she caught sight of herself. A hat is never proved until you see yourself in it unexpectedly and are both surprised and reassured. She smiled at herself and reached up to take it off. It was all right.

"What a beautiful color. I don't imagine you bought that hat in Montana!" Mrs. Randell said.

"Yes, I did. It was made by a French milliner."

"Really!" Mrs. Randell laughed as though a French milliner in Montana were a joke. *Easterners don't think any good can come out of the West*, Mama had said.

"You will want to freshen up a bit before dinner and then come down," Mrs. Randell directed. "Don't bother to unpack, Jennie will be up to do it for you."

After Mrs. Randell had gone Pamela moved around on the blue carpet on tiptoe, looking at everything: the little bedside lamps, one on each side of the bed, and the sofa with four fancy lace pillows, and the dark red silk comforter at the foot of the bed. The bathroom opened out of her room so it must be hers. She wished Ruby could see it. "Deserted duck pond," Ruby would call it, as she did the big washtub at the ranch that she used for baths.

It was too warm in the room. Curtains as heavy as the quilt Ruby sometimes tacked over the window at the ranch when

[77]

they had a blizzard were drawn across the windows. They opened like curtains on a stage when she pulled the cord at the side. She raised the window that was set so far in from the outside wall that the rain could never spatter on the pane. The night and the weather could never come very close here. The radiator beneath the window sent up so much heat it made a screen against the night air at first. Pamela stood there until she could feel the cold finally creeping through.

"We want you to feel entirely at home, my dear," Mr. Randell said. "One of the family, just as Alan was at the ranch."

But Alan never was; he never wanted to be. Had he told them he was?

The Randells were sorry they both had to go out after dinner, but she was doubtless tired after that long trip. Perhaps she would like to go to bed early. There were books in the library, a phonograph, a stereopticon in Mr. Randell's den under the stairs and she must be sure to go out into the conservatory, the chrysanthemums were so lovely now! Mrs. Randell would have to find some young people her age; did she play the piano? "Just go anywhere you like; you don't need to be timid because Chloe and Jennie, the cook and second girl, will be in their quarters," Mrs. Randell said.

"It's going to be so nice to have a daughter in the house." Mr. Randell put his arm around Pamela's shoulders. "I'm expecting you to take me down to the office in the mornings and come for me in the evening."

The Randells are so friendly you will feel perfectly at ease with them, Pamela, Mama had told her.

But Pamela didn't feel quite at ease with them. It was rather a relief to be left alone. She wondered what Alan was like when he was at home. The grandfather clock in the hall tolled the quarter hour and the sound made the house seem empty. She walked slowly through the downstairs rooms, touching with her eyes books in the library she might read, the phonograph, the piano. She went over to it and played the first bars of "Juanita."

The conservatory opened just off the music room. The door

[78]

had a stained-glass window like the window on the stairs. When she opened it light from the hall shone through the stained glass and showed a tree, green-leaved and heavy with red fruit. She traced the fruit with her finger. They must be pomegranates like the fruit in the basket Mr. Randell had brought last spring. The air in the greenhouse, strangely fresh, strangely fragrant, came around her like the sudden freshness of a warm chinook wind at home, but there was no wind here. Every plant and fern stood stock still, like flowers at a funeral. The conservatory was dark except for the street lamps. Maybe gaslight was bad for plants. You could come in here any time and pick flowers, even in winter. The earth-cold smell of them led her to the chrysanthemums and she touched a big curled-mop head with her fingers. Uncle Jeb Moore had had chrysanthemums shipped in for Mrs. Moore's twenty-fifth wedding anniversary.

The clock tolled the half hour. It was rather strange to leave her alone the very first night. Mother wouldn't have left Alan. She wished he were home.

Standing inside the glass house she could see the lights from the house across the street and the street itself, in between the big dark trees. It was very different from the street at home. A cab passed by rolling smoothly on the smooth pavement. A man walked briskly on the sidewalk and when he passed under the lights she could see the round stiff crown of his hat, like Wrenn's father wore. Then the street was still.

Mama had said, *When I go back east, I always feel as though I'd come home in a way. You will, too. After all, all our roots are in the East.* But she was different from Mama.

Pamela walked back out of the conservatory and closed the door behind her. Jennie, the second maid, came down the stairs and said, "Good evening, M'am," looking at her with round curious eyes.

"Good evening," Pamela said. She wished she would stay and talk, but she hesitated to ask her to. The door to the pantry swung after her. The clock intoned another quarter hour. She might as well look at the stereopticon views.

Mr. Randell's den was a warm green room with the biggest leather chair she had ever seen, twice as big as Papa's, and a roll-top desk as big as the ones in the courthouse at home. She found the stereopticon and a taboret piled with boxes of pictures and selected Paris rather than Africa or India or historic Boston. Then she saw the picture over the desk; a framed photograph, too palely gray to be distinct, but even across the room the outlines had a sharp familiarity. It was a picture of the ranch; that was King Butte in the distance. At the bottom in white ink was printed, Rocky Mountain Cattle Company. Below the long picture was a smaller one showing the ranch house with Mr. Randell and Slim and Papa on the steps, and Ruby standing in the doorway. She swallowed quickly. Why should he have these pictures here? He was president of the Rocky Mountain Cattle Company only. . . . The ranch house looked dilapidated in a picture. It wasn't really like that. Papa was wearing his old hat. Ruby had her apron rolled over her arms so it must have been dirty and she didn't want it to show. The brim of Slim's hat was so wide you couldn't see anything of his face but the chin. Mr. Randell seemed out of place standing there. The ranch looked bare-naked in the picture. Not a tree showed. When you were really there you saw the stand of aspen by the river and that big old cottonwood by the corner of the barn and the mountains over to the north. They were so faint in the picture they looked like clouds.

She didn't want to look at the stereopticon views of Paris after all, so she went on up to her own room.

Those three weeks will be an experience you'll never forget, Maybelle Lacey had said.

That was true, Pamela thought soberly, as she sat on the train on her way home, and sorted out her impressions. She never, never would. Beside her in a paper bag was the blue hat with the American beauty ribbon, and on her feet were the button shoes of russet leather that Mrs. Randell had bought for her. On the window sill so it could get air, along with the cinders, through the crack under the window was the corsage of rose-buds that Mr. Randell had given her. And he had kissed her on the station platform, holding his hat in his hand, with his gray curly hair blowing in the wind. "You're your father's own daughter, my dear," he had said, which was a compliment be-cause she had heard Mr. Randell telling Mr. Archer that Charlie Lacey was a "prince of a man." "I want to get Alan out there again. The rattlesnake bite cut short his stay last summer."

And of course Mrs. Randell had kissed her good-by. Mrs. Randell looked a little like a mink, she thought, like the one Slim had trapped at the ranch, with a little face and little ears and dark eyes and fur. Or was it that Mrs. Randell had a mink coat with dozens of little tails and claws?

She liked Alan best, which was odd because she hadn't liked him at the ranch last summer. But he was different here. He was better looking in his own Eastern clothes; almost, handsome. He was a little bit like his father, especially when he spoke to the coachman. When he talked about the ranch, he had sounded as though he had had a great time. "We used to ride every afternoon," he had said one night at dinner and he asked how "old Slim" was. "He was a card, wasn't he? And Ruby was a pippin!" as though they were old friends of his. She had known then that he had never told his mother and father how he had hated it there. She began to wonder if she had just dreamed that he had rushed out of the cookhouse in a rage, or that she had seen him lying unconscious on the ground after the rattle-snake bite. He still carried the snake rattles that Slim had sent him when he was in bed at their house.

"They're my luck charm," he said. "Before an exam I shake them in my hand like this."

It made her uncomfortable to think of the Thanksgiving dance the Randells gave. Mama would love hearing about it; the orchestra hidden by palms in the end of the library and flowers everywhere and the caterer and waiters to serve the chicken salad and ices and cakes. She had felt fine standing next to

Mrs. Randell in the receiving line, in the blue satin dress of Mama's that Miss Bell had made over. Mrs. Randell introduced her as "our young friend from the West." She had thought at first that they had given the party for her at the end of her visit but then she heard people saying that the Randells always gave one every Thanksgiving. She could tell by Mrs. Randell's quick dark eyes moving over her that she looked well. She could tell it, too, by Alan's glances.

"Who would ever believe it if they saw you out at the ranch last summer? Only thing the same is that lock of hair that was bleached in the sun," Alan said. Her fingers reached up to tuck the telltale strand under but he said, "Don't; I like it." He brought up his college friends to meet her and they seemed to know all about her already as she knew about them from listening to Alan last summer. When the short, red-headed one was dancing with her he said, "I'd like to come out to your ranch this summer, may I? Randell thinks he owns you."

But she remembered sitting on the window seat on the stair landing with Janie Mason, that girl with the black hair and velvet dress, and Sally, and Mrs. Randell's niece, Jennifer. The boys had gone to get refreshments for them and the girls were talking of people and things she didn't know so she had felt silent and stupid.

Pamela's eyes moved along the stitching of her russet boots and followed the dear little amber buttons, but her mind wouldn't be distracted. The boys had come back and somehow she found herself talking, making them all laugh so Janie Mason kept saying, "Did you really? Oh, I'd have died!" And the red-haired boy said, "No wonder you went out west, last summer, Randell! Old Teddy Roosevelt had the right idea with his Rough-riders, didn't he?"

Of course, she hadn't *really* taken Chuck's place as night rider at the roundup camp, but she had been on roundups and she almost believed it herself as she told about it. The part about the wind and the dark and the cowboys singing and the campfires burning low was true enough. You had to make it sound exciting or people weren't interested in the West.

"Wasn't there any other woman on the roundup?" Sally asked.

"Oh yes, Ruby was there; Ruby is the foreman's wife. Alan knows her," but she didn't look at Alan.

"I should say I do. You should see her!" Alan said, smiling at Pamela as though they had a secret.

"Did you ride on the roundup, too?" one of the boys asked Alan and she had explained quickly that roundup came in May and October. People in the East really didn't know anything at all about ranching.

She remembered now how the Randells' niece had licked the ice off her spoon with a delicate red tongue and said, "Do you live right on Uncle Ralph's ranch?"

She had hated that. Alan knew she did. The ranch was theirs as much as the company's; more, because Papa had owned some of it before there ever was any company, but she only said, "No, we live in town."

"Oh, say, I wouldn't want to be out west and live in town," one of the boys said.

Alan explained, "A Montana town is pretty different from Buffalo; you know, false fronts to the stores and plenty of saloons and saddle horses tied out in front and every now and then a little gun fight." So he was making up, too.

"How about Indians?" Sally asked.

"Oh yes, we still have Indians in town sometimes, from the reservation," she had said, not bothering to make them sound colorful or exciting. It was her fault, she supposed, she had started talking about home, but now they sounded belittling. They wouldn't think much of Brandon Rapids. It was horrid the way you could be part of a group one minute, laughing and talking, and the next, way outside by yourself. And coming from the West did make a difference. She wished she had never come east to visit the Randells because now she saw The West

[83]

with her eyes and their's at the same time and it took something away from it.

Alan had taken them down to the den to see the pictures of the ranch, and the girls had shrieked at the bareness and ugliness, and she had wanted to cover it all with her arms.

"Don't you have any trees?" Jennifer asked.

"Yes, we have beautiful cottonwoods and just beyond here, where you can't see them are some lovely aspens, and up in the foothills there are some jack pines. We don't have beeches or maples, of course. You should see the view from the porch. Those are the Rockies that look like clouds," she had said, but they weren't interested any more.

"Coming to North Dakota, now," the conductor stopped to say.

"Thank you," she said politely and looked out across the white flat fields that seemed to become part of the sky, but she hardly saw them. She went right on remembering that night of the Thanksgiving dance.

"Wait for me in the conservatory," Alan had said, when he went out to help people in their carriages.

More than anything else about the Randells' house she would miss the conservatory. It was always so unexpected: by just opening the door with the pomegranate tree you could step into another world. At night it was cool and moist and shadowy. For the dance, tall iron candelabras were placed along the aisles and the little candle flames threw shadows of the plants on the wall. The smell of earth . . . loam, Mrs. Randell called it, mixed with the flower smell, and you could breathe deeper than in the warm house. When she touched the flowers they were soft and cool and unreal, almost magic. She picked a red carnation and laid it against her cheek, like a person in a play. Alan would be coming to find her in a minute. Maybe she would give him the flower, she had thought.

And then Alan came back, and they walked down to the end of the conservatory where the orange trees stood in big red pots.

"You're so different from others girls, Pam. I was thinking

[84]

that tonight with Janie and Sally and Jennifer. When you told those stories about the West with a perfectly straight face, I nearly burst out laughing. They believed every word of them."

"Well, I . . . *you* made Brandon Rapids sound like a town in the holdup days."

"Of course! I had to back you up. Can you imagine what those girls would think of Brandon Rapids?"

"You don't need to back me up. I don't care what they would think of it." She remembered how she had pinched the carnation into a red wad. Squeezing it made it all the more fragrant so she threw it in one of the orange pots. "I think I'll go to bed now. It was a lovely party. Good night, Alan," she had said.

"Don't go yet, Pam. I won't see you till summer." Alan caught hold of her arm. "If I go to Europe next summer, I won't see you then."

She had been so surprised that he had any idea of seeing her next summer. "Why, you hated it; why would you want to come back again?" she had asked. She had thought he was going to say . . . she pushed the cinders on the sill down in the crack under the train window. "Maybe Pam is a reason," Rose had said that time. But Alan said, "Oh, I didn't exactly hate it; not after I got home and thought about it. Chaps at school are always asking me about it; I make a good story of it . . . all the yarns your father told and Slim . . ."

She had thought of the red-haired boy saying, "Randell thinks he owns you." What had Alan said about *her?*

". . . I wouldn't let Slim or Ruby or any of them get my goat another time. I suppose it got under my skin because I wasn't used to that sort of ragging. I'd like to go back and show them."

He was trying to apologize for last summer. But he wouldn't be any better another time. He couldn't handle Slim just by calling him "old Slim" and saying he was a card. Couldn't he see! He didn't understand them any better than he had then. She had felt suddenly sorry for him. And then he had given a funny little laugh and said, "I don't mean that's the real reason why I'd be going back, Pam."

When she glanced up at him, he was pushing the stick with the Latin name on it deeper into the dirt of the flowerpot, and he was frowning.

"Ever since you saved my life, Pam, I've felt . . ."

"Oh, that!" she had said quickly because that wasn't what she had expected him to say and, anyway, that was over and done with. "Your mother will be wondering where we are. We ought to go and say good night," she had said.

"Wait, Pam. May I write you?"

"Why, yes, if you want to." And then Alan had blown out the candles and they had gone back into the house. She wished now that she hadn't interrupted him.

The next morning at breakfast there was the note for her at her place. Mr. Randell had gone to take Alan to the station and she and Mrs. Randell had sat together at the table.

The note read: "I didn't finish what I wanted to say. I'll have to come out to the ranch next fall when I get back from Europe. I'll find a way. Love, Alan." She had it folded in with her handkerchiefs. It was funny that he sounded so much more sure in his note than when he was talking to her.

"Alan felt so badly about having to go without saying good-by this morning, but I told him you were entitled to your beauty sleep," Mrs. Randell said. "How did you enjoy the party?"

"It was a very nice party," she had said, wondering what Mrs. Randell would think of Alan's going out to Brandon Rapids again. What would she think of his writing "love" in his note?

And then after a little space, in a voice like Jennifer's she had asked Mrs. Randell about her reservation for home.

"Dear, dear, don't you like the East any better than that?" Mrs. Randell had said in a teasing tone.

"I don't like it as well as the West," she had said.

You'll just hate to leave there. I always do, Mama had said, but she didn't. When she changed trains in Chicago and saw the sign TRAINS FOR THE WEST in the station it meant her, like the sign SENIORS did when she went back to school last fall.

It was snowing out the window, little fine grains of snow, coming down so fast you couldn't see anything else. The conductor lighted the lamps in the train it was so dark.

"I guess people get lost in blizzards like that!" the man across the aisle said to the conductor.

"Yes, sir!" the conductor shook his head. "Pretty rough country out here! Makes a person think about the folks that made it out here in the covered wagon."

Pamela held her hands tight together, her eyes out the window, playing the game they played most often as children on their street. She was shivering under the canvas top, moving her shoulders with the lurching movement of the covered wagon. She had played covered wagon in the Morleys' arbor and in the hammock on the porch. The best covered wagon they ever had was an old delivery wagon from the Emporium. They were always sending someone to shade her eyes and look ahead, then run back. The play ended when they arrived to settle. It was the going that was exciting. Sometimes, they pretended to arrive and chose sites for their houses and put stones to mark them, with a big stone for the church and one for the courthouse and another for the school, but then Indians would appear or the water was discovered to be alkali and poisonous to drink, or there were already too many people there so they would pile back into the covered wagon and drive on across the prairie or through the mountain passes.

But this time she wanted to arrive, to come to her own home in her own town, where she wasn't something different. Soon it would be Christmas and Wrenn would be home. And after Christmas she might take that position in Mr. Sewall's office for a while, and after that . . .

It was 40° below zero the next morning. The train was held up thirty-five miles east of Brandon Rapids so they didn't arrive until late afternoon. The windows were coated solid with frost and the heat in the pipes couldn't compete with the wall of cold outside. "You'd know you were getting back to Montana all right!" people said with a laugh, edged with pride at the ruggedness of the Montana climate. One man on the train had

[87]

never been west before and he kept asking questions about the climate that moved the other passengers to wilder and wilder tales. "Why, I see it one winter where the thermometer never got above thirty below for three months." "It's all right if you got a good constitution and an inside job!" another man declared with a wink, and his wife contributed the information that she froze both ears the first winter in Montana.

Pamela was the first one off the train and when she found no one on the platform she dropped her suitcase and ran across to the station, flinging open the door. The people waiting there were gathered around the big-bellied stove, so busy keeping warm that they hadn't heard the train. They felt the cold air and looked up to see Pamela in the doorway, a bright-eyed, red-cheeked apparition. For an instant she looked as though she were going to embrace the whole room.

"Mama!" She rushed over to Maybelle Lacey, who was done up like a mummy with a white shawl wrapped around her head and over her shoulders. "Where's Papa?"

"He couldn't get in from the ranch. We've had a blizzard for three days and you know how that road is! Mrs. Moore offered to send their carriage down, but I wouldn't hear of keeping anyone's horse or driver out in the weather. I said we'd take a cab. What are you laughing at?"

"Oh, Mama, it sounds so like home!"

CHAPTER 9

1906

Charlie Lacey came in for J.B.'s funeral. He had heard of his death at King Butte and driven right on in, staring with disbelieving eyes at the familiar country he passed.

John Benjamin Moore had gone on one of his rare trips into

[88]

the country to see some ranchland and been caught in an early April rain that turned to snow. He came back home chilled through the heavy wool of his suit, drank a stiff nightcap and went to bed, but by afternoon of the next day he was delirious and died the fifth day, at fifty-nine. Dr. Nugent said no doc could move that fast. "Death put his horse into a dead run that time, for sure." His remark was repeated many times. Death on a good horse was easier to think of than death in the form of a blind, shuffling ghost.

Down on Main Street J.B.'s bank was closed and the plate-glass window draped with black. Men who didn't attend the funeral spoke in quiet voices about J.B. In the Silver Dollar Saloon they raised a glass to him and at the bar of the Western Hank threw out the almost full bottle of Old Taylor. If J.B. couldn't drink it, no one else was going to.

Mr. Sewall told his young secretary, Pamela Lacey, that she could have the afternoon to go to the funeral. But when she got home Charlie Lacey said, "There's no reason for you to go, Pam. I don't like funerals. When I die I want some of the boys to dig me a grave at the foot of King Butte and remember some of the good times we've had and call it quits."

"Why, Charlie Lacey!" Maybelle picked a raveling from his black suit. "But I don't know that you do need to go, Pamela. It'll be terribly crowded."

Pamela was grateful. She had never been to a funeral, but the day itself was mortgaged to sorrow. After her mother and father had gone down the street, the house seemed empty. The commonest thing, like the yellow leaf on the rubber plant, took on a mournful significance. She went back downtown to see Rose. Ever since Christmas, she had got into the habit of dropping in at the millinery shop. When there were no customers they sat on the wire-backed chairs and talked. Madame Guinard liked to have her come to visit Rose, but today Madame Guinard had gone to the funeral. It had been Mr. Moore who had loaned her money to start the shop.

"I feel awful for his wife," Rose said, twisting a piece of velvet between her fingers. "Mother made her a mourning hat and veil to wear and I took it over to her. I could see her heart is broken."

Rose had a way of saying things that shocked Pamela, and excited her at the same time; she went right to the heart of the matter.

"I just betcha she won't live long without him," Rose added. Pamela was silent, thinking of Mrs. Moore growing pale and weak. After a decent interval of sympathetic thought they returned to their own affairs.

Rose asked, "Do you hear from Alan?"

"I have once," Pamela said, thinking of the letter Alan had written from college. At the end he had written, "I am coming out there next summer and don't you forget it." But she didn't believe it.

"Do you like Wrenn better than Alan?"

"Yes, of course, but Alan's lots different when he's home."

"Nicer?"

"Ye-ss."

"Did you think Wrenn had changed much at Christmas?"

"No," Pamela said slowly. She could feel Rose waiting for her to say more, but she wouldn't.

"I guess you and Wrenn are as good as engaged," Rose said.

Color flowed over Pamela's face. "Why, what an idea! Wrenn has to finish college first and then law school . . ."

The jingle of the spring bell startled them both. Rose jumped to her feet. With the woman who entered the shop came a shrill odor of perfume. Anyone could tell at a glance that there was rouge on her face, too light a pink for her sallow skin and dark hair and eyebrows. And she wore her skirts well above her ankles.

Rose said quickly, "Mother isn't in."

"That's all right, dearie. She's got a hat ready for me. Flola at the Brown House."

Rose's face reddened. Pamela Lacey became absorbed in the hat in front of her. Both girls knew the Brown House by whispered name and by sight. Pamela had seen "the girls" out on the porch, but never one of them in the same room. Her shocked thought seemed to articulate itself in the silence.

"I'll look," Rose said.

The young woman walked around the shop on her high heels, looking at each hat; trying one on and picking up a mirror to see the back of it. Her lips were painted, too. Pamela studied her in the mirror.

Rose returned without the hat. "I didn't find it, but Mother's just gone to a funeral; she'll be right back."

"The whole town's at that funeral. Well, I'll be back, but I know the hat's here and you know I've got credit."

"I wouldn't know . . . Mother tends to . . ." Rose began but the girl turned suddenly and pointing one foot, with her hand on her hip interrupted.

"Look here, you two, just remember this. I may be a hooker, but I am because I want to be. Nobody makes me!" She banged the door when she closed it and the bell jangled a faint protest. The ugly word stayed behind. Rose looked quickly at Pamela.

Pamela picked up her bag. "I have to go." She wanted to be out of the little shop where the heavy perfume still lingered and that word that she had never heard before kept sounding in the air. But she had an idea about what it meant from the feeling of the little hairs on her arms and the prickly feeling of her scalp.

"I feel sorry for her, really I do . . . in a way," Rose said.

The ordinariness of Rose's voice struck harshly on Pamela's ear.

"Mother doesn't like her sort coming here, but they're the ones that can pay big prices for hats. They never even ask the price usually!"

Pamela straightened the hat over the featureless face of the wooden block. "How can they?" The question forced its way out. She didn't look at Rose.

"Oh, the men who . . . visit them, leave credit here. Fifty and seventy-five dollars sometimes. Mother always sends me to the back of the shop when they come, but I hear them. You don't need to say anything to your mother about her being here, though."

"No," Pamela said. As though anything would make her! The bell tinkled whenever the shop door was opened and led to quick entrances and departures, but it had nothing to do with Pamela's haste as she closed the door behind her. She walked swiftly up the street in the thin spring light. It was beginning to warm up again but she felt no warmth. You couldn't trust weather that was cold enough to chill a man to his death one day and felt like spring the next.

At the corner, private houses met the business section but tonight the houses, themselves, looked secretive. They were no different on the outside from the Brown House, except that it stood by itself over by the tracks and no one bothered to make a lawn or plant flowers. The Moores' house commanded the second corner, dark red brick with plate-glass windows that shone more than most windows. It had always looked to Pamela as though nothing could hurt it. But now folding chairs piled against each other on the porch were a dreary reminder of the funeral, and the shades were drawn upstairs. Unconsciously, she walked softly, keeping her eyes ahead of her down the street. Mrs. Moore was inside with a broken heart.

When she came to their house, she could see her father sitting by the front window, reading the paper, and enormous relief flooded through her. He was never sad or worried. He went out in all kinds of weather and never got sick. He was a "prince of a man" Mr. Randell had said, not one of those terrible men who visited places like the Brown House. She felt as she always had as a child when her father came in from the ranch; when he was home everything was fine.

CHAPTER 10

The work in Mr. Sewall's office was not difficult. Pamela could write a fair letter now on the big Oliver typewriter, or, which was more important, she could keep up with Mr. Sewall as he sat tipped back in his chair dictating ponderous sentences about the pioneers. And when, as frequently happened, the sentence broke off in mid-air and Mr. Sewall waved his cigar at her and said, "something to that effect" she finished it. Pamela had not been engaged for the business of the hardware store of which he was owner but for the purpose of helping him compile the records of the Montana Pioneer Society of which Mr. Sewall was the secretary.

Mr. Sewall was called upon to make speeches and these Pamela typed, coming to know by heart such sentences as, "We must realize that the pioneers who braved the hardships and dangers of this then unknown territory are the aristocracy of this great state and the roll of their names is a proud roll. They were guided by a dream . . . perhaps a dream of gold, a dream of peace after the inferno of civil war, of greater opportunity for their children, but a dream!"

She came to know that those who were resident in the territory before May, 1864, were a little more aristocratic than those who couldn't claim residence before December of that fateful year.

"Your people and my people, young lady, were called to a high destiny." It seemed amusing that her mother had managed that destiny by being born on May 15th of that year and that her father had happened to come out west when he was three. Papa never attended the Society's meetings, but the organization was as important to Mama as the Shakespeare or the Cosmoramic Clubs.

Mr. Sewall was in his seventies and had delegated most of the business of the hardware store to others so he was free to devote more and more of his time to the Pioneer Society. He traveled all over the state and went to all manner of inconvenience and expense to verify a record, or meet with an old-timer. All the names of the pioneers were kept in a file in his office and under each was a record which Pamela typed. The briefer ones followed the same pattern:

"Martin Francis Bailey, born in Kentucky January 10, 1838. Place of departure for Montana, Illinois; route traveled, across the plains via Colorado 1860; arrived at Alder Gulch in 1864. Occupation farmer. Last address." There was nothing of what they thought when they got here, whether they were glad they had come. The "place of departure" seemed important. The route traveled was eloquent in itself: across the plains, by steamboat, by boat to California.

"Certain significant facts become apparent . . ." Mr. Sewall dictated. "One of these is the large Southern element that has shaped the development of this state." Mr. Sewall, himself, had come from Tennessee after the Civil War. His mother's people had come from Virginia. "That the state was founded by pioneers representing such diversity of occupations, backgrounds, and stations in life is proof of that true democracy on which the country itself is founded."

Pamela held her finger above the key to see whether or not to put a period. It was hard to judge by the fall of Mr. Sewall's dictating voice. Above Pamela's desk hung a map with pins to mark the places of settlement of the pioneers. Towns long since deserted, like Bannock, were heavily populated and sometimes in the pauses, while Mr. Sewall groped for ideas or words or both, she visualized those early towns. No, he wasn't through. "The early history of this glorious state," he continued, "is still within the memory of living man, your memory and mine, but how long will that be true? Time glides past with the ceaseless momentum of the Missouri, we must record and preserve for the future before it is too late."

[94]

"A great heritage, my dear!" Mr. Sewall often said as he closed the file case.

Sometimes old-timers dropped into the office to talk of the early days and she sat quietly at her desk listening until she knew many of the road agents and actresses who trooped the state in the days of the gold camps, vigilantes, and early-day politicians. Secretly, she wished she knew someone now who was as dashing as that early governor of the territory, an Irishman named Meagher, who met an untimely death by drowning off the boat at Fort Benton.

"It must have been exciting then," she said one day after Mr. Sewall's visitors had gone.

"But very hard on the women."

"I shouldn't have minded," Pamela said, putting the cover over her typewriter for the day. "I'll mail these invitations on my way home."

On June 30th, the Pioneer Society was giving a ball for those who belonged to "that proud roll," or whose parents belonged. They were to wear old-time costumes, preferably the very ones that had seen those days. When Rose was refurbishing the bonnet Pamela was to wear she said, joking, "I might borrow that black taffeta I wore on the Pioneer Day float and go, too. I'd say my father was a card shark and I came around the Cape by boat and over the mountains from California in my tasseled boots! I bet they wouldn't dare ask me to leave."

"Oh, you couldn't, Rose!" Pamela said seriously and then stopped as Rose laughed.

"Just for fun I'd like to try. I'd ask Wrenn to take me. His mother was in the shop the other day and said he'd be home this week."

Pamela puzzled over Rose as she went down the street. You couldn't ask a boy to take you to a dance, that was the trouble with being a girl. But Rose sounded as though she really might.

One dance was a waltz and the next one was an old-time square dance that all the old people could join in.

Swing your corner like swingin' on a gate
And now your own if you're not too late.

Mr. Sewall swung Pamela around. The old people danced harder than the young ones. How funny the old dresses looked; Wrenn's mother was in her very own wedding dress. Wrenn wore his grandfather's suit that he had worn on the float.

Now swing that gal across the hall
You ain't swung her since way last fall!
Now go back home and swing your own
And leave that gal of mine alone.

"Good evening, Mr. Williams." (Mr. Williams, place of departure, New Hampshire. Route traveled, steamboat. Occupation now, cashier in the bank.) He had come for gold and ended up handling other peoples' money. Was he satisfied?

"Don't look like many of the pioneers got rich, does it?" Mrs. Manning was joking with her partner.

Allemand left with your left hand
Right to your partner, right and left grand.
Meet your own and promenade.
Go two by two, take her home like you oughta do.
Everybody swing!

Alice Reed was home from Boston. Rose said she put on airs. Wrenn was just the same. . . . "Good evening, Dr. Nugent."

There was Johnny Gates who hadn't done a day's work since he gave up placer mining, Papa said. And funny old Miss Estes who read fortunes in tea grounds. All these people were guided by a dream. What was her own grandmother's dream? Her husband didn't want to fight the North, Mama said, so he and his wife came out west. But the dream . . .

The music ended and everyone stood clapping.

"I'm glad that's over, the next one's ours." Wrenn stood beside her.

"You make me think of Pioneer Day and our float in those clothes," Pamela said.

"Only you were weeping that day, all the way up Main Street!"

"Because you were hanging my husband," she said. She had felt a certain way that day . . . she couldn't quite remember . . . riding down the street, knowing people were looking at her, feeling brave, somehow, and lonely. And afterward at Harpers' woods . . .

"It's a long time since Christmas," Wrenn said.

Pamela lifted one eyebrow, suddenly teasing. "I've been working so the time has gone by fast."

"How's your Eastern friend?"

"Alan? Oh, he's . . ." she shrugged her shoulders, forgetting this time to be arch.

"Let's leave and walk home. It's hot in here," Wrenn said. "We'll just dance out the door."

They whirled sedately around the room and out into the hall. The dance was held upstairs in the Gold Block. A long flight of wooden stairs led down to the street. Wrenn still held her hand as they went down together, Pamela's red taffeta skirt rustled over the dirty stairs.

"What's happened since I went away?" Wrenn's voice took on the warmth of the summer's night.

"I can't think of anything. You knew Mr. Moore died. That was awful."

"Yes, Mother wrote me. And somebody from the East is running the bank."

"At Christmas time Rose asked me if the East had changed you," Pamela said.

"What did you say?"

"I didn't think so then; you've been away longer now."

"It hasn't changed me about one thing, anyway."

"What's that?" Her voice was hardly audible over the sound of their feet on the plank walk.

"Don't you know?" He pressed the hand he held. "About you."

"Oh," she said stupidly. He meant . . . What did he mean?

[97]

But he went on walking beside her in silence. They were almost home.

"Let's sit on the porch." They walked past the row of rocking chairs to the swing at the end. The vines from the hanging baskets moved softly in the air. A path of light ran from inside the house across the porch but it missed the swing. It was a little like the Randells' conservatory.

"This is better than the dance," Wrenn said. "You couldn't talk in there." He laid his arm along the back of the swing just above her head. She set the swing in motion with her foot, then she leaned forward.

"We must have left the light on in Papa's study. I'll go in and turn it off." Pamela felt for the key under the cushion on the first rocker and unlocked the door. In a minute she was back. "Wrenn! There's someone in the house," she whispered. Her face in the light from the hall was pale.

"Your father isn't home, is he?"

"No, he hasn't been in since the roundup."

"Here, let me go first." Inside the hall they listened a moment. There was no doubt: someone was shuffling papers in the room at the end of the hall. Wrenn drew himself up. He walked a little stiffly. Pamela came behind him, one hand barely touching his coat sleeve. Almost together they reached the study door.

Charlie Lacey was sitting at his desk, writing in a big ledger. His hat was on the desk beside him and he wore ranch clothes.

Wrenn gave a little artificial cough. "Good evening, Mr. Lacey."

Charlie Lacey closed the book quickly as he looked up.

"Papa, when did you get home?"

"Why, hello, Pam, Wrenn. I thought you were at the Pioneer Ball. I had to get this ledger I left here. I'm just about to leave." He picked up his hat.

"You aren't going back to the ranch tonight, Papa!" The bulb under its green shade made his face look greenish, too.

"No, I've got to go down to the hotel. Randell and Bell are in town."

"But . . . you're all muddy."

"I got stuck in the mud getting into King Butte from the ranch. I got their letter and came right in." He went ahead of them down the hall. They heard his footsteps going down the walk.

"Wasn't that silly to be afraid?" Pamela said.

"Of course it wasn't, you didn't know he was coming in. I guess we startled him, too," Wrenn said.

"Would you like some lemonade?" Pamela asked as they hesitated on the porch.

"Say, that would taste good," Wrenn said almost too enthusiastically. They went on out to the kitchen but a kind of unnaturalness lingered.

"You can chip off some ice," Pamela said, giving him the ice pick. She set about squeezing lemons. Her red taffeta trailed on the kitchen floor and got in her way so she fastened it up with a safety pin.

"A scrub lady in taffeta," Wrenn said and they laughed. She took the pitcher of lemonade and danced ahead of him to the front door, but he caught up with her and held the screen door closed so she was caught between the door and his arm.

"Let me out or I won't give you any lemonade."

When he tried to kiss her she turned her head and his lips touched her ear. They were both surprised. She pushed against the door and stepped out on the porch just as the carriage stopped in front of the house and Mama got out.

"Oh, there you are!" Maybelle Lacey said. "I just thought you had gone on ahead so I came home with the Clarks. Wasn't it a lovely dance! I wish Charlie had been there."

"Papa is in town." Pamela felt Wrenn standing beside her.

"Why, when did he get here?"

"He was home when Wrenn and I came. Mr. Randell and Mr. Bell are down at the hotel and he came in to meet them."

"For pity's sake! He should have brought them to the ball. I suppose we'll have them for dinner tomorrow night. Let's see, maybe Mr. Blodgett could get me some squabs, and I'll have to get ahold of Mamie in the morning. . . . Your father has no idea of the work there is to putting on a dinner at short notice."

Pamela and Wrenn stood a little awkwardly until she went in. Pamela's hands were ice cold from the lemonade pitcher. She set it on the table and went over to the swing.

Wrenn poured the lemonade without saying anything. If she hadn't been so silly thinking someone was in the house when it was only Papa . . . Wrenn handed her a glass and she took a sip.

"It needs more sugar." She wished Wrenn would sit down. They were so quiet she could hear him swallow.

"I like it this way." He leaned against the porch railing.

It was strange to have to try to find something to say to Wrenn; she had never had to before. Then the words spoke themselves. "I'm glad you're back. It seemed awfully queer with you away."

"I thought you were so busy you didn't notice!"

She gave a little laugh. "Not quite that busy."

Wrenn sat down beside her on the swing. "I'm glad of that." His voice was so close she could feel his breath against her cheek. He kissed her quickly on the lips and held her hand between them on the swing. His hand was warm and sheltering over hers. When she moved her hand ever so little, his tightened.

"I guess I better go," he said into the silence. "Maybe we could walk out to the bluff tomorrow."

"I'd love to," Pamela said. She went with him to the steps and watched him go down the street. When he came to his end of the block he stepped out in the beam of the arc light and waved once. He couldn't see her wave back.

CHAPTER 11

But Charlie Lacey didn't want a dinner this time, he told May-belle at breakfast.

"Why, we always . . ."

"They're just out on business this time," Charlie said and drank his coffee in a gulp, as though he were at the ranch. "We'll eat down at the hotel."

"Is anything wrong, Charlie?"

"No, except that we've had a bad year; everyone has. The range was poor and we didn't have enough moisture to wet your feet. By fall things'll be better but Bell thinks they should be now." And then he was gone, banging the screen door behind him.

So there was no reason why Mrs. Lacey shouldn't go to the Shakespeare Club since Charlie wouldn't be home for dinner. They read *Anthony and Cleopatra* and afterward there was the usual discussion with a five-cent fine if anyone brought up any subject not having to do with the play, at least until the re-freshments were served.

"I can't imagine any woman, even Cleopatra, keeping Charlie from his blessed old ranch," Maybelle Lacey said, which was permissible because it derived from the play.

Lucy Moore, who was going out again now, still wore mourn-ing but she had left off the long black veil with its crepe bands. She tilted her head to one side as she said, "You know, I don't think Western men are so apt to lose the world for love as Eastern or European men are! I know the bank was as important to J.B. as I was, maybe more." Everyone laughed but then re-membering that J.B. was dead stopped a little short.

Pamela was home alone, sitting on the porch. She and Wrenn had walked out to the bluff above the river in the afternoon, just as they used to do, and lain flat in the grass with their heads over the edge to watch the bank swallows flying in and out of their holes. But they hadn't had a very good time. Wrenn didn't mention the night before; he had talked about school and what a long time it would take to go through law school, too.

"But if you like it . . ."

"Yes. Oh well, I'm going to, but sometimes I'd just like to travel, go to Europe and live there awhile and then South America. Father says there'll be a good place here for me when I'm through, but I don't want to live here all my life, do you?"

"Oh no, not all my life!" she said quickly. That sounded so endless.

"Father's always talking about the way the town's growing but it's too crude. At Harvard none of the fellows ever heard of Brandon Rapids."

"I know it, at the Randells' last fall . . ."

"I met your Mr. Randell; I was in Father's office when he came in. He's pretty nice, isn't he?"

"Yes," she said slowly. But it seemed strange that Wrenn should know him and that Mr. Randell should go to Mr. Morley's office. "Was Papa with him?"

"No, he had some other man with him, a Mr. Bell, I think."

When Wrenn stood up to go back home she wasn't ready yet. She had moved nearer to the river bank to watch the swallows looping in and out, dark as they came toward the bank, light along the edges of their wings as they flew away. Down below, the river flowed quietly toward the dam and the new power plant and on the other side the wild prairie grass was still green, all the way up the low hills. Next month it would start to turn brown. Clumps of new sagebrush stood out gray against the green and the smell of it was in the air.

"I'd like to be out at the ranch now," she said. Wrenn didn't say anything and she wondered what he was thinking. She'd have to ask Mr. Sewall if she could be away. This summer was going to be different from all the other summers if she kept her job. She wouldn't be free. It would be horrid. She had never thought of working in the summer. She didn't believe she would keep the job then, Papa wouldn't want her to.

They had walked home and Wrenn hadn't said anything about coming over tonight but she expected him. She and Mama had had supper and Mama said probably Mr. Bell and Mr. Randell would come up later though it wouldn't occur to Charlie to tell her! But anyway, she would be back in time.

Down the street Pamela could hear the tinkle of the glass prisms that hung on the Adamses' porch and every now and then the sound of the streetcar going out to the park. Kissing somebody should mean that you were in love. Did it mean that to Wrenn? Rose's mother said love was ecstasy. She went into the house, into Papa's study, and turned on the light. She had to move the big dictionary on its stand over toward the desk. Ecs . . . Was it s or c? "Ecstasy, the state of being beside oneself, as from some overpowering emotion" . . . joy, she supposed, but she didn't feel that way. There were so many meanings, as though the person who wrote the dictionary couldn't quite make up his mind. "Also mental transport from the contemplation of divine things." It didn't help much. She went out to the porch thinking about it, moving slowly back and forth in the swing. The woodbine growing up the side of the porch hid the swing from the street. When Charlie Lacey drove up with Mr. Bell and Mr. Randell she watched them get out and come up the walk, their cigar smoke coming ahead of them. They weren't talking at all. Her father held the screen door open for them and they all went in the house, then she heard the study door close.

They were still in the study with the door closed when Maybelle Lacey came home. "I wonder if I shouldn't fix some coffee and something to eat, Pamela? Did you talk to them?"

"No, they went into the house so fast they didn't see me here."

"I suppose Charlie gave them something to drink and they'd rather have that than coffee!" she said with a smile for masculine peculiarities and weaknesses. "You better go up to bed now. I'm sure they'll stay over and we'll probably have them for dinner tomorrow night. Grace Bangs gave me a recipe for chicken that I might make. It's queer Mr. Randell didn't bring something; he usually does."

Pamela brushed her hair a hundred times, sitting on the side of the bed. She went over to the mirror to see if the bleached lock still showed, but it was almost lost sight of when she brushed her hair smoothly to her shoulders, like last summer. She could hardly remember sleeping out on the porch and how hot it was, and walking across to the outhouse with Ruby, and Alan being bitten by the rattler . . . and now it was time to go out again and she would ride in the sun and get her hair bleached again. She would ask Mr. Randell if Alan were coming out this summer. She wished she were at the ranch this minute. It was close in her room. The Cheavers' house next door came too near.

"Pamela!" Mama opened her door. "Pamela, the men are shouting in the study. What do you suppose is wrong?" She was in her nightgown and had already put her hair up in curlers.

She looked so upset, Pamela said quickly, "Oh, I'm sure nothing is wrong. Mr. Randell thinks so much of Papa." But with the door opened she could hear their voices.

"They sound so angry!" Together they went to the top of the stairs.

"You gambled on making it!" That was Mr. Bell's voice. "With money that wasn't yours."

"Good God, of course I gambled." Charlie Lacey's voice roared through the house. It would have been impossible not to hear it.

"And lost."

"If you mean I can't pay it right back, but by next fall . . ."

". . . at 8% interest!" Their voices dropped. Pamela looked at her mother's face, terrible in its wrinkled fear. She hadn't stopped to put on her dressing gown and Pamela was aware suddenly of her mother's breasts under the thin material. Maybelle Lacey crossed her arms underneath as though to support their heaviness. There was silence for a moment and then they could hear Charlie's voice but they couldn't tell what he was saying.

"Go down and stand next to the other door so you can hear, Pamela," her mother whispered.

Pamela hesitated, not wanting to hear, wanting to escape from the house, away from the fear in her mother's face and the repulsive heavy look of her breasts under the white gown, and the roar of her father's voice. Her mother put her hand on Pamela's shoulder. "Go on, quick. Something's happened, I know."

She went then, stepping carefully to keep the stairs from creaking. She felt trembly inside, but she had no trouble hearing now.

"Gentlemen," Papa said in a quiet voice that didn't sound quite natural, "business is done differently in the West from the way it is in the East. It isn't a cut and dried kind of a deal with every transaction written down in a ledger. It rests on a man's word. If J. B. Moore hadn't known I was honest he would never have given me the loan."

"Certainly some of the blame for the irregularity rests with the banker. . . ." That was Mr. Randell's voice. "But you can understand how we felt getting a letter from the bank here, from the new president saying that the company was obligated to the bank to the amount of $50,000! When we knew nothing whatever about it."

"Why didn't you make the loan in your own name? If credit out here rests on a man's name that ought to have been enough without using the company's name." There was something in Mr. Bell's voice that was ugly and sneering. Pamela looked back at Mama standing on the stairway, with her hand at her throat.

"That's dishonest," Mr. Bell went on. "I don't care how you try to talk yourself out of it. You didn't want us to know how things were and that you had to borrow money! Things couldn't have been as you represented them last spring!"

Why did Papa stand it? Why was he quiet? Questioning your honor was the one thing a man could shoot another man for,

Slim said. She leaned her head against the door jamb, letting her hair fall over her face so she didn't have to look up at Mama.

"No one has ever called me dishonest before. I may seem so according to your lights, but I'm not according to my own," her father said, but he didn't shout and his voice didn't sound like his.

"If you sold every steer tomorrow could you pay that debt?" Mr. Bell cut in as though her father's honor didn't matter at all, only the money. He had a horrid cold voice.

"It's customary to sell in the fall out here . . . by this fall . . ."

Oh, why did he even talk to them!

One of the men scraped his chair back and Pamela ran lightly across the hall to the stairs. The bare treads were warm under her cold feet.

"What did they say, Pamela? What has your father done?"

"It's all about a loan at the bank, they don't understand anything about the ranch," Pamela said, hating her mother's asking such a question.

They heard the door to the study opening and Mrs. Lacey ran up the stairs like a guilty child. Pamela followed slowly. What if they did see her!

"Then we'll go out to the ranch in the morning and McBain will have a tally count . . ." They were going out the door. Pamela and her mother watched them from the front windows. Charlie was driving the men back to the hotel.

"Oh, Pamela, if your father's in bad with the company . . ."

"I hope he is," Pamela said. "I'd rather have him run the ranch by himself, just Papa and Slim. Mr. Bell and Mr. Randell act as though they own it and Papa just worked for them." *Do you live on Uncle Ralph's ranch?* that girl had asked and when they looked at the pictures of the ranch in Mr. Randell's study they thought Slim and her father and Ruby were all hired help.

"You don't know what you're talking about, Pamela. It takes so much capital to run a big ranch. As it is, everything your father makes goes back into that ranch. If I didn't have my little money from my own father I don't know what we'd do. Charlie hasn't any idea of how much it costs to live!"

Pamela's face set. She was on her father's side. She looked with distaste at her mother. Maybelle stood in front of the dresser and began straightening the disordered top drawer. The wide mirror supported by carved mahogany claws showed Pamela her mother's fretful face, and long, too-thin neck. It was hard to remember how beautiful she could look. Automatically, Pamela tried to arrange the hair in soft puffs on her head and cover the neck and heavy-hanging breasts with the net yoke and tucked taffeta of her best dress, but it didn't work. She looked away from the strangeness of her mother.

"I wish Charlie would come and tell us what's happened," Maybelle fretted. "What did Mr. Bell mean about gambling with money that wasn't his?" Then, as if sorry she had said so much in front of Pamela, her voice changed. She said briskly, "It's after midnight, Pamela, you run on to bed."

Pamela was glad to go, but she set herself to stay awake. If Mama blamed Papa she would stand up for him. She would tell him how she felt about Mr. Randell and Mr. Bell. Papa couldn't have been in the wrong. "Nobody ever called me dishonest before," he had said. She propped the pillows up against the bed head and sat bolt upright to keep awake.

The street was quiet. Over on Box Elder Avenue the trolleys to the park had stopped running. Only one arc light at the corner by the Moores' house would be on. Everything must be all right. Papa would take the men out to the ranch and show them. But uncertainty hung in the dark. She remembered uncomfortably how Papa's face had looked under the green shade . . . almost as though he was frightened by their opening the door. Had Wrenn thought that, too? "You gambled on making it with money that wasn't yours," Mr. Bell had said and Papa had roared back "Good God, of course I gambled!"

In Mr. Sewall's speech to the Pioneer Society she had liked the sentence about gambling. "The Pioneers were willing to gamble on the future; they didn't know what lay ahead in the lands of the West, but they had faith!" She felt better and turning over in bed once more, fell asleep.

There were many versions of the affairs of the Rocky Mountain Cattle Company. Mr. Bell and Mr. Randell stayed on for several days after they came in from the ranch but they stayed downtown. Everyone knew who they were and what they were about. It was known when they went to the bank that was now the Brandon Rapids Trust Co. and linked with a bank in the East. When they were seen dining with John McBain and Charlie Lacey at the hotel people put two and two together. McBain was a cattleman who had been receiver for that English company that busted up after the bad winter of '87. Charlie Lacey looked pretty glum. Somebody had it that when they got McBain to go out and take a count of the cattle Charlie was running he found Charlie was trying to pull a fast one and have his foreman shuffle the cattle so the count would be closer to the book count, but McBain was a sharp one and Scotch to boot, and up to such tricks. The report he handed in was that deception had been practiced by the manager. Not that anyone in Brandon Rapids would blame Charlie Lacey, leastways not a cattleman wouldn't; he'd come out on top if they let him alone. He'd borrowed before and paid back, hadn't he?

"As I look at it," Tom Bailey said as he set the bourbon in his glass moving slightly from side to side, "he ain't honest exactly, but he ain't dishonest, neither. It's all in the game. It was J. B. Moore's dying when he did that let them Easterners in on it and that little city feller they've got in there as president now made all the trouble. Finding out that he tried to foul up the tally was bad for Charlie, of course, but it's been done before . . . plenty."

Hank Williams measured a pony of whisky with his eye. "There ain't anything in that, and anyhow, how're you going to be sure that was what Charlie meant to do? It wasn't his foreman that was moving them cattle, as I heard it, it was one of his men that'd been riding line and hadn't been back to find out what was going on."

Everyone liked Charlie Lacey and no one took any pleasure in seeing him treated like that. The barber told Cy Acres:

"I guess they let him keep the home place, about three hundred and twenty acres is all, and his leases. If he could get credit again, which likely he could, he could buy some more cattle and run 'em up in that mountain range but there ain't going to be any more company as soon as they can get out of it. McBain is running the ranch long enough to clear things up and I guess there ain't no love lost between him and Charlie."

There was a rumor around that Charlie Lacey had used some of the money he'd borrowed in the name of the company to buy some land for himself and that wasn't quite on the square either.

"Maybe not, but look at it this way," Hank said, leaning on the bar, "if they'd left him alone and not known anything about it and come fall he'd have shipped his cattle and got a good price, in the natural course of things why he'd have paid off what he'd borrowed and made 'em plenty of profit and there'd have been no questions asked about what he owned or what he used to buy it with. Charlie wouldn't have forgot to pay the bastards back. It's just circumstances, you might say." Hank was a calm man who believed in going with circumstances. "If they trusted him enough to have him run their company for fifteen years, they oughta trust him to do it the way he wants."

Then Ned Morley came into the bar, wearing his Eastern-cut clothes, and Hank poured him his drink with a silent nod. It was said that Mr. Randell and Mr. Bell had consulted Morley in a legal way and that he had referred them to the lawyer across the hall since, as he said, he was a personal friend of Charlie Lacey's, but if he was a good personal friend couldn't he have done more than that?

"What I think is," said Sid Newton, paying no attention to Ned Morley, who was, after all, no cattleman or rancher, but a lawyer, "those Easterners want to invest their money out here and expect to make plenty more and they don't ever want to take a chance or trust anyone. Let 'em get out of the country, I say. Charlie's got his leases and his three hundred and twenty, they took the rest, or they're going to, that's what I heard."

Ned Morley seemed not to hear the discussion but he finished his drink rather more swiftly than usual. Cora Morley had told Lucy Moore that Mr. Morley was so upset over Charlie's trouble that he couldn't eat his dinner.

In the front upstairs room of the Laceys' home, Maybelle Lacey lay on her bed, a damp towel over her eyes for her headache.

"Better, Maybelle?" Charlie Lacey asked. He had come in from the ranch this noon to find her there and rummaged for something to eat by himself. Pamela was down at Mr. Sewall's office.

Maybelle shook her head without removing the towel. "Charlie, Mr. Bell and Mr. Randell came up to say good-by to me. They were such gentlemen. They said they were distressed that so pleasant a relationship should have to end, but in view of the circumstances . . ."

Charlie scowled. One hand traced the intricacy of the carving on the chiffonier drawer.

"Charlie!"

"Yes."

"And, of course, you never tell me anything about the ranch so I didn't know what they meant, only what I could gather, but they sounded as though . . ." She turned her face into the pillow with a smothered sob.

". . . as though they thought I was a crook!" Charlie Lacey snapped the words. "What do you think?"

"You know I don't think you're a . . . a crook, Charlie, but you must have done something wrong to . . ."

Charlie made a sound of disgust in his throat. "If J.B. had lived there would have been no trouble and nothing wrong, but this new jack that doesn't know anything but what he reads in black and white wants his money right now, and right now I can't pay it. And they've had someone snooping around looking into everything and they've decided that my ways of doing business aren't their ways. They've decided that because I bought a few lots with some of the money, I meant to keep it from them, and that I should have more calves . . . oh well, you wouldn't understand. Bell and Randell are so scared they'll lose some money they've put the ranch into McBain's hands and I'm out . . . or will be."

"But, Charlie!" Maybelle dropped the towel from her red eyes. "You're one of the partners of the company!"

"Yes, but there are five other partners and they want to dissolve the company and get out of the cattle business."

"But, Charlie, what will we live on?"

The noon sun finding a crack under the shades reached Charlie Lacey's blue eyes that were as cold as a piece of blue water where the ice has broken through.

"We still have three hundred and twenty acres; we can live on the ranch."

His wife sat up straight as though jerked to attention by some hidden wire.

"Charlie, I'll never go out there to live. Part of Papa's money bought this house and it's in my name!" A hysterical note sounded in her voice.

"Don't act like a goose, Maybelle; I don't expect you to go out to the ranch. Ruby would quit tomorrow if you came and she's a damn sight more useful than you would be."

Maybelle forgot to bridle at Charlie's profanity. "Oh, Charlie, how could you get into such a mess! Everyone will know about it and I won't be able to hold up my head. I've always been so proud of my father . . . your father, too. . . ."

He turned square in the doorway, filling it. "You seem to share with Bell in the idea that I've done something dishonest." His fingers found a cigar in the pocket of his shirt and then came away without it.

Maybelle turned back into her pillow with a sob. Charlie looked at her soft rumpled hair, so dark in back that no gray showed, at the narrow shoulders and little waist. Her skirt was twisted around so that one pretty leg showed a way up the calf; he had always taken pleasure in looking at his wife, but he took no pleasure today. His own words seemed to go on sounding in the room. The low rosebud ceiling held the last word there . . . "dishonest." It was like a rattlesnake that struck if it could touch you. But it couldn't.

"Well, I haven't been dishonest, Maybelle, no matter what anyone thinks or says, not in the main. I'd have let them think there were more steers than there were if I could, because it would have made 'em more comfortable about their money, but that don't prove anything. And buying those lots with the borrowed money was only a temporary thing. I figgered the money I borrowed was one-fifth mine anyway and I've taken my money to pay the boys' wages before now and not worried about how quick I got it back. You can hold your head as high as you want to!"

He waited for her to say something, but she only went on crying.

Maybelle was waiting, too. Of course, he wasn't dishonest, she hadn't really thought so, only . . .

His hand was on the newel post when Maybelle said, "As long as you didn't do anything dishonest . . . I don't care about myself, only Pamela . . ."

She could feel Charlie standing out there in the hall. A board creaked under him as he shifted his weight.

"Was Pamela home when Bell and Randell were here?"

"Yes, she let them in and I was ashamed of the way she acted. All the time I was talking to them she just stood there without saying a word, and when Mr. Randell held out his hand she put hers behind her and said, 'Good-by, Mr. Randell' as though she didn't see his hand. There was no excuse for her acting that way, after she had been entertained in the Randells' home!"

"Well," Charlie said slowly, "they've been entertained in our home, too, a good many times." He went downstairs and stood looking through the screen door at the cottonwood fluffs moving aimlessly on the June air.

Mr. Bell and Mr. Randell had a final conference with the bank president and McBain, then Randell paid their bill and picked up his bags. He wouldn't be coming back here if McBain handled matters satisfactorily, and he was going to miss it. He had liked owning a share in a cattle ranch in the West. He still had copper interests but they didn't require his coming out here. He might send Alan some time.

He had liked Charlie Lacey; he had never known anyone like him. The old gambler with his sleight-of-hand juggling of money and cattle had got pretty red when McBain faced him with his moving cattle around, but when Bell told him he'd made a mistake thinking he could do business that way, he had looked him straight in the eye and said, "You're right, Mr. Bell, about my making a mistake, but it was in ever tying up with Easterners. Your interests were never safer than in my hands." No sir, he'd never seen a man who was fired, so to speak, have so much dignity. You couldn't really get under the skin of a man like that.

"You lug your bags over to the station all right by yourself?" the man at the desk was asking.

"Yes, thank you. There's plenty of time."

Ugly enough the town was and yet he had always liked it; the fronts built as square as though made with building blocks, the half-dozen stone or brick buildings that were called "business blocks," the frame hotel, and the dirt road that he had always wanted to see in the wet season. It must be a pudding! And the winters! He had always thought of coming out here some winter to see for himself what it was like.

"It's the sky that makes the main street so different from some country town in New England, Thomas," he said abruptly to Bell. "So much of it."

"I'll be glad to get on the train," Mr. Bell said. "It's been a depressing business."

"Yes. I hope we haven't been too hasty. I can't help the odd

[113]

feeling that Charlie Lacey doesn't see yet that he's done anything out of the way. Maybe he'd have worked it out if we hadn't interfered."

Bell looked at Randell as though he had lost his mind. "Why, you can't do business that way, even if it is out in this god-forsaken country. Trust a man like Charlie Lacey and where would you end up?"

They were about a day's run out of Brandon Rapids, going through flat country that looked like desert for sure, with cactus bursting into waxy bloom all along the tracks and that blue lupine everywhere. The two men had been riding in silence for a long while when Randell said suddenly:

"I can't get that girl's face out of my mind. She looked as though somebody had slapped her."

Bell only grunted.

"Standing there with her hand behind her, not shaking hands. She's got Charlie's eyes, did you notice?" Randell persisted. "Stared right through us. I hope this doesn't make things too hard for Mrs. Lacey and the girl."

"I should think this would put him out of ranching on any big scale; a thing like that ought to pretty well ruin a man's reputation," Bell said, scowling at the bare Western country out the window.

"Maybe not, Thomas, maybe not; I don't believe he thinks it will."

CHAPTER **12**

From where Pamela sat at her typewriter in Mr. Sewall's office, she could see the newspaper stand in front of Hines's Drugstore. The light through the big red bottle in the window made the papers look like pink sheets. She had bought a paper for Mr.

Sewall on her way to work, as she always did, and glanced at it before she had her hat off. On page two a three-column headline announced in sickening black type: CHARLIE LACEY OUT AS MANAGER ROCKY MOUNTAIN CATTLE COMPANY. It was in every single paper out there on the stand!

The copy began, "Claiming irregularity in management . . ." Pamela caught her breath. Her eyes behaved badly, lingering on the words so she couldn't get on with the column, skipping so that she hardly knew what she was reading. ". . . fifteen years manager, and before that time independent rancher in the King Butte area . . . member of old Pioneer family . . . John McBain appointed temporary manager . . . company intends dissolution after sale of cattle this fall."

She heard Mr. Sewall's feet on the stair and rose quickly, covering page two by folding over page one, and then, folding the paper again, she laid it at the back of Mr. Sewall's desk. Her face was as colorless as the white blotter on her desk when she went back to her typewriter.

But Mr. Sewall said, "Good morning, my dear," as usual, hung up his coat on the hatrack and settled back in his swivel chair, as though it were any other morning.

"Two old-timers were at that ball the other night that I've been trying to get in touch with for a long time. Just type these notes." One of them has a ranch on the west side of the divide . . . really should belong to the Pioneer Society in Bitteroot County. . . ." A little color trickled painfully back into Pamela's face.

She was glad she had brought her lunch and wasn't going home at noon. Papa was still at the ranch, but Mama would go on and on. Her headache would be worse. Those men had told the paper all this; that horrid little Mr. Bell and Mr. Randell. What would Mr. Randell tell Alan? She typed Giver for River and leaned over her typewriter to erase the G.

Rose bounced up the stairs just at twelve, and Mr. Sewall put down his papers more promptly than usual, and said, "Go ahead, Pamela, don't stop to finish."

"It's real warm out, Pam, let's walk down to the park," Rose said. And Pamela went, grateful not to walk alone along the street.

"You haven't told me about the ball," Rose began. "Did Wrenn take you home? I haven't seen you since."

"Yes," Pamela said, and remembered standing in the doorway of the study. "Yes, Wrenn walked home with me. We left a little early."

No one was in the park at noon. They went past the watering trough, and sat on the bench by the B done in geraniums and little blue ageratum plants and opened their sandwiches on their laps.

"I saw him; he's grown taller. . . ." Then as Pamela said nothing Rose laid her hand on Pamela's arm. Her dark brown eyes were tender. "Pam, don't you mind about that in the paper; nobody pays any attention to that old paper." It hadn't occurred to Rose not to mention it; her mind moved directly and her words and actions followed.

"Oh, Rose, they have no right to say things like that about Papa. They don't understand how things are done out here. . . ." That *was* it, wasn't it?

"I know it!" Rose agreed briskly, biting into her sandwich.

"Why would they put things like that in the paper? Everyone will read it and believe it. . . ." It was a relief to talk to Rose.

"Pooh!" Rose said emphatically. "People know your father and, anyway, they'll forget it tomorrow."

Pamela felt more comfortable listening to Rose, looking into her earnest face. Rose's father was dead and that made it a little easier to talk to her.

"Besides the newspapers!" Rose's full red lips shaped their disgust. "You should hear Mama rave; she goes wild when she puts an ad for hats in the paper." It wasn't so much what she said, it was her emphatic voice, her way of linking her arm in Pamela's, her warmth.

Rose said as she left her at the hardware store, "Don't you care a bit, now, Pam. Come by the store tonight and I'll walk you part way home."

Mr. Sewall hadn't come yet and Pamela made things to do, filling the time. Wrenn would come over tonight and she would tell him how it really was. He mustn't think . . . but then Wrenn wouldn't. Wrenn's father and Papa were old friends.

She was looking out the window, watching a milk wagon go up the street when she saw her father, driving briskly, the way he always did. She leaned out the window and watched him get out and hitch the horses. He must have just come in from the ranch. For a moment the very sight of him, the sound of his voice saying "whoa," made everything all right. She heard Papa speaking to someone in his big voice. He was coming in here. He had never come up to the little office before. He had always poked fun at "Granny Sewall."

"Why, Papa!" He looked too big for the office, standing at the top of the stairs.

"Well, this is where you are! Pam, I'm going back out to the ranch and I thought maybe you'd like to go along. You haven't been out this spring. You tell Sewall you'll be back Wednesday. Ruby has some duds out there. I'm on my way right now."

"I'd love to." She pulled the cover over her typewriter and tidied the papers on her desk. It was only two o'clock. It would be dark when they got there, and Ruby would have dinner ready. . . . "I'll only be a minute, Papa." She put on her sailor hat in front of the little mirror. "Mr. Sewall won't mind, I'm sure . . . but didn't you just come in this morning on the train?" She went over to close the door of the wardrobe. Her father didn't answer. "Papa?" She turned around.

Charlie Lacey had picked up the newspaper from Mr. Sewall's desk and was reading it. He was reading on page two. Pamela came across to the desk. Suddenly her father threw the paper down.

"Come on, Pam. Let's get out of here." His face was a dark red.

"Papa, it isn't true, is it, what they say in the paper?" Her voice was almost a whisper. "There wasn't anything irregular about it?"

"Look, honey, suppose we talk about it on the way out. Come on."

Pamela stood still. The terrible pounding beating of her heart began again. The sinking fear in her mind made her angry. All the color drained out of her face. "I . . . I don't believe I can. I forgot . . . Mr. Sewall wanted me to do something when he came back. . . ." She hardly knew what she was saying. She wasn't looking at him but down at the desk.

"Oh, Sewall can get along all right. It won't hurt if the Pioneers don't get all filed away." His voice filled the low room. "I don't think much of this job for you, Pam, anyway. Better give it up for the summer."

"No, Papa, I really don't want to go." Now she was looking at him. She looked like her mother with her mouth set.

Charlie Lacey put on his hat. "All right, Pam," he said quietly. His voice didn't fill the room now. "I just thought you might like to get out to the ranch in the spring. Kinda pretty out there now. Well, you keep your mother company." He went on down the narrow stairs. She heard his voice but not the words as he spoke to someone in the store. She was hanging up her coat and hat so she didn't see him drive off but she heard the quick clop-clop of the team of horses. If she had gone she could have driven part way, she thought like a little girl, putting away from her mind that quick look as he went down the stairs. But why hadn't he said straight out, "Of course, it isn't true"?

Pamela didn't stop at Rose's on the way home. She walked fast, hoping she wouldn't meet anyone. But the houses were faces, suspicious, accusing, unfriendly. She had never felt this way before.

"Hello," Mama called cheerfully from the kitchen. She had recovered from her headache and was freshly dressed.

Pamela came in a little uncertainly, feeling out the house. The sun flooded through the west window of the front parlor and reached across the hall to the study. It made the stairway golden; stealthiness was impossible to imagine.

"Charlie was in from the ranch but he only stayed long enough to get himself some lunch. I was too sick to lift my head. There was no sense in his driving back out but if anything goes wrong he always wants to get away to the ranch; he doesn't stop to think what it's like to live in town," Maybelle complained. "Of course, I don't think anything is *really* wrong. . . ."

"It was in the paper this morning," Pamela said.

"Yes, I saw it, but I didn't come downstairs until four o'clock, and Charlie hadn't even opened it. It's just as well, it would have made him mad. But it doesn't really say anything except that there was some irregularity."

"No," Pamela said, thinking of her father reading the paper on Mr. Sewall's desk. But she didn't like things to be irregular.

"And Charlie told me, Pamela, that he hadn't done anything to be ashamed of."

"Did you ask him that?" Pamela's fingers pushed back the hair over her ear.

"Of course I did. And he said I could hold my head up as high as anyone."

"Oh," Pamela said with a little sigh that seemed to release a brace from her whole body.

"I knew that, myself, but it made me feel good to hear Charlie say it. I can't understand how Mr. Randell could act like that. I was just down at Lucy Moore's and I told her J.B. would turn over in his grave if he knew the way this new bank president did business, making all that trouble for your father!"

Pamela frowned. When she had left this morning Mama had been cross that she hadn't been more friendly with Mr. Randell. Now she was on Papa's side. It mixed her up.

"I just fixed us a little salad, Pam, and some iced tea. Unless you want something heartier?"

"No thank you," Pamela said. How could Mama change so fast? If Papa were *her* husband she would know; she wouldn't have to ask him.

"Mamie's coming tomorrow to do up the curtains. . . ."

Who cared about curtains? Pamela thought, then her interest focused sharply.

"There's one thing about it, Pamela, this house is in my name and it's clear; no matter what happens to the ranch we'll always have this. . . ."

Now the ground was taken from under her feet. "What could happen to the ranch?" Pamela asked.

"Oh, I suppose they could make Charlie sell it, but I don't think so. Charlie will hang onto that blessed old ranch of his if it's any way possible," Maybelle said confidently. "Is Wrenn coming over tonight?"

"I don't know. I haven't seen him since Saturday. I thought I might go down to see Rose."

"Pamela, I wouldn't see so much of her if I were you. She's a little beauty, with that black curly hair and that coloring but . . . well, she's not exactly your kind. Cora Morley asked me about her the other day. She thought she was a trifle bold asking about Wrenn as though they were old friends."

"I like her," Pamela said.

Wrenn did come. Pamela saw him from the window in her room and ran right down so Mama wouldn't go out and talk and talk. She was so thankful to see him the gladness was in her voice and shining out of her face. She had combed her hair up on her head like Alice Reed's and it felt strange and rather nice. Wrenn noticed it right away. "You look grown-up," he said.

"I am grown-up," Pamela said gravely.

They walked down to the BonTon for a sundae and the street seemed natural again. They came back and sat on the swing, and no light streamed out from the study. It was easy to talk or to be still in the soft June dark.

"Wrenn?" Pamela said at last, because she couldn't keep it back. "Did you see what it said in the paper about Papa?"

"Yes," Wrenn said in a low voice. He reached over and took her hand, lacing his fingers with hers. "Don't think about it, Pam. It doesn't make any difference."

"I was afraid you would get the idea . . . because of the other night, when we found Papa here . . ." She stopped.

Wrenn was silent, too. She held the swing still with her foot. "You don't believe that in the paper, do you, Wrenn?"

He didn't answer quickly enough and in that silence she had time to remember his saying Mr. Randell was in his father's office.

"I suppose Mr. Randell went to your father with all his lies." The word sounded ugly and brash and overwrought. The tone of her voice matched it. "I suppose you and your father and mother believe every word of it, even after knowing Papa all your lives!" She pulled her hand away from his.

"Pam, I told you it doesn't make any difference to me."

"It does to me. What does your father say about Papa?"

"I don't know what he says . . . nothing."

"But you know what he thinks," she persisted.

"He's a good friend of his, that's why he said he wouldn't handle the thing for that Mr. Randell." Wrenn said it triumphantly.

A long unhappy stillness weighed on the dark. "Because he thought Papa had done something wrong," Pamela said very low.

"Oh, Pam, don't get worked up. You know how your father is. He probably took a few chances and didn't expect to have them found out before he'd . . ."

They were luckless words. Pamela stood up.

"Good night, Wrenn Morley," she said in a small tight voice. "My father wasn't hiding anything." She went in without waiting for him to go, and ran up the stairs in the dark to fling herself across her bed. She heard Wrenn call her name twice, then he went around the side of the house and called again under her window but she lay still without answering, yet waiting for him to call again.

When Maybelle Lacey came back from visiting next door, Pamela had already undressed and pretended to be asleep, but as soon as her mother had gone to bed she got up and set her alarm clock. The train for King Butte left at 6:45. She would leave a note for Mama and ask her to tell Mr. Sewall she would be gone a couple of days. Then she got out her divided skirt and dark brown shirtwaist and felt hat and the laced boots that were too high for any rattlesnakes. It made her feel better just to touch her ranch clothes; they had a friendly, loyal feeling. She thought of Papa driving all the way out to the ranch alone, thinking his daughter had turned against him. She didn't care if he had been irregular, she loved him, and she hated Wrenn Morley.

The train crawled and stopped at the least excuse. She sat very still and held her chin on her hand watching the country that was greening over from the June rains. Probably no one would be in from the ranch and she would have to walk the five miles, but she didn't care. The conductor knew her and wanted to talk with her, but she closed her eyes and looked as though she were asleep until he moved on down the car.

It was raining when she got to King Butte, and the ground had turned to oozing, sucking mud. She stepped cautiously along the tracks to the shed that served as station and asked the man there if anyone was in from the ranch.

"Several gentlemen in and out of here last week, but there ain't been anyone since, 'cept your Pa an' he went in on the train yesterday morning; said something about driving his team back out."

"Yes," Pamela said. "I know."

"You wait around awhile an' maybe I c'd drive you if this rain don't make the roads too bad."

"No, Slim will be coming in. I'll just start out." She couldn't wait.

The road to the ranch was only two ruts through the mud with a center path churned into round cushions by horses' hoofs. It led off toward nothing but gray sky over above the mountains. The mountains themselves were white with snow and the rain was threatening to turn to snow. She tried to walk on the ground at the side of the road, but it was soft there, too.

The wild flowers were out: pink and white and bright yellow, even in the rain; blossoms only an inch high "blooming for nothing nor nobody, 'cept themselves," Ruby always said. The prickly pear blossoms showed up more, the color of amber combs, but too sharp to pick. The lupine was beginning to bloom in blue-gray clumps and white loco weed that made a horse crazy if he ate it. Pamela breathed in suddenly, not for any fragrance of the wild flowers, for they hardly had any at all, but for the clean cold freshness of the air. She lifted her head and the water dripped off the brim of her hat and ran down over her plaid jacket.

When she didn't watch where she was walking she stepped into a mud hole and had trouble pulling her foot out. She could feel the coldness of the mud through the leather and the mud stuck to the shoe laces.

It was so still! No sound of a trolley car or wagon wheels. A magpie flew up from a dead gopher close to her, croaking louder than a crow, and she scowled at its cruel beak and pitiless black eye. Once an animal had a sore on it, or was down, the magpies always gathered to pick at it. Magpies could kill a sick animal in time; they could pick the eyes out of it!

There wasn't a tree as far as she could see here, and no fences, but the land was not flat. It rolled up into a long green slope and beyond that into a rocky hill. There were new feathery clumps of sage around the rocks that would be taller than the rocks by midsummer. And over to the east, where the land cut off sharp, was the river, way down below. The road to the ranch followed above the river most of the way out.

That was the place where the Indians used to drive the buffalo over. Pamela thought of the day she and Alan had ridden there to hunt for arrowheads and buffalo bones on the shingle back from the river. Alan had said, "How could you drive a whole herd of buffalo over and let them fall down the cliff and kill themselves?" He said, "You'd have to be pretty cruel to kill animals that way." And she had felt a little ashamed that she could imagine how you'd do it . . . if you were an Indian, of course . . . yelling and riding faster and faster, with the herd of buffaloes running ahead of you. You'd just get started and then there'd be no stopping. You might close your eyes and not look once they started to fall. Slim said the sound would be like thunder and loud enough to shake the earth.

She could tell when she was halfway by the look of the rocks to the east. Some people called them the Little Badlands, and Papa had told Alan last summer about hunting cattle rustlers down in there, when he was a young man. The cattle thieves would as soon shoot you from behind those rocks as not. When Alan had asked how he dared go after them then, Papa had said, "I figured I'd shoot first." "But weren't you afraid?" Alan asked. He was always worrying about being afraid or being brave. "If I was, I didn't stop to think about it," Papa had said. He was brave. Maybe Papa had been brave to face the company gentlemen, too.

She didn't seem to mind the cold and rain so much now. She wasn't so tired. When she started out she hadn't been absolutely sure she could make it all the way, but she was now. It was easy. She walked a little faster, pulling her hat brim down against the rain, and tucking her hands into the sleeves of her jacket, almost enjoying the cold squish and suck of the mud.

Once she had thought they owned all this land, but Papa said, "Well, not exactly, but I guess if we can use it, it's about the same as ours."

When she spotted some cattle with the N Lazy Y brand that had been her grandfather's before the Rocky Mountain Cattle Company ever used it, she guessed she had about two miles more. You couldn't see the ranch buildings until you came up over the benchland above them. The cattle didn't seem to mind the rain, but they had given up eating, just stood there, waiting it out.

The mud was deeper. She slipped and fell once, and got her gloves so muddy she could feel the mud come through on her hands. Her skirt was stiff with mud, but Ruby would have some dry clothes for her at the ranch. She tried to think how warm the kitchen would be. She hadn't eaten since breakfast and she was hungry. Maybe Ruby would have some fresh bread.

The spring dusk was crowding the rimrock and had already

covered the tops of the mountains when she saw the pinprick of light from the ranch down there by the river. She tried to run down the curving muddy road, and gave it up and slogged it, heavy step by step. Somebody was down at the barn and she waved. Shep began to bark and Ruby looked out through the kitchen window but didn't see her in the dusk. She could hear Ruby saying, "That crazy hound just barks to hear himself bark."

Shep came toward her, not barking now, wagging himself in two. He put his paws on her shoulder and she hugged him, laying her cold face on his warm fur.

As Pamela climbed the steps to the high board porch of the ranch house, she heard her father laugh and then Slim counting a cribbage score. She opened the door. Slim and her father were at the far end of the room at the dining-room table.

"You got a little hasty there, Slim!" Papa slapped his knee. Slim spat into the cuspidor. The lamp on the table spread a yellow round of comfort over the shabby room, and the sizzle of ham came from the kitchen. She needn't have worried about Papa feeling bad. She closed the door and the men looked up.

"Hello," she said in a voice that was suddenly flat.

"Pam!" Papa came across the room. "How in blue blazes did you get here?"

"I took the train and walked out from King Butte."

"Good God, child, if you don't look like a calf the cow's dropped in the mud," Ruby said in her heavy voice. "Come out here to the kitchen and get your wet stuff off."

After supper, in some trousers of Ruby's, cut down from Slim's, and a wool shirt, Pamela lay on the old couch while Slim and Charlie played one more game. It was so good to be here and to be warm and dry. Then Ruby went out to set her sourdoughs for morning and Slim had to go down to the barn and she was alone with Papa.

"So you thought you'd come after all, Pam," Charlie said, holding his cigar in one hand and looking at her through the smoke.

"I wished I had all day."

"Your faith in your old Papa got a little shook up, didn't it?"

"Maybe," she said, not looking at him, waiting for him to tell her what he had told Mama. She wanted him to tell her everything was honest and right, wanted it so hard, she shivered waiting.

"Don't you worry, Pam. We'll come out on top. We may make 'em sorry they didn't hold tight a little longer. Slim and I were just figuring here . . . we may work a deal that will be a bigger thing than the Rocky Mountain Cattle Company ever was."

That wasn't what she wanted. She leaned back against the pillow, thinking how to ask him right out about this miserable thing. But he was talking about his plans. "I'm going to see Scudder, Saturday, and if he'll agree . . . I'm not interested in acting as manager at any salary unless . . ."

When her father's voice stopped she was asleep and Ruby covered her up there on the couch and blew out the light.

"Not many kids would walk five miles through that mud to see their father, Charlie," Ruby said.

Charlie's feelings tugged at the corners of his mouth. "She's a rare one," he said.

CHAPTER 13

Pamela began the summer with the feeling that she was waiting for something . . . for Wrenn to say something, to come over at least. There was a hurt place in her mind about him, and yet she had the feeling that he belonged to her; they belonged together. Next week, next month, eventually, they would come together again. It would have to be next month now. Mama said Wrenn had gone on a pack trip up the Yellowstone with the

[126]

college friend who was visiting him. He hadn't brought his friend over to meet her; Rose saw them beauing Alice Reed and Amy Wentworth around.

Maybe, Pamela thought, sometimes, she wasn't waiting just for Wrenn, but for something else, something tremendous to happen. She sat and typed pages for the book Mr. Sewall was compiling on early Montana history, but she wasn't interested. Those days were too far away even if they were only forty years ago. She was interested in her own life. She woke in the morning with a delicious feeling of excitement, and carried it like a secret as she dressed and had breakfast in the cool darkened house Mama had already closed from the sun. She was eager to be through and go out into the street, almost as though she would find there what she was waiting for.

It was hot in July. People she met walking downtown in the morning said, "It's going to be a sizzler," but she didn't mind. She liked the bright, brassy glare on the figure of Justice on the top of the courthouse, and the hot red of the geraniums in the flower beds, and the dry heat reaching through the brim of her straw sailor. People were always careful to say over and over, "Back east if it got this hot you'd be dead; back there, it's so humid. It's better this way."

Pamela ran lightly up the stairs from the hardware store to the office above with the excitement still in her.

But the little office was an oven. Pamela kept thinking of the ranch. It would be hot there in the daytime, but at night coolness would creep up from the river, and you could go up from the ranch into the hills. Mr. Sewall had said she could take a week off any time she wanted. She had been saving it for something special, but now nothing seemed more special than going to the ranch.

On her way home that evening she stopped in at Madame Guinard's millinery shop to ask Rose if she would like to go, too.

"Sure, I guess I'd like it," Rose said. "I'd hate to meet a rattle-snake! What shall I wear?"

"Oh, Rose, what a funny question. It doesn't matter what

you wear. There isn't anybody around except the men and Ruby. I'll loan you a divided skirt and you wear a shirtwaist with it."

But Rose came to the train in a wide straw hat garlanded with daisies and bachelor's-buttons. Pamela wondered what Ruby would say to it, or think of it. You could always read what Ruby was thinking, plain in her face. What would Ruby think of Rose? If she didn't like her, her face would be glum as an old board fence and she wouldn't joke or grin. You could tell right off. Maybe Rose wouldn't like Ruby, she thought anxiously. Taking someone new out to the ranch was a responsibility.

"I hope it gets prettier, it looks awful bare here," Rose said, looking out the train window.

Pamela looked without saying anything. She hadn't thought it bare. There were the mountains, pale blue on white sky today, like the picture on Mama's Japanese fan. And the creek ran beside the tracks, half hidden in the tangle of willows. She watched the red-winged blackbird swinging and teetering on a willow whip and kept it to herself as a secret.

Slim thought Rose was a "good looker." "Well now," he said as she and Pamela walked over to the wagon, "it's about time we get a chance to see some of the pretty girls they got in town!" Pamela always minded it when Slim teased her about her looks, but Rose smiled as though she liked it.

"Pam, ain't you about through with that town job? We need you out here to ride line," he said with a wink at Rose. Pamela saw the wink and was cross at him for making fun of her in front of Rose.

"You know I don't ride line," she said. If Slim knew she was angry he didn't say so. He was busy helping Rose up on the wagon seat.

The mud had dried, leaving deep ruts in the road and Slim drove across the open field instead. When they bounced Rose gave little shrieks and held her hat in front of her face to keep off the dust. "Just like the stagecoach days," Slim told her.

Pamela was remembering how it was that day in spring when she walked out.

They got off down by the corral and Pamela took Rose to see the horses.

"That's Ginger there, the cinnamon-colored one, and Calico . . ."

"Oh, that one's mine, that darling mahogany-colored one," Rose interrupted. "Come here, sweetheart."

"That's my horse," Pamela said. "Her name is Aspen, because she's never still. I named her for that little tree over by the bunkhouse."

Rose looked briefly. "What a horrid name for her. I'll call you Beauty," she said to the little mare.

Pamela climbed down into the corral and went over to her horse without a word. It seemed suddenly nauseating to her to talk to a horse, though she, herself, had always talked to horses. She made her voice gruff like Ruby's. "Here, girl," and led the horse over to the corral fence where Rose was perched.

"Oh, you darling! I want to take a ride on her before we go up to the house, Pam."

Pamela was shocked. One didn't ask to ride someone else's own horse; she would never think of asking to ride Slim's horse, but Rose, of course, did not understand these matters. Nor did one say "no" in so many words.

"She's pretty lively," she said instead. "Nobody's ever ridden her but Slim and me since she was born. I broke her myself. I'll tell you, I'll get Ginger for you to ride, and I'll ride Aspen." Pamela came back with the bridle and slipped it over Aspen's head, letting her hands speak to the mare without any words. "Here," she said, feeling generous, "you can hold her reins while I get the saddle." She led the horse over to Rose, perched on the top pole.

"I'm going to lead her outside the corral, Pam, and wait out there," Rose called in to her.

Pamela was inside the tack room when she heard the sound of hoofs and Rose calling out, "Look at me!" Pamela came out of

[129]

the barn just in time to see Rose riding Aspen bareback up past the ranch house. As she watched, Rose waved her straw hat and called out to the mare, "Come on, Beauty; here we go!"

Aspen started into a gallop. The straw hat went flying off over the horse's head so she shied. Rose was holding the reins so tight Aspen reared. Rose curled her legs around the horse's belly and leaned forward.

Pamela ran after her, yelling to her to turn up toward the rimrock so the steepness of the hill would slow Aspen down, but Rose couldn't hear. Aspen, unused to anyone clinging so tightly to her, began to buck. Pamela watched in horror and anger. Aspen had never bucked before. With each violent crowhop the horse made she expected to see Rose hurled off on the ground. Ruby came out of the cookhouse shouting to Rose to let go before she was killed. Rose was hanging way over on one side, her face against the mare's neck. She had lost the reins and was clinging to the mane with both hands. Pamela yelled at Aspen, swearing as Slim did, not knowing what she was saying. She still carried the saddle blanket in her hand. Aspen wasn't covering much ground because of her jumps and Pamela came close enough to flap the blanket in her face.

"Whoa, Aspen, whoa, I tell you," she cried out. Aspen sidestepped the blanket and Pamela grabbed the reins. Rose slid off against Pamela. The mare stood still, her neck and flanks lathered and quivering.

"Oh, I can't stand up," Rose said. She wobbled drunkenly a step or two and collapsed on the ground. Ruby and Charlie both ran toward her. Pamela looked at her without a word.

"Are you all right, child?" Charlie asked.

"I think so. I . . . I loved it." Rose's voice wobbled a little, too. Ruby and Charlie helped her to stand.

"I'll take Aspen back and rub her down. You can go on up to the ranch house," Pamela said, not bothering to introduce her to Ruby. Papa could take care of that. Pamela pulled herself up

[130]

on the mare, laid one quiet hand on her wet neck and said softly, "All right, girl, come on."

" 'By, Beauty. I'll ride you again tomorrow," Rose called after her.

The mare walked sedately enough toward the corral, but once there, Pamela pulled on the reins and rode up the hill slope until they were hidden by the clump of aspens. She slipped off the horse and, pulling up a handful of grass, began wiping off the lather.

"There, girl." She looked into Aspen's eye and saw herself mirrored back, and felt the soft nose and lips. Aspen's sweet-grass breath came warm against Pamela's neck. "You're mine, aren't you, Aspen," Pamela murmured softly, not wanting even the trees to hear her. She picked a thistle for Aspen, who ate it, prickers and blossom and all. "There!" Pamela combed the horse's snarled mane with her fingers. "Rose will never get a chance to ride you again. I won't ask her out here again, either."

At dinner at the cookhouse, Rose was the heroine. The cowboys looked at her with approval.

"Yes siree, we'll make a horsewoman out of you, for sure!" Ruby said, filling Rose's plate again.

"Pam didn't need to stop that horse for you; you had her almost licked your own self," Slim said. "I thought Pam was about the best woman with a horse I ever see, next to Ruby here, but I guess you're a reglar natcheral."

Rose's white teeth gleamed and her eyes shone as she smiled at them all.

Pamela glanced up from the meat on her plate that she had been cutting into smaller and smaller pieces, and met Ruby's eyes. Ruby knew how she felt. She could see right through you.

Rose and Pamela moved their cots together on the porch of the ranch house.

"Gee, this is nice!" Rose said. "Don't you like it, Pam?"

Pamela lay silent in her bed. Of course she liked it, it was their ranch, wasn't it? But she didn't have to talk about it.

[131]

They were quiet a long time, then Rose said, "Look at all the stars. I never saw so many."

"Mhmmm," Pamela murmured, dropping her head lower on her pillow so she could see the sword on Orion's belt. She drew in her breath quietly to catch the scent of sage and clover and the smell of the animals and the special cool air from the river, but Rose heard her and drew her breath in noisily; then she giggled.

"I can smell the manure way down at the corral."

She didn't really like having anybody here, Pamela thought. Rose spoiled it. Alan had, too. She wondered how Wrenn would be out here, but Wrenn would be fine. He was different and felt things more. He could lie and watch the bank swallows without saying anything at all for a long time. She wished she would just happen to see him to tell him she wasn't cross any more.

She pushed her feet down to the end of the cot and put her arms underneath her head. After the terrible headline in the paper it had seemed as though everything had come to a stop, but it hadn't. The ranch was just the same as it had always been. Everything in town was, too. She was over the feeling that people were wondering what irregularities her father had committed when they looked at her. It was true, as Rose had said, people forgot quick. Papa didn't seem to remember or care about the troubles last spring either. Why did she?

From the other bed, Rose said, "That Ruby kinda scared me at first, but she doesn't mean it when she looks so cross, does she?"

"Sometimes she does."

"I'd hate to meet her when she meant it. Tomorrow you must show me where that boy got bit by a rattlesnake. Do you still hear from him?"

"Oh, yes," Pamela said. "Off and on. He's abroad this summer." It surprised her the way Rose kept track of people. At first, she felt a little important in Rose's eyes, but at the same time she thought of the letter that didn't really say much.

✦

We went to the Tower of London where all those people lost their heads. London makes Dennis and me think of Boston.

Dennis was the red-headed boy. And she remembered him saying that night at the Thanksgiving party, "Randell thinks he owns you." Well, he didn't. She hadn't answered the letters since the trouble over the ranch, but Alan had never said anything about it or his father's being out here. She might write him again; it would be funny for him to get a letter in Italy postmarked King Butte, Montana.

Rose was already asleep.

The wind changed toward morning and came down cold from the Sage Hills, bringing rain with it. The rain fell noisily on the flat roof of the porch and dampened the blankets on the cots. Rose got out of bed and, bringing her blanket with her, crawled into bed with Pamela. Pamela stirred without waking. Rose slipped one arm around Pamela's waist, and they slept close together, warming each other, until Ruby came to wake them.

The next morning while they were all at breakfast, Mr. McBain drove in to the ranch in a red automobile that could be heard a mile up the road. Everyone went outside to see it. Pamela glanced at her father, leaning against the doorway. He was head and shoulders taller than McBain, who was taking off the duster he wore over his "city suit." Papa, in his old flannel shirt and vest, smoking his cigar, didn't seem bothered at all. Mr. McBain looked as red as a turkey gobbler. Having him come would spoil everything.

Ruby came to the door, pancake lifter in her hand. "You had breakfast, McBain?" She never used the prefix of Mister.

"I believe I could eat a little more after that bumpy drive, thank you."

"Well, you'll have to get somebody to hold that horse of yours and come and put your feet under the table, then."

Slim and the boys moved off toward the corral. Charlie came in to sit with McBain while he ate.

"Come on, Rose," Pamela said. "I'll show you where Alan got bitten by the snake."

"Who is that man?" Rose asked as they walked away from the house.

"Oh, he's McBain." Pamela hesitated, and then remembering that Rose hadn't believed what the paper said, she unburdened herself. "I hate him. He's against Papa."

"I didn't like the looks of him," Rose said, making a face.

"Let's go back tomorrow on the train," Pamela said. "It spoils everything having him here."

"I thought maybe we'd get to ride in his automobile."

"I wouldn't ride in his auto if he got down on his knees and begged us." Pamela kicked at a stone in the road.

"All right," Rose agreed, willing to share Pamela's hate. "Gee, I'm lame all over!"

The slow train that should have come through King Butte at noon the next day was late, so Slim left the girls there to wait for it on the bluff above the river. They had run out of talk. Rose lay on her back watching the clouds. After a while she closed her eyes. Pamela sat at a little distance, picking burrs out of her skirt and scowling as she thought of Mr. McBain. Now and then they heard a meadow lark or a wagon creaked by on the road beyond the station house.

A shadow fell dark across Rose's face as a bird swooped down to the river's edge, cutting the stillness with its shrill curli-li-li. . . .

Rose sat up. "What's that?"

"Nothing but an old curlew bird," Pam said. "Curlews always make that sound. Ruby says it's the loneliest sound she knows."

"It scared me," Rose said promptly.

"Not when you know what it is. At least, I'm not afraid of it," Pamela answered.

But after that the empty stillness was too much for Rose, so they went over to the one store kept in the front room of the stationmaster's house. They bought some dry gingersnaps and a bag of horehound drops. Then Rose's quick eyes pounced on two purses made of shells glued to a red cloth envelope and fastened by a brass snap. Inscribed on the outside in red paint were the words, "King Butte, Montana." They cost twenty-five cents each.

"I'll buy one and give it to you, and you buy one and give it to me because we're friends," Rose suggested.

"They're too little to carry," Pamela objected.

"Yes, but they're something to keep. I'll keep mine always," Rose said.

The girls were hot and dusty when they reached Brandon Rapids.

"You know what I'd like more than anything in the world?" Rose asked as she put on the floppy hat with the wreath of flowers. "I'd like an ice-cream soda at the BonTon."

"I would, too," Pamela agreed, and they went up Main Street, already tasting the sodas on their tongues.

"Do you think sodas are colder than ice-cream sundaes, Rose?"

"Much. Sundaes are more like a dessert and sodas are more like a drink. I think sodas are more exciting."

The interior of the BonTon was dim after the pitiless glare, but coolness and pungent, aromatic odors came out to them. They groped their way in the dimness toward an empty table. Four young people sat at the table in the back. Before they could make out their features, they knew them by their voices; Wrenn and Alice and Amy Wentworth, and the other one must be that friend of Wrenn's.

"Why, hello!" Rose called out as though they were special friends of hers, Pamela thought, but she was thankful that Rose was here with her.

"Hello," Pamela said. "I couldn't see who you were at first. We just came in from the ranch."

"Ugh, that sounds hot," Alice said. "It's bad enough in town."

"I look a sight," Rose murmured to Pamela. "And they're all dressed up. You haven't even got a hat!"

The others came by their table on the way out. Wrenn stopped to pay the bill so he came last. Pamela looked down at the straw she was sucking, but knowing all the time that Wrenn was turning away from the counter, pocketing his change; in a moment he would turn around. She hadn't wanted to see him the first time like this. Now he was beside them. Pamela looked up and met his eyes, then looked away quickly, glad that Rose began talking.

"I haven't seen you all summer, Wrenn," Rose said.

"Ned and I went on a pack trip. We had a great time. The guide who took us was a friend of your father's, Pam. He sure thought a lot of him."

"Oh, did he?" Pam asked stupidly. Wrenn meant . . . he was trying to make up for that other time.

The others were waiting for Wrenn outside. Pamela could see the girls' bright dresses through the black screen door; it made them seem unreal. Still Wrenn lingered. Could she just say, "I've been wanting to see you, Wrenn?"

"You should have been out at Pam's ranch. It was wonderful," Rose said. "I rode Pam's horse and can she gallop!" Rose brought her shoulders up and dropped her head back in a gesture of delight that amazed Pamela. "And we slept out on the porch so we could see the stars. I'd have liked to stay there the rest of the summer instead of this old hot town. We'd still be there if Mr. McBain hadn't come and they were all so busy."

Wrenn would know why McBain was there. He would think . . . Pamela drew on her straw, forgetting the glass was empty. It made a loud sucking sound. She turned deeper red than her sunburn.

"It must have been nice out there," Wrenn said. "Well, they're waiting for me. So long." He went on out the door with only a glance at Pamela. When he had gone, Rose was convulsed in giggles.

"Oh, Pam, I thought I'd die when you made that awful noise."

"That's what I hate about sodas," Pamela said, folding her straw over and over again.

CHAPTER **14**

Cottonwood leaves rustled on the pavement like summer's discarded wrappings. Not many more evenings to sit out on the porches of Prospect Avenue and talk in quiet voices while the rockers beat the slow time and the streetcars, two blocks over, hummed a kind of tune. Lucy Moore came up to sit with Maybelle Lacey "till its time to go in," she said. May Cheavers sat with Mr. Cheavers next door, and on the porch on the other side, Mr. Marsten dozed while Mrs. Marsten's needles made small clicking sounds in the dark. Upstairs, Pamela dressed to go to the park with the girls. Next week the park would be closed.

"I suppose Charlie will be coming in to town pretty soon now," Lucy Moore said. "J.B. used to say the street took on life when Charlie Lacey got in from the ranch." Lucy Moore's conversation worked a wistful pattern around remarks that J.B. used to make.

"When Charlie comes in this fall, he'll stay awhile. He's closing out the company's affairs, you know," Maybelle said just as Pamela came out on the porch.

Pamela walked slowly across the street to Alice Reed's, thinking about Papa. How did he feel now that everything was settled? When the calves were sold did they bring enough to make up for the loan? But Papa would never say. If he would only put things down in black and white so you could see where he really stood!

Amy Wentworth leaned over the Reeds' porch railing. "Hurry, Pam! I never saw anyone walk so slowly."

They rode out in the open trolley to the park at the end of the line. You got quite a breeze that way and you could lift your feet and let the breeze blow your skirt. You could hear the band three blocks away and the music of the merry-go-round, that was really for children, but at night grown people rode on it too. There were all kinds of people at the park, but it was all right if you went together like this.

They walked four abreast, past the cages of animals that were the side attraction: an antelope, graceful and frightened, a moose staring blindly at the crowds, his hide colorless with dust, a bear . . .

"Don't let's look at them," Pamela said. "I wish they didn't have them every year." So they went on to the merry-go-round and waited for the blaring pied-piper music to come to an end. That was when Pamela saw Wrenn Morley helping Rose down off her horse. Alice touched Pamela's arm. "Look who's there!"

"Who? Oh, yes." Pamela pretended not to have seen them. She became suddenly animated, not looking at them, hoping they wouldn't see her. She swung up on the painted horse and busied herself with the reins just as Wrenn and Rose stepped down.

"Hello, Pam!" Rose called.

Pamela looked surprised. "Why, hello." Her eyes brushed over them.

"Hello, Pam," Wrenn said.

Then the merry-go-round began to move. Pamela's horse rose on its pole, the music shrilled out its mad cacophony before it settled into a recognizable tune. Pamela's cheeks burned. She held her head high, looking straight ahead but waiting to come round again. Now she could see them, walking over toward the dance pavilion. Rose was taking excitedly to Wrenn. The ride went on forever, around and around. She didn't bother to reach for the ring.

"Did you ever expect Wrenn Morley to take out Rose Guinard?" Alice asked as they walked over to watch the dancing. "I bet they came out here by themselves, too. My mother would skin me alive if I ever asked to do that!"

Pamela was silent.

The trolley was crowded on the way back; there was no chance to talk.

"Did you have a good time, dear?" Mama called from the top of the stairs.

"It was sort of hot," Pamela said.

"Cora said Wrenn went, too."

"Yes, he was there. Good night, Mama."

Pamela sat on the edge of her bed without turning on the light and stared across at the dark bedroom windows of the Cheavers' house. How could Rose or Wrenn do a thing like that! Her two dearest friends. That was why Rose was always asking about Wrenn. "Has Wrenn ever kissed you? Has Wrenn changed?" And all the time she was trying to get Wrenn for herself.

When she saw them she would act as though it didn't matter to her. She would never let them know that she cared a snap. Anger moved in her fingers as she undressed and hung up her clothes with meticulous neatness. She brushed her hair down over her face with hard savage strokes and then flung her head back defiantly.

She lay on top of the sheet and curled her toes around the brass rods at the foot of the bed. A little light from the street came in between the Cheavers' house and theirs and rested lightly on the brass knobs.

But how did Wrenn happen to ask Rose? If it had been Alice's roommate or someone from away . . . Rose must have worked hard to get him to invite her. Maybe she asked him, herself. She wouldn't be surprised if she had. Slowly Wrenn's guilt came to seem less than Rose's, then Rose's entirely.

The next morning, Pamela ate hurriedly to avoid Mama's questions about the evening before. Once out of the house she walked downtown, staying on the Morleys' side of the street,

[139]

hoping Wrenn would come out, planning what she would say. At Third Street she turned over to Main, as usual, to pass Madame Guinard's shop. The door was open to the street but Rose and her mother must be in the back part. Some mornings she just opened the screen and called in, but she couldn't do that this morning. At noon, Rose would come up to go to lunch with her, all smiles and giggles. But noon came and no Rose, so she ate her lunch at the window of the office. It was clear that Rose was ashamed to show her face.

She met Rose two evenings later on her way home from the library.

"Hello, Rose," she said coolly.

"Oh, Pam, hello!" Rose came over and walked along with her. "Pam, don't be cross about my going to the park with Wrenn, will you?"

"Of course not, Rose. What a silly idea!"

"Wrenn came down for his mother's hat the other day and we got to talking about how soon he was leaving . . . you know, and how he hadn't been around town hardly at all. He said he hadn't even been out to the park once and then he just asked me if I'd like to go that evening."

Pamela walked silently along the street, visualizing it all, testing it for truth, knowing how Wrenn must have looked as he asked her to go.

"We talked a lot about you, Pam."

"Couldn't you find any other subject to talk about?"

Rose ignored the chilly tone of her voice. "He said you were angry at him because of something he said. . . ." Pamela looked straight ahead at the moths flying around the hanging arc light. "I said you'd get over it . . . you know, you do get angry and then over it quick, Pam; but he said he didn't think you ever would this. I'm going to see him tonight. Can I tell him you aren't angry any more? He goes back to college tomorrow night."

"He can talk to me himself if he has anything to say," Pamela said. They had come to the corner where Rose turned over. "Good night." Pamela walked away so fast she didn't hear what

Rose said. Wrenn had no business talking things over with Rose. Why would he go to see Rose the last night he was home? Pamela was almost running now, her steps on the wooden sidewalk swift in the quiet autumn night.

CHAPTER **15**

It was horrid having Wrenn Morley come to see her in the millinery shop, Rose thought. He had to sit in a stiff-backed chair and face a mirror or turn the other way and face the front door; and hats everywhere. It was bad enough having the door jingle every time he came. Taking him through the shop and up the dark stairs to the little sitting room above the shop was just as bad. Of course, her mother sat outside on pleasant evenings, with her chair against the window of the shop, and another chair beside her in case someone came along to visit, but Wrenn wouldn't like sitting there. So Rose suggested that it would be pleasant to take a drive that last night.

When Wrenn asked if he could take the horse that evening, Mrs. Morley looked up from her embroidery and said, "Dear, are you sure Maybelle won't mind? I don't believe she would like to have Pamela out riding after dark." But the blue floss she was using knotted just then and she turned her attention to that.

Wrenn knew perfectly well that his mother meant Mrs. Lacey and that she assumed that he wanted the horse and carriage to take Pamela out riding. He flushed a little but said, "Oh no. In Cambridge fellows often hire a hack to take a girl out riding."

"Be sure you are back here by ten-thirty, Wrenn," his father said. Wrenn answered with a brisk "Yes, sir" and was gone.

The little deception bothered him for the length of time it took to walk through the back yard to the stable on the alley.

He felt a little guilty about Pamela, but the thought of taking Rose Guinard out riding overcame his scruples. That afternoon last week when he called at the millinery shop for his mother he had had no idea of asking Rose to go to the park with him, but it was so easy to talk to her and her dark eyes danced so he liked to watch them. Somehow, he knew she would like to go to the park and he found himself asking her. He had never had a better time. He, himself, might not have thought of going for a ride tonight if she hadn't talked about it, but it was a fine idea.

He drove down Main Street in the early September evening and stopped in front of the window that bore the sign in gilt letters: MADAME GUINARD, MILLINERY. Rose had been waiting for him, so the door hardly jingled. Madame Guinard was there to see them off and she, too, seemed to Wrenn more jolly than most mothers usually were.

Madame Guinard really talked to him. "All these hats and Rose won't wear one! I tell her a lady always wears a hat when she goes out. Isn't that so, Mr. Morley?" Madame Guinard's black eyes twinkled.

"Well, it's so warm I don't think it will really matter," he answered quite seriously.

"See there, Mother, he isn't shocked," Rose said, and Madame Guinard laughed as though it were the best joke in the world.

"Here, then, naughty girl, pin a flower in your hair," and she picked up a little bunch of velvet forget-me-nots lying on the counter and pinned it in Rose's knot. "There!" She stood back with her hands raised to get the effect. The blue matched the blue ribbons of Rose's dress and Wrenn thought she was the prettiest girl he had ever seen.

"Oh, Wrenn, this is fun!" Rose said as they turned off Main Street. The rubber-tired wheels spun so easily over the road, so quietly; the horse's head was held up smartly by a checkrein and the tail was bobbed in a dashing Eastern manner. "Let's go out to Harpers' wood where we went for the picnic Pioneer Day," she suggested. "Would that be too far?"

[142]

"That isn't far at all, not with this horse of Father's," he said.

There was so much to talk about with Rose. He found himself telling her about wanting to stop school and go to Europe; see something before he was old and settled down.

"I want to go to Paris," Rose said. "I was born there, you know, but my parents came to the United States the next year and I can't even speak French, because Mother says it's better for her to learn to speak English."

It was so strange that they both wanted to go there; the strangeness amounted almost to a miracle that drew them closer together.

"I get through college two years from next June. I'd like to do something like that before I start law school," Wrenn said, looking down the road.

"Why don't you? You wouldn't need very much money. Mother says people in France live on half what they spend here: bread and some wine and cheese, not beef, beef, beef!" Rose imitated her mother's voice exactly and Wrenn laughed. He felt that he really might get to Paris and he had never had such a good time with a girl before.

It was not until they were on the way back that Rose said, "I saw Pam the other night."

Wrenn flicked the whip lightly over the horse.

"I asked her not to be mad at . . . you know, my going with you out to the park."

"You shouldn't have done that. I can take who I want to."

"I know, but she's my best friend. I wouldn't want to hurt her feelings."

"What did she say?"

"She said you could talk to her yourself if you wanted to," Rose softened Pamela's words.

"I guess I don't," he said. "We didn't get along very well the last time. We got into a quarrel over Pam's father."

"That business in the papers about her father was hard on Pam."

"I know. And she doesn't want anything to do with me because she thinks my father . . . Oh, well, don't let's talk about it. She's hardly said a word to me the few times I've seen her."

Rose was silent beside him in the buggy. One hand played with the fringe of her sash. She knew Pam was waiting for Wrenn to say something. She should tell him so. Pam expected him to go to see her before he left; she had been sure he would or she might not have said that with her head so high.

"I can't help that, can I?" Wrenn burst out.

"No," Rose said slowly, and then, honestly, warmheartedly, "but you ought to drop around and see her before you go away." There, she felt better, but at the same time a horrid fear bothered her. If he did, would that be the end of this?

The wheels spun with a crackling sound over the first fallen leaves that littered the road, and then revolved more and more slowly. Real trees grew here along the river; cottonwoods and willows, and box elders, full-trunked, wide-branched, old as trees grew in the plains country. After the endless prairie and naked rocks spread bare under the wide-open eye of the sky, here were hidden birds and secret rustlings, outlines of darkness as vague as yearnings and desires, tangled as confused thoughts.

One minute Wrenn had been thinking of Pam, as he had all summer, with an uncomfortable sense of embarrassment, and the next he felt only a great tenderness toward Rose. He hardly heard what she said, but the positiveness of her way of speaking made him feel more sure himself. He held the reins in his left hand and slipped his arm around her. When he kissed her very gently she turned warm young lips toward his. His arm tightened. For a moment neither of them spoke, then he said in a voice that was hardly his own, "Thank you." And the next instant he was back in his own unsure self and wondered if that was a funny thing to say. But Rose gave a little sigh and said, "It's taken us the whole summer to get to know each other, and now you're going away."

"I know," he said. "Would you write me sometimes?"

"If you'll write me right back, the very next day." She wondered if Pam had written him last year. Anyway, it was all right. Pam wrote to that boy in the East all the time.

Mr. Sewall was out of town and Pamela had the day off so she was home when Mrs. Morley came in through the kitchen. "Maybelle, I'm going to make Wrenn an angel-food cake for his last dinner and I need two more eggs." Then she turned to Pamela with an arch smile. "I guess you and Wrenn had a nice ride last night! Maybelle, I hope you didn't mind their getting home a little late."

Pamela said stiffly, "I wasn't with Wrenn last night." She went on upstairs.

Cora Morley was embarrassed. "Well, I declare! Wrenn asked to take the horse and buggy and I supposed . . . in fact, I thought he said . . . I guess he wanted to drive with some of the boys."

"We haven't seen anything of Wrenn since the first part of the summer," Maybelle said, resentment getting into her tone. "I don't think Pamela's even mentioned him for a long time."

Up in her own room, with the door safely closed, Pamela sat down at the little bird's-eye maple desk and opened the drop front. She took their class picture out of the last pigeonhole and examined it in detail, looking a long time at Wrenn, standing in the middle of the back row because he was so tall. It wasn't very good of him, but it showed his high forehead and his smile and the wave in his hair. Rose was down in the front row because she was so short. She was laughing and she had on that brown plaid dress with the ruffled yoke. Her hands were clasped together. Yes, she was pretty, but as Mama said, in a bold sort of way. Then she found herself, standing in the center of the first row because she had been the class president. She was taller than all the other girls except Phoebe Dunbar. People always said she and Wrenn made such a good-looking couple. She wasn't smiling; she remembered thinking she should look serious on such an occasion.

"You'll probably never be all together again like this," Miss

Ferris had said, "and I want you to remember always that you are the first class to graduate from the new high school in Brandon Rapids, Montana."

There was Amy Wentworth, who wrote the class prophecy and foretold that Wrenn Morley would be the governor of the state and Pamela Lacey would grace the governor's mansion as first lady. No one had laughed at that as they had over Rose Guinard marrying a millionaire and living in New York City, or Bill Kossuth owning a meat market so he could have all the frankfurters he wanted.

She pulled out the Pioneer Ball program. That was when everything had started. That was the night she and Wrenn had walked in on Papa in the study. But Wrenn ought to understand. He just talked about loyalty; he didn't practice it.

She rummaged in the little left-hand drawer until she found half of an amber comb. It was hard to break in your fingers and her teeth bit down on her under lip as she did it.

She had to hunt in all the drawers before she found the purse with King Butte, Montana on it. The shells were only stuck on and came off easily, but the red cloth lining was tough and made a horrid sound when she tore it.

There! She was through with both Wrenn and Rose for ever and ever, and she felt better.

"I imagine Wrenn will run over to say good-by after supper," Maybelle Lacey couldn't keep from saying. She stirred her tea, not looking at her daughter.

"No, he won't come. I sent him home the last time he was here," Pamela said.

"Forever more, Pamela, why? *That's* why he went with that little Guinard girl. Poor Cora's so upset she doesn't know what to do."

"It isn't anything I can talk about, Mama."

"Fiddle! All young people have quarrels. You'll get over it. Make it up Christmas vacation, or write him a letter and tell him you've forgiven him."

[146]

Pamela pushed back her chair.

"Why don't you go down to the station and see the others off, anyway? Alice Reed and John Donaldson are leaving on the train tonight, too, Cora said. It's so nice to have a crowd to see them off."

"No," Pamela said. "I don't want to."

Maybelle poured herself another cup of tea. "Believe me, Maybelle, you can be glad you have a daughter; girls are so much easier to handle," Cora Morley had said that morning, but she didn't know. Pamela had such a way of shutting up so you couldn't talk to her, just like Charlie.

CHAPTER **16**

January, 1907

"I can't get used to seeing Charlie sitting in the front window in the afternoon," May Cheavers told Maybelle at Shakespeare Club.

"He's in and out," Maybelle answered, not admitting that she wasn't used to it, herself.

"It makes a difference in the way your house keeps in order! I know what the house was like when Amos had that broken leg last winter," Amy Reed said.

They had to wait awhile before starting the reading of the play today, because several members were late, the weather was so bad. Lucy Moore sat at the window and kept parting the stiff lace curtains to see down the walk. May Cheavers was hunting a good quotation to give when the roll was called. She looked up suddenly with a smile. "Here's a perfect one for to-day, and you'd never guess it was out of Shakespeare, 'The fear's as bad as the falling.'"

"I do hope Cora comes; I asked her 'specially," Amy Reed said.

"She feels so bad about Wrenn. He was just the apple of their eye and the only son; I don't see how he could do that!" Lucy Moore exclaimed.

May Cheavers kept her finger in the book at her quotation. "If they'd only asked first, but going off that way to Butte and getting married, and, of course, the girl's Catholic and the Morleys have been Presbyterians forever!"

"I suppose Cora will want us to ask Rose to join the Shakespeare Club," Mrs. Reed said.

"Well, we won't. She's nothing but a little chit." May Cheavers closed her lips firmly.

"Cora is coming, girls." Lucy Moore let the lace curtains fall together.

Cora Morley came in with a small smile on her lips. Her eyes met each of these women she knew so well and then moved quickly away as though she might weep if she looked at anyone too long, just as others had come back to the club after some bereavement.

"Here's a seat over here, Cora," Maybelle said. She and Cora had been drawn together ever since Maybelle had confided in Cora that Pamela grieved. But Maybelle had wondered since if she should have said that. It wasn't until the interlude between Act II and III that Maybelle asked in a low voice, "Have you heard from them?"

Cora nodded. "She wrote me. She said they hated to hurt us or her mother, and you know how much hurt she was! But they knew their own minds, she said, so they went ahead. And he's going to finish college and Rose is going to work in a millinery shop . . . Did you ever? It makes Ned wild. He says he won't send Wrenn through law school."

"Act III of *Henry VIII*," May Cheavers said in her public reading voice.

> *Take thy lute, wench: my soul grows sad with troubles*
> *Sing and disperse 'em if thou can'st. . . .*

The dessert was one of Amy Reed's masterpieces and the

Shakespeare Club ate heavily to show their appreciation, so Maybelle Lacey felt it difficult to go back and get a hearty meal for Charlie. Charlie always wanted meat and potatoes and pie or pudding. Still, it was nice to come home and have him there and especially now with Pam off so much by herself. The smell of Charlie's cigar came out into the hall. He was reading the paper in the front room and he had a good coal fire going in the fireplace.

"My, I should think you'd be glad you aren't out at the ranch a night like this, Charlie! It's going to twenty below Mr. Cheavers told May."

"You can keep plenty warm at the ranch," Charlie said. He went back to his paper, but he had a disquieting picture in his mind of Slim and Ruby out there. It was pretty quiet for them. "I ain't never been on a place where there wasn't any stock, Charlie," Ruby had said.

There was Pam. Her quick steps sounded loudly on the icy walk, then on the porch, and a current of cold air pushed through the warmth of the rooms as she opened the door.

"Hello!" There was no sign of grieving on her face. Instinctively, both Charlie and Maybelle looked at her high color, her bright eyes, her young figure for confirmation of the value of their own lives. Just as they were beginning to have their moments of doubt, there was Pamela.

"I'm sorry I'm late but we're taking inventory and there's so much to do." Pamela still helped Mr. Sewall with his book on the Pioneers but she had found a place in the office of the hardware store.

"Mercy, Pamela." Maybelle didn't like to hear about Pamela's business career. She still talked vaguely of Pamela's going east to school somewhere or traveling next year.

"I like it," Pam said as she took off her coat and the scarf that went twice around her neck, "much better than the Pioneers."

"I should think so!" Charlie said.

Maybelle waited to tell her news until they were sitting at

dinner in the square dining room with the oak plate rail hand-somely decorated by hand-painted china plates. "Poor Cora had a letter from Wrenn and that girl. They're not coming back here. Wrenn's going back to school and she's going to work in some millinery store. Cora says Ned's just wild and that he won't pay for him to go through law school."

Pamela's mouth tightened. With one finger she traced the acanthus leaf in the tablecloth.

"I bet that's got Ned Morley hog-tied!" Charlie gave a sudden laugh and brought his hand down on the table so the dishes rattled.

"Why, Charlie Lacey!" Maybelle looked at him reproachfully. "Such a vulgar thing to say!"

"I'm surprised the boy's that independent. But he's got a good little girl there; any girl who could hang on her horse like she did at the ranch, remember that, Pam?" Pamela took out the plates and Maybelle flashed Charlie a significant glance.

"She can hardly bear to have them mentioned," Maybelle whispered.

"Bosh!" Charlie Lacey said loudly, pushing back his chair. But he looked more closely at his daughter when she came back in.

"If you're going out, Pamela, you go right ahead and dress," Maybelle said magnanimously, wishing now that she had just happened to mention to Cora that Pamela was going out tonight. It was one thing to tell her that Pamela grieved but another to suggest that she didn't have gentleman company.

"I'm not going anywhere tonight," Pamela said and felt her mother's disappointment.

"Good enough, Pam. Nobody in his right mind would go out on a night like this," Charlie said a little overheartily. What Maybelle said bothered him. He wouldn't like to think of Pam eating her heart out over Ned Morley's boy. Ned had always been a little too much of a strait jacket for him, but the boy might be different. And that little girl had grabbed him off, had she? But if Pam had wanted him he would think . . .

"Well, I feel mighty sorry for Cora and Ned," Maybelle said, righting her own world by her pity. "Rose has so little background." Her lips curved around the bowl of the silver dessert spoon that had come from the South.

"Wrenn's satisfied," Pamela said, and wished she hadn't said it because it seemed too true now, too much of a fact, as real as the sickening sweet taste of the canned plums they were having for dessert. Until she had said it she hadn't believed it.

They were doing the dishes when Pamela remembered. "I had a letter from Alan Randell today," she said. "I met the mailman on my way downtown this morning."

"Alan Randell!" Maybelle held her hands still, looking at Pamela. The astonishment in her voice made it sound like a little shriek.

"Yes. He's coming out here next week."

I said I'd get there. I don't think you believed me. Dad is all for it. He thinks it would be a fine thing for me to put in six months in the refinery there. . . .

"For heaven's sake! Charlie!" Maybelle called. "Charlie, Pamela had a letter from Mr. Randell's boy. He's coming out here next week!"

Pamela went on drying dishes in the kitchen. She was pleased that Alan hadn't forgotten, but she didn't know whether she wanted to see him or not. So much had happened since then: the trouble with the cattle company . . . Wouldn't it be awkward now seeing Alan? If he dared criticize her father she would set him straight about that, right in the beginning.

Papa came out to the kitchen, holding the paper in his hand.

"What's that, Pam? What's Randell's boy coming out here for?"

Did Papa mind? Did he not want to see him because of all that?

"He says his father wants him to have six months' experience in the refinery here. There's some sort of connection," she said.

"That was how Randell came out here in the first place and

got the cattle bug," Charlie said slowly, but he was thinking of something else as he talked, Pamela could tell.

"Well, Alan must come right here and stay with us. I wouldn't hear of him going any place else," Maybelle began.

"Now slow down, Maybelle, wait a minute," Charlie said.

"Pamela's heard from him right along, Charlie!" Maybelle made it a retort.

"Mostly postcards. He was in Europe all summer," Pamela explained. "He never said anything about the ranch business," she added.

"Oh, that's all forgotten by now." Maybelle's tone of voice suggested time past.

Charlie took a toothpick out of his vest pocket, which he usually did only at the ranch, and chewed it silently. He started for the sitting room and then came back.

"You let him get his own place to live," he said.

Maybelle followed Pamela upstairs. "What all did he say, Pamela?"

"That's all. He said last winter that he wanted to come out here again."

"Well, he must be pretty interested in you to make him do that! I thought he had such charming manners." Maybelle wished Pamela would read her the whole letter. She could tell so much more if she heard it.

"He didn't have at the ranch!" Pamela said. Mama's tone made her feel contrary and out of sorts, and Papa didn't want him to come; she could see that. She didn't either. It was bound to be uncomfortable. Maybe he was coming because he was interested in her as Mama said in that special tone of voice. She wasn't *interested* in him. People always said interested when they were afraid to say "love." Did Wrenn say, "I love you, Rose; I've never loved anyone else, not even Pamela"? Had going off to Butte to get married been Wrenn's idea or did Rose say suddenly, "Let's just go and get married!" She knew just how Rose would look with her eyes shining and so excited you could hardly *not* do what she wanted to. Maybe Wrenn hesitated. Maybe he wondered what she would think. . . .

"Pamela . . ." Mama stood in the doorway of her room, "I do think you should tell Alan we'll all be so glad to see him; that's just good manners."

CHAPTER 17

February, 1907

Rose looked across the restaurant table at Wrenn. He had been quiet ever since the dessert.

"Wrenn?"

"Yes, dear."

"You're not worried about things?"

"I should say not!" His face broke into a smile.

"How did your Greek go?"

"All right. He called on me. It's a good thing you made me stay awake and do it. After class I told Stephen Hobbes I was married. He lived below me in Westmorely last year. Stephen wouldn't believe me at first." She watched him closely to see if he minded Hobbes not believing it; if he had minded telling him. "I told him I'd bring him home to meet you."

"Do," Rose said. "I wish we could have him for dinner, but bring him home some evening and we could have some wine."

"He would like that, I think." Wrenn could never quite believe Rose's easy familiarity with wine, but that was the French in her. Hobbes would like Rose, too. Wrenn looked across the table now with a sense of wonder that this girl was really his wife, Mrs. Wrenn Morley! From that first night at the park he had liked her difference from everyone he had ever known. Rose had such black hair and eyes, such white skin. She was so small and quick. Her laugh was a little too sudden and loud . . . oh, not that either, it surprised him every time, that was all, but he had to laugh too when he heard it. She was so . . . so strong in her laughter and her love.

His mother had insinuated that she had "set her cap" for him. Even worse, she said everyone in town would think he had had to marry her. It was too bad but it was true that his mother had a typical small-town mind. His father had angered him more; he had said, "Wrenn, there are ways of handling these matters that are better than ruining your whole life. You should have come to me frankly instead of running off and marrying her. At your ages the marriage can simply be annulled."

He had kept his temper only because, as he told Rose, he didn't suppose they knew what love really was. He thought again of his mother crying and his father writing out a check and telling him that he would pay his regular college expenses and give him his allowance, but beyond that he would promise nothing. He wished he could forget the way his father's voice broke when he said, "Wrenn, you've never given us any worry until now. I don't want this one tragic mistake to ruin your whole future."

"It isn't a mistake, sir," he had answered. "It's the best thing that could have happened to me." He didn't try to explain to them that he couldn't live without Rose, that she felt the same way. He had felt almost sorry for them and for the house as he went down the front steps. He had put his bags into the hack he had waiting and driven down to Rose's. The street had bothered him a little, and hurting Pamela, but it was a good thing that he and Pam had quarreled or he might never have known Rose.

It had felt strange to go in through the millinery shop and up the back stairs to Rose's room. He had minded that, but Rose had been waiting for him and she put her arms around him, whispering into his ear, "Oh, Wrenn, was it very bad? Were they terribly angry? Poor darling, you were brave." And neither his mother nor father had mattered at all; he had realized that it was impossible for them to understand why he and Rose had been married.

"How was the shop today?" he asked. He disliked having Rose work. Part of the time he forgot about it because she was usually home before he was, and she never mentioned working unless he brought it up. But Saturdays he went to the shop at closing time and even her flashing smile when he came in couldn't make him feel anything but silly hanging around a women's millinery shop. It was a little place, just across from Gore Hall, and he could pretend to be looking at a book and just happen to glance over at it. In time, his mind made the shop almost a part of the Yard and nothing commercial at all.

"Do you have to study tonight?"

"I have to write a philosophy paper."

"Then we better go right back."

"No hurry. I worked on it all afternoon at the library."

Rose turned over the watch pinned to her shirtwaist and pushed back her chair. "You remember the last one took you till three o'clock."

"I remember that you went to bed and deserted me."

"I remember that you woke me up when you did come!" He met her eyes in a secret smile that gave him a sudden sense of happiness.

He paid for the meal and left a tip for the waitress but Rose had given him the money before they came in. After the first month in Cambridge she had taken over their financial matters. She had a little book in which she kept accounts, and a bag that hung at her wrist which seemed to contain all their visible wealth. He was relieved, but baffled, too. Sometimes he said, "I'll need some money today," without offering any explanation, to prove to himself that he could. And she gave it to him, but her black eyes were thoughtful. And when he spent it all with the fellows he had a twinge or two seeing her enter the item in the book under "running expenses." One thing he had learned, Rose would never reproach him for any expense but she would think about it and he would be aware of it.

At first, he had disliked the bed-sitting room they rented, with its green water-paper that was streaked from the radiator pipes, and the red figured rug and the green tasseled portieres that separated the sleeping alcove from the sitting room, but he was used to it now. Rose kept it in perfect order. She had some kind of a plant with a red bloom on it on the window sill. He hadn't noticed for some time that it was artificial. "I made it out of some hat flowers," Rose said, regarding it with her head tipped on one side in that way she had. "It's very gay, don't you think, Wrenn?" Nothing could have made him say he didn't think so.

His bedroom slippers were always under the bed, which disconcerted him when he came in, and his nightshirt was neatly rolled and hidden under the pillow sham, as hers was concealed behind her pillow. But he never let her know that this annoyed him.

The table between the windows Rose kept for his desk, with a chair in front of it. She had a rocking chair at one side in which she sat sewing or crocheting, not saying a word while he studied. At first, he couldn't study with her there without reaching out to twist a lock of her hair or hold her hand, just to hear her scold him, and move farther away. Her playful assumption that she must see to it that he tended to his work, that he ate and slept properly, amused him. He remembered how his father issued edicts at home that his mother hurried to carry out. As a child it had always seemed to him that his mother and father inhabited two separate worlds that touched only at the edges: nothing at all like this close world of his and Rose's, and this world of his seemed infinitely superior, infinitely natural and pleasant. One evening he lay crosswise on the bed translating his Greek and Rose sat beside him and fed him slices of the apple she was peeling. He couldn't imagine his mother and father doing such a thing.

Tonight, Rose said, "I had a letter from Mama; they've had terrible cold weather. Everything's black and white, Mama says."

It seemed strange to him to hear news from Madame Guinard, the milliner on Main Street. Stranger still to think of her as related to himself. But he saw Prospect Avenue in the snow, all the way up the block to Pamela's house.

"I bet it's no colder feeling than it is right here," he said.

"She made a hat for Mrs. Moore, who's gone to California for a month. Business hasn't been very good; of course, it never is until spring."

Wrenn opened his books and Rose sat quietly rereading her letter. She didn't think that Wrenn was ready yet to read her letters that began, "My dear Children." Especially, as they had had no letters from Wrenn's family except ones addressed to Wrenn alone. There were items in this letter that she thought it just as well to keep to herself: that some of the women, Mrs. Lacey's friends, of course, had stopped coming to her. "You know why! *C'est égal*." And Rose knew the quick shrug of the shoulders, the snap of the eyes that would accompany the phrase. "I made a blue velvet hat with ostrich plumes for 'one of the girls' and charged fifty dollars for it! I'm enclosing two clippings from the newspaper that may interest you." Rose read them again. There was no point in showing them to Wrenn. One was from the column known as the Spray of the Rapids:

Mr. Alan Randell of Buffalo, N. Y., who graduated last June from Harvard University, is now employed in the office of the refinery. Mr. Randell visited at the Rocky Mountain Cattle Company ranch two summers ago and narrowly survived a rattlesnake bite.

So he had come back to see Pam!

The other clipping was from the Sunday society page.

Ten of the town's young people enjoyed a moonlight skating party Friday evening last, five miles up the Missouri River. A bonfire was built and the chef from the Western Hotel served a hot repast. Those present were Alan Randell escorting Pamela Lacey, John Hyatt escorting Annie Day . . .

She could see Pamela in that bright blue coat and hat of hers. She would be very handsome. Maybe Pam would marry that Alan Randell; she hoped so. She would feel better when Pam was married, though there was no reason why she should feel badly about Pam. Pam and Wrenn and quarreled or she would never have gone with him . . . or, at least, she didn't think she would. Anyway, she loved him more than Pam ever could . . . from the very first day of high school.

But Pam hadn't forgiven her. After Wrenn went back to school last fall Pam had been as cold as ice, and never dropped in at the shop the way she used to. Now she must hate her, the way she hated that McBain. Rose remembered how Pam's face could look when she hated someone: cold and without any expression at all.

Wrenn didn't still care about her; he hardly ever mentioned her. But what if he should when they went back there to live? What if he should ever be sorry he had married her? Did he ever wish they had waited? He was very quiet at dinner, and sometimes she wondered if he felt cut off from his friends, just because he was married.

Rose tipped her head so she could study Wrenn's profile. He was sitting sideways at the desk, his elbow supported on his knee and his face resting on his hand while he wrote busily with the other hand.

"Intellectual, *serieux,*" Mama had said. "The chin *un petit* weak, perhaps." It wasn't; not to her. His face looked very strong, really noble. He was so wrapped up in what he was writing that he didn't know she was looking at him. She wished he would raise his eyes. Sometimes, his books shut her out.

She looked away from Wrenn and her eyes rested unhappily on the red paper geranium. Like last night, in Gordon Jennings's rooms when they were talking about poetry; it seemed so queer for boys, men, really, Wrenn always said "a man in my Greek class," to be talking about poetry. When they read aloud the words ran together so fast, too fast for her to get the sense. Words leaped out in the room, words you didn't usually say, like desire and flesh and soul . . . nobody seemed to notice them except her. And that poem about the running hound that Gordon had read in a strange creepy voice, that was exciting, but goodness!

[158]

She had no idea that the hound was really Christ! What an awful idea!

It was nice to go there. Gordon's sitting room was as fine a room as the Morleys' library, and so cozy with the fire. She had liked Gordon in the beginning. Wrenn said he was a very good friend of his, and wrote plays. She had liked meeting those other two men and that girl from Brookline, Timothy Allen's sister, who looked as though she would be fun, but who talked like a teacher. But then they all sat down and talked about poetry. Wrenn seemed as excited about some poem as the others were. She hadn't really heard the poem at all, she had been watching Wrenn as he sat on the floor by the fire listening to Gordon read aloud. She wished something she talked to him about would make his face look that way.

Everyone seemed to know the same poets. She had never heard of any of them. She kept hoping they would talk about Long-fellow so she could quote the part she knew from *Hiawatha*. Gordon Jennings could recite poetry by the yard; so could that girl, Annabel her name was. When Annabel got cold on the window seat and moved over by the fire, Wrenn quoted some lines to her about . . .

"Wrenn, what were those lines you told that sister of Timothy's?" Rose asked, forgetting that she was interrupting him.

Wrenn looked up and laughed. "Oh, that was from a poem Pam taught me:

> A *wind blew out of a cloud, chilling*
> *My beautiful Annabel Lee* . . ."

He went back to his paper.

Of course, Pamela would have understood all the poetry! Maybe Wrenn thought that too, when she said that awful thing. Rose got up hurriedly and took out her sewing to keep from remembering, but it didn't do any good.

She hadn't said anything all evening, hardly, and she wasn't used to sitting like a mummy. She didn't think how it would sound, and everyone else had been saying what they liked or

[159]

didn't like, and what was so bad about it, really? She had just said, "I wish poets would talk straight so you could understand them." But she had known right away that it sounded terrible. Annabel had given a little laugh and that hateful Gordon tapped her on the shoulder and said, "Methinks you don't care for poetry, little one!" Wrenn didn't say anything at all. He was busy poking the fire.

What if Wrenn thought her stupid? Maybe he wished then that he had married Pam. She couldn't stand it any longer so she went over and stood behind Wrenn, putting both arms around his head. She kissed him lightly and meant to let him go on with his writing, but he threw down his pencil and pulled her around into his arms.

"Wrenn, are you sure you aren't sorry you married me?" she whispered, not wanting even the room to hear.

"You know I'm not. Are you sorry you married me?"

She burrowed her head into his shoulder to hide the sudden, silly tears. When she didn't answer, Wrenn reached up and touched her face and felt that it was wet.

"Rose, you silly darling! What's wrong with you?"

Then she had to ask it, this one time, and never again. "You don't keep thinking about Pam?" She kept her face hidden.

"Rose, darling, that was only a boy and girl affair. I didn't know what love was then. Look at me." He lifted her head from his shoulder. "I only love you. Don't ever ask such a foolish question again."

"But . . ."

He stopped her words with his lips.

Wrenn did love her, only her, as she loved, loved, loved him. Sudden, inexplicable happiness warmed her, wrapped her, made her safe. Being loved, loving Wrenn, was . . . was ecstasy, as Mama said. But surely not Mama and Papa, like this. No one else quite like this. Telling Pam in the willow tree that time, but she had no idea what the word really meant. Funny to think so fast with Wrenn kissing her. What was he thinking at the same time? She drew away to look at him, his eyes, his nose, his dear chin.

"You have ink by your ear, Wrenn, right there!"

CHAPTER **18**

May, 1907

"I don't know why you want to take Alan out to the ranch, Pamela. When he came to dinner he didn't even mention it." Maybelle Lacey's eyes widened, her eyebrows rose, her head underlined her words with a nod. She was frying chicken for their lunch and the sizzling of the fat interrupted her. Pamela went on wrapping the deviled eggs in oiled paper.

But the ranch had been in their minds when Alan came to dinner, all the time Mama was asking about Buffalo and Europe. And it had been in Alan's eyes when he first met Papa, and in Papa's eyes looking right at him, saying, "How are your mother and father?" Alan had just said that they were fine; his father was pretty busy with the brass foundry . . . not ranching. And he had gone out of his way to explain why his father wanted him to have this experience out here at the refinery. Why hadn't he said he had come because he wanted to see her . . . if that *was* the reason. Anyway, Mama was wrong, they *had* talked about the ranch by talking about the rattlesnake bite.

"Yes, sir, I wouldn't have given fifty cents for you when Slim carried you down to the house," Papa had said. And then Alan had asked how Slim and Ruby were.

Maybelle subdued the turmoil in the skillet with an iron cover.

"Going out to the ranch was Alan's idea, Mama. He asked if he couldn't drive me out."

"But just because he thought you wanted to go. What he's interested in is you, or he would never have come back out here!"

Maybelle looked knowing and then Pamela's scowl made her add, "I hope you can find a nice, shady place on the way to eat your lunch, but I'm sure I don't remember any."

"There are plenty of lovely places," Pamela said in quick defense. "You haven't been out to the ranch in years, Mama. You wouldn't remember." Pamela's words floated back as she went upstairs.

She sang as she ran the water in the bathtub. It was a good day and it was spring and she was free from the desk at the hardware office for three whole days.

She smiled at herself in the mirror as she brushed her hair and coiled it carefully into the new Psyche knot. She looked much older than when she went east to visit the Randells two years ago.

"How old are you, my dear?" Mrs. Randell had asked. "Only sixteen, why you're just a little schoolgirl, really." She put in another hairpin.

The first time she ever put her hair up Wrenn said, "You're so grown-up." That was the night she had run upstairs and left him. Pamela's hands rested idle on the dresser edge. She looked in the mirror into her own eyes without seeing them or her sober face looking back at her. Mama was calling and Pamela went out into the hall to hear her, buttoning her shirtwaist as she went.

"You want to be ready, Pamela; you don't want to keep him waiting. I just wonder if your father got my letter and told Ruby about fixing a room for Alan. I don't think she bothers much about housekeeping."

From the front window in Mama's room, Pamela saw Alan drive up the street in his black runabout. There were only two like it in town and they were painted red. The black looked more . . . dependable, that was it. And the brass trimmings made it quite elegant. She watched him pull up the brake and get out. He took off his visored cap and laid it on the seat; she could look down on his dark head as he came up the walk. He did look different from anyone here; maybe it was the way he walked. She remembered how he had walked in his cowboy boots at the ranch and the boys had made fun of him. He glanced up suddenly as though he felt her eyes and she jumped back from the window. Why did she do that? Why hadn't she opened the curtains and waved? She went back to her room and put on her new crash duster.

She could hear Mama: "My, you're going to have a beautiful day for your trip to the ranch!"

"Yes, I'm looking forward to it," Alan said. "It was midsummer when I was there before."

"And you had such a horrible experience! I wouldn't think you would ever want to go back."

"Well, at least I have Pamela with me. She saved my life before, you know."

Pamela hurried downstairs so Mama wouldn't say anything more against the ranch or ranchers.

Alan put Pamela in the car, covered her knees with a robe and deposited her small valise in the back. They waved to Mama who stood on the front porch, and started off down Prospect Avenue with hardly a jerk.

"We can put the top up if you want," Alan said.

"I like it down much better. I'm all wrapped up."

Mrs. Reed came out on her porch and waved and the Reed twins stood stock still watching. Mrs. Moore was looking at her tulip bed as they went by. Mr. Morley had been sick this spring and the shades were still drawn. Pamela noticed each house as they passed without knowing that she did. It was an early spring and the little trees were all budding green.

They stopped for lunch along the river and Pamela took off her hat and veil and duster. "I can't even feel the wind with all that on my head." She began laying out the sandwiches.

A gray hawk swooped out of the sky, leveled off and floated motionless on the air above them. Pamela shielded her eyes and watched until the bird was out of sight. "I love the strength of their wings, but they have horrible cruel beaks . . ." She turned and found Alan watching her.

"Go on," he said, "I'm interested." But she wouldn't.

[163]

"I don't think you are."

"Well, say that I'm interested in you. That would be closer to the truth."

Pamela unwrapped the *petits fours* Mama had frosted so carefully with icing in three different colors. Did love ever begin with interest? Couldn't it just be love from the beginning? She looked off to the line of snow-covered mountains. "Didn't your mother and father mind your coming back out here?"

"Well . . ." He hesitated so long she knew they did. "Mother couldn't understand my wanting to come, put it that way," Alan said. Pamela could see Mrs. Randell with her creamy skin and dark liquid brown eyes. "But Dad could. He said he had missed coming out. And he got me the job in the office here, you know. Of course, after I start in the business next year I don't imagine I'll be able to do anything like this." He was looking down at the ground and she noticed how close together his eyes were. She wished he would look off at the mountains.

"Do you want to go into your father's business, Alan?"

"Oh yes," he said promptly. "I've always intended to. My grandfather started it and it's a pretty big thing now. You remember the office when you used to drive down with Dad?"

Of course she remembered the brick building with the brass plaque by the door. Mr. Randell disappeared into it at eight every morning and returned at five, and that was what Alan would do all his life. She had thought how different it was from her father's sudden goings and comings that depended on the weather or calves or . . . natural things, with no day exactly like the one before it.

Her eyes came back across the wide freedom of the open spaces to Alan lying on the ground in front of her. He seemed so settled. "So much more mature than anyone you know," Mama had said.

When they were back in the auto, he was telling her about the man he met on the boat going to Europe who asked right away when he heard his name if his father was president of the Randell brass foundry, so she didn't interrupt to point out again the pishkun where the buffalo were driven over. She could show him all that on the way back.

It had grown so windy he stopped to put up the top. The car bounced on the old dried mud ruts of the road and she shouted to him above the noise of the wind, "It will be better over there where there isn't any road."

He looked at her quickly to see if she really meant it, and shook his head as he drove out of the ruts. "No road at all!"

"You have to make your own out here," she screamed back.

The road was even worse from King Butte in to the ranch. She held on to the side to keep from jouncing against him and Alan held grimly to the wheel. She wondered what he would think of it when it was muddy.

"I'm afraid these rocks will puncture the tires," he worried.

The ranch buildings looked small from the benchland where the road turned down. If the aspens and cottonwoods by the river had leafed at all they made no show in the early dusk, and there was a drift of dirty snow three feet high back of the bunkhouse. There was no sign of anyone around the ranch. Then a dog's bark of alarm crackled in the stillness. And, as always, Pamela saw a head appear at the kitchen window and knew it was Ruby's.

"It looks just the same," Alan said. "Only more so this time of year."

"More so?"

"More lonely and desolate."

But they were driving under the pole gateway that leaned a little to one side so that the antlers overhead were slightly askew and there was no time to object. At one side of the gate a weathered sign announced

PRIVATE PROPERTY
ROCKY MOUNTAIN CATTLE COMPANY

and in the corner, C. L. LACEY. Pamela wondered if Alan noticed it.

She didn't wait for him to come and help her out but ran up

the steps of the ranch house. The sitting room was dark but there was a light in the kitchen.

"Well, I'll be darned!" Ruby called out. "I saw your gas wagon coming down the road but I figgered it didn't belong to nobody I ever saw so I held my powder." Ruby stood still and jerked her head forward, peering at Alan. "Good Lord, Pam, what in the world did you drug in with you? I sure never expected to see the lady cowboy back here!"

"How do you do, Ruby," Alan said, holding out his hand, sounding as though he didn't mind her at all. Pamela was relieved.

"Howdy!" Ruby shook hands with him. "Looks like you two was on your wedding trip." She glanced at the valises. The words stung Pamela's face like poison ivy and Alan colored, too.

"Didn't you get Mama's letter, Ruby? Isn't Papa here?"

"I ain't seen nothing of Charlie for the last week an' I ain't been off the joint to get any mail."

"Where's Slim?" Pamela asked.

"Drunk," Ruby said. Her mouth seemed to spew the word out in disgust and folded into a thin line that broke again to say, "Well, I'll light up." Ruby lifted the shade off the lamp on the round center table and then the chimney. As she turned up the wick Alan struck a match for her and the flaring light made a cruel mask of her face. She replaced the chimney and the shade and the light softened. Pamela was aware of the scuffed surface of the table, the old chairs, the worn-out linoleum on the floor. She had never thought of them before. She supposed they looked desolate, too.

"Alan has been working at the refinery in Brandon Rapids since February and he wanted to come back and see the ranch," she explained.

"I 'member he cried his eyes out when he had to leave it last time," Ruby said. "Well, there's sure a lot to see with one cow, three horses, and a handful of chickens. Slim went crazy with nothing to do but woman chores. I suppose you'll want some supper."

"Mrs. Lacey packed us such an adequate lunch, we're not hungry, at least I'm not," Alan said quickly. "In fact, I'm sure there's enough left for supper."

"I guess I can get together something that'll be better than Maybelle Lacey's fancy cold victuals. Pam, you better sleep in with me. I told Slim he could go down to the bunkhouse till he was sober. You can put Alan in Charlie's room tonight, unless he should get back here." She went on out to the kitchen.

"I'll show you where . . ." Pamela picked up a hand lamp and Alan lighted it for her. "I wish Papa were here, it would be different."

"Don't worry about that," Alan murmured vaguely.

She took him to the doorway of her father's bedroom and was thankful that the bed was made and the bare room in order. There was a light in Ruby's room, but Pamela felt a cold unhappiness about it. She didn't want to share this room. Ruby's belongings covered the dresser: an alarm clock, a picture of Slim in his twenties, some kid curlers, a pack of cards. Pamela glanced in the mirror and saw herself in the long duster that was badly creased from the drive. She looked too dressed up. When she had changed into the pleated skirt and shirtwaist she had brought with her she felt more natural.

It was better when they sat at the table in the kitchen, eating supper. The big range radiated heat and cheer. Ruby's kitchen was always a neat place and Alan developed an appetite for the antelope steak Ruby had fried. Her manner and voice softened when she told them about the deer that was standing right by the corner of the house yesterday morning.

"Prettiest sight you ever want to see. Ain't nothing sweeter than a deer's eye, not even a colt's," she told them. "It's too bad this danged old wind came up. This morning it was as still and peaceful as a prayer."

When they saw her putting food on a tray, Alan offered to carry it for her. "Nope. I'll take it myself. When I tell him who's here maybe he'll pull himself together and sober up."

After she had gone with a lantern and her tray there was an

[167]

awkward little silence. Loyalty kept Pamela from apologizing for Ruby or Slim or the place. Alan felt they should start right back, but he was daunted by the thought of the ride in the dark over those ruts. The rising wind beat against the log walls of the house and slid under the ill-fitting window frames.

"Listen to the wind," Pamela said. "I love to hear it out at the ranch."

Alan saw the unmistakable pleasure in her face, but the wind seemed horrible to him. It came into the room with Ruby, blowing the faded curtains and the lamp flame and the old newspapers stacked on the window sill. Ruby slammed the door behind her.

"It ain't the cold so much as the wind that makes it mean," she said.

They didn't ask about Slim, but Pamela noticed that the plate had scarcely been touched.

Pamela washed the dishes and Alan dried while Ruby set her bread sponge and washed up the milk separator. "I wouldn't trust my own mother to get them discs as clean as I want 'em," Ruby said, slipping them back on their rod and shaking them like a tambourine when she was through. Afterward she filled a skillet with popping corn and they stood around listening to the snug little pops going off like shots under the iron cover.

"The three of us sitting here reminds me . . ." Ruby began. "I wisht Slim was here to tell you this story, he gives it the works, but anyways . . ."

It was ten when they heard Shep bark and then a voice calling out to him. "That's Charlie!" Ruby said. "Here, Alan, you and Pam take that lantern down to the barn. I'll put fresh coffee on."

Ruby called out as they opened the door, "Charlie, you had anything to eat?"

"Can't remember when," Charlie said. "Got any coffee there?"

"Can't you smell it?"

Alan helped himself to popcorn. It still shocked him to hear Ruby calling Mr. Lacey by his first name. Then his eyes came back to Pamela. She was sitting over on the couch, one foot

[168]

under her, like a little girl. The light through the isinglass front of the base burner burnished her hair and her wind-burned face. Her lips were parted as though she were going to speak in a minute and her eyes were on her father. That live look was what he couldn't get out of his mind. She was like no girl he had ever met or ever would again. Take her away from this rough atmosphere . . . she fitted in beautifully when she was at his home; if she was with his mother a little more she'd drop off some of those Western expressions of hers. She was too fine to be around with a woman like Ruby. . . .

"Where's Slim?" Charlie asked suddenly.

Ruby shrugged. Her mouth pulled down. "At the bunkhouse where he belongs. I ain't excusing him any, but, Charlie, he ain't used to being alone on the ranch without any stock to speak of, or enough to do, so he has to go to work and make a fool of himself with a bottle."

"Where have you been, Papa?" Pamela asked quickly. It was uncomfortable having Alan here.

"All over creation, Pam," Charlie said, pulling off his tie and loosening the top button of his shirt. "Got just about what I went for, too, by golly! You go down and tell Slim we'll have stock here again, Ruby, if there's any in Montana worth buying!" His voice had a boasting note.

They made up a bed for Alan in the sitting room so Charlie had his own room, but Pamela still had to sleep with Ruby. When Ruby came to bed Pamela was already in the old iron bed with the covers pulled up under her chin, watching the shadows from the kerosene lamp and thinking over the day. She felt a little shy with Ruby tonight and when she heard her coming she closed her eyes as though she were asleep.

Ruby didn't start to undress right away. She pulled the straight chair up to the dresser, put her feet on the low window sill, and took out of her pocket her bag of Bull Durham and her papers. Ruby was the only woman Pamela had ever seen smoke. She wondered now why she hadn't smoked all evening and then decided she must be too upset about Slim.

[169]

Once she had a cigarette in her mouth, Ruby began taking the pins out so her hair hung down to her shoulders; her face aged with the lamp shadows on it.

The wind gave a long-drawn coyote laugh as it lunged around the corner of the house and was thrown back by the rimrock. The stillness afterward was more lonely than the crying of the wind. Ruby sat staring at nothing, her cigarette burning by itself on the edge of the dresser till she tamped it out angrily on the lid of a jelly glass. She bent over and unlaced her boots, and when she stood up her shadow on the wall was shorter than it had been.

"You asleep, punk?" she said, as though she had just remembered Pamela was there.

Pamela stirred and murmured.

"By golly!" Ruby said it the way Charlie did, "it's as cold as a rat's toes!" She hung her apron over the back of the chair, slipped her dress off over her head, then her corset cover and underskirt before she went over to the closet to get her nightgown. Her knit undervest clung to her flat chest, and her hips in the muslin drawers were only a little wider than her waist.

"Ruby, you never wear a corset, do you?" Pamela asked.

"I do *not!* What do you want to wear a corset for, when you've got your own muscles and bones to keep you in shape?" She pulled on her flannel gown and buttoned it to the neck, dropping off the rest of her clothes under it, then she raised the window wide and leaned out a minute. "Wonder how Mr. Slim likes it down there in the bunkhouse. He hasn't got any fire down there, either. That young man of yours is sitting up in his night clothes reading! I told him it was time to go to bed and he said he'd found a book he wanted to look at first. Easterners never know enough to go to bed!"

"What was he reading, Ruby?"

"Search me. There ain't more'n a half a dozen books in there. I bet your mother goes for him."

"Yes, she likes him."

[170]

Ruby gave a snort. "And you do, too! Well, I don't know why I should say anything. Lord knows, I'm a poor picker."

Pamela turned her pillow. The cold air blew into the room with the taste of mountain snow in its breath, not the frozen glacial snow but new snow falling far off on branches swelling into spring bud.

Ruby pulled the quilts up over Pamela's shoulder. "Take your time, Pam, don't go rushing off." Ruby's voice could be low sometimes and comfortable as warmth.

"I won't," Pamela said. Ruby got into bed on her side and lay quietly. The only sounds in the house were the tick of her alarm clock on the dresser, the shifting of the wood in the sitting-room stove, and the creaking of a board.

"Ruby?" Pamela asked softly in case she was asleep.

"Yes, ma'am." Ruby's voice was wide awake.

"What about the ranch? Why isn't there enough to do here anymore?"

"I was just blowing off. There's plenty to do; would be for any good ranch hand. There's buildings to keep up and fencing enough to keep a man busy all the time, but Slim ain't that sort. He's a cow man an' he's used to having someone to boss."

"But . . ." Ruby was quiet so long, Pamela said, "Things will be different next summer, won't they? Papa said he got just about what he wanted?"

"Maybe, Pam. That damn McBain did a whole lot of talking around and folks are cagey about lending money. You know how men are, your dad, anyway, an' Slim, too, always sure everything's going to turn out just the way they want. Takes a woman to look a thing square in the face. Damn me, I'm talkin' too much, again. Things'll be all right, Pam, don't you worry."

But she did worry. There was a note in Ruby's voice, a feeling about the stockless ranch that stayed in her mind. Pamela squeezed her knees together and drew them up to keep from shivering in spite of the warmth of the bed.

"Your dad knows cattle; Slim does, too. I'll say that for 'em.

They'll make out yet." Ruby's hand rested a second on Pamela's head as it often did on the neck of a nervous mare. The hand was hard-palmed, quiet. Pamela stretched her legs down in bed and turned over.

"Good night, Ruby."

"Nite, Pam."

Pamela fell thinly asleep and dreamed of rushing away in the wind. Wrenn was holding a warm cape around her shoulders, shielding her from the night. Nothing could stop them. They went down Prospect Avenue, past all the dark houses, then they were out at the ranch, running along the river. "Don't you worry, Pam," Wrenn kept whispering in her ear.

She was suddenly awake. An edge of cold came in under the covers across the empty half of the bed. She heard a step and knew that Ruby was up, putting on her boots. Ruby pulled at the extra blanket at the foot of the bed, folding it. The handle of the door turned. Ruby moved quietly through the sitting room out to the kitchen, then the kitchen door opened. Pamela ran over to the open window. Ruby carried a lantern and was going down toward the bunkhouse with the blanket on her arm.

Pamela didn't hear Ruby come back, but she smelled her cigarette and woke up. Ruby was sitting in the chair by the dresser. When she got back in bed, Pamela pretended to be asleep. Perhaps Ruby wouldn't like her to know she had gone.

There was no sign of the wind next morning, and the sun from a spring-blue sky poured down on the slowly warming earth. Overnight the cottonwood leaves had jumped ahead and the shy wild crocuses and shooting stars and pale harebells made bold patches of color between the ranch house and the corral. Waxwings flew noisily at the red dogwood bushes and Pamela saw ducks in the river when she went for the horses. She and Ruby had sneaked out together, past Alan still asleep on the sitting-room couch. Ruby went down to milk the cow. Pamela rode Aspen bareback up to the benchland where the horses always wandered in the night.

Once on the plateau at the top, she gave a long whistle and Aspen pricked her ears and set off at a gallop. All the doubts and fears of the night, of the long winter, too, were gone with the wind; only a sense of happiness, still and bright as the day itself, remained. Pamela sat quietly looking down on the weather-gray log buildings of the ranch with the mountains to the north. This was the view Mr. Randell had in his den, and her face sobered thinking of it there. But he must have taken it down by now; she might get around to asking Alan if he had. It didn't belong to him any more. Ruby went across from the barn with her pails of milk. Pamela pulled the reins a little and followed the other horses that had already started down of their own accord.

Shep lay in the sun on the warm boards of the porch and kept an eye on the breakfast table on the other side of the screen door. Ruby announced loud-voiced from the stove, "Yes, sir, ain't worth cooking if every man can't eat a dozen hot cakes!" There was nothing gentle about her this morning.

"Why, Slim, here, can eat a couple dozen!" Charlie said.

"That's on roundup; 'sides, I figger Al here needs 'em," Slim answered with his crooked grin. He looked a little peaked in the bright light and his glance met the others only briefly, but he was very clean in fresh-washed shirt and Levis.

"Al, aren't you good for a couple more?" Charlie called down the table.

"He read too late last night," Ruby jibed.

Alan laughed. "Not so very late. I found a book by Jack London over in the bookcase."

"That's sure a good one," Slim said. "I've read it four-five times."

"When you should have been doing something else, I betcha!" Ruby waved her pancake lifter.

Pamela got up to bring the coffeepot. Why did Ruby keep at him so? But everything was all right again. Papa looked rested and Slim was sober and the day was fine.

"Do you really want to ride?" she asked Alan after breakfast.

"Very much," he said. He felt quite confident; Slim had called him Al.

Charlie went down with them to saddle up. "Don't kill him off the first day, Pam," he said as they rode off. "Al, you bring her home when you get tired."

"Sure you don't want to ride with us, Papa?" Pamela asked.

"Nope. I've got to talk to Slim."

But once Alan was up on a horse again, his old unsureness came back. He kept one hand on the horn and held the reins too tight. Pamela leaned over and patted his horse's neck to calm her. "I didn't really expect to see you back here on a horse," she said. "But then, I didn't believe you would get back to Brandon Rapids, either."

Alan was too busy with his own thoughts to hear her last sentence. "I didn't do very well that summer. It was all so new, I suppose, and I didn't make allowance for the kind of simple people Ruby and Slim and the hired men were."

Pamela frowned at the "simple people." She pressed Aspen with her heels and rode on ahead of Alan. After a little distance along the bench she looked back to see what he thought of this view of the ranch spread out under the sun, but he wasn't looking. He was fussing with the buckle on his stirrup. "You know," he said when he was even with her, "I think this saddle is a little broad for me."

She paid no attention. "Look down there. Isn't it beautiful?" she asked, impatient that he didn't say it first.

"Very," he said, but the little word seemed clipped and niggardly.

"I wish we didn't have to go back to town this afternoon. I'd like to live out here."

Alan looked down at the weather-beaten buildings, dwarfed by the bleak snow-topped mountains, and the wide plain around them. Not another dwelling in sight. Even in the sun the ranch looked lonely. "I'm afraid you would find it pretty lonely," he said.

[174]

She lifted her head. "Oh, I don't think so." Would she? She thought of Ruby sitting by the dresser, smoking, staring at nothing. But she didn't mean live here alone.

"We'll get down for a few minutes so you won't be so stiff," she said. She would come out again this spring without Alan and ride with Ruby and Slim and Papa, way up on the government leases where they used to graze the cattle. They would ride hard all day long and . . .

"Too bad about Slim," Alan said.

Quick irritation flicked across her mind.

"I can understand, though, how not having anything much to do, as Ruby said, could drive a man crazy out here."

"He'll be terribly busy in another month."

"I bet he hates having your father come out and find he's been drinking. I couldn't help but feel sorry for him when your father said he was going down to have a talk with him. I imagine he'll really give him a dressing down."

"I doubt if Papa even mentions his drinking," Pamela said. "Slim knows how Papa feels about that." Her annoyance was mounting. She picked a harebell and blew the tiny periwinkle bells on their thread-thin stem so they moved a little without a sound.

"Right up there by those rocks was where you were bitten by the rattler," she said.

"I was lucky, all right. I was lucky to have you find me, Pam."

She looked at him so directly he found it hard to go on at once, but he had thought it all out. He had explained to his mother and father. Of course, they were rather opposed; he had supposed they would be, but they were remarkably reasonable. His mother had said, "But, Alan, she's only in her teens. I know she's charming in a fresh, unspoiled sort of way but she's hardly the sort of young woman who'll be a real help to you." His father had said, "I've always regretted that difficulty with Charlie; he may not be anxious to have you interested in his daughter. But he's not a small man. Pamela reminds me of him." He had stopped in the middle of the library floor and turned to look

[175]

at him. "How does she feel? Has she ever suggested that she . . . er, has inclinations toward you?"

He busied himself with picking a handful of the little lavender flowers by his foot. "Pam," he said again, arranging the flowers so the stems were all even, "I've thought sometimes that Fate had something to do with it; I mean, your being the one to save my life . . . that you were meant to be part of my life."

Pamela was frowning, looking down at the flower in her hand. It was hard to talk to her for some reason. "Pamela . . ." He leaned over so he could look into her face. "Pamela, I love you very much."

She looked at him so solemnly her eyes seemed to deepen in color. He had never noticed before that she had dark lashes and brows, not light like most light-haired girls. Her color waved up in her face. "You're beautiful, Pamela. I thought about you all the time in Europe. Dennis got tired of my talking about you." She was looking down at the grass in front of her now. "I know this is a little abrupt, Pamela, but I can only be here until fall. Do you think you might come to love me?"

"Oh, Alan, I . . . I don't think so," she said in a low voice. She should say no, once and for all. She didn't love him. He irritated her so.

"I don't mean to hurry you. It's a very important decision and you haven't had a chance to know me very well, but we have all summer and maybe by fall . . . You mustn't worry about my family, Pam. They'll get used to the idea of my loving you."

She hadn't worried about his family; she had just wondered about them. She saw Mrs. Randell in the receiving line, saying, "This is our little friend from the West." She thought of the last time she saw Mr. Randell. She had put her hands behind her when he wanted to shake hands.

"I thought by fall . . ." Alan began again.

Pamela looked across the fields to the slope of the hill. How would it look here in the fall? The grass would be faded by then, with the sage showing up in plumy gray bunches, and the Oregon grape and rose-bush pips would be deep red along the river. The

[176]

cottonwoods would be yellow gold as . . . as a wedding ring. Rose wore a wide gold ring.

"Yes, I'll know by fall," she said solemnly, not because she would feel any differently, but because it was a long way off.

"Of course, I want to speak to your father," Alan said. "But there's plenty of time for that."

"Oh yes, there's plenty of time," Pamela said. "Alan, what about your father? How does he feel now about . . . Papa and the Rocky Mountain Cattle Company? Because if he feels that Papa did something . . . dishonest . . ." It hurt her to say it, but she had to have it clear.

"He told me he regretted that whole business, Pamela; that he thought he had been too hasty."

"Did he say that!" Pamela's face lighted so unexpectedly she was radiant.

"Pamela, may I kiss you?"

"No, please don't!" She spoke a little sharply because she was startled. If he hadn't *asked*; if he had just kissed her . . . She went over to get the horses. Aspen had gone farthest hunting thistles. Pamela brought Ginger back to Alan.

"Take hold of the mane this time and swing up." She handed him the reins.

"I can get on all right," he said, a little hurt.

She sat in her saddle, pretending not to watch him mount.

"Now I've got the hang of it," he said when he was up on his horse. "You know we can come back out here some summer and ride."

It sounded as though she were really going to marry Alan Randell. She looked back along the ridge as they started back down. Now she would always remember that Alan had told her up there that he loved her. But shouldn't it be more . . . more something? But, of course, it couldn't be because she wasn't in love with him.

"You look so serious all of a sudden," he said, coming beside her for a minute. The horses were used to following each other and one always dropped behind the other so it was difficult to talk. She looked back and smiled at him instead. There was really no sense in waiting till fall to tell him she couldn't love him, but maybe it would be more polite.

CHAPTER 19

June, 1907

Maybelle Lacey said at supper Monday night, "Wrenn and Rose got home this morning."

Pamela went on carrying her fork to her mouth and moving her teeth up and down until she could swallow the tasteless morsel, but she didn't at once attempt another bite.

"Cora's been dreading it in a way, and I don't blame her. It's going to be so awkward." Cora Morley's cause had become Maybelle's. "Ned can't think of Wrenn up over the millinery shop so they're at Morleys', but Cora says she won't have them *live* with them. Of course, they haven't a cent until Wrenn gets something to do."

Pamela wondered where she would see them first.

Charlie Lacey helped himself to another slice of roast beef. He glanced at Pamela's plate and saw that she had hardly touched what she had. His eyes moved to her face an instant and away. She was playing with her napkin ring. He guessed she did still care about Wrenn and there wasn't anything he could do about it. He offered the only thing he knew.

"You want to come out to the ranch this week end, Pam? It looks good to see a few calves on it. And Slim saw Jake over at Bird Creek and hired him back, and I'm thinking of getting Bill out there again."

"Maybe I will," Pamela said.

Maybelle shook her head. "Lucy Moore's giving a party for Wrenn and Rose Saturday night, Pamela. You don't want to go away and have it look as though you couldn't bear to be here. Of course, Lucy's doing it for Cora, really."

"I don't care about that," Pamela answered, watching the way the late sun came through the green leaves of Mama's window plants, making them so much greener than they were at any other time of day. The sun shone on the painted fruit plates, erect on the plate rail, and the polished oak of the dining table between the lace-bordered doilies. She hadn't seen Wrenn and Rose since they were married. She pushed back her chair. "I'll wipe the dishes when I get back, Mama. I want to go down to the library before it closes." She couldn't just sit home this evening, nor talk to Alan, who would probably call. She had to go by Wrenn's house, and look at it, knowing they were there, he and Rose.

She felt better once she was on her bicycle, feeling the cool air against her face. It was so hot in the dining room. Riding a bicycle was the next thing to riding a horse; it made you free to go where you wanted. She rode slowly, looking at things as she passed. She had her library books in the basket; anyone could see where she was going. The trees along Prospect Avenue were taller this year, way above her head as she rode; she had never noticed before. She wondered if they would ever touch overhead as the trees did on the street where the Randell's lived.

"Hello, Dr. Nugent." He must be just getting home for supper. At seven o'clock it was as light as late afternoon, but the houses on the south side of the avenue seemed darker than those on the north side. The blue and red panes in the window of the Morleys' turret had darkened until they were both the same color now.

And then, as though she had signaled with her bicycle bell, as she used to do, the screen door opened and Wrenn came out on the porch. She couldn't *not* see him. She had to see him sometime. She barely kept the bicycle moving. Perhaps he had felt her thinking about him, willing him to come out.

He saw her right away. "Hello, Pam!" he called out. He ran down their steps to the sidewalk.

[179]

"Hello, Wrenn." She couldn't help but be glad to see him.

"Can't you come in? Rose was asking Mother about you."

"No. I'm just on my way to the library. They close at eight." Did Wrenn remember all the times they had gone to the library together? Did he remember the time she was reading "Annabel Lee"?

Wrenn was beside her now, holding out his hand, and she shook it. They had never shaken hands before. It was strangely formal.

"I guess I haven't congratulated you on your marriage," she said. "I was surely surprised."

"Oh, well, thanks. I guess everyone was surprised. How's everything?"

Everything? "Everything's fine." She held the bicycle still with her foot. There was something different about Wrenn; perhaps it was his voice; that was deeper. He was looking down at the bicycle as though the intricate design of wire spokes fascinated him.

"Wait just a minute, I'll call Rose." He ran up the steps and, opening the door, called into the house, "Rose, here's Pam." How odd it was to have Rose in there. She could hear Rose answer. He held the door open for her and she came running down the steps.

"Oh, Pam, I'm glad to see you!" Rose sounded as though they were still the best friends in the world. She was very fashionable with her hair done a new way and that high-necked light dress. She wouldn't tell Rose she was glad to see her. She wasn't. She looked right at her and said without smiling:

"How are you, Rose? Well, I must go." How did her voice sound?

"Pam's on her way to the library. It closes at eight," Wrenn said.

"I remember we were always going to the library," Rose said, as though that were years ago. "Do come and see us, Pam." Rose stepped back on the Morleys' walk. Wrenn stood beside her with

[180]

one hand on her shoulder. He looked very protective and "married." Pamela stood on the pedals of her wheel without using the seat. She turned the corner, not looking back. The street was downgrade and she could have coasted, but her legs moved round and round, faster and faster, without her knowing she pedaled. Wrenn didn't even want to be alone with her.

The library was close with all the lights on and no windows open to the June night, but Pamela felt as though she had come in out of a great wind and the roar of it was still in her ears so the close room was like a cave to hide in. She spoke to the librarian quickly and disappeared down the farthest aisle of books. She took a book from the shelf and held it open without seeing either the title or a word on the page. Her mouth was compressed and her color that had suffused her face and neck when she stood talking to Wrenn and Rose collected in two cruelly bright spots high on her cheeks, leaving her forehead white and a whiteness around her mouth. All the look of youth was lost out of her face for the instant.

"Can I help you, Pamela? We're almost ready to close," the librarian said.

"No, thank you." She put the book in her hand back on the shelf and, taking out another, carried it to the desk.

"Why, Pamela, are you sure you want Voltaire's *Philosophical Dictionary?*"

"Yes, please," Pamela said, her color flowing out again in her face.

Rose and Wrenn watched Pamela without speaking. Midway down the avenue the sun touched her head and shoulder and the soft stuff of her skirt billowing over the seat, and made the spinning wires of the wheels twin silver discs.

Rose thought: she hates me. She'll never forgive me for marrying Wrenn, but I can't help it. It isn't my fault if Wrenn fell in love with me. I didn't ever go with him until after she had that quarrel. Wrenn didn't really love Pamela, anyway. They just grew up together. But he feels bad now. I do, too.

"Let's go in, Wrenn. Your mother and father want us to play cards with them."

Wrenn thought: Pam is still angry, but she had congratulated him. He had felt queer calling Rose right away, but he wanted her to be there. Naturally, seeing Pam for the first time since the wedding kind of bothered him. Pam had that way of looking so straight at you, and lifting her head as though she were right and you were wrong. She didn't really care about him. But his eyes followed her as she turned the corner and he remembered the time he had walked his bicycle beside her while she read that poem, and her comb fell out and broke. He still had that half somewhere, or had he thrown it out when he was clearing out his drawers?

"Wrenn!" Rose slipped her arm in his as they went up the steps of the porch. "Your mother and father don't mind me as much as they did, do they?" Her dark eyes were so anxious he kissed her before they went inside.

"Of course, they don't. Give them another week and they'll love you, Rose, almost as much as I do." He was glad that he felt that way, and seeing Pam hadn't really been so bad, after all.

CHAPTER **20**

July, 1907

There is a kind of loyalty in a town like Brandon Rapids, a kind not mentioned in Wrenn Morley's valedictory address. The Morleys' friends felt obliged to see that their new daughter-in-law had enough parties given for her to look well. The society page of the Sunday *Gazette* recorded that "the Misses Reed and Marsten entertained at whist for Mrs. Wrenn Morley. The house was charmingly decorated with sweet peas in the dining room, summer flowers in the parlor, and pansies in the den." "Covers were laid for twelve at the home of Mrs. Herbert Cheavers in honor of Mr. and Mrs. Wrenn Morley." How strange to say "covers" when places were set on May Cheavers' best six-yard damask tablecloth, but the Chicago *Tribune* said "covers."

Those who rallied to the cause not only had the virtuous sense of a generous act but were titillated by certain factors in the case: that Mrs. Ned Morley would come and never show that she was not delighted by her son's marriage, that Madame Guinard would also come, if invited . . . some were inviting her, some were not; after all, it was difficult to think of her in any other way than as a milliner, but a *French* milliner was a little special and this was the West, and she did seem very pleasant, except that if you owed her money you wondered uncomfortably if she was remembering that as she looked at you with those black eyes of hers. If people expected Rose to be ill at ease they were greatly mistaken. She seemed to enjoy everything and she certainly had a new "outfit" for each party. Perhaps she had bought her trousseau in Boston, perhaps her mother made it. French, you know, and a wonderful needlewoman. Anyway, Rose was very pretty.

"Would you say pretty? Isn't there a French word, 'chic'?"

"Yes, I would say pretty, Fanny; I thought she was just plain handsome at your house!" May Cheavers told Fanny Winslow. "And I can see why Wrenn Morley married her."

Maybelle Lacey was out on the porch one evening when Pamela came home from the store. "You know, Pamela, we've got to do something for Rose. You did go together as girls and you and Wrenn Morley went out together in your baby carriages!"

The phrase "as girls" caught on Pamela's mind like a burr. "As girls" . . . that was only last summer. Were they women now? She didn't like going so fast.

"And Cora and Ned . . . our being close friends, and our families coming out west at the same time. Besides people would think you were eating your heart out over Wrenn."

Pamela smiled as she had at Alice Reed's party, and the smile was secretive and cool.

"I thought a porch party would be easiest," Maybelle said.

A cry seemed to burst out of Pamela's mind, but it made no

sound. Porches were horrible places. She had sat on this very porch that night with Wrenn and seen the light from the study, the night she told Wrenn to go home. People sat on porches and looked out at other people going by. You couldn't sit alone on a porch without looking lonely, without being lonely. She wasn't going to go on sitting here long. . . .

"One nice thing about this house, I always say, is the porch." Maybelle glanced at the hanging baskets moving ever so slightly, and the furniture freshly painted this year. "I think it would be best to have it in the evening so you can ask Wrenn and have Alan, of course, and the other young men."

Pamela sat on the step and leaned against the pillar of the porch, her hands clasped around her knees. Maybelle forgot to talk for a minute. Sitting like that Pamela looked almost, well, yes, beautiful, and like someone she didn't know at all. Her head back that way, looking off down the street as though she hadn't heard a word she had said to her. She seemed a little sad, but after she was married to Alan she would be happy. A girl was never really happy until she was married. . . . She couldn't stand it if Pamela wasn't happy. Tenderness brimmed Maybelle's eyes with unexpected tears.

Just after Pamela and Wrenn had quarreled, she had looked at her with a shade of annoyance that deepened into personal resentment when Rose Guinard married Wrenn. It would have been such a nice thing, but, really, maybe it was better as it was. Alan was a fine young man and so well-to-do. Charlie had got over minding his being Mr. Randell's son though he kept saying he couldn't imagine Pamela marrying Alan and going to live in the East. But she could see now that Pamela would never be satisfied here in Brandon Rapids. . . .

"There aren't enough boys to go round, you know," Pamela said. So she had been listening.

"But in the evening, with everybody sitting around together that won't really matter. Lucy Moore says I can borrow her Japanese lanterns and maybe Jack Donaldson would bring his mandolin and you could sing." Pamela was certainly irritating. "Well, shall we do it? I thought Friday night would be a good time. Why don't you ask Alan first and see if he can come then?"

"I think it's hypocritical for everyone to say how hard it is for Mr. and Mrs. Morley to have Wrenn marry Rose and then give parties for her!" Pamela objected.

"But how else can we help Cora? Rose and Wrenn are going to live in this town; at least, they're living here now, and Cora would feel badly if nobody called or entertained for Wrenn's wife, no matter who he married! We should drop over and call first; leave our cards anyway. Maybe we could do that tomorrow evening."

"I've already called. I stopped the night after they got back, on my way to the library." Pamela got up from the step and went on into the house.

Rose wore a cerise dress. "What an odd shade of red," Mrs. Morley said when she first came downstairs on her way to the party at Laceys'. It seemed so bright.

"Mother made it for me," Rose said.

"Isn't she beautiful, Mother!" Wrenn asked, and his admiration showed so clearly in his eyes Ned Morley found himself looking at his son rather than Rose. He looked happy, he thought with a shade of awe.

But Mrs. Morley said crossly when they had gone, "Wrenn acts just like a moth around a flame with that girl. She looks more French than ever with those earrings and that bright dress."

"She is French," Mr. Morley said mildly.

Rose's dress seemed to Pamela the exact color of the pomegranate in the basket of fruit Mr. Randell had brought, ages and ages ago, when everything was going well with the Rocky Mountain Cattle Company.

The house tonight had the same festive air it used to have when the company gentlemen came for dinner. The Japanese lanterns hung on the porch and out in the side yard, too. Music and laughter spilled out of the house.

> *Soft o'er the mountain*
> *Lingering falls the southern moon . . .*

[185]

"The punch just matches your dress, Rose," Alice Reed said, holding up her glass of raspberry shrub.

Rose laughed. "The punch is delicious, isn't it!" She had been watching Pamela, wanting to talk to her, it didn't make much difference what about, but she wanted to be friends again. It made her uncomfortable to have Pam mad. Wrenn had been so pleased about this party, but it didn't mean a thing, she knew. Pam's smile was just on the edge of her lips and she didn't look at them more than a minute, acting so busy with the party. She didn't seem really in love with that Alan, but maybe she was. It was hard to tell about Pam. Rose picked up two empty plates and started out to the kitchen with them because she had just seen Pamela disappear behind the swinging door.

"Oh, you don't need to do that, you're the guest of honor," Pamela said, meeting her in the pantry.

"I wanted to see you a minute, Pam. You were so sweet to do this for us." Rose gave a little sigh. "You don't know how good it is to get away evenings. It isn't easy to live with Wrenn's folks. We don't feel we can just go upstairs or out for a walk every evening. Of course, we won't stay there long."

"You'll be going back to Cambridge in the fall, though, won't you?" Pamela asked.

"I don't know; the man Wrenn works for here wants him to stay on. He says he has a real future. Do you think he'd be sorry if he didn't finish, Pam? I don't believe he'll go on to law school, anyway. That takes so long." There, she had asked Pam's advice; that ought to make her feel good.

"Yes, I do, Rose," Pamela answered soberly. "He'd be sorry all his life if he didn't graduate from law school." Sudden, unexpected anger came from some place, climbing up through Pamela's mind, sending the telltale color into her face. Didn't Rose remember how Wrenn had looked giving his commencement speech? How his voice had rung out!

It came in a rush, then. Rose had had no intention of telling her, but she wanted Pam to understand why Wrenn wouldn't want to go back. "I . . . I'm going to have a baby, Pam. I haven't told anybody yet, not even Wrenn. I only just know, myself." She laughed with a little embarrassment. "I don't believe Wrenn will want to go on with school when he knows." She had never noticed how Pamela's eyes could look as cold and hard as blue glass. Pam didn't say she was glad for her, or kiss her the way women did. Her face got pale all of a sudden.

"You don't have to tell him until after he gets back there, then. You could stay here with your mother. Anyway, you mustn't let him stop until he goes all the way through law school. He'd never forgive you later on. Maybe, you can get Mr. Morley to send him the way he was going to do."

"Here you are!" Alan came out into the pantry. "They're looking for you, Pamela. Some of them are leaving." He sounded as though he and Pam were giving the party, Rose thought. She wished now that she hadn't told Pam. Pam had no right to say what she should do, even if she had asked her; not in that accusing tone of voice, anyway.

Wrenn took Pamela's hand when he came up to her on the porch steps.

"Pam, this was a lovely party. Thank you." He hesitated, wanting to say something more, but Pamela said quickly:

"I'm glad you enjoyed it, Wrenn. How was school?"

He laughed at that. It sounded like a funny question to ask a married man. "It was fine," he said.

"You only have two more years before law school, don't you?"

"Only! If I go to law school," he added. "But I don't think I will."

Pam looked so serious. She laid her hand on his arm. "That would be terrible. You must go on to law school, Wrenn!" Then she turned away from him because Alice Reed and somebody named Robert came up to say good-by. He almost wondered if he had heard Pam right. But that was like Pam, he thought as he walked down the steps with Rose; Pam always got so worked up about things. He was glad Rose didn't.

Alan lingered to put out the Japanese lanterns and bring in the chairs from the lawn that nobody had used because they had gathered on the porch instead. He found the punch glasses under chairs and even on the stairway, and dried them while Pamela washed them, even though she protested.

"It gives me a chance to be with you that much longer, Pam," he said. "By the way, I talked with Wrenn about Cambridge. We knew quite a few of the same people. He seems to like it there; it's too bad he isn't going back next year."

"He isn't! I think he will." Pamela said it so positively, he laughed.

"What makes you so sure?"

"I was talking to Rose," she said, aware that she had spoken too firmly. "I think she'll see that he does."

"Oh. For a moment I thought you were going to see that he did; you looked so determined."

"You know," Alan said as he stood on the steps about to leave, "I never wanted to hurry a summer along before."

"I never want a summer to go," Pamela said.

"Just this one. I want fall to come this year. But I'll keep my word; I'll wait till then," he said with a special look that Pamela was careful to seem not to see. "Good night, Pam."

"Good night, Alan."

CHAPTER **21**

August, 1907

The annual celebration of the Pioneer Society was held at the old fort on the river this year, on the last day of August. There had been a heavy frost the week before and already cottonwood leaves, smooth and shiny-yellow as butter littered the dusty streets of the old river town. Sagebrush feathered out against the rocks on the opposite bank, the grass had turned straw-colored and the low brush was as bronzed as the skins of the Indians who used to come to the fort with their beaver pelts.

People gathered from all over the state and signed the register at the table where Pamela Lacey sat, passing out membership badges. Mr. Sewall was busy meeting old-timers and arranging for the program to start at two, right after the dinner. Where the old blacksmith shop of the fort used to be, a long trestle table was spread with red, white, and blue bunting and local ladies were laying out bowls of potato salad, crocks of beans, cakes, and coffee cups.

"Doesn't look like the old days at the fort!" a white-haired man told the women. "Food used to get so low we had to scape the barrels back in the '6os."

A man signing the record at Pamela's table called back to him, "Why, say, didn't you use to live pretty high on buffalo in those days? I thought you could just go out the door of the fort and shoot down a buffalo. And what about all those partridges and ducks!"

"Nothing high about it! We got so hard up one time we had to eat roast dog, and you can ask Josh Stevens over there."

And a little man, teetering back and forth from his heels to the balls of his feet, told Pamela, "River's pretty low. No boats'll make it back to St. Louis any more this year."

Each person dipped into the past and brought out some small detail of life in that long ago time, unrelated, yet authentic. The words Indians, prospecting, Virginia City, vigilantes mingled in the talk that floated like cottonwood fluff around Pamela's head.

"Why, I remember the time when there were so many ox teams out there in the street, freighting stuff from the boats to the gold camps, you couldn't see to the other side for the dust."

"Where did your folks go first? They had a ranch on the Madison, didn't they?"

A woman looked up from signing the register. "You're Charlie

[189]

Lacey's girl, aren't you? I used to go to school with him in Virginia City; your mother, too. Are they here?"

Pamela smiled at her. "Not Father. Mother's somewhere around."

"Your mother used to be an awful pretty girl; you've got her looks."

Everyone was out to have a good time; the better the time, the stronger the proof that coming to Montana as a pioneer had been good.

Mrs. Leslie Rumford of the Helena Rumfords came to sign. Mrs. Rumford's husband's father was in on the Shamrock Lode and built a mansion of white stone with a fraction of his fortune. She and Maybelle Lacey were girlhood friends.

"Hello, Pamela Lacey, I thought you'd be married and gone by now. Well, Mr. Right will come along one of these days; you do a little window shopping first!" Mrs. Rumford winked at her, but she meant hurry and get married, Pamela told herself. Everyone did, except Ruby.

A young man came up next and put his name down as Neale Hagen, Butte.

"Did you come in '64, too?" he asked.

" '63," Pamela told him. "My husband escaped from a Northern prison camp."

"That's interesting; so did I. Perhaps we were in the same wagon train coming out. Now that I think of it, I remember you holding the reins with one hand and that big hat with the other."

"That's right, and you were the one who shot the Indian just as he pulled me down from the wagon seat!"

And then the young man stopped playing the game. "I wish it were back then," he said. "You know, you're brought up on all this stuff, at least I was, but when you're grown-up you find all the excitement's over. If you're only a son of a pioneer you're supposed to settle right down and be a solid citizen. I find that kind of settling harder than settling a new town."

"I know," Pamela said. "I wouldn't have minded any of the hardships and I would have loved coming out to a new country." She was talking so earnestly she didn't see the Morleys and Wrenn and Rose until they were at the table.

"You're looking very lovely, my dear," Mr. Morley said in his courtly way. Pamela colored as she handed him his badge. She thought uncomfortably that it was because he knew Wrenn would keep his compliments for Rose.

"Over a hundred have registered," she said in answer to Mrs. Morley's question, aware of Wrenn and Rose standing at one side.

"Here, Wrenn, you haven't signed," Mrs. Morley said.

"They're keeping you busy, I see," Wrenn said to Pamela. The careful lightness of his tone seemed patronizing.

"Oh, not too busy," she matched his tone in lightness. Her glance rested briefly on Rose. "You've never been to Fort Benton before, have you, Rose?" Since the party at her house, she and Rose had made only the most casual remarks when they had met at other parties. She knew Rose was sorry she had told her about the baby.

"No," Rose said. "Father Morley was telling me about it in the old days. It must have been a high old place!"

"Father Morley." Every one of them had felt the strangeness of Rose Guinard's calling Mr. Morley that, but none of them gave any sign, except Mrs. Morley, who opened and closed the catch on her purse with nervous white-gloved fingers. Perhaps Rose was working on Mr. Morley for Wrenn's sake, Pamela thought.

Mr. and Mrs. Morley moved on. Rose and Wrenn lingered.

"You better sign, Wrenn," Pamela said primly. "They want a record of everyone."

"Yes, Wrenn, just because I can't is no reason. Do you remember the time, Pam, when I said I'd borrow an old-time costume from you and go to the Pioneer Ball? I feel as though I'd done that today." Then she flushed. That sounded as though . . . Wrenn reached for the pen.

[191]

"I remember you borrowed one once for the float on Pioneer Day," Pamela said. That hadn't fitted very well. Madame Guinard had to let it out. Perhaps Wrenn didn't fit very well.

"Thanks, Pam," Wrenn said, taking the badge. "We wouldn't have come if it hadn't been for driving Mother and Father down. It's a good thing we did. We had four blowouts on the way."

"And we had to stop by the river and let Wrenn wash his hands," Rose said. "You should have seen him!" Her way of saying it, her way of looking at him said so clearly that he was hers.

"How soon do you leave for Cambridge?" Pamela asked.

"I don't just know," Wrenn said slowly. "The dean has a prejudice against married students. He let me finish out the year but he may not want me back."

"You can imagine how that makes *me* feel!" Rose said, slipping her arm through Wrenn's. "If we don't go they may run out of food and I'm starving." She was in a hurry to move on.

"That's right," Wrenn said. "May I bring you a plate, Pam?" Wrenn's eyes held hers for an instant. She almost said yes, to bring him back again so she could say more about school, then she saw Neale Hagen bringing her one. Rose nudged her elbow. "Look out for the lady-killer. He has a way with him! We've just been talking to him." She rolled her eyes and smiled meaningly at Pam, as she and Wrenn went on.

What did Rose mean? What a common thing to say!

"I was a little slow because I had to stop and kill this wild turkey," Neale said with a smile, going on with the game. Pamela took pains to be especially gay because of Rose's remark.

"There were some Indians here while you were gone, but I kept the cabin door barred."

During the long speeches, laden with flowery oratory and heavy with reminiscence, Pamela had time to look beyond the broken dobe walls of the fort to the river and think about Wrenn and Rose. Maybe Wrenn was sorry he had married so fast. Rose hadn't cared a fig about his career just so she had him. She didn't care if she ruined his whole life. She must have told him about the baby by now. Pamela's face that had been so tranquil and young a minute before tightened. She was frowning at her own thoughts, and her lips were closed too firmly to form a sweet curve.

"Can't I drive you back to Brandon Rapids?" Neale Hagen asked when the old-fashioned dance that brought the Pioneer celebration to an end was over. He had managed to dance four out of the six round dances with her.

"We're going to stay overnight at the hotel and go back in the morning," Pamela said.

"All the better. Will you walk down along the river with me and we can decide which gold camp to strike for? I'll drive you back in the morning. I have a car that will hold seven. I can't say that it's all paid for, but I have it in my possession at the moment. That sort of thing never worried the pioneers, why should it worry me?" Pamela laughed in spite of herself. She was aware of her mother watching her from the other side of the hall, as she went out with Neale. She waved back and smiled as though she couldn't see Mama shake her head.

"I have a better idea," Neale said, as they crossed the main street to the river side. "Why don't we marry quickly and then go the rounds of all the gold camps? You can dance . . . I know that after tonight . . . and maybe sing. I'll win a little money at faro on the side; I'm pretty good at that, and in the meantime we'll see what each camp has to offer. And if we don't like them we'll push on to San Francisco!"

There was no sense in him. She laughed. "I don't believe in marrying quickly."

"You don't!" He stopped in the path and looked at her as though horror-struck. "I believe in marrying quick, getting rich quick, dying quick, before old age can catch up with you."

The lights from the hotels and stores across the street were bright enough to show her his face, irregular featured, jutting chin, dark hair brushed back in a kind of peak, and the dark eyes she had noticed this morning.

"Don't talk that way; it scares me," Pamela said.

"Not you! I looked at you and I said to myself, there's a girl who may get mad, may break her heart, but she'll never be scared."

"Why would you think that?"

"Oh . . . the way you hold your head, with your chin up, and the clearness of your eyes, and the quick way you picked up the act . . . I don't know, don't ask me why. I know, that's all."

She was pleased, but she changed the subject. "Life was quick for that Irish governor of Montana who was drowned along here somewhere."

"Meagher, you mean?" Neale said quickly. "He's my private hero. Wanted for rebellious conspiracy in Ireland, governor of the Montana territory at thirty-seven. It's funny that you should mention him."

"No. I'm secretary to Mr. Sewall. I know the history of the pioneers very well."

"What a dead-and-gone job for you to be doing."

"What do you do?" she asked, suddenly curious.

"Well, right now, I'm a labor organizer, stirring up the miners so they'll insist on their rights. It's the kind of a job I fancy Thomas Meagher might have tackled with gusto. The rest of the time I do various things. At the moment I'm just out of a job. My mother hoped to make a priest of me but I didn't have the vocation. My only vocation is for living. Let's go down here to the river."

The lights from the town tossed bright coins onto the river where they floated without sinking. They were larger than the pennies dropped on the water by the stars, but not so bright. The rest of the river was dark without being black. Pamela went over to the edge and dabbled her fingers. It was almost warm. She wondered if Rose could be right about Neale Hagen. She hadn't liked the way he spoke so lightly of being out of a job.

Neale knelt and thrust both hands in the water up to his

elbows, splashing the water up on his face. Then he stood up and shook back his hair.

"Good old Missouri, that's known more avaricious men than most rivers: fur traders, gold seekers, land grabbers, people wanting something for themselves. That's why it's drowned so many; I don't think it cares much for white men. You know the pioneers were terrible takers."

"The river's avaricious, too. Every year at the ranch it takes away the land. After the river goes down you can see how it's clawed at it, not caring what it drags with it."

"No," Neale said slowly. "It isn't taking it for itself. It doesn't keep it; it's just surging so hard it pulls some of the soil along with it, but that's not the same. Now in summer, it's too sluggish for me. Only, that's when it does most of its drownings, of course."

A chill came up from the river and pressed in against the warm dry air of the land so she shivered.

"Come," he said. "We can walk quite a ways along here." He took her hand. In places the sand came over her champagne kid shoes, in others the sand was damp and firm. She didn't care about her shoes nor that her skirt had dragged in the sand, nor that her hair was blown in the wind.

> We are the music-makers,
>   And we are the dreamers of dreams,
> Wandering by lone sea-breakers,
>   And sitting by the desolate streams . . .

His voice seemed to come from a little way off, gentled by the low ripple of the river. The sadness of it was unbearable until he slipped his arm around her waist and they walked wonderfully together along the shore.

> We, in the ages lying
>   In the buried past of the earth,
> Built Nineveh with our sighing,
>   And Babel itself with our mirth:
> And o'er threw them with prophesying
>   To the old of the new world's worth;

[195]

> *For each age is a dream that is dying*
> *Or one that is coming to birth.*

She was no longer Pamela Lacey, but part of the human race, part of all sadness and all beauty. . . .

> *But we, with our dreaming and singing,*
> *Ceaseless and sorrowless we!*
> *The glory about us clinging*
> *Of the glorious futures we see,*
> *Our souls with high music ringing . . .*

He broke off and pulled her suddenly so close she could feel the hardness of his body against hers, and his teeth bruised her lips. Then, gently, he stood apart from her.

"Are you angry?"

"No," she said.

"Nor frightened?"

"No." She laughed, the idea seemed so foolish.

"What did I tell you! That was a kiss and embrace for the souls of all the pioneers who ever loved along the Missouri. Not the avaricious ones, though! They wouldn't understand taking only a kiss." He drew her hand through his arm and held it as they went on along the dark shore in the shelter of the bank.

"Tired?"

"No. I could walk all night."

"So could I. I did one night to see if I could. Ugh!" The sharp smell of decay came to them, choking them. "That's far enough. I wonder about the souls of people who dump carrion along the river."

Before they climbed up the bank to the street it seemed natural that he should hold her close again and kiss her lips, gently this time. They walked silently along the board walk to the hotel, midway down the empty street, and Pamela didn't care that their feet sounded loud at that hour. She felt neither clandestine nor guilty, but rather quite gay.

"Good night," she whispered as he held the door of the hotel open for her.

"Are you hungry? I know where . . ."

[196]

She shook her head. "I'm really not."

The wide face of the wall clock registered three o'clock. No one was at the desk. She went up the creaking stairs to the second floor and down the dark corridor to Number 21.

Maybelle Lacey sat up in bed. "Pamela!" she said sharply.

"Yes."

"Pamela Lacey, where did you go with that man?"

"I went walking along the river, Mama, and it's very late."

There was such a queer note in her voice, Maybelle blinked her eyes in the dark, trying to see her. "You didn't even tell me where you were going! I shook my head but you didn't see me."

"I know, but you like to have me go out, Mama." Pamela sounded as though she were making fun. Maybelle came entirely awake.

"That Neale Hagen is a wild young man, Pamela. He's no good at all. Mrs. Silvester told me about him. She said she wondered at your dancing so much with him. Was he . . . did he behave himself?"

"Of course, Mama."

Pamela lay wide awake. She felt too excited, too happy to sleep. Phrases of the poetry came back to her . . .

> We are the dreamers of dreams,
> Wandering by lone sea-breakers . . .

This was what she had been waiting for: this excited feeling, and the sound of poetry in her ears . . . no! not for any feeling or any words. She had been waiting for Neale, this one person out of all the world.

What if he was a "wild young man"? Some people couldn't understand a man like Neale. Rose couldn't. Alan would be horrified by him but Papa might like him. It didn't matter if no one else liked him; she did.

A young man alone didn't have to stick to one job. When he found what he really wanted to do, it would be different. She wondered if he had any family . . . there were so many things she wanted to know about him. They would have time to talk on the way home, lovely exciting talk mostly, in the front seat. The others would be in back, but she must ask him. . . .

The next morning Mama had to call her twice before she heard her. Then she remembered she was going to see Neale and got right up.

"Look how wrinkled that dress is! You can't wear that, Pamela. It's a good thing you brought your dark green in case of rain. It's awfully dark for such a warm day, but that can't be helped."

Pamela put on the dark green dress obediently and smiled to herself. Neale would laugh, too, about the wrinkles. She could hardly wait to see him.

The dining room was nearly filled by Pioneers. Pamela was thankful Mrs. Silvester wasn't there. It made no difference to her what she might say about Neale, but it would make it harder to persuade Mama to let him drive them home. It would be better to have Neale suddenly appear and ask them. Mama would be so surprised and she might say yes without remembering all Mrs. Silvester had said. Neale had such a way with him. Neale would win her over. She remembered with annoyance that that was what Rose had said. She sat facing the dining-room door so she could see him first if he came early.

"The train goes at nine, Pamela. You go up and get our bag," Maybelle said.

Pamela ran up the stairs, but she lingered a few minutes looking out over the street from their bedroom window. Why didn't he come?

She carried the bag down and stood it on the long front porch of the hotel. From there she could see the river, lazy and blue today. How different it looks from last night, she said to Neale in her mind. You can't see the shore where we walked, but there is the place where we climbed down. No one else in the whole town walked along the river last night, no one but us. Was he going to come?

Mr. Sewall came toward her, his everlasting notes in his hand. "Here, Pamela, I'll want you to put these on cards in the file. Wonderful gathering wasn't it?"

"Yes, indeed, Mr. Sewall." But her eyes were on the street.

"The street's almost as crowded as it used to be!" Mr. Sewall was talking to someone else now.

She hoped she would see Neale swinging up the street before he saw her. He would be smiling, and he would probably tell her the ox team was ready. No, he would drive up, of course. "I can't say that it's all paid for, but I have the car in my possession." The remark glanced across her mind like some insect that looks big in front of the eye but too tiny to bother with at a distance. There were one, two . . . five automobiles down the street. Perhaps one of them was Neale's. She might just walk down the street a little way.

"Mr. Carter is going to drive us over to the station in his surrey, Pamela" Mama had her hat and veil on and was buttoning her gloves. "It's so nice of him."

She couldn't leave yet. Pamela's eyes searched the street again. She was the last to get in the surrey. As they drove along the street she watched everyone on the sidewalk. Now they were coming to the last automobile on the main street. It stood in front of a saloon. Four or five men stood around the door. The ladies in the surrey looked away but Pamela stared. Her hand lifted and then dropped again quickly. One of the men was Neale. But he looked so different in the morning light, so much older. His hair hung over his forehead. His tie was pulled to one side and his collar was open, but it was his face that seemed so different. There were the jutting chin and the dark eyes but his face was so . . . so softened. He walked unsteadily over to the car. As the surrey passed he looked up. His glance seemed to pass straight over Pamela, but he bowed elaborately to the whole carriage. One of the men in front of the saloon guffawed.

Pamela stared straight ahead down the street. She hated Rose for being right.

Fall, 1907

In September, Pamela read the item in the paper aloud to Maybelle.

Mr. and Mrs. Wrenn Morley have left for Cambridge where Mr. Morley will continue his studies at Harvard University.

"Oh yes, didn't I tell you that, Pam? Cora says Rose just insisted on Wrenn's going back to school. He had a real good opportunity here and he wanted to stay, but Rose said she'd never forgive herself if he didn't graduate. Ned is so pleased with them, he's going to pay his tuition and raise his allowance. He thinks Rose is a wonder, all she's willing to do."

"I'm glad," Pamela said. She wondered if Rose had told the Morleys about the baby.

"Well, as I told Cora, they might as well make the best of it. Wrenn's married and there's nothing they can do about it."

It was always awkward when she met Wrenn or Rose on the street, Pamela was thinking, or at some party or sitting on the Morleys' porch; they pretended it wasn't, but it was. Yet now that they were gone the town seemed empty. It was different this fall from last fall, or was each fall of your whole life different from every other? Each spring, each winter.

There weren't many of her class left in town. After all, two classes had graduated since theirs. Most of the girls were married or moved away. There had been a flurry of excitement over Alice Reed's engagement to the boy who visited during the summer. Alice was having a Christmas wedding, but, as her mother said, she was already living in Oregon in her mind.

Mary Marsten had married the tenth of September and gone to live on a ranch in the Judith Basin country. "I don't know how I'll ever stand living off on a ranch after living in town all my life, but that's all Bob cares about, except me," she added proudly. "Think of me all alone off there when the snow comes!"

"There isn't anything I'd like better," Pamela said. She thought of being at the ranch with the snow falling softly, steadily, closing off the road. But with whom? With Neale? she mocked at herself. Then she went back over the whole encounter, for the hundredth time.

He hadn't really said a word about love. He had just kissed her and held her close because they were there together and it was that sort of night. She couldn't fool herself.

Tonight when Pamela came home Mama told her about Amy Wentworth's getting married; Amy, who the class prophecy said would take up medicine, had gone to California to study nursing and married someone who was curing from tuberculosis. "Mrs. Wentworth is afraid she'll spend her life taking care of him. She must be crazy!" Maybelle said.

"I don't know," Pamela said. "Maybe she loves him."

"I'm certainly surprised to hear *you* say that," Mama said pointedly. "After the way you dangle Alan on the string."

"Why, I don't anything of the sort," Pamela said crossly.

"Well, just remember that when he is gone, there won't be anyone to do things with and go places with. You'll miss him."

"Anyone would think there wasn't anything in life for a girl but getting married!"

"It's mighty important, I can tell you." Maybelle began setting out supper on the kitchen table.

"What if you're not in love with anyone?" The question stood stark in the middle of the kitchen floor. The cupboard doors with their discreet buttons looked reproachful at letting such a thing out naked.

"When someone loves you as much as Alan obviously does you, Pamela, you'll learn. It wouldn't be hard with anyone so considerate and patient. I think he'd make you very happy."

"But you didn't have to learn."

Maybelle gave a little laugh that left an arch smile on her

face. "No, I could hardly wait for Charlie to ask me. He was handsome, Pam. You can imagine what he was like. I never knew what he was going to do next. When I was young the young men were more . . . Oh, I don't know! I suppose it was such a new country then and they were so ambitious and daring!" There was that tone in Mama's voice that made her seem younger than she was.

"I thought surely Charlie would be in before this. Here it is the middle of September. But I suppose now he won't be in until after roundup."

"I might ask Alan to drive me out to the ranch this week end," Pamela said. "I think he would like to go again before he goes east, and I haven't been out to the ranch since last spring."

Pamela pushed open the screen door and went slowly down the walk. Dark was coming earlier this month. She felt alone as she walked up the street. It seemed incredible that people had loved each other enough to marry and build each of these houses on the street, while she, Pamela Lacey, walked down the street alone. She wasn't going to marry Alan, and he would go soon. If Neale Hagen . . . but don't think about him. If Wrenn had only waited, if they hadn't quarreled over Papa . . . but Wrenn was married to Rose and they had gone away and left her here.

She wondered if anyone else had walked up this block of Prospect Avenue and felt this same kind of panic. In other towns, but not here. The houses hadn't been built long enough; the town wasn't that old. In the whole block there wasn't a single person who hadn't been in love and married.

It was dark and suddenly she began to run, as she used to do when she was still in school. If people were out on their porches they would think it was a child running home. They couldn't hear her long skirts swishing around her knees. She ran until she was out of breath and her heart pounded against her chest, and it hurt her to swallow, then she turned around and walked back home.

[202]

Alan was there on the porch with Mama. She heard his voice and saw his white flannels through the lilac bush. Tonight she would have to tell him she didn't love him . . . that wasn't what he asked; he asked if she would marry him, but she wouldn't. She walked slowly across their lawn, stepping on the fallen leaves that already littered the grass, hearing the leaves.

"There she is now," Maybelle said.

"Pam!" Alan came to meet her. His voice was warm and eager. "If I'd known which way you went I would have come to meet you."

As they came up on the porch Mama went in the house too obviously, Pamela thought.

"It seems like fall tonight," Pamela said and was surprised when she had said it.

"Yes, Pam. Are you sorry?"

"No. The summer was long enough."

"It was for me, I know," he said.

A little pause spread between them as they sat on the swing. Pamela started it in motion with her toe and they moved gently back and forth. Mama had lighted the hall light and the drop light in the dining room, but not the parlor light. Pretty soon she would bring a pitcher of lemonade or call out from the hall that she had made it and then go tactfully, ever so tactfully, and hopefully, upstairs.

"The summer's made me know, Pam, how much I love you, if I didn't know already."

"I . . ." Pamela began. She couldn't marry him without loving him. She must tell him that now. But she waited for the wagon coming down the street to get by; it made so much noise. It was a buckboard and it was stopping in front of the house. Why, it was Papa.

"Whoa!" Charlie Lacey called out.

"Hello, Pam, Alan," Papa's voice was different. It was tired. He sat down in the first rocker, letting his weight into it slowly.

"I was going to ask Alan if he would drive me out this week end. You haven't had roundup yet, have you, Papa?"

"Nope, Pam, I don't have any cattle to round up, unless I help with Ackers'."

"You said the steers were already on the ranch; the last time you were in, you said that!" Sharpness lined her tone.

"I started buying 'em, Pam, had some of 'em on the place, but the bank decided not to give me the loan. It wasn't Higgins's fault; he promised it, but he just couldn't do it. Banks are pretty cautious since the panic last year."

"That's so, sir. I know money in the East is very tight," Alan put in.

Pamela hardly heard Alan. Papa sounded so . . . so beaten. And maybe it wasn't the bank, maybe it was because people didn't want to lend the money to Papa after the Rocky Mountain Cattle Company trouble. But Papa wouldn't see that. He wouldn't admit it if he did.

"Did you have to take back the cattle you had bought?" she had to ask.

"Sold 'em. Didn't seem to be any other way, and I had a chance to lease the land to Curly Ackers."

"Slim?" she began.

"Slim's got a job over at the Diamond R till after roundup. Ruby's out there still."

Pamela saw how it must be out there. She saw Ruby rolling herself a cigarette and staring out the window over the sink. She could see Papa coming back, disappointed.

"I came in to meet Jeff Butler, tomorrow. Well . . ." He put a hand on either arm of the chair and pulled himself up wearily. "I'll go in and see your mother." It was the sound of his voice that frightened her.

"We could drive out anyway, if you'd like to see the ranch," Alan said. "I'd like another try at the riding."

If they went out to the ranch, she could talk to Ruby. Ruby was the only one you could trust. Papa had been so sure everything was fine, last spring. "No," she said. "There isn't any point in going if Papa isn't there."

When Pamela turned off the lights and started upstairs, Maybelle came out in the hall.

"Pam?"

"Yes, Mama." Why did Mama always ask that way; who else could it be?

"Your father's gone to bed. Things haven't gone well at the ranch. He had to lease it. I guess it's been leased ever since summer."

"I know," Pamela said, and then with hardly a pause, she added, "I'm going to marry Alan, Mama. He wants to be married in November."

"Oh, Pamela! Darling, I'm so happy for you." Maybelle put her arms around Pamela and walked down the hall with her to her bedroom. "I think he's such a fine young man; so dependable and safe!"

"Yes," Pamela said, trying not to mind her mother's arm around her. "I think he is." She remembered her father talking to Mr. Bell and Mr. Randell, saying "I don't suppose the cattle business is *safe*," making safe sound prissy and careful and beneath you. But she liked things safe and dependable, turning out just as people said they would. That's the way they would be with Alan. "We'll be very happy, Pam," Alan said as though it were a promise.

"He wants me to visit his family for ten days, right after he gets back. His mother is writing us, but I told him I didn't think I could."

"Of course you can, Pam. But I wouldn't want you to stay any longer than that because if you're married in November there will be so much to do. We'll have a church wedding, of course, and the reception here. Chrysanthemums are beautiful for a wedding, bronze ones with yellow cottonwood leaves. And you can wear my wedding dress."

The excitement in her mother's voice buzzed around her head like a late fly. Pamela walked away from it but she didn't try to put an end to it. She would be gone from here soon, away from Mama and Papa and this house and the street and the town, and she was glad.

PART TWO

1912-1918

"Some people are molded by their admirations, some by their antagonisms."

CHAPTER 1

Spring, 1912

"*Très jolie!*" Rose said as though she were in her mother's millinery shop, using one of the little French phrases Madame Guinard kept, as it were, in a box back of the counter because they had often the effect of a charm upon her Montana customers. "Wait, let me tie your veil a little higher."

Cora Morley submitted happily to the ministrations of her daughter-in-law's skillful fingers. She was never so sure of her appearance as she was after Rose had approved. Now that Rose and Wrenn and little Stephen lived so near she could ask Rose's opinion at any time.

Rose stood on the porch watching Mother Morley go down the street. She could never get used to the difference between her impression of her before she had married Wrenn and now. When Mrs. Morley used to come into the millinery shop she had seemed hard to please, turning down a hat with such decision, and taking silver dollars out of her pocket book as though she didn't bother to count them. And, of course, she didn't. Rose was always shocked at the hazy idea Mother Morley had of what she spent. So it was all the stranger that she had to ask Father Morley for every cent and sometimes held back a few dollars on this bill or that to pay the maid of all work. She consulted Rose about what to wear, countered with another suggestion, and then always agreed, and her greatest worry seemed to be lest she displease Father Morley and Wrenn.

It was strange, too, to know that Father Morley, who always looked so calm, could get so irritated if his tea wasn't piping hot or the juice of the roast beef didn't run red with the first prick of the knife. The Morleys' house had awed her so few years ago, with its red and blue panes of glass in the rounded turret window and the jigsaw work all across the upstairs porch, but now she knew that that fancy woodwork had to be painted this spring to preserve it, even if it was a terrible expense, and that the room behind those red and blue panes was hard to heat.

Thank goodness they had their own apartment after living three months with the Morleys when they first came back from Cambridge, and in Brandon Rapids' first really nice apartment house too.

Rose walked back up Prospect Avenue to the Pioneer Apartments feeling pleased with herself that she had pleased Mother Morley by dropping in to see her new outfit. Mother Morley would be even more pleased if she took Stephen up the street just as the Shakespeare Club was breaking up so all the members could see and admire him. Having a grandson had done much to reconcile Mother Morley to Wrenn's marrying her, she knew very well, though the Morleys still thought it outlandish that she had named the baby Stephen after her own mother, Stephanie Guinard.

Rose's face that had kept its roundness took on a speculative look, black eyes shrewd, the full red underlip caught by small white teeth. From something Mother Morley had said, or not so much said as intimated, she had an idea that the Shakespeare Club might be going to ask her to join. She didn't care about the club especially, since they only read the plays and didn't ever act them, but the Shakespeare Club was important in Brandon Rapids. And though Brandon Rapids was not the center of the world and never would be to her, it was now, while Wrenn was "getting established" as Mother Morley put it. If they hadn't come back here in the first place . . .

Without any warning, the old resentment darkened her mind like the ink which the deep-sea squid lets flow through its body to color the water around it. If it hadn't been for Pamela, she thought for the hundredth time, she might not have egged Wrenn on to finish law school. That first spring in Boston he had talked of going to Europe; he had a chance to get a job in a steamship office in Paris. There was nothing she had wanted to do more, but she didn't want Pamela Lacey to think Wrenn's marrying her had spoiled his career. She liked the idea of Wrenn's being a lawyer, except that it had taken three more years of school, but she certainly never meant to have him come back here to practice. She hadn't planned on Father Morley getting sick so he had to retire, and how could she ever have guessed that Wrenn, himself, would change so? That he would become so interested in everything here. Now he said all the things his father said when they first came back, said them as though he had thought them up, himself: that he had a real opening, that the town was growing, the West was opening up with the railroad and the homesteaders flocking in and the wealth here. "In ten years' time, Rose, at the rate it's going, I'll be able to take just the cases I want."

In ten years' time she would be thirty-three and still here. Oh well, if Wrenn really wanted to live here, it was all right. It was Wrenn she cared about. She had told Mama yesterday, "I love him more all the time." And Mama had said, "It's a fine thing Wrenn Morley is the one he is; you have it so bad, if he were a good-for-nothing gambler you'd love him just as much." Would she? Maybe. She couldn't imagine not loving Wrenn. But she couldn't imagine him being a gambler, either!

The front hall of the Pioneer Apartments was pleasantly warm after the chilly April day. The red carpeting and the imitation marble walls of the foyer resembled the regal stage settings used by visiting stock companies at the Opera House. A long mirror fronted the entrance and gave back a vivid image of a young woman with black hair and eyes and white skin smiling at herself. She stepped into the self-operating elevator feeling very elegant as she rose slowly to the third floor.

✦

At Shakespeare Club everyone was talking about the sinking of the *Titanic* the week before. The drama and tragedy of it made the play they were reading pale by comparison.

"Yet isn't it really significant," Amy Reed was always seeing the significance in things, "that we were reading about the shipwreck in *The Tempest* when this occurred?"

Cora Morley said, "Ned was saying this morning that it would have been a good deal more merciful if Astor and Guggenheim and some of those men had been saved instead of those poor women from the steerage; they won't know how to speak English and their husbands were drowned and how will they ever manage in a new country?"

Maybelle Lacey waited until time for refreshments to tell them about Pamela.

"When, Maybelle?" Lucy Moore asked.

"Just this morning! I was upstairs sewing and I looked out the window and there was Pamela coming up the walk as though she were just coming home from downtown."

"I don't see how you could tear yourself away to come today."

"I wouldn't have, but Pamela says she's going to make quite a little visit."

"How does she look?" Cora Morley wanted to know.

Maybelle enjoyed the moment. "Just fine. She was in black, which scared me at first, but she says black is very fashionable this spring."

"All black?"

"White gloves and shirtwaist."

"She's been married three years now, hasn't she?" May Cheavers said.

"Five!" Cora Morley answered for her. "I know, because Wrenn's been married six."

"Maybe she's . . . ?" May Cheavers asked in a low voice but with raised eyebrows.

"I wish she were," Maybelle answered, and her eyes met May's. A smile at once wistful and knowing touched both women's mouths. "Of course, she wanted to surprise me, but if I had just known I'd have asked Mr. Osborn to go to the hotel for the little time she was here. He has Pamela's old room."

"She didn't know you were renting rooms?"

"No. She doesn't like the idea but, of course, with Alan's position she can't imagine needing to. But renting to gentlemen like Mr. Osborn and Mr. Bates isn't like renting to just anybody."

"Well, I think you're wonderful to do it, Maybelle." It was Mrs. Reed who said it this time; someone always did say it.

Pamela was glad that she had arrived on the day of the Shakespeare Club.

"It only lasts a couple of hours, Mama; of course, you'll go. I'll be busy unpacking the whole time you're gone."

But she hadn't expected to find roomers in the house. "They're almost never home in the daytime," Mama had said, but she felt their presence. She stood in the doorway of her own room, not wanting to go on in. It looked smaller than she had remembered it, low-ceilinged, alien. Ties hung on the inside of her open closet door. A silver shaving stand occupied the corner of her dresser. A cigar box balanced it on the other end. She thought of what Mama had said.

"They're both such gentlemen, Pamela, who feel what a privilege it is to live in one of the town's fine old homes. Mr. Osborn says that in a hotel he could never hope to get the real atmosphere of the West. You'll just sleep with me in my room, and Charlie can sleep on the couch in his study the nights when he's home. You know that has a good box spring."

"Does Papa . . . doesn't he mind having roomers here?" she had asked. Surely, Papa wouldn't stand for roomers in their house. She wished Papa were home. Mama, of course, but it was Papa she had wanted to see so badly.

"I don't think he's crazy about it," Mama had said slowly. "But I notice he doesn't mind when I have a little money for things. He's buying cattle for Robinsons' of course, but that isn't like operating a big spread, you know." Something in Mama's tone kept her from wanting to ask anything more about Papa.

"Where's my old desk?" she had asked.

"That was too small for a man to use, so I put it up in the attic."

The attic, of course. She would move up there. She wouldn't think of moving in with Mama.

When she went up to the attic after Maybelle had gone, she opened the front window and sat on the floor looking down on the street. The trees had grown. The one in front of the house came as high as the window sill and she could see the swelling red buds against the sky. In Buffalo the trees were deep green and full-leaved by now. The forsythia and tulips were almost past. Alan had counted a hundred and forty-eight tulips in the back garden this year.

It was hard to come to a stop. All the way out on the train she had felt herself moving west and her mind moving faster, ahead of the train, urged her on. Her wanting to be back here had been so sharp she couldn't sleep at night; sometimes, lying awake, hearing the high shriek of the Buffalo trolleys, the motorcars that seemed to run all night there, and Alan's even breathing, she had seen everything about this street, almost more clearly than she could see it now, because then she could see the whole length of it at once.

The houses were no period at all, though Alan called them "Western Gothic." Someone had built a bungalow in the vacant lot next to Moores' since she had been away. Squat, heavy, it seemed to glower from under its porch at the older houses. She remembered that night at dinner when they had guests and Alan was talking about Montana. She had heard just the end: "The mountains are magnificent, but you should see those raw Western towns; they're really ugly." He had caught her glance then and said, "But they have beautiful women in those towns, one, anyway!" Then he had bowed down the table at her and everyone had smiled and clapped. She had hated it. She supposed the towns *were* ugly, the houses and the public buildings and the mud streets, except when the light shone on them in a certain way. Late in the afternoon, like this, when the sun got too far down to be glaring, the warm radiance changed even Main Street, but it wouldn't be any use trying to tell Alan that, if he had never seen it for himself.

She was glad the spring was late. She was here in time to watch it come. Already the bare cottonwood branches had a new lightness to their gray bark, as though green, spring blood ran underneath the bark. The sky was warm with a clear light. At five o'clock at home, in Buffalo, that is, the light was green shaded, falling in gold patches across the close-trimmed grass of the park or in the back garden, through the cut-leaf birch and the Japanese maple and the copper beech that Alan's father was so proud of. A cottonwood could be as lovely as a beech tree.

The Emporium's delivery wagon passed and her eyes decorated the E with affection. It was just as she remembered it. Then Dr. Nugent got out of a new motorcar in front of his house, but his bag looked like the same old one. When a girl wheeled by on a bicycle it seemed as though she saw herself going past, before she had ever been married or gone away.

The last time she had been home, three years ago, Alan had come, too. They had only stayed two weeks and they had been so busy going out for dinner, and to church, being Mr. and Mrs. Alan Randell of Buffalo, she had not had time to feel like herself. It was in winter and Alan thought they shouldn't try to go out to the ranch for fear they might get snowed in.

But Papa had come in from the ranch. The train was two hours late because of the snowdrifts. Papa was out on the platform waving his hat and he jumped off the train before it stopped and lifted her right up off the ground. She remembered so well when he was shaking hands with Alan he had said, "How's this squaw of yours?" Squaw had an unpleasant sound to Alan and he looked it and that just spurred Papa on. "Oh, I tell you, there's something to be said for a real full-blood squaw like you've got, Alan," and he went on talking about friends of his who had married Indian women till poor Alan didn't know what to think. Papa was terrible when he saw he could string somebody. "Well now, I'll tell you, I thought quite a bit about marrying a squaw myself when I was a young man; squaws'll do all the work and they'll never leave you. . . ."

Pamela got up from the window and pulled her old desk out from under the eaves. It did look absurdly small and secretive and somehow virginal. She opened the drawer. Everything was there, just as she had left it, but she closed the drawer again without touching anything. If she moved that couch over by the window she could lie in bed and look out. The marble-topped table and the horsehair covered chair that they had had on the float gave this end of the attic quite a furnished look. Mama wouldn't like her sleeping up here but she couldn't help that.

Whenever she heard voices on the street below she went over to the window. This time it was no one she knew, just two middle-aged women coming down the street together. But her eyes followed them, seeing the way one woman let her bag swing from her hand, her blue dress, the brown coat of the other, the movement of their heads as they talked. The light touched the cheek of the woman on the inside and polished the black coil of hair under the hat of the woman beside her as they turned toward each other. It gave them a . . . a vulnerable look. She wondered suddenly whether they were happy, what had happened to them. Then they faced straight ahead and the sun, striking them full in the face, made their features heroic for a minute. Everything seemed more than it was in this strong Western light that she wasn't used to any more.

She was making up her bed when a child's voice came clearly up to the attic. "Why didn't we stop and see Grandma, Mama?"

"Because they're having a meeting, Stephen."

Pamela stood at one side of the window to look down, and her hand fingered the jabot at her neck. Rose and her little boy were walking slowly down the street just as she had seen them so often in her mind that she was hardly surprised. Only, the boy was taller than she had thought he would be, but, after all, he was five. He had a cart that he pulled by a rope. His hair was bobbed across his forehead and he wore a white sailor suit. His black-stockinged legs looked so sturdy from here. Rose was heavier; striking, of course, not really pretty except when she smiled down at the little boy. What had Wrenn seen in her that made him fall in love with her?

The little boy sneezed in the sun and lifted his face so Pamela could look down on it. He was more like Wrenn than Rose. Rose didn't even look at the house as she passed.

Pamela was still by the attic window when Maybelle came up the walk with a stranger. He must be one of the roomers, she decided.

"My married daughter, Mrs. Randell, is here for a little visit," Maybelle said. "She came to surprise me on my birthday."

Mama's birthday was the twenty-second of April; she had forgotten that. Mama was giving the man her full history.

"Pamela lives in Buffalo. Her husband's father is president of Randell and Whitcomb Brass, and I imagine her husband will be someday. I'm so anxious to have you meet her . . ." Pamela heard the front door close, but she waited to go down until she heard Mama calling from the foot of the stairs.

It seemed to Charlie Lacey as he drove up his own street that he was always leaving or coming home. He could have slept out at Sid Walsh's place tonight. Sid wanted him to stay and play a little poker; he'd have had a good time all right, but while he was sitting there before supper, having a short one with Sid he decided to hit for home. Everything about that old ranch house of Sid's made him think of his own place. Of course, Sid's was a little more fixed up. Mrs. Walsh lived there all year round and their kids boarded in town during the week, but the boys coming up from the bunkhouse for supper and Sid's foreman telling him about that calf made him . . . well, say it once, nobody could hear it. Made him homesick, like a kid.

"How're you making out buying cattle for Robinsons', Charlie?" Sid had asked him. "Fine, Sid, fine," he had said. "They're a good outfit. If I'd have known as much about them when I was shipping cattle as I do now I'd have sold everything to them."

"You like it, Charlie? As well as ranching?"

Damn him, he wasn't going to tell Sid how he felt, so he said, "Well, I'll tell you, Sid, out on that ranch of mine I never got to see anybody and I kinda like getting around and seeing everybody in the cattle game, seeing their stock." And he did. It wasn't bad now in the busy season, but last winter there hadn't been much he could do but drop down to the Western and talk to ranchers who happened in. This next winter he was going to go out and live at the ranch; batch it if Ruby and Slim weren't there. That would be better than putting in the time here in town.

Charlie drove around to the barn and put his horse up before he went into the house. He remembered Maybelle wouldn't be expecting him but there would be something in the icebox. All the lights were on with these roomers of hers. He never would get used to having strangers in the house; Maybelle did it as much to have someone there as for the money. Remembering that was the only way he could stand them. He dropped his old jacket on the storm porch and kicked off his galoshes, which were caked from the mud of Sid's corral, and opened the kitchen door.

"Maybelle!"

"Papa!" Pamela heard him from the front room and came running like a child. "Papa, I was afraid you wouldn't be home tonight."

"Well, if it isn't Pam!" He didn't pick her up off her feet or give her a bear hug, just kissed her and stood back looking at her. "Where did you come from, girl?"

"Oh, I just came. I told Alan I hadn't been home for three years and I had to go this summer." Papa looked heavier. He was actually gray on the sides above his ears. The gray didn't look real but as though it had been powdered on for a play. She had been thinking all the way back on the train about seeing him.

"Papa!" she said, trying to realize it harder. They went together into the parlor where Mama was and that Mr. Osborn. Papa put his arm around her, and he was as big as she remembered and the smell of the cold air and his cigar and a faint good horse smell hung around him just as she had remembered.

And then everyone was talking at once; Maybelle telling how she looked out of the window and saw her, and Mr. Osborn saying he had heard so much about her and was certainly glad to meet her, and Papa asking about Alan and saying he was going to stay over at Sid Walsh's but something must have told him to head right back home. Well, this was something like it having Pam back here . . .

"I believe I have your room, Mrs. Randell, and I'd be glad to move down to the hotel while you're here if . . ."

"No, indeed, Mr. Osborn, there's plenty of room . . ." Maybelle said.

Pamela said, "Oh, thank you, I have my bed all made up. . . ."

But they were interrupted by Charlie saying, "That's very thoughtful of you, Mr. Osborn. We would appreciate that. If you and Mr. Bates would do that we would be greatly obliged." His tone indicated that they would do it.

Mama was frowning. "Charlie, we can't ask . . ."

Mr. Osborn said, "I'm afraid it's a little late to arrange it tonight, but the first thing in the morning." He hadn't expected to be taken up on his offer.

Charlie sat down in the Morris chair and lighted his cigar. "Now let me look at you, Pam. You look as though you'd come off winter range but we'll grain you up good." His tone and manner showed he had finished with Mr. Osborn. Pamela was uncomfortable, but she sat down beside Papa. Mama walked with Mr. Osborn out to the hall.

Maybelle came back into the room. "Charlie, you shouldn't have done that. Mr. Osborn is just as nice as can be but you can see he's put out. He really is an exceptional person and I'd hate to lose him permanently."

"Exceptional! There's nothing exceptional about him. Let him go. I'm not going to have two strangers all over the place when Pam's here. By God! I've tripped over them long enough."

Pamela saw Mama's eyes flash, then she shrugged in a manner

Pamela used to try to imitate in front of the mirror because it seemed so grown-up.

"Very well, Charlie, if the financial advantage doesn't matter to you, but please don't raise your voice so they can hear everything you say, and don't swear!"

Pamela's eyes moved away from Papa and Mama to the bookcase. On the top shelf, just as it used to be, was that book about the Vigilantes and next to it *Grant's Memoirs* . . .

"I bet it seems good to you to be back in Montana, Pam!" Charlie said.

Mama drew up her rocking chair. "And she's going to make us a real visit, Charlie!"

CHAPTER 2

Now that she was back in her own old room it still seemed alien. She had washed the curtains and spread, and brought down the bird's-eye maple desk from the attic in a kind of frenzy to have the room just as it used to be, but it continued to seem smaller than she had remembered it; she hadn't used to think of it as either small or large, for that matter, but simply as her room. She lay awake at night and remembered Wrenn calling from the walk below the side window after they had quarreled, and the night she had come home from the trolley park and seen him with Rose. She thought of the day she had dressed for her wedding here and hurried upstairs to change into her "going-away suit" with Mama helping her and saying, "You look so happy, Pam; you look just radiant" and she had looked at herself in the mirror as she put on her hat (which wasn't as pretty as the ones Madame Guinard made but she wouldn't go to *her*), and her eyes hadn't quite met her own.

In the mornings she woke early and noticed things she had

never noticed before, how the blue rose border was uneven on the wall at the foot of the bed, and that in the framed sepia print of Christ and the doctors Christ didn't look as though He even heard their questions. The corner where the rocking chair used to be was taken up by her trunk. She had been going to move it down to the cellar, but Mama said, "Why don't you just leave it there, Pam. It won't be in your way." So she had left it. Later she could move it down; she avoided going into things with Mama.

"How long are you going to be here, Pam?" Mrs. Cheavers had asked yesterday. She had answered honestly enough, "All summer, I hope." "And will your husband be able to get out?" "I'm afraid not; they're enlarging the plant and he's very busy." "Oh! Well, isn't it nice for your mother and father that you can be here!" "It's very nice for me."

The third morning after she arrived Mama had tapped on her door. "Asleep? I've got something here I know you've been waiting for!" and she had handed her the letter from Alan. Mama had waited for her to open it, but she had been very slow about it, asking about people in town, saying that she hadn't heard Papa go off early this morning, until Mama said, "Well, I'll leave you to read your letter and then breakfast will be ready."

And even after Mama went downstairs she let the letter lie on the bed without touching it, looking at Alan's handwriting, seeing him writing it at the office after his secretary had gone. She dressed before she could bring herself to tear the envelope open. Then she took it over to the window and read it.

Dear Pamela:

It seems incredible to me that you could do a thing like this, going off so melodramatically, leaving a note behind. Real life is always different from a romantic schoolgirl dream but surely you know that I have never had any thought of anyone but you and that I am entirely devoted to your happiness. You say that the sinking of the Titanic *made you realize that our life together just wasn't enough. What can you possibly mean? Reading about*

*that tragic shipwreck was too much for your sympathetic nature.
I am absorbed in my work that is true but never so much so that
I lose my awareness of you. You must feel that all my family is
devoted to you as well as our many friends. You have made a
real place for yourself. It is my hope and prayer that we shall
be blessed with children and when that time comes life will seem
richer and fuller to you.*

*Stay a couple of months and then come back home to me,
dear. In the meantime I shall say here simply that you hadn't
been west in a number of years and felt that you should get
back to see your family.*

With my tenderest love,

Alan

Her eyes went back to the sentence about the dream and she
remembered Mr. Sewall's speech. The pioneers all had a dream
when they came west. She didn't know whether she had one or
not, anyway it was no romantic schoolgirl dream. She knew just
how Alan would say that. She put the letter back in its envelope
and went down to breakfast.

"How's Alan?" Mama asked as she poured herself another cup
of coffee and sat down while Pamela ate her breakfast.

"Fine," Pamela heard a voice say that had no connection with
her own.

"I wish he could come out."

"He's enlarging the plant; he couldn't get away just now."

"My, I hope I can get east next fall and visit you. I feel as
though I'd been there from your letters, but still it's not like
seeing everything."

"Alan wants to build next spring," the other voice said. "His
father has given him a lot."

"How lovely! And I suppose it has trees on it?"

"Yes. Quite a few. There are really two lots, and there's a big
beech tree," she added, thinking how Mama would love it. Mama
would like everything about the life in Buffalo. But after living

with Papa she wouldn't find Alan exciting. When she looked up, Pamela saw a knowing smile on Mama's face.

"It sounds to me as though you feel you need a larger place because of a new member of the family on the way!"

Pamela had picked up her coffee cup. Maybelle's expression was wasted on the bottom of the Haviland cup. "No," her own voice said. "I'm sorry to disappoint you."

Disappointment was in Mama's voice. "Oh! Well, I hope you don't wait too long. I thought maybe that was the reason you came back this spring. I was thinking maybe I would go on when the baby was born."

"No," Pamela said again, picking up a crumb beside her plate.

Maybelle studied her daughter's face in the morning light, wishing she would say more. She couldn't come right out and ask her why she had no children. Really, she believed it was easier to talk to Cora Morley or Lucy Moore than her own child.

"Mama, wasn't the sinking of the *Titanic* a terrible thing?" Pamela said unexpectedly. Maybelle was startled.

"Terrible. We were talking about it at Shakespeare Club. Those men were certainly brave."

"Yes," Pamela said softly. "I keep thinking of the boat out there in the middle of the sea, in the dark. The orchestra kept playing, you know, gay music like 'Alexander's Ragtime Band,' right up to the last. Some people didn't know they were sinking until the orchestra played 'Nearer My God to Thee.'" Pamela was sitting back in her chair, looking out the kitchen window. Her face bothered Maybelle, it was so . . . so intent. "And in a couple of hours there was nothing at all, just sea and darkness."

"I know it; perfectly dreadful!" Maybelle murmured, vaguely upset by Pamela's going on so about it, and her disappointment that Pam wasn't going to have a baby. She had felt sure. Cora kept saying, "Wait till you have a grandson, Maybelle. I tell you, we just think the world of that little one of ours!" When she saw May Cheavers at the back fence she went out and left Pamela by herself.

The sinking of the *Titanic* did make a difference to Pamela.

[223]

It made life seem so . . . valuable. Why couldn't Alan see? All those people were drowned and here was she, Pamela Lacey Randell, still living. She didn't want to waste any of her living.

When she had washed and dried the few dishes she went through the house to the front porch that looked naked and exposed without the swinging baskets and the vines, or the swing and porch chairs. It was too cold to stand there without a coat but she stayed, shivering a little in the cold air.

Then she saw Papa driving up the street just as he used to, in the buckboard behind old Lupin. His big gray hat shaded his face and his shoulders stooped comfortably forward as though he didn't think about them. She noticed the way he held the reins in a half-opened hand on his knee and she knew before it happened where Lupin would leave off trotting and how the wheels would sound revolving more slowly. She went down the steps toward the curb.

"Hi, Pam. I thought you might be up by now. You don't keep ranch hours back east, I can see. I'm going out to the ranch. You want to come along?"

"Of course I do. I'll be ready in a minute." This was what she had been waiting for. She wasn't back home really until she had been out to the ranch.

"No hurry," Charlie said as he got out of the buggy. "I'm going to have a cup of coffee first and a piece of that pie we had last night if there's any left."

This was what she loved, Pamela thought as she went upstairs; doing things unexpectedly, not being in a hurry or caring when you got some place. "But, Pamela, you have to keep to a schedule," Alan was always saying.

Maybelle cut a piece of pie for Charlie. Then she went over and closed the swinging door into the pantry. "Charlie, you'll have a chance to talk to Pam on the way out. See how things are between her and Alan."

"Why, what did she say?"

"Oh, she hasn't said anything in particular, but that's just it.

She got a letter from Alan today but she didn't offer to read it to me. And she isn't going to have a child. It sort of worries me."

If Maybelle hadn't said that, Charlie thought as they rode along, he could have enjoyed this trip with Pam, but now Maybelle had him worried.

"I'll have to stop at Tom Bailey's place and look at his cattle, Pam. You know where it is, you turn east after you come to hangman's tree and it's about a quarter of a mile off the road."

Pamela nodded. She did seem quiet. He had thought she looked a little peaked when she arrived, but she didn't now. She had grown prettier, if anything. He had asked her about Alan; he couldn't do that again. "Your mother says you heard from Alan today. What did he say?" He tried out the sound of the question in his own mind, but it sounded prying. This business of having a child was something for her mother to talk to her about. When he got a chance, after the first one was born, he'd put in a word then; tell her he'd always been sorry they hadn't had more children; a boy or two. Not that Pam wasn't as good as a boy, but then he'd have had him with him. Cal Jessup passed them in his Overland making so much noise Charlie tightened his hand on Lupin's reins, just in case she should get scared. Then he had a good idea.

"How does Alan like his new Hudson?"

"Oh, very much. He sold the horses this year."

"Have you tried driving it yet, Pam?"

"He bought his mother's electric for me."

"Well, that was nice. It wouldn't do for country driving, I imagine, but you probably don't do much of that there."

"No," Pam said.

Charlie looked away across the rolling flats that were only just beginning to green up and gave up trying to question her. "Too bad you didn't come just about two weeks later so there'd be some color in the country."

"I like it this way. Everything's too green in Buffalo."

"Course that's the way I feel. I like it any time. Last time I was out some homesteaders that took a claim beyond the second coulee, 'member?" He felt her nod. "Well, they had their brand new plow out and they were working away, having a hell of a time 'cause the ground was still frozen on the north side there. And when the man saw me he walked over and said, 'When do you figger to start your plowing?' I told him I didn't figger to start while I was in my right mind. He sort of stared and didn't know what to think. I said, 'I figger to raise cattle if too many homesteaders don't mess up the place.' "

"Are there many homesteaders near us?"

"Not right around us. I got Slim and Ruby to take out claims. They're going to prove up on 'em this summer and sell 'em to me, I hope."

"I wish I could take out a claim," Pamela said.

Charlie lifted the reins and chirruped. Lupin laid back her ears in reproach. Lifting the reins would have been enough. "You see, Pam, you'd have to have a little shack of some kind built on it and then you'd have to live there three months. You couldn't hardly do that unless Alan plans to come out and spend his vacation and I don't imagine he'd take to the idea of spending it out in a shack."

"He wouldn't, but I would. I know the piece I'd like. Maybe Ruby would stay with me."

Charlie scowled at the sky that looked like the new canvas top on a chuck wagon; just as white, and lashed down tight to the rim of the prairie. He liked a sky to be blue. "Can you stay long enough, Pam?"

"Oh, I might."

Charlie turned off the road at Tom Bailey's. There wasn't time now to go into it, besides when a man used that tone you didn't go on asking questions. Prob'ly Pam was the same way, but he worried about what Pam meant by that all the way over to the corral.

Pamela watched her father talking to the men down there. They liked him, she could see. He slapped his hat against his knee as though he was mad about something. Mr. Bailey was telling them something now, and pointing out across the field. They must be talking about the homesteaders.

She watched her father walk over to a steer and lay his hand on his rump, as quiet and easy as though he were walking up to a horse. He walked around the animal and then stepped off to look at the bunch they had in the field near the corral. She saw him nod his head. He knew cattle, Ruby always said, but you could tell that by just watching him. The wind was blowing so he had to take off his hat and his hair blew up into a kind of crest, and his profile seemed cut into the white sky. He was taller than the three other men who stood listening to what he was saying. He had a notebook he was writing in and the men were nodding their heads. He put the notebook away in the pocket of his shirt and took out cigars, handing them around. Somebody must have made a joke because they all laughed and one of the men slapped Papa on the back. She wished he hadn't given them cigars; it made him seem like a salesman. He wasn't a salesman, he was a buyer. Either one wasn't the same as a rancher.

"Nice cattle?" she asked as they drove away.

"First class. I'd like to own that bunch he had in the field there." Some note in his voice or the way he looked away as he said it so that his voice seemed to come from far away told her that he hated this job of going around from place to place buying cattle for the Livestock Commission.

"You do have some cattle though, don't you?"

"Yes, a few. We lease the grazing land to Ackers for half the calves. Slim's working for Ackers now, but he and Ruby stay at the ranch except times they need Ruby to cook over there. They ought to cut free from the place but they don't. Kind of waiting till I get going again."

Charlie chewed on his cigar, then he threw it so far it fell in a thicket of wild rose bushes and started a hen pheasant. Pamela watched her flying across the road just ahead of Lupin. She thought of the large framed paintings in Mother Randell's dining room of pheasant and wild duck tied up by the feet. She had never liked them.

"Pam, I've been thinking of writing Alan to ask him if he would like to go into the ranching business . . . I mean as an investment. Perhaps he has some friends who would be interested. . . ." Pamela turned so suddenly with such a startled expression he didn't finish his sentence.

"It would be a unique opportunity for some Easterners who are interested in the West. . . ."

"No," Pamela said sharply. "Alan wouldn't be interested after his father's experience!" Her voice was almost shrill.

"Well, all right, I just thought . . . there's nothing to get excited about, Pam." He was glad when Pamela looked away. She was as worked up as Maybelle got over things.

"I should think you had had enough of Eastern partners." It sounded mean and taunting in her own ears but she couldn't keep it back. How could Papa have thought of such a thing? He must be crazy. All the good, proud feeling she had had when she was watching him look at the cattle disappeared. "What if you had bad luck or, or something, and they lost what they'd put in?" the question came out explosively.

"There's no reason why we should have bad luck. With a little capital I'd plan to buy the best bulls available and I've got the grass . . . after all, my dear, I know a thing or two about raising cattle and after my experience buying for Robinsons' I'm in a position to sell pretty advantageously."

Pamela stared at the road ahead without seeing it. He sounded so confident, almost boasting. The way he said "my dear"!

"Oh, I suppose there is always a little risk, but, after all, Pamela, nothing is completely safe in the world."

Pamela bit her lip in her sudden, fierce, hopeless anger. Didn't he remember anything? That was what he had said that time to Mr. Bell and Mr. Randell and she had thought it was fine and brave. But that was before all the trouble. She had married Alan because she wanted to be safe. That was Papa's fault.

"Don't ever ask Alan to invest in the ranch. *Ever!*"

[228]

Charlie was puzzled. She was so excited all of a sudden. Her eyes snapped as though she was mad. There must have been some trouble between her and Alan. Maybelle had guessed there was. When Pam got around to tell them, she would. If Alan hadn't treated his girl right . . . Charlie reached out and laid his big hand gently on Pamela's. And suddenly Pamela was crying against his arm, crying so hard her whole body shook.

"There, Pam, it's all right. You're back with Papa now; everything'll be all right," he murmured as he had used to comfort her when she was a child. At first, Pamela seemed to cry all the harder, then she sat up straight again and they drove the rest of the way to the ranch without talking.

"Well, bless my saddle sores! Look what the wind blew in!" Ruby came down the steps to meet Pamela and hugged her. "I was looking out that window when I see Lupin and the buggy and I was thanking my stars I made bread today for Charlie. Then I see he had someone with him an' a woman an' I like to died trying to make out who it was. Didn't dare dream it could be you, Punk!"

"Oh, Ruby, I'm glad to see you!" Pamela said. "Papa stopped at the corral but I couldn't wait."

"Well, I should hope not! Riding in all that wind you look as though you'd cried all the way from town. Danged old wind! I hate a spring wind, comes in all the cracks."

Nothing had been changed in the ranch house, except that Ruby had braided a new rug to go in front of the base burner and the curtains seemed to Pamela to have shrunk another inch above the sills.

"I'll have to give you venison stew, Pam, but I got fresh bread. Slim ought to be back pretty quick. He's over at Jorgensen's bunkhouse trading a .45 revolver he bought second hand. You know Slim, he'd trade me, if he got a good price."

When Ruby had gone on out to the kitchen Pamela went over to the window that faced the river and way beyond it King Butte. Nothing changed about the view. She watched a ball of tumbleweed, as big as a bushel basket roll across the bare stretch of ground and land in the river and then float with the current until it caught against the root of an old cottonwood tree.

"You haven't even got your hat off!" Ruby said.

"Oh, I was just looking around first. I believe I even missed seeing tumbleweed back east," Pamela said as she turned away from the window.

"You miss queer things when you ain't happy," Ruby said. "So that professor of yours let you come west for a change!"

"Well, I came anyway, Ruby."

"Better take off your hat and stay awhile," Ruby said, pulling the string of her tobacco bag tight with her teeth.

"Did you leave him for good?" she asked, yellow-gray eyes almost crossed as she looked at the cigarette paper she was sealing with her tongue.

"I don't know yet." Pamela took off her hat and jacket.

"Do you love the lady cowboy?" Ruby lighted a match with her fingernail.

"I didn't ever really love him," Pamela said, her eyes on the slow movement of the river.

"That's the worst thing a woman can do, Punk. It makes me ashamed of myself that I never taught you any better. It's worse than a lot of things people think is worse. Unless you both know it and then it ain't right."

Pamela looked over at her, apprehensive as a guilty child. There was no color about Ruby, her skin and thin lips and hair were gradations of gray that only made her eyes more yellow. When those eyes met hers, Pamela looked back to the river.

"He's very kind and good, Ruby . . ."

"I know. I seen him here. Wouldn't hurt a flea and says 'pardon me' every time he moves. You oughta be ashamed of marrying that sort when you know he loved you." Ruby's voice was quieter than it usually was but it had such a fierceness in it; Pamela hadn't expected her to speak like that. She hadn't meant to tell her all this and here she was hardly in the house and Ruby was scolding her.

[230]

"You think I should go on with him then?"

Ruby seemed intent on her smoking. The room was still except for the sound of the wind and then she heard her father's voice call out Slim's name. When she was a child she would have rushed out the door and run down to the corral. She couldn't do that now she thought, hankering after being a child.

Ruby walked over to the airtight stove, lifted its cover and dropped in her cigarette stub. "I didn't say that, Punk. What are you going to do if you don't go back to him? I don't think much of that store job you had. If you was a man now I'd say you oughta take ahold of the ranch, but I never seen but one lady rancher and I wouldn't have give two cents' worth of tobacco for her. Either way, you'll pay for what you done, I know that." She went out to the porch and gave a falsetto yell that echoed back from the rimrock. "Come and get it!" Then she went on out to the kitchen.

Pamela had a feeling of being left in the lurch. What a queer word, "lurch." Her mind busied itself with the word. She followed Ruby out to the kitchen. "You left me in the lurch," she said, but Ruby made no answer, only lifted a cover from a pot and tried the potatoes with a long-handled fork. Her face from the side looked sad to Pamela.

Slim was different. He was always jolly. He started talking as he opened the door. "Where's that Pam that sold out to the East? All the trouble I had raising her up to be a cowgirl an' then she goes off and gets married and lives in the city!"

"Slim, it's so good to see you!" Pamela said, shaking his hand.

" 'Member how I used to swing you right up on my shoulder? Guess I still could; it don't look like you put on too much weight. Betcha I can still get my two hands around your waist." He made as if to try.

"Here, now, Slim, I'm watching you!" Ruby called out. Charlie's big laugh filled the kitchen and everything was just as it used to be.

"What did you get for your gun?" Ruby asked when they were

sitting around the kitchen table, the big nickel-plated oil lamp spreading a yellow circle of warm light over them.

"He didn't do so bad, Ruby. By golly, he's getting sharper," Charlie said.

"Don't tell me he brought home another glass-eyed roan-colored yearling like the time he traded a gasoline saw," Ruby said.

"No, sir, you told me never to bring another horse back from a trade, Ruby, so I didn't. That's the way to get along; never do nothing your wife says not to. I said on the way home, this'll sure please the little woman!"

Ruby's mouth turned down in distrust. "What did you get?"

Slim winked at Pamela. "Yes, sir, I'm sure pleased with this trade. Course I hate to let a good gun go, too. I feel real bad about that, but then when I think what pleasure this is going to give Ruby!"

"You tell me, Slim, right now or you won't get another thing to eat!" Ruby reached over and picked up his plate.

"Say, you know, I ain't got much appetite tonight. I forgot to tell you but they have their meals right on time over there at Jorgensen's and they asked me to set down with them." Ruby slumped back in her chair. She rolled herself a cigarette and affected indifference.

"There now, I don't like to see a woman quivering with curiosity like that; 'tain't good for them, is it, Charlie?"

Pamela had forgotten this kind of teasing. She laughed out of relief to be back here.

"You're right, Slim. If I was you I'd wait till morning. Ruby'll be feeling stronger in the morning," Charlie said.

"No, I guess I better tell her or she won't sleep a wink. Ruby, I traded that beautiful old-time .45 Colt revolver and a new saddle blanket for a Overland engine and what's left of the body."

"What's that?" Ruby asked sharply.

"An automobile. Red Moyer bought it new and first he got it stuck in the mud an' then he run it into a tree an' he decided he'd stick with hosses, so he traded it to me. What do you think of that!"

"Not much. I think you'd be better off if you stuck to horses!" And Pamela remembered how Ruby always sounded cross when she talked to Slim. But she didn't mean it. Ruby loved Slim. She wouldn't have married him if she hadn't.

"What's the matter, Pam? You're just sitting there looking serious as a church door and not eating anything," Charlie said. Pamela laughed quickly in self-defense.

CHAPTER 3

"You'll do wonderfully, Wrenn. I wouldn't be surprised if Mr. Hill was so impressed he asked you to be attorney for the railroad."

Wrenn smiled but since Rose was intent on tying his white tie the smile met his own eyes in the mirror. "He's more likely to ask me after he's met you. You're beautiful tonight, Rose."

Rose's quick fingers touched the side of his face just long enough to give a suggestion of a caress. She glanced in the mirror at herself in her black lace. Mother Morley had reported that Pamela had said black was very smart in the East. She leaned nearer to the mirror to fasten her earrings and remembered Pamela saying, "Why, your ears are pierced!"

"I suppose Pamela Lacey will be there," she said.

"Oh yes, I imagine so," Wrenn agreed. "Mother said she looked fine, didn't she?" He was rather glad that he was going to be toastmaster tonight. Pam would hear him.

"She's thinner," Rose said, thinking with dissatisfaction that she herself had been plump ever since Stephen was born and now she was pregnant again. Queer that Pamela had no children. Pam would see how successful Wrenn was. The paper

[233]

yesterday had said, "The toastmaster for the great occasion will be that promising young attorney, Mr. Wrenn Morley." Pam must have read that.

"We'll have the cab drive down to the station so Stephen can see the train come in, then we'll drop him home and go right to the hotel to be there to welcome them," Wrenn said.

At 7 P.M. most of the town was gathered at the station to see the arrival of the special train from the twin cities. It came out of the spring dusk with a loud clanging of the bell and mysterious sissing of steam. Then the Elks' band struck into the raucous strains of "There'll Be a Hot Time in the Old Town Tonight" drowning out the cheers of the crowd. The dignitaries crowded onto the platform and the mayor and members of the Brandon Rapids Chamber of Commerce mounted the train to meet them. Along the side of the train a banner, slightly worse for the snowstorm it had gone through in North Dakota, bore the words NORTHWEST DEVELOPMENT LEAGUE.

Lights were on in the parlor car and the diner, and vases of ferns and pink carnations hung between the windows. The polished mahogany reflected both lights and flowers and the silver and linen napery dazzled the waiting crowds. Most of the curtains were drawn in the sleeping cars but one left open part way showed a Pullman bed made up with sheets and pillowcases whiter than any home linen. The trip was intended to boost the settlement of the country, but those who took it had no thought of enduring any of the privations and crudities that would await the new settlers.

"Those two cars are the private ones belonging to the presidents of the Great Northern and the Burlington roads," Wrenn pointed out to Stephen perched on his shoulder.

Rose was searching the crowd for a glimpse of Pamela. When she saw her, Pamela was standing with her mother and father at the edge of the crowd. The light from the station platform fell on them so she could see Pam clearly. Pam was laughing at something Mr. Cheavers had said and she tilted her head in the way Rose remembered. She was bareheaded and a comb or an ornament sparkled against her light hair. She was arranging a white veil around her head and Rose saw that she wore elegant elbow-length white kid gloves. Mrs. Lacey was in evening dress but Mr. Lacey wore his everyday clothes.

Without really meaning to, Rose said, "There's Pam, Wrenn, over there."

"Let's go over and say hello and then we must leave," Wrenn said.

Of course he would want to see her right away, but then, they had to see her sometime. Why should Pam's coming home make her feel so uncomfortable? After all, she and Wrenn had been happily married for six years. Pam was just an old school friend. . . .

"Yes, sir, this is really a big day for Brandon Rapids!" Mr. Cheavers said as they came up.

"It may be for Brandon Rapids but it isn't for the country," Charlie Lacey's voice boomed out. "What's it for except to stir folks up to go homesteading and cut up the range. They can't make a living on any little hundred and sixty acres of dry land and they'll spoil it for the rest of us."

"Hush, Charlie!" Mrs. Lacey said. "Oh, Wrenn and Rose! Pamela, look who's here!"

Rose was unaware of what she, herself, said as she shook hands. "Yes, this is Stephen. It's his bedtime but his father thought he should see the special train. We think he's a pretty nice boy!" How cool Pam was; how elegantly slender. Mrs. Lacey was always telling Wrenn's mother how happily married she was, how wealthy. . . .

"I hope to stay quite awhile. I haven't been back here for three years, you know," Pamela said. "I see you're the toastmaster, Wrenn. It will seem quite like commencement all over again."

"We're at the Pioneer Apartments, Pam," Rose said. "You must come and see us. Come over for coffee some morning so we can talk about old times." There, that was the right note. "Did you know that Alice is . . . yes, I'm coming, Wrenn. We'll see you all there."

"Mr. Lacey's an old die-hard," Wrenn said in the cab. "He won't have any part of it." He didn't mention Pamela. She wouldn't, either. They were both quiet. Stephen kept up a little sing-song, "choo-choo train, choo-choo train" that bothered Rose because it was so tuneless.

"You can see that Pam's not much interested in Brandon Rapids any more," Rose said, but they were home and Wrenn carried Stephen into the house.

The banquet room at the Western was handsomely decorated with palms and flowers from the greenhouse, but everyone said it was too bad they couldn't have great sheaves of wheat to carry out the theme . . . the theme of . . . oh, you know, Plenty, and all that. The band played so loud you couldn't really talk but everyone was bowing and smiling and watching the visitors. Waitresses moved swiftly through the crowded room. It was very pleasant sitting here at the head table with the president of a St. Paul milling firm next to her, Rose thought, and the president of the Burlington Railroad on her other side. Now Wrenn had risen.

"Since our distinguished guests are going west tonight, we shall begin our program at once." Rose had been nervous for Wrenn but she needn't have been. His voice was so natural. He liked doing this. He must be like this when he was in court. She looked down the table and saw his hand resting on the tablecloth, long-fingered, well cared for, not even trembling.

". . . and first I want to introduce to you our distinguished guests . . ."

Her eyes wandered to the white satin badges on most of the men there. "Zone of Plenty" was printed in gold on them. Then her eyes came back again to Pamela, sitting with her mother and the Cheavers way over in the corner of the room. What did Pam think seeing her sitting up here? She wasn't looking at her but at Wrenn. Her face had that same listening look it used to have at high school when Pam sat up in the front row and she sat two aisles over and three seats from the back. What was she thinking about Wrenn?

One speaker sat down and another rose. They all paid tribute to the vision of "that great Empire Builder, James J. Hill" and to the opportunities of Montana. And in Seattle they would pay tribute to the opportunities of Washington, as they had praised the rich soil of the Dakotas in North Dakota last night. They bandied statistics about.

"*Do you know,*" demanded one of the railroad men, "*that 2,344 carloads of settlers' property bound for Montana passed through the twin cities last year? It is safe to wager that in ten years' time Brandon Rapids will equal St. Paul, itself.*"

But still, Rose thought, she would rather live in St. Paul, or New York, or back in Boston. Maybe Pamela was thinking she was glad she didn't live here.

Wrenn presented a gold-painted key to the visitors. He had brought the key home and Stephen had kept asking how it could be the key to the city when there wasn't any door.

Each visitor responded with lavish praise.

"*When I asked Mr. Savage to tell me about Brandon Rapids he gave me what I consider not only an accurate but an adequate picture. He said, 'the women of Brandon Rapids are so fair the stars are envious, the horses . . . for they still know what fine horses are there . . . the horses are so swift they make the wind roar in rage, and the whisky in that town is so pure it is a virtue to be intemperate!*'

"*Do you wonder that I had to come out to see for myself?*" The laughter was so loud the speaker had to wait to continue. "*But now that I am here I want to say this, that all these virtues pale beside the spirit I find in this Western city; it is the spirit of push and development that takes hold of things and gets them done!*"

Enthusiasm enveloped the room like some fragrant ether; people breathed it in, smiling at each other. The men felt confident, proud of their sagacity in choosing Brandon Rapids as a home. The women thought happily of the near future when there would be spreading shade trees as far as you could see along the paved streets and no dust blowing in their faces and sifting into their houses, because the prairie would be moved so far back by the hundreds of new homes built there.

The man beside Rose was the next speaker. He pushed back his chair and then the ice-cream dish and water glass from his place as though he needed plenty of room. Rose glanced up and noticed how he dropped one thumb into the pocket of his white waistcoat and thrust his head back as though finding his thoughts on the ceiling. She could see the soft folds of his neck sagging fleshily into the opening of the turn-back collar.

"*It seems to me*," he said, his voice coming from above her, "*that the remarkable thing about this town is that it is a Man's town. A young man's town. And when I say that I mean no discourtesy to the fair ladies present. Rather I mean to say that I have seldom seen such masculine vigor in a comparatively small city. Where are your old men? Where is your cemetery? It makes me feel young and full of vigor just to be here. . . .*"

Well, yes, it really was true, when you stopped to think about it, Rose thought. There were plenty of middle-aged but not so many really old people. Even Wrenn's mother and father were really only in their fifties. With the chair pushed back she could see Wrenn. A little smile curved his lips and he seemed to be studying his water glass. Now he was looking at his watch that lay on the table in front of him. The men wanted to be on their way to Seattle by 11:30. Wrenn rose. His voice was a relief after the heavy juicy voice of the visitor.

Rose sat erect, listening with all her being. Pride warmed her blood and sent a becoming flush under her usually white skin.

Wrenn seemed to hesitate. Rose felt the change in his voice as quickly as she felt him turn or sigh in bed beside her. That wasn't what he had meant to say. When he had read his remarks to her he had said, "There, that should make the old boys beam." Where was that sentence about "a city of a hundred thousand by the middle of the century, a busy metropolis serving the vast agricultural area reaching to the Canadian line"?

He must have forgot. Why had he said "however the future turns out" as though it might not turn out well? She glanced over at him. The chandelier above the speakers' table shone down on his light hair that even the briskest manipulation of his military brushes could not make lie straight. It was a private comfort to her that he would never be fat. Father Morley was a very handsome man still, except that he was sick.

". . . and as our guests journey on through the night our good wishes will go with them. We hope they will return before long to see many of the prophecies made tonight gloriously fulfilled." He sat down and hurriedly took a sip of water.

Then it was over and the president of the Burlington road was saying what a privilege it had been to sit by her. She would have to wait till they got home to ask Wrenn what had happened, whether he didn't feel well. A twinge of worry etched a hairline on her forehead, even as she smiled at the compliment.

Pamela realized how long she had been away from here when she looked around the banquet room of the Western. She knew most of the faces but she had nothing to say to any of them. On the way in, Mama had done most of the talking. "A great treat to have her home! I should say. We're going to keep her as long as we can. Yes, I think she looks fine. Pamela, you remember Mrs. Vane." All she had to do was smile and nod, and murmur, "It's lovely to be here." But she felt remote.

The hotel that had used to seem so very grand had shrunk. All the women always averted their eyes as they passed the swinging half door to the bar but she looked coolly in this time, catching a glimpse of the painting over the bar, of the bottles and the polished wood; it was just a small place with hardly any mystery at all.

"Don't you want to sit nearer? There's a table over there."

"No, let's sit back here with the Cheavers, Mama." From here she could look at Rose and Wrenn without seeming to stare. Rose sat talking to the man on her left as though she enjoyed it. Her diamond earrings sparkled as she turned. They must have been a gift from Wrenn. Maybe Wrenn liked pierced ears. Did Rose really suppose that she would run over for a dish of reminiscences? She would say, "I remember how you schemed to get Wrenn to take you to the park; I remember seeing you together climbing down off the merry-go-round, and how you got him to take you riding the night before he left for school; as though it had happened just last summer. I remember more than that, I remember how you said 'can you and me be best friends.'"

But Wrenn . . . he was standing now, tapping on his glass with a spoon. He did look a little older; he had the same smile. He was looking straight at her as though he were talking to her. A funny thing to think when he was married and so was she, but she did think it. No one could know; no one could read her thoughts; they were safe inside herself. "Did you ever wonder about what other people are really thinking underneath what they are saying?" she had asked Alan once. He had scowled at the idea. "No, I can't say that I did; I'd feel that was none of my business." But how could you help it when you knew how different your own thoughts were from what came out in your words.

Why had she said that about its being like commencement tonight? That must have sounded sentimental and childish. Wrenn's speaking made her think of his commencement speech, that was all. He had read it to her in Papa's study, and it was about loyalty. And then he hadn't understood the way she felt about Papa.

The oratory floated in the close air of the banquet room like brightly colored balloons, threatening to fill the room and shut off all air.

Now Wrenn was introducing the next speaker. She liked watching him. How had he learned to speak so easily? But, of course, he was used to it now. Mama sent her the clipping about the case he had won for the rancher. She would like to see him try a case in court. What would he say if she went to him about a divorce?

The speeches were growing more and more fiery. Each speaker seemed to try to surpass the golden prophecies of the preceding one. Mr. Cheavers leaned over to her. "If they were offering Montana for sale tonight, everyone would sure buy!"

Pamela nodded, but she was watching Wrenn. He sat looking down at the table in front of him, smiling a little at something the speaker was saying. Once she saw him look at his watch. Now it was his turn to speak. He seemed to hesitate, then he looked across the room. His voice was quiet after the others, as though its very quietness questioned the truth of the prophecies the others had made.

"I want to tell you a rather ironic little story," Wrenn began simply. "Last winter I defended an old codger charged with manslaughter. He had graduated from Harvard back in the '60's and come west after the war to make his fortune. By the time I met him he had lost most of what he had made and, in spite of my efforts, he was convicted. I dreaded seeing him after the verdict, but do you know, he managed a rueful sort of smile and said, 'Morley, I might not have ended up this way if I'd stayed back east, but I'm still not sorry I came out here; it's the best country there is and I've had my nickel's worth of fun in it.'"

People laughed a little uncertainly, not quite sure about the point of the story. Wrenn's face had been serious, now he was smiling. It warmed Pamela and she was smiling back across the room at him. Did he see her?

". . . after all," he was saying, "the most precious ingredient that we have here in this Western country is the loyalty all of us feel. However the future turns out, nothing can diminish that spirit."

What had he said? One word detached itself from his sentences, touched a nerve. She couldn't remember the rest of the sentence. She tried to go back and fit it into context, but it was too late. She repeated the word to herself, compressing her lips so they wouldn't move. The word was loyalty, just as it was that other time, in the commencement speech. Why had he said it tonight? He must have said it for her, he must have wanted her to know that he remembered. Or had she drawn it out of him by saying that about his commencement speech? It was as though she and Wrenn had come quite close and spoken to each other across all these people. He was still talking. . . .

"As our guests journey on through the night our good wishes will go with them. We hope they will return before long to see many of the prophecies made tonight gloriously fulfilled." His voice had lost its quietness; it was like the other speakers' voices.

Pamela was slow standing up, not wanting to go just yet, but the celebration was over.

"Why, Pamela Lacey, I saw you come in with your mother and I couldn't believe my eyes. When did you come?" The room was full of bustle. The band was playing.

The visitors were anxious to get back to their train now, to the palatial private cars with the waiters pouring Scotch and bourbon. "Bourbon is the Western drink . . . no, I'll take it neat. We'll go through the pass over the divide early in the morning. Most beautiful scenery in the world; you'll think you're in the Alps. By tomorrow we'll be out of this god-forsaken desert country. Trees tomorrow; plenty of water in Washington."

"Half the town's out there, watching the train pull out. No wonder! They never see a main-line train in here. Oh, they will in time; no doubt about the future of the town, no doubt at all, but it may take time."

"Yes, sir, high-class people in there, mostly Eastern and Canadian; quite a few Southerners. Plenty of wealth already. That young Morley was a bright young fellow, handsome wife, born in Paris, she told me. Morley's pioneer stock. Next few years, folks from all over Europe will be taking up land out here, even Russians. The West's a regular melting pot."

When Maybelle and Pamela came out in the lobby they saw Charlie smoking a cigar, sitting in one of the big armchairs. He wore his soft gray hat and the coat and vest he wore every day, with trousers that didn't match.

"Charlie! looking like that with everyone in dinner clothes," Maybelle murmured. Pamela smiled at him, thinking that he looked the way she always thought of him.

"What's the matter? I wasn't in there. A man don't have to get a white tie on just to sit out here in the lobby. Besides, I thought you might like to be driven home."

"Charlie, everyone was there. I said to Pamela I wished you could have heard the speeches."

"I heard 'em, right here. A lot of hot air. To hear 'em talk you'd think the town was going to grow overnight. It's a wonder they can bear to leave it if they feel that way about it. I got the horse out in the alley so if you go out front, I'll drive around."

CHAPTER 4

Summer, 1912

For once Charlie Lacey was glad to be in town. It was so dry in the country the dust covered everything. The grass on the range was poor and the cattle showed it. He had even felt sorry for the damn fool homesteaders this afternoon as he drove back to town, sorry and disgusted with them at the same time. They looked so little grubbing away at their fields under all that sky, like grasshoppers or ants.

The house in town was cool because of the way Maybelle kept it shut up all day; it felt good. He took the paper out on the front porch and read while there was any light, but when it grew too dark he was content just to sit there with his feet on the railing and look out at the shadowed street. The hanging baskets hung still he noticed and those jingle-jangle prisms on the porch across the street made no sound at all.

The screen door whined as Maybelle stepped out on the porch. Her white dress stood out in the dark like the white petunias in the hanging baskets, and there was a flowery smell from the lotion she always rubbed on her hands after she did the dishes. "Charlie, do you know that Pam has been here since the end of April?"

"Well now," Charlie said. "That's not quite four months. She said when she came, she was going to make us quite a visit."

"She's upstairs writing a letter now," she said in a voice just above a whisper.

"To Alan?" Charlie asked.

"Well, I don't know, but I think so. She got another letter from him yesterday but she went right upstairs with it and didn't say a word till I asked her how he was."

"What did she say?"

"She said, 'Oh, he's fine. He's out at the lake with his family.' I wouldn't wonder if she hasn't been a little bit homesick for Buffalo and all; she's kind of moped around and been up in her room a lot, and last night she took a long walk after dark."

Charlie gave a noncommittal grunt, and relighted his cigar.

"Well, all I know is she's awfully closemouthed about him and his family and everything there. You'd think she'd be anxious to talk!"

Not since Maybelle used to talk to Charlie here on this porch about Pamela's birth had they been so close. They were like two conspirators together.

They heard Pamela's quick step on the stairs and were silent, Maybelle rocked busily and fanned herself with the newspaper Charlie had let fall to the floor when he finished with it. Charlie struck another match. The screen door's whine was cut short, it was opened so quickly.

"It is cooler out here, isn't it!" Pamela said. "I'm just going down to the corner to mail my letter." Her voice sounded light-hearted, almost eager.

[244]

"I don't think there's anything wrong, Maybelle; you just imagine it!" Comfortable relief heartened Charlie's tone.

"I'm sure I hope so. It's getting so that people wonder about her staying on. The girls were asking me at Shakespeare Club if she was going to spend the fall here."

"Let 'em ask; it's none of their business," Charlie pronounced. Then they saw her light dress moving through the dark as she came back. "I felt kinda sorry for those homesteaders next to the ranch . . ." Charlie began, to fill the silence as Pam came up the walk. She sat on the side of the steps as she used to do. Charlie forgot about the homesteaders. Down the street they heard the Marstens' front door close and an automobile backfired over on Higgins Avenue. "It must be nearly ten; about my bedtime," Charlie said.

"I know you've wondered," Pamela began. Her voice was too light in the absorbent dark of the summer night. It didn't sink in, the way it should. Her words hurried so Charlie had to lean forward to catch them all. "I'm not going back to Alan. I wrote him tonight."

This was what she had feared but now that she heard it said aloud Maybelle was shocked. "Why, Pamela Lacey, how dreadful!"

"What was the trouble, Pam?" Charlie asked gently. "Was he . . . he hasn't been unfaithful to you, has he?" Sweat came out on Charlie's forehead so he had to get his handkerchief out to wipe it off. It was hard to ask your daughter a thing like that, but that must be it; what else could it be? Alan Randell hadn't looked to him like a double-dealer, but you couldn't always tell about the quiet upright-looking ones. And even if he was . . . plenty of women stayed married to their men even if . . .

"No. Alan loves me, in his way." Again the light words bobbed on the surface of the listening dark, refusing to sink, like corks on the water.

"Well, then . . ." Maybelle's voice soothed a naughty child. "Now you've had a good vacation and you go back and everything will be fine. You've certainly been lonesome for him, I could see that," Maybelle went on, trying to turn her hope into a fact by the confidence of her tone.

"No, I've decided. I'm not going on living with Alan when I don't like it. I've only got one life and I'm not going to spend it that way."

She awed them into silence for a moment, she was so sure. Then Maybelle said, "But, Pam, what does Alan think?"

"He thinks I'm unreasonable and he's hurt and he keeps saying if I'd wait until we had children, but I'm so thankful we haven't any so I'm free. And he'll marry someone there in Buffalo and be happy; happier than he is with me."

Charlie mopped his forehead again and then sat holding the damp handkerchief between his hands. "Let's go into the house," he said sternly, and went in first, letting the door bang behind him. Maybelle hurried after him, but Pamela continued to sit on the step, leaning against the post, her hands clasping her knees. Now that she had made up her mind and written Alan, she felt quite calm. It would bother Mama and Papa and she was sorry about that, but it couldn't be helped.

"Pamela, Papa wants to talk to you," Mama said from the door.

Pamela smiled idiotically as she faced them in the front room. "That's all there is to say about it. I won't change my mind. I've been thinking it over ever since I left there, and I wrote him tonight that he can divorce me."

Maybelle sat down in a chair and began to weep. Charlie scowled at Pamela. His voice had lost its sternness.

"Haven't you been happy with him, Pam?"

"I haven't been really unhappy," she said, not smiling, her mouth firm, "but I haven't been sure that I was alive. I mean, my days didn't mean anything." She lifted her head and looked back at him. "It's just that it isn't enough. If you don't understand, I can't explain. I don't love him enough, he doesn't love me enough, though he thinks he does. And it isn't just that; it's that I don't do anything that really matters. I can look ahead and see what I'll be doing next year and five years from now and the day before I die and I can't stand it!" Her face contorted in an expression of such unexpected anguish they were silent for a moment.

"But what are you going to do, Pamela?" Her mother stared at her as though she had never seen her before.

"I'm going to get my old job back for a while . . . I'm not just sure what I'll do."

"Are you going to stay here in Brandon Rapids?" There was a cold edge to Maybelle's tone.

"For a while, unless you would rather I didn't."

"Of course we want you here, Pam." Charlie went over to her and put his arm around her, trying to pull her head down against his shoulder but she stood straight. Then Maybelle said, "But, Pam, I don't see what Alan has done!"

Pamela's shoulder drooped wearily. "He hasn't done anything, but I can't go on living with him." They seemed to stare at her, so did the room and the bookcase and the bay window where she had stood for the wedding reception. The room was too hot, too close. Mama was crying and Papa went over to comfort her.

"It's too hot to go to bed; I'm going to walk a few blocks," Pamela murmured. They didn't stop her. She had a sense of running although she wasn't.

Even this, going out of the house at ten o'clock at night would bother Alan. "Perhaps in Brandon Rapids, Pam, but hardly here in Buffalo. Why don't you walk around the garden. It's rather lovely, at least I think it is." Always that hypocritical deprecatory tone of voice. If he only once boasted and didn't care how it sounded . . . like, like Papa.

"Come with me, Alan. I feel like walking."

The little perplexed frown on his forehead, half amused, half irritated; the hesitancy. "I was going to do a little reading tonight."

"Oh, never mind," she had said and gone to walk in the garden, from the bed that had only white blooms to the blue bed, from there to the grape arbor and then over to the big beech tree and climbed up in it. After a while, Alan had come out on the porch and called and she had slid down quietly, ashamed suddenly of having him think her childish.

Most of the houses were dark now, or the lights had retired to the bedrooms on the second floor. It was so hot the windows were opened wide and even the shades were not pulled way down. At home, in Buffalo, that is, there were shuttered blinds on her bedroom windows that you could close by turning a little brass handle at the side. She had never tired of wheeling the blinds inward, watching the laddered shade fall upon the blue carpeting, if it was daylight; knowing the stripes of light that fell upon the lawn if it were night, but sometimes she felt sad as she swung them open to the morning, knowing how little they had closed in.

There was the time she had wakened in the night and clung to Alan in a panic of loneliness and said, "Love me, Alan, so I can't even think." And she could feel the embarrassment in his voice when he said:

"You get too high-strung, Pamela. It isn't good for you."

She had asked him why he loved her, one time, and he had talked about her hair and eyes, things that had only a little to do with her. He had said then that he loved her because she was so sincere and brave, and he talked about her saving his life. She was sick of remembering that, and it didn't mean anything, anyway. He didn't love her for any of her faults, but they were part of her; her impatience and her restlessness, and worst of all to Alan, her lack of system. She reached up and rubbed the back of her neck that began to feel tight and stiff again, the way it did sometimes sitting across the room from him, or having Sunday dinner at the Randells'. She moved her shoulders as though to free them.

To Alan love was something you felt for your wife. It was a satisfaction, never, never ecstasy. Rose's word, that she could never quite forget. But she couldn't say to Mama and Papa, "I'm leaving Alan because we find no ecstasy in our life together." And she hadn't been able to say it to Alan for a kind of shame and fear that he wouldn't quite know what she was talking about. They never said anything to each other that mattered; really mattered.

She had given up hoping to have him know her, or understand how she felt about . . . small, important things. Like the way the house here in Brandon Rapids and the house at the ranch had always divided her thinking. Maybe, if she could have told him about the night she stood outside the door and listened to his father and the other men in the cattle company and Papa, maybe then the fear that could still blow through her mind like a cold wind might be shut out forever, but she couldn't because Alan would want to go into all the business details and then he would pass judgment and decide, as he always did, with his father. He wouldn't even think about what it had meant to her. There was no use trying to tell him.

She had tried to see with his eyes. "Alan, when you were a child, what were you like? I don't mean what you looked like, I mean inside." For when you loved someone you tried to know and keep alive the tender child-part of him, so it wouldn't be completely lost.

"Well, I guess I was like most boys. . . ."

"No, you weren't," she had said sharply. "No one is really exactly like anyone else. Tell me something about yourself that you remember, something you thought or loved or were afraid of."

He had thought her silly, but finally he had remembered that he used to hate twilight on the way home from school in winter. "I used to run until I saw the lights behind the curtains in our house," he said.

"Did you?" she had said slowly, feeling his fear, but thinking how different they were. "I always liked the twilight, but out at the ranch it was best; it was like a lake that spread slowly down out of the sky. . . ." It had been so good to talk this way with Alan, but he had interrupted.

"By the way, Pamela, did you return Mrs. Rudyard's call, today?"

She had felt her hands raised foolishly, drawing the lake of twilight from the sky. "Yes." As a matter of fact, she had made the call.

It was all her fault; she had written Alan that. She had married him without loving him, because . . . her thoughts moved hesitatingly but some part of her mind held them to the line, made them go on toward the unpleasant truth . . . because she had been afraid. Afraid of this same street where everyone had someone to love and be loved by. Afraid of . . . her mind balked again and held back, but she nudged it ahead. Afraid of Papa's confident assurances that didn't turn out. She wasn't any more. She didn't put any faith in them, that was all. And what was there about this street to mind? There were other ways of living besides being married to someone. It needn't be a loveless life. Hadn't she loved . . . whisper it then, but let your lips and tongue move over the name . . . hadn't she loved Wrenn all this time? And Wrenn had as much as said that night, in the middle of his speech, all that he could say.

"You'll pay for what you done," Ruby said. All right, she would pay, whatever she had to, but she was not going back to Alan and the Randells and the red brick house in Buffalo. She had made a terrible mistake but there was no reason to go on with it. She would make a life for herself here, depending on no one but herself. Unconsciously, she was walking faster. There were no houses for a few blocks and the sweet dry prairie air came softly across empty space to her. She felt excited as she hadn't for a long time.

Walking so fast, she almost ran down the hurrying little figure scooting along so close to the edge of the sidewalk.

"Why, Miss Bell, good evening!" Pamela said as she recognized the seamstress who went out to sew.

"My, you give me a start! Hello, Pamela Lacey. I should call you by your married name." Bright curiosity sparkled in the dark. "And who should I meet but Pamela Lacey, out walking all by herself!" she would tell tomorrow, her mouth full of pins and her fingers moving swiftly over her sewing.

"No, just call me Pamela Lacey; that's fine," Pamela said, turning back now.

CHAPTER 5

"It would be better for you to get the divorce, Pamela. People are apt to judge from that who is in the wrong," Wrenn said, turning his pipe in his hand as he spoke, keeping the surprise he felt out of his voice.

"I am in the wrong," Pamela said, looking back at him so fiercely he glanced down at the papers on his desk. "I have no grounds. He has; he can plead desertion."

Wrenn let the moment's silence stand. As though Pamela felt it asked for some explanation, she said, in a lower voice, with the fierceness going out of her eyes and leaving only dullness there, "I can't go on living with him."

And he believed her. But how could this man, this Alan Randell, stand to let her go? "You have written him that you wanted it this way?"

"Yes, I told him he would be hearing from my lawyer in a few days." Her eyes moved away from him out the window. The clear north light allowed no softening of any line or expression; it outlined her head tipped back ever so little in its small flat-brimmed hat, her firm mouth and strong nose and brow. He had never noticed how much she looked like Mr. Lacey, but he remembered that color high on her cheeks. For a moment he was so drawn to her that all sense of the strangeness of this circumstance dropped out of his mind.

"I like your office. You can see both the river and the mountains from here," Pamela said into the silence.

"Yes, I like the view," he murmured.

And then Pamela stood up and held out her hand. "Thank you, Wrenn, for taking care of this for me."

"I'm only sorry, Pam, that you should have this experience."

Her mouth twisted a little and then folded more tightly together before she said, "Don't be; it was my own fault."

"I can hardly believe that," he said now in his professional lawyer's voice. "I think you are being unnecessarily noble in your attitude about asking no support, nothing at all. There must be certain things you would like to . . ."

"I wouldn't take anything, but don't make any mistake about this, Wrenn. Alan Randell is a fine and honorable person, a devoted husband. This is going to be very hard for him. He's going to feel it as a personal disgrace, but I can't help that."

"I shall get this letter off. . . ." She didn't look as though she had been through an ordeal, she looked very well. What did she feel? What would she do with her life? Pamela Lacey, divorced.

He walked with her to the elevator. But it was difficult to get back to work. He dictated two letters to Miss Ames and then let her go. He would write this letter out longhand first, anyway. It wasn't so much Pamela that bothered him as the tragedy of the thing; this was the first divorce he knew at first hand, the first divorce among their kind of people in Brandon Rapids. A devoted husband, she had said. Then why? If he were getting the divorce for her he would have gone into that, but as it was, he hadn't wanted to ask. When he did ask her how long she had been considering this move she had said that about the *Titanic*. "After I read about the *Titanic*, I decided." He remembered the porch party Pam gave for them years ago. That was the first time he had met Alan. They sat on the step and talked about Harvard. He had struck him then as a good sort, like the chaps you met back there, a little older than Pam. Pam might be pretty difficult to understand sometimes. By the time he left the office he was wondering if he couldn't act as mediator, perhaps. Pam was too fine a girl . . . woman, rather, to break up her marriage without more grounds than she seemed to have, unless she had chosen this way to protect her pride.

He stopped in at the Western Hotel on his way home. It had come to be a sort of meeting place for some of the younger men, though some of those who had gone to school back east had an idea of forming a Gentlemen's Club—perhaps a University Club. A good many of the wives and children were in the mountains this time of year and their husbands took their meals downtown. He thought with secret pleasure of Rose saying, "Go away for a whole month without you! Why, I'd die, Wrenn! Stephen is just as happy here and I'm happier!" Besides, Rose was having her baby in September.

It was pleasant to know nearly everyone in the lobby. Rose had wanted to settle back east, but not for him. If your family were pioneers in a place, you kind of wanted to stay there. As that man with the Development League had said . . . "It's a wonderful thing to be young with the country and grow with it." Wrenn Morley's mind had carved out a groove of thought that it slipped into with the same comfort that he slipped into his father's big leather spring rocker that was now his property.

Ken and Bill Wood and Stevens weren't there yet so he idled over his drink waiting for them. Just off the bar a poker game was going on. From where he stood he could see the cards fall.

Hank shook his head. "Been going on since two o'clock," he muttered.

Wrenn stepped toward the archway to see who was playing; Pam's father was one of them. He was playing with his hat tipped back on his head. His coat was off and his vest unbuttoned and he had a stub of a cigar in the corner of his mouth. But there was something slack about his face. For a darting uncomfortable instant he was standing with Pam in the doorway of Mr. Lacey's study. How could he ever have thought that Pam looked like her father?

"What are you trying to do, cut yourself in on a hand of

poker this time of day?" Matt Stevens clapped him on the shoulder.

Wrenn laughed. "Where in the world were you? I'd just about given you up."

It was stifling in the second-floor apartments at the Pioneer. Wrenn tied the white curtains into a knot in each window before he came to lie on top of the bed beside Rose.

"Thank heaven we'll be moved back home next week at this time. I remember there was always a breeze in that big front bedroom of mother's."

Rose was slow to speak, then she said, "I've loved this place. I sort of wish we weren't going to move." Perhaps this was the time to tell Wrenn how she dreaded going to live in the Morleys' big house with Mrs. Morley there, though she was a sweet old thing.

"I know, but you'll like it when we get there. I like the idea of Stephen growing up there and having my old room and I can use the barn to put the auto in."

"It will be different though," Rose said, moving her head so it rested on Wrenn's shoulder in spite of the heat.

"No it won't," he promised, smoothing down her dark curly hair. We can be just as much alone as we are here. Mother understands that; I've talked to her about it."

Rose smiled to herself in the dark. She could imagine Wrenn, putting it so gently that his mother wouldn't have any idea what he meant.

"I always hated being an only child there. Pam did. too. We used to talk about it when we were very young. Now Stephen won't have that," Wrenn said.

"What a funny thing to talk about . . . I mean when you were children."

"Well, we only lived a block apart, you know, and we played together all the time. Pam was in to see me today."

"At the office?"

"Yes, she's not going back to her husband."

"She isn't!" Shocked amazement vibrated through her voice.

"She doesn't say very much, but she was very positive about it. I thought, at least I hope, maybe I can persuade them to think it over, anyway."

"Is Pam going to stay here, then?"

"I imagine so."

"I thought Mrs. Lacey said she was so happily married and her husband was so well-to-do?" Would she like Pam living here again? Rose lay still thinking about it, Wrenn moved away and lay with his arms folded under his head, forming phrases in his mind. "Knowing Pamela Lacey as well as I do, I can understand. . . ." "Because I am such an old friend I am writing not only in the capacity of Mrs. Randell's legal adviser. . . ."

CHAPTER 6

Madame Guinard looked at her daughter as she sat on the low rocker by the window, nursing the baby. With the wholly dispassionate eye that Stephanie Guinard had always turned even on those she loved, she noted the beautifully rounded young breast framed in the fresh dimity ruffle of her peignoir, the dimpled elbow, and the sulky charm of the face bent over the baby. When Rose pouted that way she looked like a child.

"I never will be asked to join the Shakespeare Club now, with Pamela Lacey in it!"

"Is she in it, or her mother?" Madame Guinard asked.

"Oh, she is, too. As soon as they knew she was going to stay here they asked her, of course."

Madame Guinard rocked and looked around the front bedroom. The red and blue panes of glass in the turret end of the room where the bassinet stood overlaid the fern-gray pattern of the carpet with oriental blossoms, bold colored in that mauve and blue bedroom. The high-backed walnut bed was covered with a Marseilles spread, and Madame Guinard thought of the town in France that she had known so well as a girl. That the very finest spread made in a certain factory in Marseilles should grace her daughter's bed in Brandon Rapids, Montana, pleased her. The embossed pattern of the spread, so cunningly woven by those intricate machines, seemed to make a design out of the happenings of her own life. And a design was better than to have all the things that had happened lying higgledy-piggledy in your memory; it made order out of chaos and she liked order.

Madame Guinard's glance came back to the baby who was her grandchild.

"I wouldn't let the Shakespeare Club worry me, Rose," she said. "What do they do? Gossip and eat, no doubt. Very little Shakespeare!" The gesture of her hands made light of the Shakespeare Club and all its activities.

"Oh, Mother, it isn't just that! It's that Wrenn Morley's wife should be asked to join. I mind it because of Wrenn. Mother Morley says one blackball can keep you out, and, of course, Mrs. Lacey has always been able to do that."

Madame Guinard made a face. "Don't be a goose, Rose. Your husband will go so far his wife won't need to worry about any invitation. They'll be begging you to join before you know it."

"And I'll refuse when they do ask me."

Madame Guinard shrugged. "Well, then!"

The sleeping child's mouth dropped away from the breast in contented satiety. Rose carried her over to the bassinet that had been Wrenn's as a baby. Her lips lost their pout as she bent over her. "I don't care, really, only I don't know that I like having Pam Lacey come back here to live." Quick color sprang like a rash over her neck and face. Madame Guinard's shrewd black eyes caught that color and the uncertainty in Rose's voice, but she chose not to comment. Instead she said something to please her.

"You're not so plump as you were after Stephen was born."

But watching her daughter, she remembered Pamela going past the shop the other morning. You had to look at that girl when you saw her: something about the way she held her head. You could put any old hat on her and it would take on style. Madame Guinard glanced at Rose's neck that was creamy white with a necklace crease at the base and remembered the Lacey girl's thin column of neck with cords showing through the skin like the wires of a hat frame under velvet; not really showing, only enough to give the velvet form and line. The way she walked was a thing to see, too, not the little hurried steps women often used, nor any languid strolling, but as though she liked walking. She had gone to the door and smiled at Pamela. The way Rose felt had nothing to do with her own likes or dislikes.

"Good morning, Madame Guinard," Pamela had said, not the way her mother always did, remembering she was a milliner, nor as though she thought of her as Rose's mother but just for herself. She didn't look sorry about her divorce, either. After Pamela had gone by she had watched her, wondering why Wrenn Morley had chosen Rose instead of Pamela. In her own mind Stephanie Guinard always allowed her thoughts complete freedom without any sense of guilt if they sometimes penetrated a little far or a little critically into other peoples' lives; it was the only thing that made living alone in this small town tolerably interesting.

"There's Wrenn, now, just turning the corner," Rose cried out. She tied the sash on her dressing gown more tightly, touched the stopper of her perfume bottle to her neck and hair and stooped to look in the mirror. There was no trace of a pout in that face now, only eagerness, Madame Guinard noticed.

"I'll run along, Rose." Madame Guinard gathered in the extension neck of her black satin bag and snapped the silver top securely down on it.

"Won't you stay for dinner, Mother? I wish you would," Rose said, but she hardly thought what she was saying as she hurried by, her taffeta skirt under the soft Swiss gown rustling as she went, and Madame Guinard heard her running down the stairs.

There was no doubt about Rose's love for Wrenn. That was it! That was what Rose had that Pamela Lacey didn't have, perhaps. Love . . . not for the human race, nor even her mother nor her children so completely, but no, only for one man. Madame Guinard nodded her head with her thoughts. It was better, that, than a talent or beauty for a woman, except that if a man threw it away, or if he died, what was left?

Madame Guinard sighed a little as she went over to look at the baby again. She lingered a few minutes to enjoy this large sunny bedroom before she went back to her small quarters above the store. Besides she wanted to give Rose and Wrenn a little time. She would like to stay for dinner tonight, but it was always a little stiff with Mrs. Morley there. Rose always invited her when she stopped in, but sometimes she seemed relieved that she didn't stay.

"Hello, Mother Guinard." Wrenn was standing at the foot of the stairs, his arm around Rose. "Why do you go just as I come?" She could feel Wrenn's liking for her through his carefully reproachful tone. "My other mother," he often said, but it made her lips twist ever so slightly. He tried a little too hard.

"I had to come to see your young daughter. Be sure you don't spoil her," she told him. Always the same tone of voice: merry, bridling, gaily admonitory. But already, she could feel their attention leaving her.

"Good-by," she called, tilting her head to one side, smiling airily, but at the same moment a wave of loneliness choked her.

"Good-by, Mother Guinard, and don't you dare run off next time just as I come," Wrenn said. He played a thing too long.

"Good-by, Mother. You call me tomorrow, and see if you can make a sailor cap for Stephen, won't you?"

Now she wished she had stayed. If Rose had just asked her again . . . but Rose was always saying how nice it was when Mrs. Morley was invited out and she and Wrenn were alone.

She stopped to talk to Stephen, who had a rope around the iron post of the fence and was playing horse.

"Don't you want to come down and have dinner with Grandma, Stevie?" she asked with sudden eagerness.

The little boy turned his face up to her with Wrenn's smile, but he shook his head. "I'm going to eat with my mama and papa and we're going to have pie. Blueberry pie!"

She would just have an ice at the BonTon and maybe a cup of tea when she got home. She really didn't feel like having a regular dinner tonight.

CHAPTER 7

1914

Pamela tried not to look at the Morleys' house every morning as she passed it on her way to the hardware store, or she tried to glance up at it and not think about Rose and Wrenn. She told herself it was childish, just because they lived so close. When she was in Buffalo she hadn't thought about them, hardly at all. The children were different. The first year she was home little Cora was born and she had kept track of the baby carriage out on the porch. Stephen started to school that first year, too. He was a shy little boy and it took him a long time to make friends, but now sometimes he waited for her and walked down to the next corner with her. She had taught him to call her Aunt Pam.

But there was enough in the office of Sewall's Hardware Store to occupy her. In these two years she had quietly taken over the office work and all the ordering of bolts, nuts, screws, of barbed wire, sheet-iron stoves, and washtubs. And she had put in a line of cheap cut-glass dishes and plain china for hand painting. To strangers she was "that bright young woman in the office." To those who had always known her, she was Pam Lacey. The Randell had been dropped off like an old bent nail, no longer serving any purpose. Mr. Sewall did less and less about the store and left more and more to Pamela. Jed Parsons, who was fifty himself, and had been with Sewall for twenty-two years, complained about it to his wife, but filling out an order for something out of stock so bothered him that he always took it to Pam to check in the end. And it was Pamela who talked with the homesteaders who came in to buy their first supplies, and back again to buy more, this time on credit.

"Mr. Sewall is out just now, perhaps I can help you," the interview usually began and the homesteader found himself telling the young woman at the desk exactly where his land was, how much he had done, what luck he had had with crops, while the clear blue eyes took in every detail of his clothes: the faded unironed shirt, the patched overalls, the broken-down shoes that were never intended to be worn in relentless clay mud, before they came back to the sunburned face and crusted eyes and sugar lips. Sometimes Pamela Lacey made a curious request before charging a bill of goods. Sometimes, she said, "Bring your wife in with you before we finish this list; she may need something else." And often when she came in . . . the music teacher from Newark, New Jersey, or the Methodist minister's wife, or the tuberculous young woman who had taken a homestead because the life was so healthy . . . Pamela tried to convince her that she should sell out and go back home. "You know you're going to have to carry all your water! . . . It's too hard a life. You can't make a go of it without more help." But usually the determined homesteaders didn't believe her.

Once Mr. Sewall interviewed a homesteader at his big desk across from Pamela's. When he was through he said to her, "Open an account for this man, Pamela." Pamela picked up her pen and wrote on the sheet in front of him, "I wouldn't do that if I were you."

Mr. Sewall scowled and said, "Here, I'll do it." When the homesteader had gone off with his goods, Mr. Sewall came back to the office. "I liked the cut of his jib, Pamela. What made you say that?"

Pamela adjusted the sheet of paper in her typewriter. Her mouth pressed together and twisted ever so little to the side. "I don't know, something about his voice; the way he talked. He had too big plans."

"God Almighty, Pamela, that's what this country needs!"

"Men who can take a chance!" Pamela said, mimicking his enthusiasm. "Men who promise more than they can do." And there was something about the pale sharp look of her eyes that kept Mr. Sewall from saying any more. When the bill was still unpaid a year and a half later Pamela had written across the top, "Just what this country needs," and left it on his desk.

It startled kindly old Mr. Sewall. He wondered if Pamela Lacey was one of those suffragettes. There wasn't an easier-going man anywhere than Charlie Lacey; he'd give you the shirt off his back.

Pamela paid board at home. At first, Maybelle had said, "You don't need to do that while you're here."

"But I'm going to stay here; live here, Mama."

"You'll find Mr. Right one of these days and be off, I know!" Maybelle said, trying not to see Pamela's unsmiling face. Charlie said, "No, Pam, this is your home; I'm not going to have you paying board." But Pamela paid the same amount that Maybelle's roomer had paid, plus five dollars a week for meals. She put the new bills in an envelope on the sideboard under the cut-glass vinegar cruet and the next day the money had disappeared.

As Maybelle said to Cora Morley, "We don't want her to pay anything, but it makes her feel independent." Cora duly reported to Rose and Wrenn at breakfast the next day. "That's the way she was about her divorce," Wrenn said. "I tried not to charge her anything. I told her I was glad to be of any help, I felt so sorry that she needed me in that capacity, but she insisted."

Cora Morley shook her head. "Not many women would feel

that way. Well, I've always said Pamela Lacey was one girl in a million."

Rose broke her toast in small pieces and ate it without butter because she was gaining again. She had meant to keep back part of the grocery money this month to pay for that suit at the Emporium, but maybe she wouldn't after all, though goodness knows, that was the way Mother Morley had always managed. Mother Morley had said long ago, "I wouldn't bother Wrenn too much about the bills, dear. Men don't understand that you have to have certain things."

Rose rang the bell for Hazel to clear the table. "Pamela manages to dress very well, anyway," she said.

Pamela Lacey was invited everywhere. "Pam, dear, I wish you didn't have that old job, I wanted to ask you to my card party." "Pam, we won't have dinner till seven so you'll have plenty of time to change." "And I've asked you, Pam, for that new young lawyer who's moved to Brandon. He's unmarried, and I hear he's very smart!"

"Pam, will you come to dinner, Thursday evening? I've invited Rose and Wrenn Morley, but you don't mind them, do you?"

"Of course not. What a funny idea!"

"Well, I just meant . . . I remembered he was an old beau of yours."

"Of course, I'll come." Pamela's voice had a way of sounding very clear and high and as though she spoke in an empty room to test the sound of her own voice.

A hostess enjoyed giving her out-of-town guest a quick description of Pamela . . . "married a wealthy Easterner . . . he built her a beautiful home in Buffalo, and then, my dear, she came back . . . divorced, nobody really knows why except maybe Wrenn Morley . . . some people say she was in love with Wrenn, but he married the daughter of a milliner here in town . . . you'll meet them tonight. Oh yes, they're terribly happy."

At such dinners, Rose, who loved food, was seldom aware of what she ate because she was so much more aware of Pam across the table, and more aware of Wrenn than Pam. She knew when he put back his head and laughed at a funny story Pam was telling about the hardware store. Rose thought with resentment that Pam always made her job sound as though it were full of amusing happenings and as though she, herself, were quite a businesswoman. It was at Dr. Nugent's that she heard Pam say to Wrenn, "You are going to run for representative, aren't you, Wrenn?" They were waiting for the tables of bridge to be arranged and everyone was standing around. Rose was talking to Les Keller, but she heard Pam just the same. Wrenn laughed and said, "Do you think I ought to?" "Of course, I do, Wrenn. We ought to have someone in the legislature who knows it isn't always true that the sun rises in the East." He had laughed again and said, "That would be hard to prove, don't you think?" "No. Not for you, Wrenn," Pam had said. Rose hadn't heard any more but it seemed to her when she glanced across the table at Wrenn that he was still thinking about what Pam had said. He certainly wasn't thinking about the cards.

"I heard Pam talking to you about running for state representative, Wrenn," Rose said that night when she was undressing. "I didn't know you were thinking about it." She couldn't keep an injured tone out of her voice.

"It's mostly talk. Some of the fellows think I should. Would you like to spend part of the winter at the capital?"

"How did Pam hear about it?"

"I suppose down at the store."

Rose thought about it while she brushed her hair and went in to see that Stephen and Cora were covered. She tiptoed downstairs through the dark house to turn off the tap she heard dripping in the pantry sink, and stood a few minutes at the front door looking out at the arc light above the street, thinking about Pam and Wrenn. If Wrenn did run and won, it would be spoiled for her because Pamela Lacey had urged him to do it. She wished Pam had never come back here.

"Rose, anything the matter?" Wrenn was waiting for her at the top of the half-flight of stairs.

"Just that old cold water faucet again. I must . . ." He put his arm around her and they stood together in the dark so close she heard the beating of his heart as though it were her own. He was so dear to her; what if she should lose him? What if something should happen to him? An irrational fear caught at her mind, chilling it like a sudden draft. When Wrenn loosened his arm gently she tightened hers. "Wrenn, are you all right?" she whispered.

"Why, of course, dear, but we might go on to bed instead of catching our death of cold out here, don't you think?"

Under his teasing words the fear disappeared and she could say lightly, "Don't run for representative, Wrenn. Don't let's change anything."

CHAPTER 8

1916

The hardware store smelled of iron, tin, and dusty floors, freshly mopped. Pamela washed her hands at the single faucet in the back storeroom and took off the paper cuffs she tied over her sleeves each morning. If she could hold on until she said good night to Mr. Sewall and walked around his cuspidor for the hundredth time, and spoke to Ben Kearns who wasn't quite right but right enough to mop floors and look at her with a simple loose leer when she passed, she would be out of the store where she could take a deep breath. As she went through the store she let her eyes run over the counters like fingers, barely touching the nails, twopenny, fourpenny, tenpenny; then the screws, brass and nickel-plated. Hinges came next.

"Night, Miss Lacey!" Ben called out. It had taken him all this time.

"Good night, Ben," she said again and reached the door.

But the street was the same as it always was, except that it was cooler than last month, and the sun was farther down behind the four stories of the Western Hotel. Farnhams had taken their awning down for winter and the Emporium was showing women's winter coats. The BonTon had Halloween decorations in their window and Hagemans' shoe store displayed handsome new cloth-topped button shoes.

"It's just a deadly little Western town," she said aloud in her mind. How had she let herself be caught here like this? She had always expected better things . . . great things, really, of herself. And she hadn't done them. People in Brandon Rapids had been surprised, too, when she came back here to live; when she took back her job at the hardware store. They had expected better things for her, too, their voices said, their lingering look, but by now they took her living here as a matter of course. How quickly people, your friends, accepted your fate for you, she thought. How quickly you began to accept it for yourself; which was worse.

Half a block down the street, Bunny Welch stepped out of the bank building where he had his insurance office. He was waiting to walk home with her. Bunny, who lived with his mother and was a good, sober young man, inclined to plumpness, with a mouth curved like a girl's and moist brown eyes that seemed to stick to you when he looked at you. Bunny Welch had come to Brandon Rapids after she had left, but by the time she returned he was one of the town's most promising young men. Bunny had come from Utah, "but not a Mormon, oh my no, not since they gave up polygamy!" he always said, rolling his moist brown eyes. Bunny was twenty-eight.

He stood there smiling, calling out greetings to the other men who came out of the bank building. Older men liked Bunny Welch; they felt he had "good sense." Older women invited Bunny for dinner when they invited Pamela Lacey and said, "Wouldn't it be a nice thing if Bunny and Pam . . ." But Pamela just looked bored when they tried to tease her about him. Still, Pamela Lacey must be twenty-nine or thirty; she wouldn't have too many more chances. Feminine eyes looked wise.

"Hello, Bunny." That absurd name irritated her. Anybody who would let himself be called Bunny!

"You know what I told you about that German submarine in the Newport harbor?" he began. "Well, right outside the three-mile limit she began sinking vessels!" He tapped his newspaper significantly. "We'll be in the war, you mark my words!"

It was not necessary to comment when Bunny expounded on the news. This was the way he would orate to his wife, Pamela thought without amusement. They walked along together, Bunny seizing her elbow and helping her across the street at the corner. Bunny would go all the way up Prospect Avenue and linger at their walk and hope to be asked in for dinner. Mama would love nothing better, and hurry around and put on a fresh cloth and open a jar of pickles or brandied peaches.

"And if there's a war, I'll have to go. The married fellows are the lucky ones; if it comes to a draft they'll take the bachelors first." She wouldn't rise to that.

"If war is declared, I think I'll volunteer as an ambulance driver," she said.

"You don't even know how to drive!" he scoffed like a boy in school who couldn't stand to have a girl get ahead of him, she thought; a fat boy.

"I'm going to buy a car in the spring," she said coolly. "I drove Alan's . . . my husband's car quite a few times."

The mention of her husband reminded him of her divorce which he tried not to remember because it bothered his mother so much. He made his tone very jocular. "I can't wait to see you going down Main Street at sixty miles an hour! I've been think-ing of buying a Maxwell, myself," he added. The talk of cars took them all the way to J. B. Moore's house on the corner of Prospect. Lucy Moore was coming down her walk.

"I'm going to keep Cora Morley company," she told them. "With Wrenn and Rose away so much of the time, she's left alone a good deal."

"I guess Wrenn Morley's asked to speak everywhere since he was elected representative," Bunny said.

"I imagine so," Pamela answered.

"Yes, sir, he's going a long ways. The barber was saying to someone in the chair just yesterday, that he expected to see him governor of the state some day."

Pamela made an assenting noise. But it was Rose she thought of instead of Wrenn, Rose as the wife of the governor. She could see her in an evening dress the color of a pomegranate, and long white gloves, standing in a receiving line. She wasn't listening to Bunny until he said, "I see your dad's home." Then the old childlike rush of eagerness crowded out the thought of Rose and she walked a little faster.

Charlie sat forward on his chair on the porch. "Well, Pam, I've been sitting here waiting for you!" His big voice boomed out across the street. "It's getting cold, too. Hello, young man!"

"Good-by, Bunny," she said quickly and turned up the walk, glad to be rid of him, but he followed to talk to Charlie.

"I thought you weren't coming till tomorrow, Papa?"

"Oh, I move right along when I get started home," Charlie said. He was in high spirits. "I've had about all the traveling around I want. With the war ahead of us I want to get back to the ranch and start raising beef." He sounded full of business again, as though he had plans and were going to carry them out.

"The way it looks to me," he said, tipping his chair back and bracing himself against the front railing, "Wilson can't help but change his tune. If he don't, the whole country'll be up in arms."

And Bunny followed right along. "That's what I was telling Pam on the way home." What pleasure men got out of repeating their earlier statements and talking about things that didn't concern them personally, Pamela thought as she went on in the house, without inviting Bunny to stay.

Charlie took forty winks after supper, sitting in his chair on the porch. When Pamela came out after the dishes he was sound asleep and his heavy breathing made the dark lonely. She thought of putting the afghan over Papa, it was so chilly on the porch, but she didn't do it. It made him seem too . . . less strong, as though he had changed from the Charlie Lacey who used to throw his saddle down anywhere out on the prairie and sleep comfortably. She had always been proud of his hardness.

She went to the library tonight because he had told Bunny she was going out. Where else was there to go in Brandon Rapids in the evening, alone that is? Tonight, the Pioneers met, but it made her squirm to see Mama presiding, and she had typed the report that Mr. Sewall was giving. There were the moving pictures, but Bunny might go by himself. Douglas Fairbanks was in the picture and a Pearl White serial, but even if Bunny wasn't there, there was something shameful about slipping into the movies alone at her age. If she were older, Mrs. Moore's age, or younger, but at her age she felt self-conscious sitting there alone when the lights were turned on. Everyone her age was married and sitting with her husband in the evening, going up to give the baby a drink of water or tuck him in. "Do come over some evening, Pam, we don't do anything," but if she went they were surprised, and she was bored.

Going to the library in the evening was safe, only it closed at nine. Still you could walk home slowly afterward with books under your arm. And if you met someone you knew, you could say, "I'm on my way home from the library."

Once, she had met Wrenn there. He was bending over the table, looking up something in an old newspaper. She stopped by the corner of the table and said, "Hello, Wrenn," so quietly no one could hear. The color had rushed into his face and he had looked glad.

"Hello, Pam."

"You look as though you were doing research," she said quickly.

"Yes, you turn up some queer bits in these old newspapers." How queer and stilted they were; worse than when they were in their teens.

"You always did haunt this place, Pam. Do you still read poetry?"

"Yes. Don't you?"

[268]

"I'm afraid I don't very often. Briefs have been more my reading diet."

As though that were the reason, not Rose! If she and Wrenn had married, they could have shared so many things. Did he ever think of that?

"I know you've been busy, Wrenn. You've done so well." What a stupid flattering thing to say! She had mocked at herself as she said it.

"Well, I must go. Cora's had croup and Rose gets worried about her." Now he was acting married and calling on Rose's name as though he was afraid he would forget her. "Good night, Pam. It was nice to see you here." Nice! His face was changing; it was stronger, less boyish. People spoke of how stern he looked in that murder trial last spring. He had made a strong speech about the law being the modern vigilante organization and won the case. They said Rose went to court every day and sat in the back to hear him. People said how devoted she was. Maybe they said she was there, too, once, way over at the side of the courtroom. Rose had seen her there. Rose had smiled, but quickly and then looked serious again the self-conscious way people did at funerals.

Tonight, Wrenn wasn't at the library. Only the librarian sitting under the green-shaded lamp, as neat as one of her own library cards, making order itself seem to be life, and a boy and girl of high-school age sat over at the long table, whispering. There was someone in a white dress in the aisle between the bookstacks where she, herself, had once fled.

Pamela walked slowly along the bookshelves, reading titles to herself. The library was like the fruit room at home, she thought. Filled with preserves, preserved love and romance, and jellied courage and spiced adventure. If you couldn't get fresh, if it was out of season, out of reach, you took these. She couldn't touch a novel tonight. She wanted fresh fruit. She didn't want to read about somebody else. Pamela Lacey, what was happening to her? All day, she could hardly find herself. She couldn't go on like

[269]

this: working at the hardware store, walking home with Bunny Welch, eating supper with Mama and Papa, facing the evening . . .

"Are you finding what you want, Pamela?" the librarian called out, just as she had that other time.

"Yes, thank you." But she wasn't. She never had. What had she wanted? Quick color lined her skin as she stood there alone by the shelves. She took down Whitman's *Leaves of Grass* from the poetry shelf so the librarian could see that she had a book in her hand, and bent her flushed face over it. She had read it in the first place because of the title. . . . Grass, bluejoint, buffalo, stem grass. Slim said grass was what made a ranch. Whitman called grass the beautiful uncut hair of graves. Indian graves on the prairie, pioneer graves of people who came out because they wanted something they didn't have, but they never found it.

She liked the roll and push and surge of Whitman's poetry, and the ideas, daring ideas people in Brandon Rapids didn't own to having. Only Rose did. Way back when she was a girl she had said that about ecstasy. Wrenn didn't need to read poetry now, perhaps. Pamela turned the page quickly and formed the words she read with her lips to keep her mind on them.

> *Prodigal, you have given me love, therefore*
> *I to you give love! Oh unspeakable passionate love.*

Not the kind of love Alan gave her; she gave Alan. . . . It was better to come back here and live alone. She turned the pages with a loud slapping sound. She felt mean and poor in her own eyes. Her love hung heavy on her like her own breasts and as useless. She ran over the printed words as though hunting a hiding place for her thoughts.

> *Where sun-down shadows lengthen over the limitless and lone-*
> *some prairie,*
> *Where herds of buffalo make a crawling spread of the square*
> *miles far and near,*

Where the hummingbird shimmers, where the neck of the long-
lived swan is curving and winding,
Where the laughing-gull scoots by the shore, where she laughs
her near-human laugh . . .

This was better. This was like being out at the ranch.

There was a rustle in the library. The boy and girl went out holding hands. The white dress in the stacks belonged to Letitia Adams. She spoke to Pamela as she went by, overpleasantly, overeagerly, carrying a red-bound novel in her hand, preserved love to feed on.

Pamela pushed Whitman back on his shelf and hurried out of the library. She should never have come back here to this town. There was no life here for a girl alone, once you were grown. She had thought it would be fine to be back here, with an independent job, but it wasn't. It was tight and lonely and . . . somehow humiliating. There was nothing to keep her here, really. Why did she stay? If she could go out to the ranch to live, but there wasn't enough to live on. She wouldn't like the ranch alone. . . .

If she took the money she was saving for a car, she could go away. She could still fit herself for something, even at twenty-nine. She could volunteer to the Red Cross for overseas work. She was strong and tireless and she could work. Eagerness leaped in her mind like a sudden wind. And she would be doing something that was really needed. It was unthinkable that she should go on here at her little job when she could be helping in Europe. That was it, the need was so great; she was going because she was needed, not because this place was intolerable. She wasn't tied down by a husband or children, she was free to go where her country, well, if not her country, Belgium or France needed her. If the United States did go to war then all the more reason.

When she met Mary Marsten and her husband, she forgot to say she was on her way home from the library. She just said hello and hurried on, impelled by her own racing thoughts.

CHAPTER 9

1918

At first, the war had seemed far away from the sagebrush prairies and the ranchlands that ran up into the foothills of the Rocky Mountains; a long way from the Western towns that were rapidly outgrowing their two-story false-front buildings on Main Street, and the easy money days when no one picked up any coppers he got back in his change. The war was way off overseas between those foreign countries that were always harboring grudges against each other anyway. It might mean something to those Eastern cities but out West it was only a speck so far off on the prairie that you could hardly tell whether it was man or beast or a clump of sagebrush. But while you watched, that speck came so near and loomed so large its shadow fell dark as the wing of a hawk flying over your own ranch.

Ranch hands, loose-jointed, easygoing fellows who hardly ever read the papers, were saying after supper at the cookhouse, getting out their Bull Durham to roll a cigarette, or taking the toothpick out of their mouths and caching it in their vest pocket, "Guess I'll be joining the army. Figger I'll leave my saddle right here till I get back." And they were gone without a thought to the fall roundup.

Slim went. He came in to town and stopped at the hardware store to say good-by to Pamela, as set up as though he'd been drinking, but he hadn't. He had promised Ruby again that he wouldn't touch a drop.

"Where's Ruby? Didn't she come with you?" Pamela asked.

Slim shook his head and pulled at his left ear. "She says she's got more important things to do." His mouth cracked into a grin. "She's a daisy!"

Pamela remembered the last time Ruby had come into town. She had whirled around on her swivel desk chair to see Ruby standing in the doorway of the hardware office. She wore her usual housedress with the jacket of her suit over it and a faded green scarf tied over her head. After talking a while Pamela had said, "Stop over at our house, Ruby, and I'll be there a little after six. I'll phone Mama."

Ruby's mouth had twitched. "I see myself sittin' and drinkin' afternoon tea with Maybelle Lacey."

But when she was almost home Pamela had seen Ruby from way down the street. She was sitting on the steps to the porch, and she was alone. She sat as she did at the ranch, shoulders slumped, head back a little, looking down the street as though it were the field she saw from the ranch. No town woman sat like that. When Ruby had seen Pamela coming up the walk, she had made no sign, just waited.

"Didn't you tell Mama you were here?" Pamela asked.

"Nope. But if I know your ma, she's looked out and seen me."

"Come on in the house, Ruby," Pamela said.

"You came together!" Maybelle said. "How do you do, Ruby." Mama's tone was always like this when she spoke to Ruby or Slim or someone from the ranch. It grated on Pamela. "I'm so sorry Mr. Lacey is out of town on business."

"I was hopin' Charlie might get back before I left," Ruby said.

Dinner was just as Pamela had known it would be. Mama talked too much, about nothing that would interest Ruby, calling Papa Mr. Lacey and in that same tone of voice. Ruby said almost nothing and ate with a wooden face, her eyes darting out quick and stealthy to see whether Pam was using her fork or a spoon.

"I trust you aren't accustomed to very hearty meals at night, Ruby. When Mr. Lacey is away, Pamela and I prefer just soup and salad and a dessert." Mama knew very well Ruby wouldn't like a fruit salad. There were almonds in it, and, at first, Ruby took them out and put them on the saucer of her tea cup.

"Oh," she said suddenly, "them's nuts; I thought they was pits."

[273]

"Are you in for some shopping, Ruby?" Mama asked, ignoring Ruby's remark.

"No, ma'am, I ain't," Ruby said, offering nothing more.

When Ruby had finished, she stood up. "Thank you for the victuals," she said stiffly.

Pamela wished Ruby had come; it seemed a long time since she had seen her.

"Slim's a damn fool," Charlie Lacey said at dinner that night, swearing in the presence of his women, which he didn't usually do. "He's too old in the first place. The army doesn't want forty-two-year-olds. He'd do more for his country if he stayed home and raised cattle. As far as the ranch goes, Ruby can do everything he can and then some."

Bunny Welch went off to officers' training camp, proud now that he had decided to go. He drove Pamela out along the river to Harpers' woods before he left and told her that in times like these he realized that her divorce didn't really matter, and asked her to marry him. They sat on the old wooden picnic table where Room 21 of the Brandon Rapids High School had once spread their pies and cakes and little French tarts.

"Oh, Bunny, I'm sorry, but I couldn't," Pamela said, looking off along the shore, trying to keep the horror she felt at the thought out of her voice. She wondered how she had ever told Alan Randell she would marry him.

Three clerks from Sewall's Hardware left for the army.

"For a time, there, I was afraid I was going to lose you, Pamela," Mr. Sewall said. "It was a lucky thing for me that your mother had her heart attack. I'd be losing my right hand if you were to go. You stay by me, Pamela; you won't be sorry."

Pamela smiled faintly and clattered away at her typewriter so that she couldn't hear any more.

The world needed more wheat, more beef, and banks became attentive, even gracious, to the rancher who needed a loan to buy more seed or one of those big unwieldy combines, or more cattle. Charlie Lacey bought a hundred head of feeder calves. When hands were scarcer than hens' teeth he managed to pick up a crew of six men, all of them over fifty, east of Main Street at places like the Maverick. Ruby's mouth twisted way over to the side of her cheek, her nostrils dilated and she looked at Charlie from under lowered eyelids when he brought the men out.

"There you are, Ruby, you always said it wasn't worthwhile cooking unless you had a crew."

"You don't call *them* a crew, do you?" Ruby snorted. "A bunch of drunken bums is what they are."

"You're darn right they're a crew. I never picked a deadbeat to work for me yet."

Charlie had no time for buying for the livestock commission these days; he was going to be back on the selling end.

Every woman in Brandon Rapids who could knit was doing her bit. Maybelle Lacey could sit in the parlor and knit, even with her bad heart. Only one woman had turned in more sweaters to the Red Cross and that was Madame Guinard, but then, she was French. The Shakespeare Club rolled bandages at their meetings now, while only one person read. They had given up refreshments to support Mr. Hoover's conservation program, so they accomplished a good deal. Of course, if someone did have a box of candy or a plate of cookies . . . but that was different from the days when they used to serve timbales and tortes and Lady Baltimore cake in an effort to outdo each other.

Everyone was busy; everyone was organized . . . to knit, to make speeches, roll bandages, collect money, staff the Red Cross and Soldiers' Home Protective Society offices. Everyone wore buttons, badges, and special uniforms and murmured the same slogans.

Mrs. Wrenn Morley was asked to head the Red Cross. She demurred at first, and then accepted.

"You think I should, don't you, Wrenn?" she asked at dinner one night when they ate without the children or Mother Morley.

"After all, Mother Morley is here to keep an eye on the children and I do have good help as long as Hazel is here. Of course, it will be a terrific job and a big responsibility, but I just think I ought to do what I can. There's going to be a Soldiers' Home Protective Society, too, but that's not as big a thing . . ." Rose's eyes sparkled. She grew more handsome all the time, Wrenn thought. But in that high-necked dress, with her added weight, she looked almost formidable. It was like a disguise that only he could see through to the slim young girl he had married.

"I think you're just the one for the job," he said, thinking how naturally things fell into order around Rose: the house, the attic that he remembered used to be a catchall when he was a boy, his own drawers, underwear in neat piles, boiled shirts wrapped in tissue paper, collar buttons, cuff links, everything in its place. Bills, even items from the newspaper she thought he should see, clipped and laid under the weight on his desk. Besides, it would be good for Rose to be busy while he was in the army.

Rose took a spoonful of the blancmange and tasted it with relish. "I suggested that they ask Pamela; she would be fine for it, and her life seems so sort of dull."

"Pam has her job, of course. She practically runs the place, you know," Wrenn said. He was never quite sure how Rose felt about Pam.

"I think she could manage that part, but Pam doesn't get along too well with people. The Red Cross will have to use everybody and she's so apt to seem a little impressed about being one of 'our pioneer families.' I remember that about her even at school. Mrs. Lacey has that same high and mighty air, which *is* funny when you think of Charlie Lacey!"

"I used to think Mr. Lacey was about the most wonderful person I knew, when I was a boy," Wrenn said. "When I was little, I wanted to be a rancher like he was instead of a lawyer."

"Why, Wrenn, you never told me that!"

"Mr. Lacey seemed much more exciting than my father," Wrenn said with a gentle smile of apology to his father. "He was so big and healthy, the way I felt a man ought to be out here."

"But he never really has pulled himself together since the company put him out, has he?" Rose said.

Irritation twitched at Wrenn's lips. Rose had a way of saying things so bluntly. Yesterday, she had said, "Isn't it queer that being a lawyer, your father would have left your mother so badly fixed. Except for this house she really doesn't have anything!"

"They left Charlie Lacey pretty well strapped," Wrenn said. "As a matter of fact, if they had backed him a little longer he might have made money for them."

Rose made a quick exasperated tch with her lips the way Madame Guinard did. "People are so shortsighted. Have some more dessert, Wrenn?"

Wrenn took a second helping. Yet he did know what Rose meant about Pam. He thought of her standing on the porch that night saying, "Good night, Wrenn Morley. My father wasn't hiding anything!"

Wrenn folded his napkin and pushed it slowly into its ring. He didn't look at Rose as he spoke. "Dear, I went around to the recruitment office today . . ." He tried to keep his voice casual. He could feel her looking at him and knew just how her eyes would grow darker in that way they had. She wouldn't say anything until he was all through.

"I just can't not go, Rose."

"But I thought since you're thirty, Wrenn . . . I suppose that doesn't make any difference if you *want* to go."

"I hope to be sent to officers' training camp. . . . I won't know for a week or so." The dining room seemed strangely still and he wished the children would come in. He wished he hadn't told her just yet.

"Stephen will be excited. He asked me yesterday why you weren't in the army," Rose said. "I told him you could do more here, making speeches. I think you could, Wrenn, really." She brushed some imaginary crumbs off the tablecloth. "Your mother will be awfully upset." Not a word about herself. She went ahead of him into the library and stood by the front window.

"Do you think you can manage here without me for a little, Rose?"

"I suppose so." She sounded sulky. He couldn't quite make her out. He stood close to her, not knowing what she was thinking.

"Wrenn."

"Yes, dear?"

"I wouldn't want to live if, if you were killed," she said very low, without turning around from the window. "I wouldn't. I'd kill myself."

"Darling, don't talk like that. Nothing will happen to me." He tried to put his arm around her but she pulled away.

"You're my whole life, Wrenn," she said in a strained, almost angry voice.

"Rose, you're mine, too. You know that." It came over him as he said it that it was entirely true. Without Rose . . . why, without Rose . . . Then she was sobbing against him, and his own eyes were wet against her head.

CHAPTER **10**

"It just goes to show," Mrs. Moore said to Rose, "how well women manage when they do take over. J.B. always said he didn't want women in the bank, but he never really tried them. Nowadays, there's a woman at almost every window. Well, that makes 8,750 four-by-four-inch compresses, and 7,355 nine-by-nine-inch compresses we've shipped to headquarters this month!"

"That's splendid," Rose answered a little absentmindedly. "You'll have your report ready to give at the board meeting tomorrow morning, won't you? I have to have it then, even though Pamela Lacey won't be able to be there. A morning meeting is so much better for everybody else, and she can send her report over. We can't arrange the meeting just for one person."

Mrs. Moore lingered, but Rose had already reached for the telephone. She talked to Pamela more often by phone than in person. Pam seemed too busy to drop around to Red Cross headquarters and she certainly wasn't going to go over to the Soldiers' Home Protective Society office. It still surprised her that Pam had taken that job with all she had to do, but, of course, she only kept her office open in the afternoons. The Red Cross office had to be kept open all the time and every evening. Talking to each other from offices only two blocks apart subtly changed their voices. It was as though they talked blindfolded, without the softening effect of a smile around the mouth or eyes. The conversation easily became clipped, terminated too soon or lasted too long.

"Pam!" Rose began. "I find I am going to have to hold the board meeting tomorrow morning because so many can't come in the afternoon or evening. I know you can't make it then but if you'll drop your report in this noon, I'll ask someone to read it."

There was nothing in the words themselves to offend, only some vibration of the voice, some note of officiousness.

"Very well," Pamela said. Nothing in her words, only some cadence of annoyance. Then her voice freed itself from annoyance. "I was just about to call you, Rose, about a girl who is here in my office."

"Yes?" Interest lifted her tone.

"Her name is Elsie Reddich. She works in the Emporium and she came to ask for a loan to pay her expenses to Camp Lewis to marry a soldier there before he is sent overseas."

Rose hardly waited for her to finish. "Isn't it amazing what

[279]

they'll ask for! Well, you tell her that the Red Cross can't lend her money for anything like that and I don't think the Soldiers' Home Protective Society should either. We'd have everyone wanting to borrow money just to go and visit their soldier boys!"

"She said she heard the Red Cross had lent money to one woman so she could go to see her husband who was dying and, as she put it, this seems just as important."

"Oh, that's absurd, Pamela. We can't establish any such precedent."

Pamela's voice was cool. "I suppose it's a question of whether we are dealing with individuals or precedents, isn't it?"

"Of course, I can take it up with the board, but . . ." Rose said.

"Feeling as you do, I don't imagine it will do much good to put it up to the board. I notice that you are pretty apt to make it clear when you present something to the board just how you want them to decide it."

"Now wait just a minute, Pam. That isn't so."

"Perhaps not, but that has been my impression."

For a long minute there was silence over the wire. Neither one was quite sure of what she wanted to say next. When Pamela had picked up the phone it had simply been a matter of wanting to help a young woman if she could, one of the many cases that filled her new file case, and then, in some inexplicable manner, she was personally involved with this girl. She picked up her sharpest weapon.

"I can remember the time when you couldn't wait to marry yourself, Rose. It's too bad you can't remember how you felt."

"Aren't you being rather personal, Pam?"

"And truthful." The words seemed to speak themselves out of her mouth. "Well, you take it up with your board and let me know. I'll see what we can do here."

Rose came part way. "Pam, what I mean is that we have to be very careful not to incur criticism from the public for the way we spend funds. . . ."

"I see," Pamela said. "Anyone who does anything out of the

ordinary incurs criticism. I thought the important thing was how much we could help. I can't talk any longer, Rose, this girl is sitting here in front of my desk waiting for an answer." She hung up the receiver.

The girl's eyes hung on her face as she turned away from the phone. They were large brown eyes, still moist with tears. She was a pale young woman with masses of brown hair, insecurely fastened up on her head with large bone hairpins. All the time Pamela had been talking on the phone, the girl had busied herself with trying to lay two brown cotton gloves exactly upon each other, finger for finger. Now she held them in one nervous fist.

"They won't give it to me!" she said in the tone of one receiving a death sentence.

"Mrs. Morley doesn't feel that the Red Cross can lend you the money but she is going to talk it over with her board."

"But you don't think that will do any good. Miss Lacey, I gotta go. He's going overseas and I can't let him go before we're married. He wanted to be married before he left and I said no, but I was wrong." She wiped her nose with her gloves. "You wouldn't know how I feel, Miss Lacey."

"Yes, I would know," Pamela said. This girl was going to her love, before anyone else could take him away from her. She was running down a lonely dark street. Pamela knew well enough.

"This office only gives money for food or clothing or fuel, but perhaps we can give you money to cover your food while you are away from work; that's legitimate enough, and I . . . I will lend you money for your ticket," Pamela said in a dry voice.

The next noon Rose called Pamela at the store. "Pam, thank you for getting your report over. The girl who brought it must have been that girl. She was certainly appealing. I would have liked to talk to her but she went out too fast." Rose's tone this morning was warm, friendly.

Pamela waited.

"It was a fine report. I could see the board was impressed.

[281]

You didn't send any notation about this girl's request, but I did take it up. I didn't tell them how it seemed to me, but all but one felt the same way . . ."

"Oh, never mind, Rose," Pamela interrupted.

"No, listen, Pam. I got to thinking how right you were that I couldn't wait to marry, only Wrenn swore he'd leave school if I didn't marry him before he went back and, of course, I couldn't see that. Anyway, I want to lend the girl the money myself. . . ."

"That's generous of you, Rose, but I lent her the money. She left on the sleeper last night." Pamela drew little marks on the paper in front of her.

"Oh, Pam, you shouldn't do that!"

"Well, it's all taken care of. Tell me, did they beat last month's record for bandages?"

CHAPTER 11

Fall, 1918

On her way home from the ranch Pamela drove slowly thinking about Ruby. Ruby had wanted to go right back after Slim's funeral. "You don't think I want to stay in that woman's town, do you?" Ruby had asked as they drove toward the ranch. "Don't like to leave Slim there either, except he's way out on the edge. I'd have buried him out at the ranch, but you can't tell, you might not always be able to hang on to the ranch."

Pamela had waited for Papa to say something to that, but he didn't. He might not have heard, of course. He felt so bad about Slim's death, he hardly said a word all the way out.

"We'll get out there in time to get supper; I'd rather do that," Ruby said. "Charlie'll need something to eat and them three bums of his." They had driven silently most of the way, Papa in back and she and Ruby up in front, with the car curtains buttoned on because it was so cold. Once Ruby had burst out, "Damn fool to go off to the army in the first place. I told him he'd get killed, but I never thought it'd be by getting sick in camp before he ever seen a battle."

She could feel Ruby dreading the empty ranch house as they drove into the yard. Charlie helped her out of the car and Ruby let him without a word. That had shocked her.

"Slim never got onto a ranch of his own in all the years he talked about it," Ruby said as she went up the steps to the house.

"I always felt this one was part his, Ruby," Charlie said. "I think Slim felt that way, too." But Ruby shook her head. " 'Tain't the same, Charlie, you know that."

"Well, it would have killed Slim to know we aren't even going to make the interest on the loan this year. He's saved that, anyway," Papa told her.

The ranch had looked sad and lonely. It was cold for September, cold enough to snow. The ground was so bare it needed something to cover it. From down on the road King Butte didn't seem to have a blade of grass, and the grass on the fields was grizzled brown. They had seen some of the steers standing lean and droopy as they drove in. "Raising them for shoe leather, Pam," Papa had said. "They look about as good as the homesteaders' wheat did, at that."

When Papa wasn't booming something his voice didn't seem to belong to him. She had always wanted him to tell things just as they were, but when he did it hurt her.

She had been ashamed that she was so glad to get away. She had a cup of coffee with Ruby, standing by the kitchen window, both of them looking out toward the butte. She had tried to think of something to say to Ruby, or tried to touch her to comfort her. Women comforted each other with their arms, but she couldn't seem to do it, so she stood there going on with her own thoughts. Then she looked at Ruby and saw tears on her face. It was so terrible to see Ruby cry she put her arms around her easily and said what she had been thinking as she stood there. "Ruby, you loved Slim; you never married him without."

Ruby had sniffed hard. "You're damn right, Punk, but a woman's a fool to love a man like I did that one." She put another stick in the stove and clattered the teakettle back over. "Might as well cook onions, tonight; I'm bound to snivel anyways. Whyn't you stay overnight and get up early in the morning and drive back?"

But she couldn't. She wanted to get away from Ruby's grief and her father's heavy gloom. She had the feeling that Ruby knew she wanted to get away when she came out on the step to see her off, but all Ruby said was, "Watch out for jack rabbits, Punk!" When she looked back, Ruby was standing in the doorway waving . . . like that time, driving home from some place, from the class picnic at Harpers' woods, that was it, a woman had come to the door to watch them go by, and waved and she had felt sad, without knowing why. This time the woman had a name and she knew why she felt sad.

Pamela had never driven back to town from the ranch at night before, but doing something, going some place, made it easier to put the sadness of the last few days farther from her. If she stopped, if she stayed out there at the ranch, it would settle down on her again. This Maxwell automobile that she had bought from Bunny Welch before he went into the army was like her old bicycle. It gave her the same sense of freedom. She was making almost thirty miles an hour; the ranch and Ruby's face and her father's worries were left behind.

This was the way she would have driven in France, in the dark, across rough ground like this. Only there would have been shells bursting and enemy soldiers waiting around the next curve. . . . She drove faster, sitting up very straight and stiff, holding the wheel steady against the jounces.

The road was so bad she had to put her whole attention on straddling the baked mud ruts that looked like canyons in the wavering headlights of the car. The wheels slid into the trough of the rut with a violent jerk. Then the lights went out. At first, she couldn't see at all and sat blinking at the sudden darkness. The motor seemed to roar louder in the dark. Then the sky above the dark shoulder of mountains grew lighter. It was a kind of luminous dark that had a visibility all its own. Sage and thistles and mullein stalks stood up from the earth like fenceposts marking out the road. She let the brake out slowly and inched forward. You would have to drive in the dark if you were driving an ambulance in France. Oh, she could have done it, she knew she could. Nothing would have been too hard, too terrifying. You knew in yourself what you could do. Maybe, even yet . . . Mama was all right again if she was careful and didn't go up and down stairs too much.

Then she thought of Papa. He had said, "I'll ride down as far as the corral with you, Pam." When she stopped to let him out, he said, scraping the dirt off his boots on the edge of the running board, "I was just wondering, Pam, if you could lend me a couple hundred to meet the interest on the note I've got coming due. I can't sell the cattle yet, not the way they look; they wouldn't weigh enough."

She had hesitated. To have Papa ask her for money made her feel hopeless. She wasn't going to refuse, she was just stalling a minute, catching her breath. And then Papa said, "You've got your car paid for, Pam, you could borrow more than that, and you've got almost enough in the bank."

But she had only just finished paying for it.

"I'll give you a second mortgage on the ranch, Pam," he had said. "Just to have it a business proposition." An image of her father standing in the headlights of the car stayed with her. He hadn't shaved since early morning and his beard showed white against the color of his skin. The white shirt he had worn to the funeral didn't look right on him. His shoulders sloped too much in it. But it was his eyes that bothered her.

She stared ahead into the dark; her neck was stiff from peering forward so intently. There was no use thinking of going off to France, the folks needed her here. Mama counted on her board money, and now Papa. She drove carefully around the curve into the four corners of King Butte to see if she could find someone who could fix her lights. The game she had played about driving in France seemed a childish thing, only an escape, not really patriotism at all when you looked right at it.

CHAPTER 12

Rose was frightened, and she wasn't used to being frightened. She didn't show her fear except in her wide dark eyes above the gauze mask. She sat at the big desk with the telephone, looking like a slightly more rotund and motherly version of the Red Cross nurse in the poster on the wall back of her.

The Red Cross office that had once been a clothing store was the picture of organized activity. A volunteer secretary typed at the smaller desk next to Rose's. At a long table at the end of the room women in white aprons, Red Cross veils and masks, sorted clothing that other women were constantly bringing into the room. The conversation had a way of dropping into a whisper that penetrated every corner, and then rose again to a subdued murmur.

Rose was reading the typewritten copy she had prepared for the newspaper when a woman came up to her desk.

"When I got to that address the man had died," she said in a low voice.

Rose looked quickly away from the fear in the woman's eyes. "Why don't you stop for the rest of the day," she said briskly. "We can find someone to take your calls this afternoon. You go home and sleep." Her mind lingered over the word sleep. She had a headache herself, and she couldn't think of anything better than sleep. But there wasn't any time to spare. When the woman had gone, she picked up her pen and changed the number six to seven so that the sentence read: "There is a total of 165 new cases of influenza this week and 7 deaths." She laid down her fountain pen and clasped her hands together; they felt cold.

She had told Mother Morley to stay in bed again today just to be on the safe side, and Hazel would call her if she were any worse. Mother Morley often felt poorly; that didn't mean she had the flu. It was just her headache that made her worry about her. And the children hadn't been out of the yard since the epidemic had started. There wasn't any safer place; there wasn't really any other place to go.

It did her good to think of what Mama had said. "You won't get it, Rose. You've always been healthy." And when she had said, "What about you, Mama? You're working twice as hard in that community kitchen as you do in the shop," Mama had made a face and said, "Me, I'm not afraid. What have I to lose? The flu can only keep me from being an old lady. Better I keep busy making soup; nobody is going to buy hats now."

If Wrenn hadn't gone; if he were only here now! She picked up the list of bandages packed and shipped and tried to put her mind on the neat rows of figures. What if Wrenn were to get the flu at camp? That husband of Ruby's had died of it. The paper said there were hundreds of sick soldiers. She couldn't breathe with the gauze mask over her nose. She reached up and untied it, holding it away from her face so she could take a deep breath, then she retied it more tightly. She didn't suppose she really needed to wear a mask when she wasn't making bandages, but if she didn't, then the women were careless.

"Oh, Mrs. Morley, I meant to tell you . . ." The secretary came over to her desk. "We got Miss Lacey to drive that truck to Big Fork. I called her office to see if they knew of anybody who could take it, and she said right away that she would. She left after lunch."

"She can't be very busy in the office if she can get away like that," Rose said. How like Pamela to do the dramatic thing. "That was a job for a man," she added.

"We couldn't find any man. But Tom Griffith is driving the other truck. I guess everybody in the town must be sick. They said a hundred and ten and there can't be many more than that in Big Fork."

When the phone rang beside her, Rose jumped. She had liked the phone ringing in the beginning; liked new things coming up all the time, making decisions, answering questions, thinking at once of what to do, but this morning it sounded ominous.

"Red Cross office, Mrs. Fenwick speaking," the secretary answered.

As though she knew it would be for her, Rose stretched out her hand for her own extension. "Did the doctor say she had the flu? He must be crazy; Mother Morley couldn't have had it for three days," she said into the phone. "Hazel, you can't go before I get home. You can't leave the children. I'll be right there." Her hand trembled as she hung up the receiver, but when she saw the frightened look in the secretary's face, she said quickly, "Mother Morley hasn't felt well all winter. I'm sure it's nothing serious, but I'll go home and see to things."

There was no taxi, and Rose had to walk home on legs that had become strangely unsteady. Mother Morley might be sick, but she would be better tomorrow, she told herself. Little Cora had hardly been sick a day in her life; she had been perfectly well this morning, how could she get sick in a couple of hours? It was just Hazel's imagination.

Hazel met her at the door, all dressed to leave.

"Go along then, but it's absurd to think it's healthier out on your ranch. I think you're very foolish to go," Rose said crossly. She was relieved to find Cora on the sofa, holding her doll the way she always did. And she always had high color; it wasn't fever. But she picked her up and carried her upstairs to her bed before she went in to see Mother Morley.

Rose had never really looked at Mother Morley. Their eyes had always met and moved on. Now Rose looked steadily down at the thin face on the pillow. The skin was sallow; had it always looked that way? Mother Morley dusted it with rice powder and a little dab of rouge, too pink for her skin, so you couldn't tell. Was it right for her to breathe so fast? She had always avoided touching her, but she laid her hand on her head and brought it back quickly.

"Mrs. Morley's got it bad," Hazel said as Rose came back downstairs. "The doctor's coming again as soon as he can. I sure hope the rest of you don't get it." She closed the door with a bang, and Rose was left alone.

Where was Stephen?

"Stephen?" Rose ran back upstairs. "Cora, where's Stephen?"

The child opened her eyes and looked at her without answering. Rose undressed her and went to call Madame Guinard. They didn't need her at the community kitchen as much as she did right here.

"To the hospital? Was she sick? Why didn't you call me?" Rose cried into the phone. Mother of God! Mama was sick, too, and they had taken her to the hospital.

"Stephen!" she called from the back door and saw a movement in the box elder tree against the back fence. "Stephen, come down out of that tree. Mother hasn't time to hunt all over for you."

"Is Grandma going to die?" Stephen's fair head and anxious face looked down at her from the crotch in the tree.

"Of course not, Stephen. Don't be silly. Come right down and help me get supper."

The little boy swung out of the tree, hanging by his arms for a moment before he landed lightly on the ground. "I climbed up in the tree so I wouldn't get any germs. I tried to take Cora, but she got scared and cried."

It was close to midnight when the doctor came back to see Mother Morley. And afterward Rose followed him downstairs and sat down facing him.

"How could she die like that? I talked to her this morning." Her words came out in a whisper.

"That's the way they do, like flies," the doctor said wearily.

[289]

"The little girl's pretty sick; you want to watch her." He wanted to startle Mrs. Morley out of that stunned look. "The boy seems all right." He didn't like the way she just sat there. He picked up her hand and felt her pulse.

"You better get to bed, yourself, Mrs. Morley. You're tired out. I'll get someone to come over here tonight and stay with you," he said confidently, but he didn't feel confident. He was trying to think whom he could get.

"Yes, I'm very tired," she said, shaking her head so he could see how tired. He mustn't go and leave her here alone. If he left her, she would be sick, right here. She couldn't see him clearly; she felt him getting farther and farther away. He was opening the door. "You better sit down and rest yourself," she said, but her voice didn't seem to come out very strong.

"I don't like to leave you, but I'll get someone here, Mrs. Morley. You get right up to bed." The door closed the way it had behind Hazel.

Rose sat staring at the door. She had undressed and put on Wrenn's big flannel bathrobe with his last letter in the pocket for comfort. But when her hand touched it now, she had forgotten what it was. She took it out and tried to read the address, but it blurred too badly to make out, and she let it lie on the hatrack. Then she heard Cora crying.

"Mama's coming, baby. Here, Cora," she called. She pulled herself up the stairs by holding onto the banister.

Pamela saw the lights streaming from Rose's house a block away and looked at it curiously as she drove past in the big truck. It was odd that she thought of it as Rose's house now instead of Wrenn's, but then a house did seem to belong more to the woman than the man, any house. There had been a picture of Wrenn in uniform in the paper. She had meant to cut it out, but she had forgotten and the paper was thrown away. You couldn't think of anything but the flu these days.

Mama had left the door unlocked and she let herself into the house and made some coffee. She ate a cold boiled potato and a piece of meat loaf she found in the icebox, and spread jelly on a slice of bread, a regular truck driver's lunch, she told herself. She wasn't really tired, and not sleepy at all, only hungry.

It had been exciting driving the truck. She hadn't known for sure that she could do it when she said she would. "Say, you're all right," Tom Griffith had told her when she helped him with the tire. And when she had smoked a cigarette with him, he had said with a grin, "You're a regular sport, aren't you!" She hadn't smoked since the time she tried one of Ruby's, and Ruby told her not to let her catch her doing it again till she was all "growed up." If she wasn't now at twenty-nine, she never would be!

She had shut the door of the kitchen so she wouldn't wake Mama, and she didn't hear the phone right away. She had to run to get it.

"Miss Lacey," Dr. Boyd said, "I tried to get a nurse to go to Morleys' but there isn't one in town that isn't busy. And then I had to go out again, and when I was coming back, I saw your light. I wondered if I could get you to take a hand there?"

"Who's sick?" Pamela asked.

"Old Mrs. Morley died, and Mrs. Morley and the little girl are both sick, and Madame Guinard's in the hospital. I'll get over in the morning, and I believe you better wire Mr. Morley. Mrs. Morley'll be a lot sicker by morning."

"I'll go right down," Pamela said.

You did all kinds of things in an emergency like this, but still, Pamela wondered if Rose would be glad to see her, if she would want her there. She rang twice before she saw Rose coming down the stairs, bundled in a big robe that must be Wrenn's, and her face red from crying or fever. She wasn't quite sure Rose knew her. Rose opened the door and said in a strange, thin voice that lacked any of her usual positive manner, "Cora's upstairs in my bed, and she's very sick." And when they went past a closed door she said, "Wrenn's mother is in there. She's dead."

Pamela tried to carry Cora back to her own room, but Rose

clung to her so she left them both in the big bed in Rose's room, and sat by them in the dark. Rose seemed to sleep a little, but when she woke she was delirious and kept calling Mother Morley. She didn't know when Pamela took Cora from her. The little girl was barely breathing and even her head under the soft dark curls seemed hot against Pamela's face. Then she heard Rose scream and ran back to her.

Rose was sitting up in bed, holding her head with both hands. "I told you we had to have more workers!" she cried out.

"We'll get them, Rose. Now lie down," Pamela said, wishing she knew what to do. "Not really much you can do," the doctor had said, "but they shouldn't be alone down there." Rose thrashed around the bed so violently, Pamela sat on the edge and tried to hold her still. When she finally dropped off to sleep, Pamela went down to send the wire.

"Your mother died this morning. Cora and Rose dangerously ill. Come at once," she read off to the telegraph operator.

"How is it signed?" asked the tired voice over the phone.

"Signed? Oh, sign it Pamela . . . Pamela Lacey."

Pamela sent Stephen down to her mother's in the morning without telling him about his grandmother's death.

"Will you take me out to your papa's ranch if I stay till Mama gets well?"

"If there isn't too much snow, we'll go out there and stay a week," she promised.

Little Cora died two nights later. Rose was too sick to know. Pamela was alone in the house with Rose all week. The doctor shook his head and said she might not make it either, but Pamela set her mind against that. She sat up all night sponging Rose's body. It was hot again as soon as she had finished, and she began all over again. When Rose's lips got that dry look, she held the glass of ice-cold lemonade to her lips, feeling triumphant if Rose swallowed as much as a mouthful. The doctor said it might help, might not, but she had to do something. In a strange way, Pamela felt she was not Pamela Lacey, and this wasn't Rose Guinard; they were two living women fighting against some common enemy. When a person was so sick, she almost lost any identity but that of a human being. But after the worst of it, when the fever went down and Rose lay sleeping peacefully, Pamela was back in her own person, Pamela Lacey who had nothing in common with Rose Guinard.

She had plenty of time to sit by the bed and think about Rose. Did Wrenn look at her when she was sleeping and think her beautiful? "Beautiful in a bold sort of way." She didn't look bold now, nor beautiful, either. She was too pale, and her eyes were closed. Pamela stared at the closed eyelids, waiting for them to open. Rose's beauty lay in her eyes. When they opened, she would tell Rose that Cora had died. Her eyes would be red with crying then. But when Rose woke she only said, "Try to drink a little tea, now, Rose."

Pamela was closing the window Friday morning when Rose spoke. She turned quickly.

"I've been sick," Rose said. Her eyes seemed to search Pamela's face. They weren't beautiful so much as frightened, childlike, like little Cora's.

"Yes," Pamela said, "but you're better. You're going to get well."

It seemed odd that Rose didn't ask about the children or Mother Morley, or how Pamela came to be there. Her eyes followed Pamela around the room. After she had drunk the tea, she closed her eyes again and seemed to sleep. And Pamela sat in the chair by the window and drowsed, herself.

"Weren't you afraid to come here and nurse me?" Rose asked suddenly.

Pamela opened her eyes. "No. It sounds queer, almost sinful, but I feel indestructible, as though nothing could happen to me," she said. She felt so strong beside Rose, but it was a relief to have Rose better, to have her talk.

"Mama wasn't afraid either, but she said she had nothing to lose," Rose said slowly. For the first time she sat up against the pillow by herself and pushed back her hair as Pamela brought warm water for washing. "Is Mama?"

"She's better, Rose," Pamela said, but she was wondering if it was because she didn't have much to lose that she had felt safe from the flu. She said aloud, "Your mother loves life; that's too much to lose." But she was saying it of herself. But why should she love life? her mind went on asking as she dried Rose's arms. That was just a cliché. Life didn't love you. And yet, loved life was right. She loved the whole business of it, even this being equal to things, driving that truck, taking care of Rose, keeping her alive.

"I hate sickness," Rose said. "I never could stand to be around sick people," and her eyes filled with tears.

"You're getting well now," Pamela said briskly. It bothered her to see Rose cry like that. Rose was always so sure of herself.

Sunday morning, Wrenn came. Pamela had thought of his coming and that she would be the one to meet him, but she was out in the kitchen fixing Rose's lunch, and he let himself in with his key. He looked so worried, she said, "Rose is coming along fine, Wrenn," before he could ask, "and Stephen is at Mother's."

"What about the baby?" The khaki uniform made Wrenn's face so colorless. His voice sounded husky.

"Cora died, Wrenn." Her words seemed too blunt. She wished she could hide his stricken face against her shoulder, but she stood there with her arms hanging hopelessly against her apron, remembering how Wrenn had hated the dull look of death in a shining trout. He seemed to be waiting, so she said again, "Rose is better every day, now. She seems to know about your mother, but I haven't told her about Cora. Better wait until she's stronger."

She let him go up alone and went back out to the kitchen. She would take Rose's tray up and leave some lunch for Wrenn, then she would go. She had grown so used to this house in the last week, getting meals, turning out the lights at night and opening the front door to the morning, she had tried to imagine to herself how it would have been if she had married Wrenn and this was her house, with Wrenn going out and coming in, but she never could. And now that Wrenn was back and she could hear the murmur of his voice and Rose's, she wanted to be gone.

Wrenn came out to the kitchen to find her. "Pam, I can never thank you for all you've done . . ." His voice broke. He sat down at the kitchen table. She stood by the sink, drying her hands.

"You don't need to, Wrenn."

"I just can't believe the baby and Mother are gone," he said. "Rose knows about Mother and Cora. She thought Stephen had died, too." His face startled her; it was so haggard.

"Oh, Wrenn, I should have told her then. She didn't ask about them, and I thought it was better to wait."

Wrenn's fingers tested the edge of the pine table for smoothness, moving slowly back and forth. His head was bent over as though he gave his whole attention to the work of his fingers, but he said in a low voice, "Rose said if I'd been here it might not have happened."

"But you know that's absurd. You couldn't have kept them from getting the flu. Nobody knows how you get it."

Wrenn went on smoothing the table edge. "You took care of the funeral and everything, didn't you, Pam?" She could feel the effort he was making to speak quietly.

"No. I couldn't leave Rose. Mr. Cheavers took care of everything."

"I didn't even get overseas. I might better have been here. Rose is right," he said.

"Don't talk that way, Wrenn. That's so futile." She was impatient with him. When he looked at her, his face lay too open in its sorrow. She looked away, suddenly diffident, not wanting to share this intimacy of grief.

"I've got to get hold of myself before I go back up to Rose," he said. She laid her hand on his arm in pity. "Stephen is going to be so happy to see you, Wrenn. I'll call Mama and tell her to let him come up, but I don't suppose he better come in the house yet."

She wondered at her own voice talking on so naturally, as if nothing had happened. She went out to the hall and phoned, but all the time her mind was testing its new knowledge, articulating it quite clearly: she didn't love Wrenn Morley. She no longer cared that he didn't love her.

When she came back to the kitchen, Wrenn was standing by the window. She went on quietly preparing Rose's tray, having nothing to say. They both heard Rose's voice that had grown a little querulous in her sickness.

"You go on up, Wrenn. I'll bring the tray." She poured the broth carefully into one of Mother Morley's delicate Haviland cups, then she carried it upstairs.

"I can't bear to have you out of my sight, Wrenn," Rose was saying, and Wrenn said, "I want to be right here with you."

"There you are, Rose," Pamela said, coming in with the tray. "You look better already. I'm going to run now." Her eyes slipped quickly over them both. "Let me know if you need me. Don't come down, Wrenn."

She hadn't been out on the street for seven days and the air seemed too sharp after the dry warmth of the overheated house. After the curtained rooms, there was too much light, without any warmth. It made her wince. The street was strangely empty on a Sunday afternoon, and she was conscious of her heels making loud empty sounds.

She came to her house, but she couldn't go in just yet and answer Mama's questions. She half expected Mama to see her from the window, but she went on by as safely as though she were invisible.

When she was beyond the houses, she turned across the open ground that always seemed to stretch way to the far line of mountains. The October grass was pale and sucked dry of life. It ran over the vacant lots and the open prairie until it was lost against the gray, empty sky. Burrs caught against her skirt as she walked, and milkweed rattled when she brushed against it. She picked off a pod, already emptied by the wind, and held it in her hand. It was a shell, not a sea shell, but a dry-land shell, that had once been filled and now was empty. She played with it, curving her fingers around the brittle husk, then she crushed it in her hand and threw it away. If she didn't have her love for Wrenn, then she didn't love anyone, anyone at all.

She rubbed her hands together to warm them and pushed them down in the pockets of her coat. She walked slowly, hardly looking where she was going.

But what had happened? How could she look at Wrenn today and know that she didn't love him any more? If she had married him and they had grown together . . . love had to have something to make it grow. It couldn't exist on nothing. Or was she one of those people who couldn't love anyone?

Almost everyone was in love. All those girls who came in to ask help at the Society loved some soldier, and that was the thing about them that gave them dignity. And all the books and all the songs . . . "I love you truly . . . tru . . . ly, dear," and all the movies were about people in love. What was the matter with her?

Maybe it hadn't happened just today. Maybe she hadn't ever really loved Wrenn. Unconsciously, she covered her mouth with her hand as though she had spoken aloud, but she made no sound. She had been a girl with a dream about love that she had hugged to herself all these years, and she had given the dream the name of Wrenn. It was plain enough if she looked squarely at herself. She kept walking, thankful that she was alone. There was no one she wanted to be with.

She stopped just in time. Someone had started to dig a cellar hole, and the ground fell off sharply to a depth of eight or nine feet, but the edge was hidden in the dusty grass. This was no place to come to walk any more. What was she doing wandering around out here like a romantic schoolgirl! She might get the flu after all, if she got chilled this way. She pulled her coat around her and hurried back to the street.

When she walked into the house, Maybelle was frightened by the dull look of her face and her mussed hair and the pieces of dry grass clinging to her coat.

"Pam, what happened? Are you sick?"

"No, I'm all right; I'm just tired," Pamela said.

PART THREE

1926-1941

"Shut, too, in a tower of words, I mark
On the horizon walking like the trees
The wordy shapes of women . . ."
　　　　　　　—Dylan Thomas

CHAPTER 1

1926

"In New York, Paris, everyone wears the cloche!" Madame
Guinard pronounced. "Just like this, way down."

"It looks like a pail turned upside down," Pamela laughed.
"I can hardly see out from under it."

"I cut it off a little, there! That's what makes it smart!"
Madame Guinard tipped her head to one side, scissors in hand,
as she backed off to get a long view of the point she had cut.
Her hair was still a glossy black, a little purplish in the strong
Montana sun, but that sun was not often allowed to rest on it,
nor on the dead white complexion.

"And nothing on it?"

"Nothing, but *nothing*." Madame Guinard waved her plump
hand. "You don't want any ornaments. Women go to the five
and dime and buy ornaments. I tell you honestly, Pamela Lacey,
it is exactly right on your bobbed hair. And that color green is
good . . . like that book everybody is reading."

"Oh, I'm nothing like the girl in *The Green Hat*." Color
quickened her face. It surprised her that Madame Guinard
should have read that book. She had read it in her own room
at night with the sound of Papa's snores and after Mama had
finished her sleepless prowling around the house.

Madame Guinard's shoulders rose like a collar around her

head and dropped. "Maybe not, still, a green hat is . . ." she rolled her hands. "How shall I say . . . interesting."

"But the girl in that book was just young." Why did she go on about the book?

Madame Guinard pushed her face forward so that it was very close to Pamela. Her black eyes snapped. "You are young. What is young? It is what is in the inside: spirit, courage, hope, love . . ." she spit the words out one after the other. "I hear how you pay that mortgage on your father's ranch!"

Again the color rushed up under the green cloche. "Oh, I couldn't have done that if Mr. Sewall hadn't willed me the hardware store. It was nothing I did myself."

Madame Guinard's lower lip curved up over her upper one. "Most womens after they sell the store would put their money in good safe investment. They wouldn't go buying an old ranch. That takes nerve." She clashed her scissors together.

"Wrenn advised me to invest the money, and I'm not sure he isn't right, but I wouldn't like to see that ranch go out of the family," Pamela said. It was better than saying as she had to Wrenn, "I love that ranch." He had probably told that to Rose, and Rose had pitied her because she had no husband to love.

"Then you keep it. That's right!" Madame Guinard said. Her face became shrewd with curiosity. "Is your Papa going to run it for you?"

"Papa will be a great help, of course." And she was going to try to keep him out there all summer, but Papa was too content now to sit in the lobby of the Western and talk about the old days. "I'm going to run a dude ranch. That's why I'm going east to try to interest Easterners." She had said it enough times now so that it began to seem sensible. It had sounded preposterous in the beginning.

"Good. You bring those Easterners here, and I'll sell them hats!" Madame Guinard joked.

"They would have to be cowboy hats. They're going to rough it. They're going to sleep in log cabins and eat in the old cookhouse and ride . . ."

"And pay for doing that?" That was what Ruby had asked, and then she had added, "Where you going to get these fools?"

"Of course, they're going to pay," she said to Madame Guinard. "People will always pay for a new experience. They do it all the time."

Madame Guinard moved one of the little chairs nearer and sat down. "How many you plan to get?"

"I don't really know whether I'll be able to get any!" Pamela said, "but I have some names of people to see in New York. I'd like to get at least ten." She had difficulty seeing them out at the ranch and a little panic when she tried to think what she would do with them once they were there; but first let her get them.

"You charge them how much? Maybe twenty-five dollar a week?"

"Thirty-five! This is to be a money-making proposition."

Madame Guinard laughed. "That's right! Time to close the shop anyway; you stay and have a little glass wine so we can drink to your—how do you say—your dude ranch!" She pulled the shade at the window and locked the door. "This prohibition where you have to lock the door before you take a little sip of wine!" Her teeth clicked together in disgust. She brought out a tray with a decanter and two small glasses. Pamela started to take off the green cloche.

"No, keep it on. I like to see you. You don't look like Brandon Rapids, Montana, sitting there. Maybe you should wear pants and cowboy hat when you talk to these New York people about your ranch!" Madame Guinard teased. "There, this is imported sherry. Rose wanted some one night for her dinner party. I tell her this is too good to waste on politicians. Here's to your ranch! May it make you plenty money and bring you great pleasure! It is very great pleasure to be independent and know you do it yourself."

Confidence warmed Pamela as she sipped her wine, and a sense of excitement. She and Madame Guinard had something in common; the were both independent of other people. They made their own way without a husband. She hardly saw Madame Guinard's wrinkles or the gray close to the roots of her hair, only her bright eyes and gay laugh and quick interest that made it easy to talk to her.

"You have seen a ranch like this?" Madame Guinard asked.

"No, but I have heard of one in Wyoming that has been running for a good many years, and there are two or three in the mountains west of here. I'll have to work it out as I go along."

"You will be pioneer in dude ranches!" Madame Guinard laughed. The word "dude" tickled her every time she said it.

"Wait till you see the pamphlet I'm having printed. It begins: 'Enjoy the true hospitality of the Old West!' " Pamela took off the green cloche in a wide gesture of welcome. Her short-cut hair fell back against her neck; her eyes brightened.

She looked as though she were still in her twenties, Madame Guinard thought, but she was the same age as Rose, thirty-eight, maybe a year younger. That girl there was one of those lucky women who look young a long time and keep their straight figure. Rose was too plump, but she was pretty enough. Madame Guinard glanced over to the wall where the newspaper picture of Wrenn and Rose was fastened by a hatpin to a velvet pincushion. It had been taken in Florida and underneath, the caption ran "Vacationing under Sunny Skies." They could do things like that. Besides his private practice now Wrenn had the contract with the company. He was a pretty important man.

"The only trouble is that I've got to go ahead and get the ranch ready before I'm sure of my people," Pamela was saying. "That means quite an investment."

"Don't you worry; they will come! You have to gamble. I gambled when I open this shop," Madame Guinard said positively, but she was thinking that she had had a husband to pay for her bread and butter. She wondered again why Pamela Lacey had left her husband and come back here to live. Not many women were strong enough to make a life alone.

"Well, I'm going to try it," Pamela said. "If I make enough, in a few years' time I may go back into straight cattle ranching."

"Where you going to stay in New York?" Madame Guinard asked suddenly, to put an end to such talk.

"Oh, I'll get a room; I don't care where."

"No!" Madame Guinard said. "Stay at big hotel and have people come to see you there. Then they think you have a fine successful ranch. You don't want to tell them you just start. Rose and Wrenn will be in New York by then; I ask them to get you a room where they stay."

"Oh, no, I don't want to bother them," Pamela said.

"And why not! Didn't you take care of them and save Rose's life? Maybe they like to have chance to pay you back. Listen to me, Pamela Lacey, you can't be like that if you're going to get somewhere with a business. I write them tonight."

After Pamela had gone, Madame Guinard had one more little glass of wine before she put the decanter away in the cupboard back of the pile of uncut felts. She sipped it slowly, remembering that Rose had said after the flu: "I imagine Pam was glad to do it for Wrenn, not me. She was always in love with him, you know." In that moment Madame Guinard had not liked her daughter because she had seemed so . . . triumphant that she had Wrenn. She was triumphant about Wrenn's success, too. Rose never spoke of the baby any more. She was like that about anything that hurt her.

Pamela's confidence lasted all the way up Prospect Avenue. The soft wind of yesterday's chinook had swept the snow off the street, and the air was touched with spring. All winter she had said, "I'm going back east in the spring. In the spring I'm going to New York," and now spring was here, and she was going.

Of course, it would be a help to meet Rose and Wrenn in New York and, naturally, they would be glad of a chance to repay her for that time during the flu epidemic, something more than the fitted leather suitcase they had given her. "Dear Pam, this is only a token . . ." Rose had written on the card. But when she thought of that time she always remembered how she had felt that afternoon after Wrenn got back, walking up this street.

That afternoon had made a difference in everything. She had worked harder, after that; what else was there to do? The hardware store had done well, and she had bought up the two homestead tracts next to the ranch and helped Papa when he did so badly with his cattle those years after the war. But what was that?

"I don't feel I'm getting anywhere," she had said to Ruby one time when she drove over to the ranch where Ruby worked. "Whatever made you think women get anywhere, Punk?" Ruby asked in disgust. "They just keep busy and grow older; don't learn much, either." She wouldn't take that. She was going to get somewhere before she grew older. Where was somewhere? It was independence and satisfaction, and she was going to make some kind of a life for herself. She was going to make enough money so she didn't have to worry about debts. No, that wasn't enough either. She was going to get to the place where she didn't need to depend on anyone. And if she was lonely, no one would ever know it.

She was glad when she saw Papa sitting by the parlor window. For a minute she didn't remember that he hadn't been away except to drive downtown in his old model T Ford and sit in the lobby of the Western.

"You don't mind, Papa, if I run the ranch as a dude ranch?" she had asked.

"You own it, don't you, Pam? You can do what you want with it." She had tested the note in his voice. Did he mind not having it in his name? He didn't really own anything but a few shares of stock in a worthless mine . . . that was about all. But she had put all her money into the ranch, and it had to belong to her if she was going to do anything with it. That was it, not that she didn't quite trust him.

But what made her think that she could make it pay? She stood still with her hand on the gate, looking at Papa there in the window. She was starting out right, in the good old Lacey way, by borrowing. If no one came to the ranch to use those four new cabins and all those horses she had bought, she would go broke. Or suppose they did come and didn't like it? It was too late now to give up the idea. She might as well stop worrying she told herself and went on into the house.

"You are certainly late enough, Pamela," Maybelle Lacey said, and Pamela remembered this was the night of the Pioneer Society meeting. "Aren't you coming to the meeting? You know you should after Mr. Sewall's putting in his will about your carrying on the aims and principles of the Pioneers."

"He should have left the money to you," Pam said, smiling.

"If he had, I would never put it all back in that old ranch of your father's that's lost us enough money now." Maybelle had started to say it lightly enough but a deep bitterness about their pinched circumstances got into the words and flashed in her eyes. Charlie Lacey pretended not to hear her as he came out into the dining room.

"I'm pioneering in dude ranching right now," Pamela said quickly. "Papa, if I decide to go to the expense of having a bathhouse, do you think I could pipe the water from that spring up there in the alders?" Papa would like to be asked.

"Course you can, Pam, and then put in a stove to heat the water, and you'll have it good enough for any tenderfoot."

Maybelle left them sitting at the table talking plans. When Pamela did the dishes, Charlie came out to the kitchen and sat down to talk.

"I always thought I'd get a fireplace built in that old shack some day," he said. "With those windows on the end, you must get that whole view up the river. Course when we first built that cabin, we weren't thinking about views; we were thinking about warmth."

"We've done a lot since you've been out, Papa. Do you want to ride out with me this week end?"

"Well, I might, Pam," he said slowly. Then his face livened

in a grin. "I'd sure like to hear Ruby's views on these changes. I'll tell you; I'll make the coffee about six, Pam, and we'll get a good early start and eat breakfast out at the ranch."

"All right, Papa," Pamela said, smiling.

"Do you really think Pam can ever make a success of it, Wrenn?" Rose said when they came back up to their hotel room. She crossed her knees under the short, tight skirt and then uncrossed them and thought of Pamela's long, shapely legs that looked so well under her leather riding skirt.

"I certainly hope so," Wrenn said. "I thought Mrs. Wellman was sold on the idea. If she goes for a month and takes her whole family, that's five right there."

"I had an idea that Lucy Wellman might be interested, and she has plenty of money and friends, so I thought if we invited her to meet Pam . . ." Rose had the pleasant glow common to patrons and the successful manipulators of other people's affairs.

"I thought they were all impressed with Pam, herself," Wrenn said.

"Oh, yes, I'm sure of that. Pam does make a very good impression." Rose was still in the role of manipulator. She and Wrenn had invited the friends whom they knew in New York to a tea to meet Pamela; a rather nicely done little affair, she felt.

"I could see Jennings liking the sound of the ranch, all right," Wrenn said. "He would certainly have peace and quiet for his writing there, if that's what he needs."

Rose felt the same uncomfortable feeling she had had that other time, years ago, when Gordon Jennings had lifted one eyebrow and smiled down at her as though she were an amusing idiot. She wished Wrenn hadn't invited him. If he did go to the ranch, he would stop off in Brandon Rapids on the way through and stay with them.

"What does he write?" she asked, thinking that next time when she saw him she could mention it.

"Oh, I don't know. He wrote a book about Harvard that was dreadfully funny at the time. I might have known he would like Pam."

"Why?" Rose asked.

"She's so different from most women."

Different from me? it was on the tip of her tongue to say, but she caught it. That was too coy. She knew, really, what Wrenn meant. Pam had always been different. She had an instant's vision of Pam's turning around so quickly in her seat at school that her long light hair fell over her shoulder in a fan of fine strands, her eyes sharpening as she said to Bill Kossuth, "You have to have something different if you want to win a prize." But what prize had poor Pam won?

"That was clever of her to wear those ranch duds to the tea. She was quite striking," Wrenn said.

"That was my idea. She was horrified at first. When I saw she had them here, I said, of course, she should wear them. Easterners love that sort of thing."

"How on earth did she happen to bring them?"

"Oh, she had some vague idea of having a table in the lobby of the hotel with her boots and spurs and hat to attract attention so people would stop and pick up one of her folders. But you know that wouldn't stir up any wild excitement!"

Wrenn was taking his papers out of his brief case as though he wanted to get at them. When Wrenn was busy with law work, she was left alone. She could read, but often she didn't have anything she wanted to read. Or she could write letters. But it seemed a pity when they were in New York. . . . She got her stationery and took it back to the bedroom to write Stephen, but after she had uncapped her fountain pen, she held it without writing, thinking about Pam at the tea.

After all the help they had been, they wouldn't need to feel so indebted any more to Pam for taking care of them during the flu. Of all people, why Pamela Lacey had to be the one, she had said to Mama. Mama had said, "Don't be so small, Rose, that you can't take such kindness with good grace." Maybe she was small, but it did make her uncomfortable.

And it was hard for Pam to take things from her, from both of them, she could see. She had been a little stiff when they had first talked about giving the tea for her so she could meet a few people who might be interested in the ranch. Pam probably wouldn't have agreed if Wrenn hadn't proposed it. He had done it very well, as though he, himself, wanted to see if Eastern people would take to the idea of ranch life. She had watched Pam watching Wrenn. Pam could look at a person when he was talking without moving her eyes away from his face.

Pam put you off with that manner of hers when she said, "It's very kind of you and Rose, but I feel it's more than I want anyone to do." "But we want to, Pam. My goodness, we're thrilled at your idea!" she had said, and Wrenn had put his hand over Pam's on the table and said, "Don't talk that way, Pam, with such old friends," as though he were reaching back into all the things they used to do together before she had known them. That was probably why Pam agreed.

"May I go up to your room with you and see what pictures of the ranch you brought that you could show at the tea, Pam?" she had asked.

And Pam had said in that cool tone she could get into her voice, "Why, of course, if you're interested." But once she was there, it had been like the first time Pam took her home to find a costume to wear on Pioneer Day. When she saw Pam's riding skirt and boots and spurs lying on the chair she had known right away that Pam must wear them to the tea.

It had been a good idea. Pam looked wonderful with her light bobbed hair and the worn leather things, and the starched white shirtwaist. Pam said her spurs had belonged to Ruby's husband, and they were sterling silver. Gordon Jennings had called Pam an American version of Joan of Arc . . . or was it a Western version? He had probably taken her to dinner tonight. Well, that would be a treat for Pam, poor thing!

When she first looked at the pictures Pam had brought along, she had really been appalled: pictures of the mountains that looked so bleak they were enough to scare you off, and one of her horse and the old log house at the ranch, and one of that big butte and a profile of her father, of all things, that made him look like a cowhand. She had wondered then how they would strike Easterners, Mrs. Wellman, for example, but they acted crazy about them, when she showed them at the tea.

"Look at all that space!" Gordon Jennings had said in a funny hushed voice that made people laugh, but he had said, "No, I mean it. What do any of us know about living with all that space around us? You'd have to be big to stand it." He always made her uneasy; you never knew when he was going to sound as though he were saying lines in a play, or reciting poetry.

"Do you go out to this ranch often, Rose?" Mrs. Wellman had asked. And she had said right away, "As often as we can. We're crazy about it. It's the most beautiful place in the world, really." Pam had the queerest expression on her face, but she must have been pleased to have her talk it up.

"We slept out on the porch of our cabin, and the air was simply intoxicating!" she had told them. Well, she and Pam had slept on the porch that time. "And it's so peaceful there!" She had certainly done her best to sell the ranch to them.

Pam didn't follow it up at all; she just stood there with a little smile around her mouth. She had told Pam afterward that she must talk it up more and make people feel that they couldn't afford to miss such an experience.

"I'll take a lesson from you, Rose," Pam had said. "But I'd rather just show them the pictures of the ranch and answer any questions. I don't want them to be disappointed."

"Well, heavens, you couldn't just pass around pictures and expect to get enough people to make it pay!" If the Wellmans and Gordon Jennings did go, it would be because of Wrenn and her, not anything Pam had said.

Gordon Jennings seated himself across from Pamela. "Everyone was admiring you as you walked through the dining room."

Pamela laughed. "You know, walking into the room, I felt exactly as I did years ago, riding in a float down Main Street. I was wearing my grandmother's clothes then and pretending to be the wife of a road agent who was going to be hanged. I really felt like that woman, but, at the same time, I was aware of the people on the sidewalk watching me. Rose was on the float, too," she added.

"I'm sure she was dramatic. I thought she was going to swoon over the delights of your ranch. Has she really ever been there?"

"Oh, yes, she's been there," Pamela said lightly.

"I can't quite imagine her out there against all that sky. On the other hand, I seem to see you against that background right this minute."

"That's because I'm wearing these clothes," Pamela said, but she was secretly pleased. Rose had sounded too "girlish," somehow . . . like the time in the drugstore. Rose had raved about the ranch in the same exaggerated way. She wondered if Wrenn remembered that, too.

"No, it's not the clothes," Gordon Jennings was saying. "I think I'm going to have to come out this summer, along about the fifteenth of July . . ." He spoke very slowly, planning it out as he spoke. "I'll make a reservation just for a week at first. It isn't quite my sort of thing, but I may stay the rest of the summer. I want to see if it's the country that's made you the way you are."

"It's the soil," she said, smiling back at his serious face. "Gumbo Lily, they call me." She felt a warm sense of confidence. Of course, people would want to come out to the ranch. At the tea she had had such terrible misgivings. There was something so . . . false about the whole idea. She couldn't imagine any of the people at the tea out at the ranch. What would Ruby think of that man who asked if the ranch dietitian could follow a diabetic diet? What would she do with those people if she got them out there?

But, of course, there was plenty to do. It couldn't help but be a success. Gordon Jennings' sensitive mouth and warm brown eyes, his high forehead and thinning dark hair became the features of a typical ranch guest, interested, humorous, admiring.

"I feel sure you will need to come for a month, at the very least," she told him in mock seriousness. She lifted her foot a little because the spur she still wore had caught in the heavy hotel carpet.

"This ranch was once a real old-time cattle ranch?" he asked.

"Yes, indeed; my father used to run fifteen hundred head of cattle in the shadow of that butte I showed you," she boasted.

"And now you're going to run Eastern dudes."

She laughed, but she hadn't liked it.

CHAPTER 3

"Hadn't you better go slick up the riverbank, Pam? You don't want them guests stubbing their toes on a dead fish carcass!" Ruby stood in the doorway of the living room watching Pamela set a pitcher of pine branches at the side of the fireplace.

Pamela's grin, Ruby thought, was very much like old Charlie's. It was a good thing to kid her, she'd gone like a steam engine ever since she got back from New York, driving even the old Finn who built the new cabins twelve to sixteen hours a day. It was funny Nurmi would take it. But folks always liked to work for Charlie and they did for Pam. Course, Pam worked harder herself than anyone, cleaning, scrubbing, oiling logs and running back and forth to town for supplies, and then sittin' up half the night out here by the fire writin' folks about the place.

"Ruby, I do feel guilty about having you do all the cooking

without anyone to fix vegetables or wait on table or anything."

Ruby took her time answering, sealing her cigarette and getting it lighted first. Then she sniffed so violently it contorted the muscles of her nose. "I ain't never had any trouble yet feedin' a mess of cowhands, I guess these Eastern folks ain't going to be any worse. But keep it plain, Pam, don't ring in any tablecloths and salads like your ma makes, cause that's a horse of a different color altogether. The way you got it fixed won't be hard." Ruby glanced over at the long trestle table Pam had had Nurmi build of cedar boards and that she had rubbed until it had a dull shine of its own. It was already set for the Wellman family who were to arrive in time for dinner the next day. "I don't go for some of the things you done, Pam, but that bare table looks good to me—that is, it would if you didn't have that bowl of sagebrush in the center of it.

"Well, I guess I'll go take me a shower." The bathhouse with its shower and toilet was a source of great delight to Ruby. "Don't worry, Pam, I'll be in there so early in the morning they'll never guess I been there." Halfway to the door Ruby stopped again. "Slim would get a kick outa having those heads he shot around the room." Pam had had the plaster ceiling taken out and opened to the rafters of the roof so the old log house that used to seem low-ceilinged had a feeling of height. Way in the peak the head of a buffalo brooded sulkily over the room. And from the opposite peak a mountain goat looked down in remote tranquillity. Ruby had objected when Pam took up the old linoleum and had a new floor laid. "That's plain foolish, Pam. If a floor's sound it don't matter if the boards are slivery." But Pamela wanted a new floor under the Navaho rugs she had bought. Charlie had got them for her from some old friend. "I remember I slept on that one there, Pam, one night when we stopped in his place in a blizzard."

The two bedrooms were left as they were, one for Ruby and the other for Pamela but Pam's was more of an office than a bedroom with a desk crowded in under the window and bills pinned to a nail above the desk and correspondence in a cardboard file.

She had offered the room to Charlie but he preferred a room in the old bunkhouse. "Then I can play cribbage with Luke if things get thick up here," he had said. Luke was to be stable boss in the new order of things. Ruby and he sparred whenever they met but they got along. "I guess I can put up with him same as I can those pesky gnats," Ruby said.

"Well, I s'pose this is our last night of peace." Ruby had come back from the bathhouse, looking very clean with her hair pinned on top of her head and her face shiny. "Tomorrow night the damn guests'll be all over the place . . . you understand Pam that if one crosses the doorsill of my kitchen they're a goner. I'll run 'em out at the point of a butcher knife. And you better go to bed, too, Pam, if you're going to keep them guests company."

When Ruby had banged her bedroom door, as she did all doors, Pamela let her qualms that she had kept out of her voice and face and mind all day creep back. She tried to see the woman she had met in the hotel in April out here at the ranch. Or that friend of Wrenn's who was a writer. How could they possibly fit in?

When she looked over at the wall by the door she missed the secretary that used to stand there. Oh, not really missed, it had been hideous. And the old couch she had slept on so many nights as a child was moved down to the bunkhouse. Of all the furnishings only the big kerosene extension light, which used to hang down over the round oak table and now shone on the trestle table, was left. Even the wallpaper was gone and the room was covered with the burlap she and Ruby had put up themselves. It looked the way she had seen it in her mind's eye, and it was ready. Why did she keep thinking about the way it used to look? That old ugly, comfortable room belonged to her childhood, when Papa ran a real spread and Slim was living. That time was gone and there was no use hanging on to it. She would have to serve it up for the guests for local color. That day at the hotel, Mr. Owens had said, "I hear your father was a big cattle operator. The thing that interests me is that it was a real ranch in the beginning."

Not a make-believe ranch like it was now! And one woman had said, "I suppose you rode from the time your were walking! I've always wanted to learn to ride as the real old-time Westerners rode." Could she teach riding?

"You put a man on a horse an' after he falls off a few times he'll learn or he'll give up and walk, that's all I know about it," Slim had told Alan that summer, years ago. She would make sure she was out of Ruby's hearing when she tried to teach the Easterners to ride.

Through the window that faced the ranch road she saw the lights of a car. It was late for a visitor. She stood with her hand on her hip, watching the light just as Ruby always did. That must be Stephen.

"One of them guests is headin' down here under his own steam, Pam. You want me to help you get that red carpet rolled out?" Ruby yelled from her room.

"We're not getting out any carpet till tomorrow, Ruby. I think it's Stephen, anyway."

"Now there's my idee of a real good experienced hand!" No one could be as sarcastic as Ruby. "I look for him to get bit by a rattlesnake the first week."

Pamela went out to meet him without bothering to answer Ruby. Ruby went too far with her talk; she wondered if she would be a problem with the dudes; whether she would even be nice to them, but she couldn't get around to talking to Ruby about it. On a regular ranch anybody could say what he pleased and, of course, that was the only kind Ruby had ever had anything to do with. It seemed to Pamela that she had worried all week about things that had never bothered her before.

She hadn't seen much of Stephen since he went away to school, but Wrenn had asked her to let him come out and work this summer and, after all Wrenn and Rose had done she couldn't refuse. "It'll do him good to be outdoors," Wrenn had said. "I want you to pay him wages, Pam, so he'll understand he has to work for them, but I'll deposit them to your account." That was fair enough when she was just starting and didn't know how much use he would be.

And Rose had said, privately, "Stephen's a dear, but you know how college boys are, he gets on Wrenn's nerves sometimes; Wrenn is working so hard these days."

"Hi, Aunt Pam!" a boyish voice called through the dark. "I've got a lot of stuff with me but I'll leave it in my car tonight."

When he followed her into the house he gave a long whistle. "Holy smokes, what a stunning place!" He walked around the room, looking at everything and came to stand in front of the fireplace. She was pleased.

"I don't see how you've done it; it was just a little old ranch house when I came out here as a kid, remember Aunt Pam? You brought me out right after the flu epidemic. And now it's fixed up like a regular dude ranch. The ranch has sure come full circle since then, Aunt Pam."

Anger streaked across her mind for an instant at his glib way of talking. "Full circle" had a sarcastic sound, like something Ruby might say. But there was no sense in being angry at him.

"Stephen, you see those old branding irons hanging there? That brand was in the first list of brands. Now, if I take you on as a hand, you'll have to remember to call this the N Lazy Y, not a dude ranch!"

"O.K., but let me call the people who come out here dudes. That's what they are, playing cowboy. There's a fellow in my class at Harvard who asks me about the old days in the West every time he gets a chance. When I told him one time, I don't know just how I happened to, but anyway, that my grandfather was a vigilante he almost sat on my lap and begged me to tell him more. They really go for that sort of thing back east."

Stephen didn't look very much like Wrenn, she decided, watching him as he talked, but he was a good-looking boy with a quick smile and Rose's dark eyes. Wrenn was never so assured . . . or was he? Stephen must be nineteen; Wrenn was married to Rose when he was nineteen. . . .

"Is Charlie, I mean Mr. Lacey going to be out here all sum-

[317]

mer?" he asked, reddening at his slip of the tongue. "I remember him teaching me to ride."

"He'll be here some of the time, anyway," she said.

"You oughta have him, just for atmosphere. I think he's co-lossal!"

Pamela stood up. "I'm going to have to put you down in the old bunkhouse, Stephen . . ." She must stop getting irritated with him, but he managed to say things in such a way . . . Charlie Lacey for atmosphere! "When Papa is here . . . he'll be sleeping down there too. You can have a great time together."

"Gosh, yes, if I can just get him yarning about the old days."

The sweet June air had smoothed her temper by the time Pamela walked back up from the bunkhouse. For the first time in her life she was going to spend the whole summer out here. And in the fall, would stay late in the fall and maybe part of the winter. This was hers. The . . . dudes wouldn't matter. She would give them a real experience, show them the "hospitality of the Old West" but they were just guests; they would go away and she would still be here. She pulled the thong latch on the new log door Nurmi had made for her, because you couldn't put a draw latch on the old door. The fire had burned down and it was dim in the room, too dark to make out the buffalo head up high in the peak of the roof. The smell of pine boughs lay on the warm air and the sharp breath of sage. She stood still, touching the room with her eyes. No place had ever been so much her own.

"I wonder if that green cowboy aims to get *me* yarning about the old days!" Ruby called out through the thin wall. "I can see where I'm goin' to have to rub the fresh paint off'n him, right now."

CHAPTER 4

There was no telephone yet at the N Lazy Y. Any wires had to be carried out from the railroad station at King Butte. The station agent couldn't leave until after the train from Brandon Rapids came through and nobody seemed to be going out that way, so he was glad to see Pamela Lacey standing there on the platform about ten minutes before the train was due. He got the wire right out of his desk and took it to her. He knew what was in it; nothing either good or bad, just about some friends of hers that couldn't come for a visit, so he stopped to pass the time of day.

"Ain't seen Charlie for quite a while. You tell him to stop in when he comes out," he said.

She didn't say a word. She used to be a sociable kid as a long-legged girl tagging along to the ranch with her Pa, but being back east and growing up had changed her. She didn't look too healthy either, such a bad color. Well, she must be . . . let's see, close to forty; not young any more. The station agent went back into the office.

Pamela put the wire in the pocket of her skirt and walked over to her car, feeling as though her skirts dragged against her limbs. She drove slowly up to the store where Stephen was giving her order for last-minute supplies and stopped the car and sat there staring at a placard advertising Copenhagen Snuff.

Stephen came out with a wide smile on his face. He wore his new Stetson and blue jeans with a red bandanna handkerchief in the back hip pocket as a special touch for the dudes. His smile gave way to amazement.

"Aunt Pam, didn't they come?"

"They aren't coming." She listened to her own words as she spoke, not really believing them.

"You mean, not at all?"

"No. Not at all. Mr. Wellman's mother wants them to come to the Cape, and as she is old, they feel they must give up their trip to our wonderful ranch this year." She smiled when she finished, a tight-mouthed little smile.

"Why they ought to be shot!" Stephen's indignation reached through her feeling of numbness. "Didn't they pay anything when they made the reservation?" He dumped his groceries on the seat he had brushed off for the sake of the Wellmans' city clothes, and came over to Pamela's side of the car.

"No. They said they would come, and I believed them. I'm not very bright, Stephen. I wonder if the others will change their minds."

"Who comes next?"

"Gordon Jennings, a writer, is coming two weeks from now to stay for one week and see how he likes it. I haven't anyone else for July but you see I expected the five Wellmans for the whole month."

The boy's face was troubled. "You know that fellow I was telling you about, Aunt Pam, who's crazy about the Old West. I could write him and tell him what a wonderful place it is and maybe he'd come. His old man's a regular Babbitt but he's got plenty of money. It disgusts Jake."

Pamela managed to laugh. "That would be fine. His money wouldn't disgust me just now."

"Shan't I drive?" he asked. He had driven in.

"No, Stephen, I believe I'd feel better if I had something to hang onto for a while, you know?"

"Sure I know. You must be ready to bite tacks." He got in the other side and offered Pamela a stick of gum. "Mother doesn't chew gum; I suppose you don't."

"Yes, I think I will, Stephen, instead of tacks."

But they were silent. Pamela drove with her eyes on the ruts of the road. She was busy subtracting five times thirty-five dollars a week from her calculations. She had counted on the Wellmans! She wouldn't have had the extra cabin built except for them. She could have put up a tent for the children. She shouldn't have done so much; she should have waited. She could have done without a new floor and taking out the old ceilings. Maybe she could have managed without that sorrel mare. She had no business gambling on their coming, investing so much in the place.

Papa had made suggestions she wished she had taken now. "I should think you could fix up the bunkhouse and let that do for one guest cabin, maybe two; you could cut it into four little rooms and Luke and the boy and I can sleep in a tent this summer." But she had gone right ahead and taken a chance! Just like Papa. Charlie Lacey's girl, she was!

It was easy to take a chance when you wanted something enough; you expected things would work out the way you planned and so you went ahead, and sometimes you were disappointed. That had been the way it was with Papa; she had never understood so well before. He must have driven over this same road, knowing the cattle company was going to be dissolved, or that the cattle wouldn't bring much. He hadn't done any crying about it. You had to take a chance yourself and lose before you could understand somebody else.

"Aunt Pam, let's not tell Ruby these folks aren't coming at all. I mean, she'll just say I told you so. She thinks everything about having a dude ranch is phooey."

"Ruby would guess, Stephen, you can't ever fool her." But she minded Ruby's watching from the window and seeing her come home alone. On a sudden childish impulse she stopped at the corral, murmuring something about wanting to look at the new sorrel mare. "Will you put the car in the shed, Stephen," she said so she could be alone and put off telling Ruby a little longer. The mare was a four-year-old and she had named it Aspen for the Aspen she had as a girl.

When the mare saw her, she came over to the gate and Pamela rubbed her ears and worked a burr out of her mane. When she held her hand out, Aspen mouthed it gently. Pamela didn't talk to her or call her names but she twisted her fingers in the coarse hair and rubbed her hand over her neck. No need to keep her in the corral all day now so the Wellmans could see her best horse. She opened the gate and the mare followed her all the way up to the pole fence that enclosed the ranch house.

Pamela glanced quickly at the long table, but the table had been cleared. She went on out to the kitchen. Ruby had her back to her and was busy at the stove. The table was set with four places.

"Hello, Ruby."

"Hello, Punk."

"They aren't coming."

Ruby sniffed. "Good enough. I didn't like the sound of 'em, needing an extra room just because him and her can't stand it in the same room. They oughta started in a soddy like I did with the whole family in one room." She clattered the cover on the kettle.

"Pam, you can't trust Easterners. Slim always said they're a different breed of cats. They think they want to come west and then when you got all ready for them they lose the notion." Pamela poured herself a cup of coffee and stood by the stove, only half listening, but comforted a little by Ruby's heartiness and the hot coffee.

Ruby filled her own cup. "Any decent person gets to a place if he says he will. You see, Pam, city folks ain't never fed stock so they had to be there on time to do it, nor milked . . . nothing like that. They just go and come, go and come when they want!" Ruby moved her head from side to side. "You call Steve and Luke, Pam, an' I'll dish it up."

Luke never said anything. He came in and sat down. Stephen looked quickly at Pam and took the seat across from Luke. "Gee, it looks good, Ruby," and then he was embarrassed remembering that the fried chicken and biscuits had been intended for the dudes.

"Stephen, why don't you take Aspen out this afternoon. You might look at the fence along the homestead. Luke, you need to see why the spring water just trickles into the trough in the corral." She made her voice brisk, matter-of-fact.

"I was thinking I might go fishing this afternoon," Ruby said between puffs of her cigarette. "You've kept me so gol-darned busy this spring I ain't even wet a hook yet. I might get enough trout for supper."

"Why don't you, Ruby? Trout would taste good," Pam said, but she wasn't thinking of trout; she was wondering if she put an ad in the New York papers if it would bring any guests. Not in July. The whole month would be a total loss. She would have to pay Nurmi for his carpenter work; she couldn't ask him to wait for his money, but she could let the lumber bill wait and the bills for oil and varnish . . .

"Hell, Punk." The front legs of Ruby's chair came down with a bang. "You don't want to fuss around with dudes. Let's get some cattle on the place. You can make a loan. You ain't got any mortgage on this place now. It don't look quite right without a mortgage. That's what I been missing. You take out a mortgage and get you a couple hundred head; get Charlie to buy 'em . . ."

"Gosh, Aunt Pam, why don't you? I'll work without any wages . . ." Stephen said. Luke chewed.

Pamela's eyes moved out through the kitchen door. Ruby saw her glance. "That's no waste, Pam. You just got it fixed up the way you want it to live in yourself. You can close that big barn off, in the winter, anyway. You can live out here all year round like a regular rancher."

"It isn't as simple as all that, Ruby." Pamela's tone of voice closed the subject. She pushed back her chair. "Better go right ahead," she said to Stephen and Luke. She had invested too much in the dude business to throw it overboard now.

She walked out of the house, across the little bridge over to the guest cabins. The beds were all made. Towels hung on the wooden rods by the washbasins. There were flowers in the Wellmans' cabin, paintbrush in one room, lupine in the other. She took the flowers out and threw them in the alders back of the cabin. Then she closed the doors and went on down to the corral, not quite sure what she meant to do.

[323]

Stephen had left Aspen for her. He wasn't like Rose, she thought. Since the horse was saddled and waiting, she might just ride a little way up above the ranch so she could look down on the whole spread. She had kept herself so busy she hadn't been on a horse since she got back from New York. She had hardly taken time to look at the early wild flowers that would be gone now in another week, nor marked how far the snow had drawn back from the pass on Wild Cat. Other years there wouldn't be so much to do; it was just the first year that the date of the dudes' arrival jumped out of the calendar and swallowed up all the other June days so you didn't know where the month had gone. It wouldn't be like this every year . . . would it?

She let the reins lie slack on Aspen's neck, slack as her own thoughts. Her mind was tired of making decisions and figuring costs and wondering how things would turn out. Her eyes moved up to the top of Wild Cat Mountain and touched the snow still holding there, ran down the loose scree to the fringe of jack pine and lost themselves in the aspens; then they came out again on the open ground. The grass was good this year, and nothing on it but the horses. The ranch buildings always looked small in all that space.

The ranch house was just as brown and small and weathered as ever. The stone chimney had been added but it didn't look new; stone never did. The raw ends of the new logs in the guest cabins and the ranch house porch jumped out at you, but the stand of aspens mercifully hid the bathhouses. She looked down to the barn and the corral and the long low shed where Slim used to shelter the weakest calves in a cold spring. Nothing was crowded at the ranch, plenty of room for ten more dude cabins, at a good distance from each other. You could enlarge the corral there, too. . . .

She watched a deer move out of the aspens, graze along the edge and disappear across the field without seeming to see her, but a sharp warning came from a magpie who flew angrily over her head.

Deer, elk and antelope come down to graze in sight of the ranch. The cry of the curlew is heard or the drumming of a pheasant in the tall grass,

the brochure on the ranch read. Aspen raised her head and then went back to eating, Pamela sat so still. From up here the river didn't seem to move at all . . .

Because the site for the ranch was chosen in an early day, it lies along the Missouri River.

She wished she had never written a word about the place if she was always going to think of what she had said when she was out here. She had had the brochure printed on rough brown paper, with photographs of the ranch in sepia, because the man in the New York printing place had said, "We always use this sort of thing when we want to suggest 'class.' " She wheeled Aspen around and set off across the open meadow that skirted the rocky base of the butte.

"Come on, Aspen," she whispered and gave the high, falsetto cry Slim had taught her. "The Indian yell" Slim used to say. The mare pricked her ears and was off, across the wide unfenced acres.

The air was cold along the edge of the mountain when she started back down. She came out of the aspens where she could look down on the ranch. Smoke rose from the chimney. Then she made out Papa's old car. She pricked Aspen with her spurs and galloped all the way to the cabins. Someone had opened the door of the Wellmans' cabin again. She rode on down to the ranch house fence.

Two women sat in the pole chairs Nurmi had made. Charlie Lacey sat beside them. Then Stephen came around the corner of the porch.

"I'll take your horse, Aunt Pam. Charlie and the dudes have been waiting for you for an hour." He winked as he took the reins from her.

"Pam, Miss Gilespie didn't know how to reach you so she

called the house in town when she and her friend got in on the train and I brought them out," Charlie explained after he had introduced the two women to her.

"Gilespie" . . . she had never heard of anyone by that name.

"They learned about the ranch from the railroad company, Pam, and they thought it sounded interesting. Miss Gilespie used to come out to Montana with her father when she was a girl. He was a construction engineer for the railroad."

Miss Gilespie and Miss Davis were spinsters, in their fifties. By their sitting there they seemed to impart the atmosphere of an Eastern hotel to the porch of the N Lazy Y.

"We've had the most fascinating time talking to your father," Miss Davis said. "And your mother was so thoughtful as to give us tea. We discovered she's an Easterner, too, and from the South; that made us friends right away."

"And we're to be the first guests this season!" Miss Gilespie said. "My, this is a beautiful place."

"I was just telling them about the spring we had five hundred and eight calves and the snow was two feet deep on the level ground, Pam," Charlie said. He settled back in the chair beside them as though he had entertained dudes on this porch other years . . . as, indeed, he had. Weren't the company gentlemen dudes, after all, Pamela thought.

Pamela went into the house. The table was set and a fire burned on the hearth. Ruby was out in the kitchen.

"You sure got your dudes," Ruby said, crimping the edge of the pie she was making. "I wish they was two prime white-face heifers instead."

Pamela stood in the doorway. "I've decided to buy some cattle, Ruby. I'm going to borrow some more money and buy sixty to seventy head. It looks empty from the butte up there."

"You better have 'em out where I can catch sight of 'em from this window if I'm going to be feedin' dudes in here all summer. And get Charlie to pick 'em, Pam. He knows cattle." Ruby slid her pie into the oven and slammed the door.

CHAPTER 5

1931

Pamela stood in the kitchen at the ranch drinking a cup of coffee and watching the wind blow the filigree spheres of dry tumbleweed across the ground to lodge transiently against the posts of the corral fence.

"She's your mother, Punk, even if she is Maybelle Lacey," Ruby said. "You can't do nothing but go down there, as I see it."

"I'm coming back as soon as I find someone else to keep house for them. I'm not going to stay there; I've got too much to do here, Ruby; you know that."

Ruby sniffed. "Yup, you got all them letters to write to every dude that ever showed her face out here, an' that fancy booklet you're putting out."

"I want to get Nurmi started on the new dude cabins, too."

Ruby scratched her head, and her mouth twisted into a grimace. "Did you see all them boudoir lamps Luke's made out of deer legs? And them bedside tables with elk legs holding 'em up? Some night, one of those precious dudes of yours is going to wake up and reach for something on the table and touch the fur leg and fall into a dead faint. Don't know as I'd care for it, myself."

"Dudes love that sort of thing, Ruby. The more skins and rustic touches in the cabins, the better. I meant to show you the pins I'm going to have for sale with the brand made out of copper."

Ruby snapped the head of a match into flame under her thumbnail and lit her cigarette. She hadn't taken pains rolling it, and it had a lumpy appearance. "If you didn't acshally raise some prime beef on this place, I'd say they oughta take that brand away from you. A brand was something you had to have in the old days, something you was proud of; it wasn't to be made up into a gewgaw."

Pamela set her coffee cup down on the sink board. Ruby nettled her. After all, Ruby was making a better salary now than she had ever dreamed of, and she wasn't working as hard either. Of course, Ruby never meant half she said. She remembered Rose saying that time, "Ruby isn't as stern as she acts, is she?"

"Well, I guess I better go," Pamela said. It was better not to try to talk to Ruby when she was in this mood. By the time she came back, Ruby would be over it.

The town looked dreary as she drove in to it in the early afternoon. The April light clothed it too thinly for the cold wind. The trees on Prospect Avenue were sharp and loveless in their bare state, and the houses stood up in reasonless angles and cupolas and bows from the dirt-blown street. How narrow the lots were! And with all that open land beyond! You could chalk that up to the visitations of the Northwest Development League that had boosted real estate beyond its value. Each house crowded so close to the edge of its lot there was no more than room for a lilac bush or a scraggly hedge on the side, and the trees stood guard in front of the houses to keep them in their narrow space.

The Morleys' house seemed less cramped because it stood on a corner with the vacant lot next to it. It had been painted last fall. Rose had put a brass knocker on the front door that caught the light even on a day like this. The name Morley was engraved across it. It was the only doorknocker on the street. The old-fashioned patterned lace curtains in the big front windows had given place to plain ones that fell in sheer folds, and upstairs white curtains with fluted ruffles were looped with careful precision at each window. Rose had managed to get a touch of elegance in the old house, Pamela thought as she drove past, or was it just an air of prosperity!

Maybelle opened the door for Pamela. "I thought you were sick in bed from your letter, Mama."

"I was, but that woman was no earthly good, Pam, and I had

[328]

to let her go, and then there was nobody here to do for Charlie, so I had to drag myself around."

It seemed to Pamela today that she went from irritation at the ranch to irritation at home. She carried her galoshes out to the vestibule and slipped off her coat without answering.

Maybelle looked at her in her wool pants and flannel shirt. Pam could wear trousers better than most women, but she didn't like them on her. She didn't like her hair cut short either, but it was no use to say anything; Pam wouldn't pay any attention to her. And she was going to be cross when she told her why she had written her to come in.

"Now we'll have to go through all that again, trying to find someone else," Pamela said. "You can't be without someone."

"Anybody would be better than that woman," Maybelle said, one hand fingering her collar. "But the main reason I wrote you, Pam, was because the Shakespeare Club has its annual meeting tonight, and I'm retiring as president, you know, and . . ." She forgot what she was going to say when Pamela's eyes flashed like that.

"Mama, you made me drive all the way in from the ranch just for that! You wrote 'come at once' and I supposed you or Papa was really sick and that Mrs. Dobbs had left, not that you had told her to go."

"You seem to forget, Pamela, that the Shakespeare Club has stood for a good deal in this community!"

Pamela's mouth twisted. "Where's Papa?" There was no use talking to Mama when she used that lofty tone of voice.

"Downtown some place with some of his old cronies, I suppose." Maybelle moved a little uncertainly into the other room. It upset her when Pamela was cross. But, anyway, she did want her here. Pamela would be surprised when she saw how the club felt about her mother. They were going to give her a gift, May Cheavers had hinted to her; at least she had said she better "be prepared." She guessed she better take just a little nap so she'd feel well tonight.

Pamela was in no hurry to change out of her ranch clothes.

They expressed her aloofness to everything here. The steam heat was stifling after the stove and fireplace heat at the ranch. The house here in town no longer seemed spacious when she came back in, the way it used to. It seemed small and cluttered, cut up into rooms that were no more than cubbyholes. The ranch was her home now. The Buffalo house never had been; that belonged to Alan, and this house had always been Mama's. The ranch used to be Papa's. He must have felt the way she did about it, and she had taken it away and made it hers. She always had an uneasy feeling about the ranch, as though she had no real right to it. But Papa couldn't have held on to it if she hadn't taken it; she had gone over this so many times, and yet the half-guilty feeling was still there. She might go down for Papa. That would please him.

The lobby of the Western was full tonight. The bar was closed, of course, because of prohibition, but all the big barrel-backed chairs were filled and the air was thick with cigar smoke. People stood by the swing doors, waiting out of the wind for the streetcar.

Pamela saw her father at the end of the room, talking to a man she didn't know, who had an Eastern look to his clothes. Papa was settled down as though he had no thought of going home for hours, his chair tipped back against the pillar.

"I hear you're out of the cattle business, Mr. Lacey," the stranger was saying as she came up.

"What made you think that?" Papa asked, and Pamela stood still, listening. "I'm still in the business, in a small way. Got about a hunderd, hunderd and fifty top-grade calves out there. They're not so many, but they're better grade; these are all purebred stock. My daughter's running the spread. Course I do all the buying and picking and keep an eye on it. When we're ready to sell next time, I'll let you know. I'd kinda forgot about your outfit."

"You do that, Mr. Lacey." The man was pulling out a card to give him.

"Hello, Papa," Pamela said. "I thought you might like a ride home."

"Well, hello, Pam. Isn't this a humdinger of a wind! Blowing the wheat farmers right out of the country." His voice boomed out so loud, people turned to look at him, nodding or smiling when they saw who it was. Everyone knew him, old Charlie Lacey, old-time cattleman. Charlie walked out to the car with her.

"You must have had a good beating coming across the flats the off side of Spring Creek, Pam, but I thought your mother would get you in some way!"

"It wasn't too bad," Pamela said, unconsciously copying the offhand tone Charlie always used. "I came down because of Mama's letter, but it was just as well because I wanted to ask you what you thought about buying a few more calves to feed through the winter. Jorgensen's selling the hay he put up, cheap. We might bring them up to about a hundred and fifty, say. Hank could take care of that many with Luke to help." Her eyes were on the streetcar tracks that ran as straight as lines on a ruled sheet of paper.

"Depends on, Pam, what you mean by cheap." Her father's tone was sharper than she had heard it in a long time. Jorgensen wasn't selling the hay very cheap, but she could buy it. She'd have to take out a loan for the calves, and she might not build more than one new cabin this year, but for once she could back up his claim; make every last word of it true. Her lips folded together in a tight little smile of satisfaction.

Pamela hadn't been to a Shakespeare Club meeting in years, and it was ridiculous for her to go now, but helping Mama get dressed in her best black crepe, she had a sudden sharp awareness of how much it meant to her. It was uncomfortable to look at things through someone else's eyes, and she hadn't done much of it since she stopped trying to see through Alan's. Since then she had looked only through her own; it was easier.

"Pam, do you think I should wear this brooch?" Maybelle

[331]

stood in the doorway of Pamela's room, and Pamela was a girl again, sitting at the piano looking at her mother all dressed for the dinner for the company gentlemen and thinking how beautiful she was.

"Yes, I do. Here, let me fasten it for you," Pamela said gently.

"You're not going in that old suit, Pam!"

"That's all I brought except my ranch clothes. I hardly have anything but suits, as a matter of fact. I don't go in for these women's things, you know."

"I think it's too bad, too," Maybelle said. "You'll be sorry when you're older, Pam."

Pamela had a feeling of crowding herself into too small a space as she followed Maybelle into the Reeds' parlor that was already filled with the members of the Shakespeare Club, most of them Mama's age.

She sat in the hall beside Mrs. Moore, but after Mrs. Moore had asked about the weather at the ranch and she had told her, they fell silent, and Mrs. Moore turned to talk to someone on her other side. It was hard to think of small things to say. Ruby was the only woman she talked to in the winter. What did women say; they were all talking so busily. She leaned a little forward, setting herself to listen. But they were talking about people she didn't know; someone was ill and someone was better. Those who had husbands were fond of quoting them: "Well, John says . . ." Someone else was painting her dark woodwork green to match the walls . . . She could say, "I spent last week rubbing oil on the logs of the dude cabins," but no one else here lived in a log cabin. She had an uncomfortable sense of being outside. Would she be sorry when she was older?

"Why, there's Rose Morley!" Mrs. Reed hurried to open the door.

They must have taken Rose in after Mrs. Morley's death, Pamela thought. Mrs. Reed sounded so pleased, almost honored that she had come, and Mrs. Reed hadn't liked to have Alice go with Rose years ago.

"When did you get back from Chicago, Rose?" Mrs. Reed was asking.

"Oh, Wrenn and I came in this morning . . ." Wrenn and I, Wrenn and I . . . or had she really said it only once? "And I remembered the annual meeting tonight."

"What a stunning outfit, Rose! You didn't get that here!"

Pamela had forgotten how women exclaimed over clothes. "Stunning" was a woman's word. She saw Rose's pleased smile. "No, I must admit I didn't. When Wrenn was busy, I went shopping." Pamela saw her diving in and out of shops on Michigan Avenue. Sitting at the counter, pulling on her white gloves, giving her name and address: "Mrs. Wrenn Morley, 600 Prospect Avenue, Brandon Rapids, Montana."

"Hello, Rose," Pamela said quietly.

"I can't believe you're here, Pam! You're as bad as I am about coming," Rose said.

"I know. I don't believe I've been to a meeting since you became a member, but I came tonight with Mother." Did that sound petty, reminding Rose how long it was before she was invited to join? She hadn't meant it to sound like that. Mrs. Reed moved a chair beside Pamela's for Rose.

There was the usual flurry over quotations with which to answer the roll call. They made no pretense of learning them any more, just read them from the printed page. "Here, girls," Mrs. Moore said, "do you have yours or do you want to look one up? We won't bother to read a play today with the annual meeting and all." She passed out books.

Pamela turned the thin pages.

How bitter a thing it is to look into happiness through another man's eyes.

That would have done once, but not now. She was past that. Rose's happiness wasn't for her. How silly the women sounded, quoting poetry like schoolgirls; they managed to get the same sing-song into their voices. One or two made a point of saying their lines from memory. Mrs. Biddle closed her eyes and clasped her hands like a child. Rose would be next. Pamela waited to hear what she would choose.

> Silence is the perfectest herald of joy:
> I were but little happy if I could say how much.

In that warm, throaty voice of hers, it became her own personal experience. Pamela made her voice brisk:

> Now my soul has elbow-room.

She felt triumphant as she said it, removed from this room full of women and their little domestic lives, and wanting no part in them.

"Isn't it amazing what you can find in Shakespeare!" Ethel Evans said when the quotations were over.

"How's Wrenn?" Pamela asked finally, as though the question were forced out of her.

"He's fine, but so terribly busy. I hardly see anything of him unless I go with him." She loved his being so busy, Pamela thought. It gave her a feeling of importance. "But we're going to run away to California for two weeks, just the two of us. . . ."

"That's a good idea," Pamela said. Rose had grown too portly to talk of running away.

"Don't you get lonely out there practically by yourself all winter, Pam? I know you have Ruby, but she's . . . well, not exactly your own sort. Honestly, I'd think you'd go crazy," Rose said.

"No, I find myself terribly busy, as a matter of fact, getting ready for the next season. And Ruby is quite a person." Did Rose suppose for a minute that she would *say* she was lonely!

"I suppose you're looking forward to going to New York soon to get dudes?"

"I don't know that I'm looking forward to it; it's hard work, really."

Rose didn't say anything to that; perhaps she knew she was irritated. They really had nothing to talk about any more. Being happily married didn't always make a woman more interesting.

[334]

"And now . . ." Mrs. Reed stood in the doorway between the rooms. "I have the very great privilege of presenting to our dear charter member and former president, Maybelle Lacey . . ."

Rose leaned over to whisper to Pamela, "I wish Mother Morley were here. Shakespeare Club meant everything to her, you know, and she thought the world of your mother."

Pamela wondered if Rose had ever guessed that it was Mother Morley who had kept her out of the club so long.

"Look, Pam, your mother's thrilled," Rose said above the clapping. "I suggested giving her something more personal, but most of them thought a painting by that cowboy artist would be something for her to hand down."

But Maybelle was disappointed by the painting. "This is more for you, Charlie, than it is for me," she said when they got home. "I wouldn't want to put it any place but in your study."

"Well, say, that's pretty good." Charlie held it at arms' length and inspected the painting. "That's a chuck wagon at roundup and there's a horse that's got out of hand and going to smash right into the cook fire. J.B. would have liked that, but I'll tell you someone else would get a kick out of it, too. Give it to Pam to take out to the ranch. Ruby'll think that's pretty darn good!"

"I'm certainly not going to send it out there for Ruby. It will go right over your desk, Charlie. But wasn't that a funny thing to pick out for me? Here, Pam, you put it somewhere for now." Maybelle's voice had lost its indignation. She was too tired to care, even about the Shakespeare Club.

"Rose was saying they think the world of you, though, Mama," Pamela said quickly, changing Rose's words a little.

"It was nice Rose was there when you were," Maybelle said.

"Oh, in a way." Pamela's shoulders moved slightly. "We don't have anything in common any more."

CHAPTER 6

1936

When the pack train was ready to start for the mountains, Hank always led the way up past the ranch house so Pam could see them off. She made a little ceremony of departures and arrivals, and it gave the dudes a chance to take pictures. She had at least twenty of the best ones framed, each with the date and destination written in white ink: "Pack trip to the Heart River Country, Aug. 1932"; "Goose Creek Fishing Trip, Sept. '34." She was watching for the trip that was going out this morning, so she could come out on the steps at the right dramatic minute. It was a little like being on a float, she thought sometimes. The dudes often took her picture standing there; she had put one of the snaps in the front of this year's ranch brochure.

She glanced in the mirror. Her hair that looked so simply cut, she always had styled in New York. Then all summer Ruby could trim it for her. Her white shirt of imported flannel had the N Lazy Y brand embroidered in navy on the pocket, and her dark blue jeans were tailored to order even though they were made of denim, wrong side out so they had that subtle weathered look from the beginning. Every season she watched the dudes arrive with the "ranch clothes" they had bought in Eastern sports stores; bright shirts and bandannas and fringed jackets, cheap felt hats complete with chin strap, and terrible riding pants, and saw them revise their ideas while they were there. She was playing with the idea of opening a shop in the old calf shed where dudes could buy the right sort of clothes. It could be very cleverly done, and you could make at least forty per cent on most things. Ruby didn't think much of the idea. Ruby went right on wearing her housedresses that she seemed to buy prefaded; the new ones looked so much like the old ones. "Slim never liked pants on a woman, les' she was on a horse," Ruby always said.

They were coming now! Pam picked up her buckskin jacket and went out on the porch to meet them. "I wish I were going with you! It will be beautiful up there at the falls. You never saw anything lovelier," she said to them all. "Do you have plenty of film? You'll see deer coming down to that little lake in the evening." As she said it, for their benefit, she really saw the deer moving quietly out of the trees, and she wished she were going to be there, but not with dudes. Papa and Slim had taken her up there the first time.

Her eye ran quickly over the pack horses; it took so many more than it used to. Hank growled about it. In the beginning, she had made a virtue of roughing it, but now she felt she had to give the dudes as much comfort as they could get at any other dude ranch. She had explained it to Hank. "I won't argue with you, Pam. You're the boss," he had said, but he had been disgruntled on every pack trip this season. Well, she *was* the boss, and she had to do what she felt was best.

She went over to the young bride who was a trifle nervous on a horse. To make her feel better, she went through the business of looking at her cinch and having her rise in her stirrups so she could check their length. She caught Hank's eye as she was doing it; a cold eye it was. Hank had already checked every horse. He was smiling sarcastically over at her. She must remember to say something to him later, explaining that it was just to impress the poor thing.

"You're all set?" she called over to Hank. Hank twitched his lips without answering. He never wasted words. She had to explain him to the dudes when he wasn't around. "He's the real thing," she had told Mr. Seavers one night. "He's worked for some of the biggest outfits in the country." (Cattle outfits, not dude ranches.)

"Just a drifter, you mean," Mr. Seavers had said in his heavy businessman's voice.

"No, indeed, not a drifter. You don't understand the Western cowboy, Mr. Seavers, I'm afraid," she had said.

She always gave the dudes a thumbnail sketch of all the people who worked for her; "the outfit," she called them, making them very Western and colorful, but she did particularly well by Ruby and Hank, and Papa, if he was around enough for the dudes to get to know him. If you were going to have people remember your ranch and come back year after year, you had to have plenty of "characters" and atmosphere; she had learned that.

"On your way, then!" she called out now, raising her hand. "And bring me back a sign you've been there; bear grass, or paintbrush, something that grows on the other side of the divide, and some tall tales of your adventures!" Her voice was slightly raised, slightly dramatic, and yet the dudes loved it. Hank was scratching the back of his head in embarrassment, she could see, but he knew why she did it. Curly, who had the string of pack animals, gave a regular mountain yodel, and they were off, the dudes waving and holding their reins too tight, all excited, you could see. It was a pretty sight, a train of fourteen riders, and the seventeen pack horses, winding up through the aspens.

She went back into the house and out to the kitchen. Let's see, that would leave only twenty-one dudes for lunch. She must plan something a little special for those who didn't go on the pack trip. Luke could take the three youngest dudes along the river to the buffalo pishkun to hunt for arrowheads, and tonight she might get Ruby to cook steaks out over the fire for everyone here. They kept the old chuck wagon equipped for that sort of thing, and Bob and Barry could sing cowboy songs for them afterward by the fire.

"Pam," the dude whose name was Fitz called out to her from the desk where she was addressing post cards. "Pam, I would have gone on the pack trip if I'd thought Hank would give me a decent horse, but he always palms off some dreadful nag with a hard gait on me."

"Oh, I'm sure you're mistaken about that, Fitz. Why don't you let me pick a horse for you, and we'll take a little ride together this afternoon. Western horses always seem so different at first," Pamela said soothingly.

[338]

So there would go her afternoon, but the morale of the ranch was only as good as the enjoyment of the last single female, she always said. It amused her to realize that she had been running a dude ranch long enough now to have some clichés to which she resorted; ten years last spring.

This afternoon when she took Fitz for a short ride up to the bluff above the river, Fitz said, "It must be so desolate here in winter," and Pamela was back on this same ridge with Alan on a June morning years ago. It seemed to her that he had been her first dude.

"No, it really isn't," Pamela said. "Now try to sit back in your saddle and take the jounces in your shoulders. You're not going for a ride in the park, you know; you're going to be riding all day after the cattle. Easy does it . . . like this."

She had to come back up from the fire that evening to get the phone call. It wasn't like the old days when they had to go to King Butte to get a message. The wire wasn't too good, but it was kept busy by the dudes with their long-distance calls. She expected to hear somebody wanting to make a last-minute reservation. She couldn't take anybody; they were full way into the end of September.

"It's very urgent. I must get in touch with Pamela Lacey at the N Lazy Y," a strained voice at the other end was insisting. It sounded like Rose.

"Hello, this is Pamela Lacey." She had to shout.

"Pam?" The voice seemed far away, only vaguely familiar. "Pam, this is Rose. Can you hear me? Your mother died this afternoon, Pam. Your father asked me to call you. He's here with us. Can you come right in, or do you want Wrenn to drive up for you?"

"I'll drive in. Tell Papa I'll be there as soon as I can."

"Well, we all got to die sometime," Ruby said when Pamela told her. "If Maybelle goes to the east coast of heaven, she'll do all right. What was she—seventy-five or closer to eighty?"

"Seventy-four," Pamela said. "Papa's seventy-seven, but you'd never guess it, would you? I'll try to bring him back out here with me. You take care of things here, Ruby, and don't tell any of the dudes what you think of them; you have an interest in the outfit, you know, and the dudes are partly yours, too."

Pamela had the whole trip in from the ranch to get used to the thought of Mama's death, but it still seemed incredible as she turned up Prospect Avenue. She hadn't been in town in late August for a good many years, and the thick-leaved stillness of the summer night fell heavily on her mood. She hadn't noticed before how the trees almost touched overhead on their street. It must have seemed to Mama like the streets back east, at the last. But it was so walled in. The porches of the houses came so close to the sidewalk. People didn't seem to sit on their porches the way they used to do. It shocked her that there was no light in their house; Mama wasn't there, and Papa was down at Wrenn's. Papa had left the door unlocked, of course. She stepped inside still half expecting to hear Mama come to the head of the stairs and call.

She had been a disappointment to Mama all the way round, it seemed to her; not marrying Wrenn, and then getting a divorce from Alan, and having no children . . . there was no use going back over things. She and Mama had been two different women, that was all.

She changed out of her ranch clothes and turned on the lights in the hall and the parlor and even upstairs, so it wouldn't be so hard coming back. Then she walked slowly down the block to Rose and Wrenn's, not anxious to get there. Wrenn was away so much of the time, she was thankful that he had been home just now for Papa's sake; for her sake, too. She wouldn't have gone there if only Rose had been home. But then Rose wouldn't have been; she always went with Wrenn.

Rose came to the door and put her arm around Pamela. Pamela held herself aloof inside that arm. Rose was sincere enough in her kindness; it wasn't that, but she was possessive, even of someone else's grief. "I know just how you feel, Pam, dear," Rose said. "Pam, dear" . . . it grated, and she didn't know herself how she felt. How could Rose?

"How is Papa?" Pamela asked.

Rose shook her head. "He's all broken up, Pam. Your mother died so suddenly. It was such a shock." The phrases were so trite the meaning ran out of them as though from a sieve.

Papa and Wrenn were sitting in the library, smoking, hardly talking at all. Wrenn came out to meet her. "Hello, Pam. I wanted to drive out to get you, but Rose thought it would take longer; of course, it would."

Of course, Pamela thought, but she would have liked that. They would have talked about things: the situation of the country and how the ranch was going and perhaps come back to the days when they were children. Wrenn took care of all her business affairs. They had come into a new relationship, something that had grown naturally out of that time when Wrenn read her his valedictory speech—something calm and intelligent and without hurt. She found herself quoting him sometimes when she talked politics with the guests at the ranch. "My old friend, Wrenn Morley, has the opportunity of seeing at first hand . . ." Friend out of lover, only he never had been her lover except in her own mind.

"Here's Pam, Mr. Lacey," Wrenn said, raising his voice.

"Pam! I'm glad you've come, Pam." Papa held her hands tight. He couldn't seem to say anything more. She had never thought of Mama as mattering so much to him. Mama had said so many bitter things about the ranch, but Papa seemed to have forgot all that. Papa's grief made the three of them feel like children again, outside the world of their elders. It drew them together for the minute.

They sat together around a card table in front of the fire. Charlie Lacey ate his supper because he always ate at mealtime. The others toyed with their food.

"Wrenn and I often eat dinner here in front of the fire," Rose said, and Pamela saw them here as though she looked through the glass window of a store at some delight that was not hers. What did they talk about when they were alone here by the fire? About Stephen? But Stephen was married and living in the East now. And Wrenn's work, of course. "Wrenn and I were saying how much your mother did for the community," Rose said in a silence. Pamela made no comment, because she doubted if they had said that.

"Yes," Charlie said. "Maybelle was always interested in improving the town."

They were standing together out in the hall when Rose leaned over and brushed Wrenn's shoulder. "I must have got some powder on your coat, dear." Pamela noticed how her hand remained there on his shoulder, pink-nailed, possessive, caressing. Only Rose would do something like that, in such bad taste, really, she told herself. Wrenn frowned, then almost absent-mindedly he laid his hand over Rose's as they stood there.

Charlie shook hands with Rose and Wrenn. "Thank you both. Old friends are a great help at a time like this," he said, but his feeling clothed the worn-out phrases so no meaning was lost.

Pamela repeated her thanks, her voice so much lighter than Papa's, her feeling thinner. Her eyes met Rose's briefly, and Wrenn's. Again they were like children brought together by their elders' grief into a pattern of close friendship. Were they old friends, or old enemies, she and Rose?

When they reached home, Charlie said, "The Pioneer Society wants an obituary of your mother for the paper tomorrow. They gave me this write-up, and they thought maybe we would want to add a little something to it. You do it, will you, Pam. I believe I'll go on to bed; I'll just sleep in the study tonight." After a few minutes, he came back out. "Your mother was very proud of being a Pioneer, Pam, don't forget that. She didn't like it that I joked her about it."

Pamela sat at her old bird's-eye maple desk that seemed absurdly small and girlish after the big table she used at the ranch, and read:

Maybelle Bottsford Lacey was one of the first children born in Virginia City, Montana territory, in 1864. Her parents came from Virginia, her father having been an officer in Lee's army. He was wounded in 1864 and came west.

She remembered taunting her mother with that once. "He didn't like it there any more so he came off out here," she had said. She was sorry now for the way she had said it, but it was true.

They became leaders at once in the new community, helping to build the first Episcopal church and school. Winfield Bottsford was one of the Vigilante organization which brought law and order to the new West.

Her eyes slipped along the familiar phrases that fitted so many of the Pioneer obituaries that they made a stereotyped pattern.

Maybelle Bottsford was sent to St. Louis to finishing school, and married Charles Langford Lacey, son of another pioneer family of Virginia City, in 1881. Mr. Lacey engaged in cattle raising in the King Butte area and became a prominent leader in the early cattle industry.

Not dude ranching—the real thing. Should she put in: "This family ranch, maintained somehow through the grueling winter of '85 and again in 1907, in spite of the burden of debts and mortgages and difficulties with the Eastern company that once owned a portion, their daughter has now converted into a smart dude ranch where Easterners may play at living in the Old West"?

Mrs. Lacey has been active in the Pioneer Society of this city, having held the office of President for the last seven years, retiring only recently on account of ill health.
She was the type of woman who brought the culture of the East to flower in the new Western land and sought always by her own example to cherish and hand down the heritage of courage and endurance characteristic of the Pioneer tradition.

Smooth, flowery phrases that would please her mother, and Mr. Sewall, too. "They lived their dream, Pamela; that was what made the West. That is your heritage as the daughter of the Pioneers!" She was back in the little office above the hardware store, hearing Mr. Sewall's voice swell with fervor, interrupted only by the sound of his sudden expectoration.

And what did it mean, any of it? What truth was there in it? What culture had Mama brought but a belief that things in the East were a little nicer than out here in the "crude West." "In the East, Pamela, people have meals on time, and, of course, they dress for dinner. . . ."

And that heritage Mama cherished: stories of the old days when everything was bigger and more exciting than the present. When did they stop telling about the hardships of those early days? . . . "We had to save our bath water and use it again to wash clothes in." "He had an Indian wife or two before he married, but then, of course, there weren't enough white women to go round in those days." When did they begin to tell about the glorious old days when men and women were so much braver than they are now, and every woman found a man to love?

How did that heritage of the Pioneers help the sons and daughters? It taught them how to live when life was exciting, not when one day followed another in a routine of working a hardware store: how to live when you had found your lover, who loved you, not how to make your life rich and full and sweet when you were that awkward person known as a spinster.

What could she add to Mama's obituary but bitter phrases? And what good was that? Mama's obituary was part of the Western Myth, and myths were always larger than life, just as the cowboys of Papa's day were a race apart from the rodeo-riding small-town boys who wore bandannas and yellow riding boots and glass-studded belts.

Mr. Sewall had willed her the hardware store because he felt she would carry on the myth, and what had she done? Helped explode it by making a dude ranch out of the N Lazy Y.

No, she had nothing to add to the neatly written clichés of Mama's obituary. Let it stand as it was, with love to Mama from Pamela. She took up her pen and wrote, "Mrs. Lacey is survived by her husband, Charles Langford Lacey, retired rancher, and by one daughter, Pamela Bottsford Lacey, of . . ." she hesitated, not of this city, no, "of the N Lazy Y Dude Ranch, King Butte, Montana." That was the truth, and there was the dude ranch that poked fun at the myth. She wasn't hiding it, and she wasn't ashamed of it. She slipped the obituary into an envelope and addressed it to the paper.

CHAPTER 7

September, 1940

"Well, they've gone, Ruby!" Pamela came back into the kitchen from seeing the last dudes off. There were four hunting trips booked but for three weeks there would be no dudes on the place.

Ruby was standing by the sink, rolling a cigarette. She made no move to pour her a cup of coffee so Pamela got herself one. That was Ruby's way of expressing her disgust with dudes and dude ranches. Sometimes, when some dude came very late for breakfast, Ruby was like this, seeming not to hear at first and then moving so slowly as she scrambled an egg or poured a cup of coffee. Yet the dudes were always crazy about Ruby. They sent her cards at Christmas and left large tips for her at the end of the season.

"Yup," Ruby said finally. "Best bunch of suckers yet." She took off her apron and dumped the contents of the two large pockets upside down on the kitchen table. The money fell with a noisy clank, bills in among the silver and one fluttered down to the floor. Ruby stooped down to get it and unfolded a twenty-dollar bill. Without any change of expression, her cigarette drooping a little from one corner of her mouth, she counted aloud, "Three hunderd and ten and four-fifty from that fussy little flippet of a Mrs. Brimsley makes three hunderd and fourteen and fifty cents."

"That's wonderful, Ruby. Now do something special with it."

Ruby gave a snort. "I'm figgering on it."

Pamela finished her coffee, and lighted her own cigarette. She had been so busy this season she hadn't had any time to sit down and talk with Ruby. She let the silence grow between them, relaxing into it. She was ready for this. She almost wished there were no hunting trips planned. She and Luke and Ruby and maybe Hank could take one by themselves. Go up over the divide and into the Sage Hills country, take a week for it . . . "I thought maybe you and Luke and Hank and I might get in a little hunting trip, Ruby, just ourselves. You haven't been on a horse all summer."

"How could I? Three meals a day, not counting lunches to go out and 'just a little something to go with the drinks, Ruby, you know,'" Ruby mimicked the high voice of one of the dudes.

"You did have pretty good help this season, didn't you think? I thought next season, I'd hire four college girls for waiting on tables and doing the cabins and we might get a second cook to help you, Ruby, who could do all the salads; you hate that part." She saw Ruby's mouth twist. "I'm so wound up I can't come to a dead stop. We have all winter to plan next season." She waited for Ruby to give her shrill "whoop-ee" she gave sometimes when the dudes were gone, to say something, anyway, that would match her mood. "Ruby, they've gone, do you realize that? We've had the best season we've ever had and we're alone, except for Luke and Hank."

Ruby grunted.

"I'm going to spend the whole winter up here this year, Ruby. Papa would be better off up here, too, I think," she said more slowly. The last time she had tried to bring him he had said,

"You know, Pam, I think I'll stay in town. I'm just kind of a curiosity for the dudes out there; in here I've got some old friends around town that are the same kind of article."

Ruby ground out her cigarette in the ash tray so hard she seemed to be boring a hole. "Pam, I guess I might as well tell you now before you get to making so many plans. I hate to do it worse than anything I ever done, but I've made up my mind."

Pamela looked at Ruby in amazement. Ruby was sitting on the table trying to roll a new cigarette but her fingers trembled so she spilled the tobacco, and her mouth was trembling, too.

"Why, Ruby, what on earth is the matter?"

"Pam, I know it won't seem right to you after you cut me in on the ranch and made Hank head of the outfit and all, but I don't like a dude ranch and I don't like the damn dudes, and Hank don't either, and we've made up our minds to quit. We're going to tie up together and hire out on a reglar ranch somewheres till we can find a few acres of our own." Ruby slid off the table and walked over to the window, turning her back on Pamela.

Pamela's face was colorless. Her hands were clasped around the coffee cup so tightly the knuckles were white. She stared at Ruby's back. In the still kitchen they could hear the bawling of the calves, only this week cut off from their mothers.

"I'm sorry, Pam. Sorry as hell," Ruby said to the window. "But you can get someone. Country's full now of wranglers and ranch cooks that want to hire out to an outfit like this. And you can take your time and find the right ones."

"Do I understand that you and Hank are going to be married, Ruby?"

"That's the general idea. I told Hank there's no fool like an old one; course, I'm the oldest. He's seven years younger than me, but he thinks we can make a go of it." She turned around and faced Pamela.

"I suppose then you are marrying Hank because you love him?"

Ruby went over to the sink, held her cigarette stub under the water faucet, then carried it to the stove and dropped it in before she answered. "I had that coming, Punk. No, it ain't love like I have for Slim, but it's some kind of thing that'll do. Hank understands how I feel."

"I see. Well, the ranch doesn't mean much to you, I guess. And it gets pretty dull spending the whole winter up here with me. When had you and Hank planned to leave?" Her eyes moved away from Ruby and rested on some object out the window. She pushed back her hair and shaped it around her head in a careful gesture of indifference.

Ruby worked the button on the front of her dress in and out of its buttonhole. A painful red blotched her face. The muddy yellow color of her eyes was diluted by the moisture that brimmed them.

"Hank and I figgered about the first of December we'd pull out, 'less it makes a big difference to you, Pam. That would see you through the hunting season pretty well."

"How thoughtful of 'Hank and you' to give me so much notice. No, nothing makes any difference to me."

Pamela walked out of the kitchen and through the big room of the ranch house. She was conscious of the signs of dudes: a discarded letter left on a chair, a match book from some night club in New York, a forgotten glass on a window sill. The ashes from the big fire they had had last night had blown out on the hearth, but she let them stay there. Then the lamp made of an elk's leg on the table by the couch caught her eye, the small hoof painted the shiny black of a girl's patent-leather pump, the slender furred leg supporting on its top an electric bulb mercifully hidden under a parchment shade. It seemed the epitome of all the artificial features of a dude ranch, the thing that was driving Ruby away. Pamela jerked the cord from the wall and hurled the whole lamp, bulb and shade and all, hard against the rocks of the hearth, then she walked out of the house with quick, hard-heeled steps and took the path that led up through the aspens. Ruby heard the crash and came in from the kitchen. She watched Pam from the window, biting the back of her hand to keep from crying.

Hank saw Pam climbing the hill and came to find Ruby. "She walked like she was mad, and you look like you was crying so I guess you told her."

"Yup." Ruby wiped at her eyes. "She's mad at me for the first time in her life. She smashed that there lamp and then she took off out of here like she was going to climb to the top of King Butte before she stopped to take a breath. It would be just like her to stay out here by herself all winter, with Luke to help feed and do chores. She'd go crazy all alone."

"Be lonely, all right," Hank said. "I spent a winter alone over in the Bitteroot sheep-herding oncet."

"It's worse for a woman by herself," Ruby said. "They're really lonely. Come right down to it, I s'pose that's part of why I'm marrying you, Hank; I want to be honest with you."

"I figgered that was part of it. Same with me. Maybe it's the same with everybody. Don't let that worry you, Ruby."

"I'm worried about Pam," Ruby said, scowling to keep her eyes from filling again.

"Well, she's fifty; old enough to figger out what she wants. Nobody's making her live off out here. If she'd kept this a regular ranch, maybe she'd have kept you and me. I like her first-rate, but she's different when she's got to talk and act for them dudes. You got any more coffee?"

Ruby poured him a cup and one for herself. "She won't give them up after the season she's had this year. With the war on folks can't go to Europe so they're crazier about this country than ever. What'd you get in tips?"

Hank blew three smoke circles in succession; the kind that made the yellow-haired dude girl squeal when she saw them. "A couple of dudes left an envelope with my name on down at the saddle room. The rest I told I didn't take tips. I'm no damned stable boy!"

Ruby's mouth moved to one side and she sniffed. "I took 'em, every little bitty one, an' I got three hunderd and fourteen dollars an' fifty cents. I'm going to put that into a papered Hereford bull." She gave a short, loud laugh. "That's pretty good, ain't it? Bull! D'you catch, Hank? Paid for by folks that fall for any bull you want to shoot. Slim'd get a laugh out of that." She went into the other room to get the binoculars that hung by the window. Standing there, she ranged her view over the rimrock, up past the aspens onto the rocky ground of the butte, itself.

"There she is, sittin' up there on that rock, looking off to nowhere and lonely as a damned curlew."

"Stop worrying, Ruby. She's gotta figger it out by herself, anyone has, man or woman."

Ruby grunted. "You can say that again. Get a real quick fire going for me, Hank. I'm going to make a pie for her when she comes back."

CHAPTER 8

November, 1940

Wrenn was late coming back up to their room in the Copper House, but Rose was used to that on trips with him through the state. He was always apologetic when he did come, but there was no need to be. She didn't mind waiting, and she liked the unexpectedness and excitement of the trips.

They always had the best room in the best hotel in each town in Montana. Sometimes that wasn't much. The Bonanza near the Idaho line was nothing but a frame building with thin partitions and one bathroom to a floor, but they had filet mignon there, prepared by a cook who had once been a New York chef, but taken to drink and drifted west. And even in a place like the Bonanza there were interesting people who had business with Wrenn, legal matters and, lately, political. Rose loved the talk about oil wells and mines and ranching. Sometimes Wrenn seemed too . . . oh, dignified and a little stiff, and then she tried to make up for it by her own warm interest. And afterward she said to Wrenn, playfully, "Darling, don't act as though you were remembering that you came from one of the first families of the pioneers!" Sometimes she had a chance to murmur, "Don't be so serious, Wrenn. Tell them that lovely story about the racoon and the beaver." But Wrenn was easier with people than he used to be. She never would forget what that old lawyer had told him once. He had said, "Morley, you've got plenty of ability and brains to be governor of this state, but you haven't got enough human warmth to matter to people." That had bothered Wrenn. "He's right, Rose. I don't have," he had said.

"Don't be silly, Wrenn, you can have; you just have to act a little more interested in people you meet." The lawyer had died since, but she wished he could know Wrenn's reputation for thoughtfulness. Of course, people didn't know that it was she who reminded him. "Ask him about his wife, Wrenn. You know she was sick for so long." "Remember the trout he put on the train for us when we went through Whitefish. Be sure to tell him how good it was." She had been a help to him; more help than Pamela would have been.

Rose went over and opened the window because the room was too hot. It didn't matter if the snow made a sissing sound on the big copper-colored radiator and sprinkled on the carpet. There was heat to waste in the Copper House. They always had this corner room on the sixth floor. It was high enough up so you could look way above the crooked street over to the mountains. Mountains were fine in summer but too cold looking in winter. How did Pam stay out there so late at the ranch with nothing to see out her window but that bare butte and the mountains behind it? She had asked Stephen that, and he had said, "Oh, Mom, you can't understand Aunt Pam. She likes staying out there." Rose shrugged ever so slightly, as Madame Guinard did. Perhaps she couldn't understand Pam, but she was sorry for her. When she felt sorry for her, she liked her better.

[351]

Rose moved the tasseled cord of the shade back and forth with one finger, remembering the time she had said to Wrenn, "Pam has a mind just like a man's, hasn't she?" And he had said, "No, I wouldn't say that. She has an awfully keen mind. And fair." After all these years, it still bothered her to have Wrenn praise Pam.

When the phone rang above the sissing of the steam, she felt like a lady in a play, crossing the yards of heavy red carpet to answer it. She often felt that way when she was off on these trips with Wrenn. This would be Wrenn telling her to have the bags taken down and meet him in the lobby, or maybe saying he was bringing someone up to talk a few minutes before they started out. She never knew.

But it wasn't Wrenn; it was a Mr. Neale Hagen who had urgent business with Mr. Morley. If he could just see him for a few minutes. . . . Rose's voice became formal. "I know Mr. Morley intends to leave right away. He has already been detained, but I will certainly tell him, and then if you will give me your phone number, he can call you before he leaves town. I really can't promise, Mr. Hagen."

She wondered what his business was as she wrote down his name and phone number. He had sounded as though he knew her. Of course, lots of people knew them whom she didn't know, but she made it a point to remember names because Wrenn was so poor at it.

Hagen . . . ? She watched the tasseled cord on the shade moving now with the draft that blew in around the loose-fitting window, trying to remember. Wasn't he that man they met years ago at Fort Benton? Of course he was, and he hung around Pam and danced with her most of the evening. Now she remembered all about him. He was that labor leader in Butte who stirred up so much trouble last year. But, of course, he might have a good many votes in his pocket . . . not that Wrenn would put it that way. Wrenn was always talking about principles. . . . "You see, dear, the principle involved . . ." He made so many speeches all the time that sometimes, even when he was talking to her, getting undressed for bed, he sounded as though he were still making one. But maybe he better just see the man.

Wrenn called as she had expected and wanted to start right off. "The snow's drifting. We'll just stop for a sandwich and go right out. You call him and tell him I can't see him this time."

"It would only take a minute, Wrenn. You can find out what he wants and then put him off until later. I think I would. No, up here would be better, more private. It might be conspicuous in the lobby if . . . you know."

She heard Wrenn's step in the hall. It seemed to her sometimes that she was always listening for it. "You sound as though you're going to break into a run the next step," she told him. "Don't hurry so!" But she liked his hurrying, the kind of dash there was about everything he did. He would win the election; she felt it in her bones. She could tell by the way he flung the door open and smiled that he had been pleased with his conference.

"I hope you aren't going to mind being stuck in the canyon all night, Mrs. Morley, because we just might be!" he said, holding her face between his cold hands as he kissed her.

"Maybe we better stay overnight and go in the morning."

"Oh, no, we'll get through; I've got to be in court in the morning. But I'm going to cut this interview you've fixed up for me pretty short."

Mr. Hagen was on time. Rose opened the door for him. She remembered him right away when she saw him. He looked older, handsome though, in a way.

"I'm sorry, Mr. Hagen, that we are so hurried, but Mr. Morley says the snow is drifting already, and you know what it will be in the canyon!"

"I know; I've just come over the other way." But he smiled at her as though he didn't take it too seriously. She remembered telling Pamela that he was a lady-killer; he still thought he was.

Wrenn was asking him to sit down. Now that he was here, Wrenn acted as though there were all the time in the world.

That was his way. She lingered, pretending to be busy with her dressing case at the opposite end of the room so she could remind Wrenn of the time. If Wrenn wanted to be alone with him, she would know. Without ever agreeing on them, they had signals.

She put her hat on in front of the mirror; Mama had really been inspired when she made it. The pheasant feather was amber against the beaver. "Beaver for you, or maybe leopard; gray squirrel for Pamela Lacey," Mama had said. Still, the beaver did make her look larger. Her eye moved over to Neale Hagen in the mirror and caught his eye, then quickly down to her gloves on the dresser. He had been watching her, but he went right on talking to Wrenn.

"Morley, I want you to go with me to talk to a bunch of miners tonight. I tried to get you sooner, but I didn't get in town. . . . I'll drive you over there. If you come tonight and talk to them the way I think you will, you'll have twice that many votes and besides that it can mark the turning point in relations between . . ." There was a kind of intensity in his voice that made her glance hurriedly over at Wrenn.

"I could get you back here about two, unless the storm gets much worse; three at the latest," he was saying.

"I'd like to," Wrenn said slowly, "because I really have their interests at heart, but I don't want Mrs. Morley to be snowed in on the road and . . ."

She saw Mr. Hagen's mouth twist ever so little. He lifted his hands as though weighing something in them, something light.

"Wrenn," she interrupted gently, "don't worry about me. If you feel it's an opportunity you don't want to miss. I mean . . ."

She felt rather than saw Mr. Hagen's glance. He said quickly:

"I do think it's an opportunity. It's important both to the men and to your husband, Mrs. Morley. I want them to see the kind of man who's running for governor. It's important to the state, too, for that matter."

Wrenn was catching fire now. His eyes were that extra-bright blue they took on when he was interested. "I suppose we could make an early start, as soon as I get back, perhaps," he said. Now he was in that mood when he felt he could go without sleep or meals and work all night. She loved him like that. "If you'll drive me over, I'll go," Wrenn said.

"I want to go with you. I don't mind the cold, and I don't want to wait here." Rose smiled at Neale Hagen.

"Mrs. Morley, it's going to be a rugged trip. I don't like to seem ungallant, but the meeting is going to be held in a barn of a place, and there won't be any other women."

"No, Rose. It's nonsense for you to go. You get some sleep, and we may start out as soon as I get here."

"I can't see . . ." she began, pouting a little. Wrenn had his mind made up, she could see. He came over and put his arm around her. "Good night, darling. I'll wake you when I come." The old saying that went way back to the nights when he used to study late won her over.

"Go on then. Mr. Hagen, take good care of him."

"I surely will. I wonder if you remember that we met before, Mrs. Morley?"

"Of course," she said. "At the Pioneer celebration at Fort Benton. I remember you were very much enamored of Pamela Lacey." Now why had she said that!

"Indeed I was. She was a most unusual girl."

"She's a very fine woman," Wrenn said, "and a very bright one. She's turned her father's old cattle ranch into one of the most successful dude ranches in the West."

"Wrenn has helped her with the business side of it," Rose put in. A moment ago they had been in such a hurry to leave, and now they stood talking as though Pamela held them there. Neale Hagen didn't say anything, just looked thoughtful. He was that romantic sort.

"Well," Wrenn said, "if we're going . . ." And then they were gone, and the room seemed too empty to stay in. Rose hung up her coat and hat and opened the suitcases she had closed. She picked up her handbag and went out to the elevator. She might as well use up some of the time by having dinner. And after dinner she would call Mama and have a chat. Mama would worry if they didn't get in tonight. The wind was blowing so hard the snow sounded like sand against the glass pane, and the sissing of the radiators had sunk to a puny whine.

She was surprised at all the people in the dining room on a night like this, eighteen or nineteen at one large table. When she asked the waitress about them, she said they were the Dude Ranchers' Association, and then she noticed their clothes: fancy shirts and some of the women wore pants. . . . Wrenn wouldn't be seen dead in Western rigs. It was odd that Pam wasn't down for the meeting, but probably the snow kept her away. Pam must be one of the most successful of them all.

While she ate the steak that was too big, but the safest thing on the menu to order, she thought about those friends of Gordon Jennings who had had dinner with them before their train left. Pam had taken them into the mountains on a hunting trip. Gordon was always sending people to Pam's. One of the women had raved about Pam. "I never saw anything like her," the woman had said. "Imagine a woman taking out a hunting trip in the first place! She wrangled the horses in the morning when it was so cold the water was frozen along the edge of the stream, and then came back and did a good share of the cooking. And she looked so fresh, I felt simply haggard."

"She had some wonderful stories of the early days. I guess her father was a big cattleman and fought the cattle rustlers back in the eighties and all that," one of the men had said. Rose could hear Pam making old Charlie Lacey sound like a regular Western hero.

"Of course, she charges all the traffic will allow and a little more," the other man had said. "How was it she put it? I thought that was pretty good, something . . . oh, I know, she said, 'If you want to feel like the pioneers in the untouched wilderness, you have to endure some of the hardships and hardships cost something.' She holds you up all right, but she gives you a great time."

It was amazing, really, that Pam should have made such a

[356]

success, such a solid financial success. . . . Charlie Lacey was always up to his neck in debt. Of course, Wrenn had helped her. He had advised her all along. She did think Pam imposed a little; she knew how busy he was. She didn't know yet whether Wrenn ever charged her . . .

Rose took a taste of the mince pie and laid down her fork. She shouldn't have ordered mince. She might have known it would be made of elk meat. You needed to add plenty of brandy if you were going to use tough elk in a mince pie.

Over her coffee, she went on thinking about Pam. She and Pam never really said much to each other when they talked. Sometimes when she was with her, she felt so dumpy beside Pam's long slender look, and a little stupid when Wrenn talked to her about, oh, about forest conservation or something. Other times she felt so lucky beside Pam she tried not to think about her; the way you tried not to think of some penniless drunk you saw on the street when you were driving to a dinner party. It made you frightened to be so happy yourself.

There was something about being with Pam that made her use Wrenn's name all the time: "Wrenn and I had to laugh . . ." or "Wrenn and I had such a good time in New York . . ." She heard herself, but once she was started, she had to finish her sentence. And to say "Wrenn and I" was like saying a charm. No one could touch her once the charm was said.

. . . Wrenn would be there by now. He would be talking to the men. She knew just how he would look; you could tell by his face how sincere he was, and how much he cared that they understand exactly where he stood. That was the thing that would make him win in the end; that people felt he was sincere; and he was. She wished she had made them take her along so she could be sitting now in the back hearing him.

Pamela slammed the door and started the car in motion down the road from the ranch that had not even faint shadows to suggest a traveled road. She might very well be sorry she had started; she might be stuck any place between here and the

Copper House and have to spend the night in the car, or walk miles through the snow or slide off the road for that matter. There was no real reason why she had to get to the Dude Ranchers' meeting; none of them could tell her anything she didn't already know, and she could just as well read the report of the meeting later on, but it was a reason for going to town! She couldn't settle down to the winter at the ranch the way she used to when Ruby was there.

The windshield wipers were useless against the crazy popcorn dance of the snow; she lowered the window and tried looking out into it. It was better the other way, but the snow felt cool and good against her face.

What would Alan think of the flats in this weather? She had thought of him more lately. Of Wrenn, too. When you were alone for weeks at a time, you had to gather around you everyone who had made very much imprint on your mind. You had to go back over things; the silliest small things you wouldn't think you'd remember. Like the time she had the birthday dinner for Alan, the kind of little intimate dinner he liked, very carefully planned. Suddenly he had leaned forward and looked at the Japanese iris in the pewter bowl and said, "Pamela, there's no water in the flowers!" Said it accusingly, all out of proportion to the deed. And she had said, "So there isn't. Heavens, how awful! I went to answer the phone and forgot it. Quick, pour your glass in before they perish!" managing to make it somehow funny so that everyone laughed, everyone but Alan. And afterward, when everyone was gone, Alan was still displeased. "Really, Pamela . . ." he had begun, and she had cut in quickly, "Really, Alan, it was rude of you to mention the water. The damned flowers would have lasted through dinner." She had said "damned" on purpose.

"Don't be rough, Pamela!" he had said. "You sound as crude as Ruby." Alan gave it a certain sound that made rough sound worse than dishonest or immoral or unkind, and he couldn't say anything against Ruby to her.

"I don't happen to find Ruby crude," she had said, and known

beforehand that he would say next, "Don't be childish, Pamela."
She had been childish, of course. He had made her so. Oh, no,
she could never have gone on with Alan. It didn't trouble her
to know he was married again. His mother had sent her an
announcement and she had written him that she wished him
great happiness. She remembered the woman; a pleasant quiet
person with a tranquil face who would be right for him. She
hadn't been tranquil, yet she craved tranquillity, but it was always outside herself, in the mountains, on the ranch.

Why did she keep remembering unpleasant things? Life was
half remembering and as many things you didn't want to remember as those you did. Think of something pleasant. Think
of Wrenn last summer, asking her what she thought of his running for governor, asking her almost anxiously, caring what she
thought. She had known Rose was listening, not liking his asking
her, and she had said, "What does Rose think?"

"She didn't like the idea in the beginning, but now, I think
she likes it," he had said. Yes, Rose would. But Rose would be
thinking about the change it would make in their living, not
what Wrenn could do. She had answered honestly, "I think it's
fine, Wrenn, if you're strong enough. You'll have a lot of things
to fight in this state."

She had seen that faint unsure look in his eyes, and then he
had smiled and said, "Well, I can try!" It looked as though he
would have a chance. Papa said he'd be elected. It would be
interesting to see him, and Rose, too, in that role. If she had
married him and been the governor's lady . . . there was one
thing about it, she would certainly keep him from making a
speech like that last one of his that was in the paper. He knew
very well he could never give the farmers all he promised! But
he probably wouldn't like having his wife criticize his speeches;
he didn't like having his valedictory speech criticized! Well, he
was safe with Rose; Rose thought everything he did was perfect.

After the dark snowy road, the lighted hotel looked good to her.
She was glad she had come. She felt like a celebration. Mel

Gardner of the Diamond T met her in the lobby. "I said you'd get here by midnight, Pam, and you're just fifteen minutes late. I was telling Ben Davis a little thing like weather wouldn't stop you! But I was scared when they said at the desk you hadn't put in for a reservation. Couldn't have a dude ranchers' meeting without you, Pam!"

Pamela laughed. "No, I decided to come at the last minute. Maybe they're filled up."

"They better not be. If they are, you can bunk down with my wife, and I'll find a place."

Other ranchers called out to her as she crossed the lobby to the desk. She knew she was a little dramatic throwing back her fur coat, pulling off her gloves. She was more successful than most of them. They said, "Look at Pam Lacey at the N Lazy Y; look what she's done."

"How's the snow up your way?" someone asked.

"Not too bad," she called back over her shoulder. Never admit the going was hard, easy does it; that was the Western way.

"I didn't write in for a reservation. Do you suppose you can find a room for me somewhere?" she said to the desk clerk. She wrote her name on the pad he pushed toward her, "Pamela Lacey, the N Lazy Y, King Butte."

"Yes, Miss Lacey," the clerk said respectfully. "Fact is," he leaned a little toward her, "we can give you the big corner room on the sixth floor, best room in the house." There was something in his manner that arrested her.

"How does that happen?" she asked. "I thought you'd be full." And then she saw the look of the man's face that had completely wiped away the usual jovial lines and left the forehead puckered, the eyes shocked. Something was wrong.

He looked down at the pen she had handed back to him. "The Morleys had that room. I keep it for 'em whenever they come. They've been here the last two nights."

"The Wrenn Morleys?" she asked, but, of course, he meant the Wrenn Morleys.

The man nodded. "Mr. Morley was driving over to Butte tonight with Mr. Hagen to make a speech, as I hear it. Mrs. Morley was waiting for him here." He glanced up at Pamela and dropped his eyes again.

"Yes?" Pamela said, impatient with his deliberate manner. "What happened?"

"They went off the road over by Horseshoe Creek an' Mr. Morley was killt. Musta been early in the evening, but they couldn't get word to Mrs. Morley till about two hours ago. Somebody came by, fin'ly and brought Mr. Hagen an' . . . an' the body back."

Pamela stared at the man. "Hagen? Neale Hagen was with Mr. Morley?"

The man nodded. "Hagen was pretty bunged up and white as this blotter. I guess his arm was broke, but that was all. He was shaking like a leaf when he asked me to call Mrs. Morley's room. Guess you was a friend of the Morleys by the look of your face."

"Yes," Pamela said. "We grew up together. Where is Mrs. Morley?"

"Some friends of theirs that Mr. Hagen called tried to get her to stay with them, but she insisted on going back to Brandon Rapids, in the snow and all, so they drove her. She acted like she didn't know what she was doing; half crazy, you know. It was a terrible shock to her. An' they took the body home right behind her." He shook his head. "Ain't that a terrible thing?"

"I can't believe it," Pamela said slowly.

"Course they'll read about it in the paper tomorrow morning, but I haven't told anyone else yet. It'll put the kibosh on their dude association doings. Everybody in the state thinks a lot of Wrenn Morley."

Pamela stood in the corner room on the sixth floor that had been the Morleys' and looked around her. The maid had straightened it; there was no sign of former occupancy. Rose had heard about Wrenn in this room. Neale Hagen had told her here. Pamela glanced in the mirror almost as though she would see Rose's reflection still held there. She glanced down at the dresser top and saw the light drift of powder on the scarf that the maid had missed, and thought of Rose brushing powder from Wrenn's shoulder that time. She remembered how possessive her hand had looked and how Wrenn had covered it with his, and they had stood there like that.

Pamela picked up her coat and bag; she couldn't stay here. She would drive back to Brandon Rapids, too. Maybe there would be something she could do.

The lobby was nearly deserted when she went back and left her key at the desk. "I won't be staying after all," she said, avoiding the curiosity in the night clerk's eyes.

"Being friends of yours, I guess you're pretty shook up, too," he murmured sympathetically. "There's another one an' I can't blame him! He won't stay at the hospital an' he says he don't want a room." Pamela glanced in the direction of the clerk's headshake. Neale Hagen sat in one of the big chairs in a dim corner of the lobby. His arm was in a sling, and an ugly bruise distorted the side of his face. He smoked a cigarette and stared across the room without seeming to see anything. There was nothing in the slumped heavy figure that reminded her of the young man she remembered. She felt his wretchedness, then she remembered that he was alive and Wrenn was dead. She went on out of the hotel into the snow.

It wasn't too bad driving on the highway. The snow came down steadily, like a curtain between you and the night, but it wasn't blowing. She could understand how Rose couldn't stay there, how she had to get home. Pamela drove fast, watching for Rose's car ahead of her around every curve, but, of course, she wouldn't overtake them. They had had a good two hours' start. On a curve the lights of the car shone full on one of Wrenn's posters nailed to a telegraph pole. MORLEY FOR GOVERNOR it said, and there was Wrenn's face. She hoped Rose hadn't seen that. "She acted like she didn't know what she was doing, half crazy, you know," the man at the desk had said. She didn't wonder. She couldn't believe Wrenn was dead; how could Rose believe it? What would she do? Madame Guinard would be there when she got home, and Stephen would come. . . .

Maybe she should have talked to Neale Hagen. Maybe he could have told her something Wrenn said that she could have told Rose. But Rose wouldn't want to hear Neale Hagen's name. She wondered how Wrenn had happened to be driving with him. It was strange that Rose had stayed at the Copper House alone. She always went with Wrenn.

Rose and Wrenn had always been so . . . devoted was the word people always used. How would Rose manage now?

And how could this have happened to Wrenn just now, when he had so much ahead of him? Rose was looking forward so to his being governor. Rose . . . her mind kept going back to Rose.

Lights were on in the Morley house as she drove down Prospect Avenue. It was the only lighted house on the block, just as it had been the time of the flu, but the bedroom on the corner with the turret was dark. Pamela stopped the car and went up the steps. She hesitated to ring, and when she tried the door, it was unlocked. The familiar hall had a startled silence about it that made her feel like an intruder. She had no right here. Why had she come? But before she could leave, Madame Guinard came down the stairs.

"Madame Guinard, can I . . . I came to see if I could do anything."

Rose's mother shook her head. "There is nothing no one can do." She rubbed her hands as though trying to warm them. "I've given her something to sleep. . . . I don't know, Pamela; I don't know if she can stand this."

"Could I . . . would it be any help if I stayed here tonight?"

"I will be here. No one can do any good to Rose. She don't want any human being, only Wrenn."

Pamela stayed awhile with Madame Guinard, sitting out in the kitchen. She made coffee, and they drank it, holding their hands around the hot cups. Every now and then Madame Guinard tiptoed upstairs to see that Rose was sleeping. When she came back, she said, "She is sleeping, but tomorrow she has to wake up again."

Then they sat silent again.

"Wrenn was thrown against a tree and killed quick; he didn't have time to know," Madame Guinard said. "I tell Rose it is better than he be crippled or have terrible brain injury, but she just cry all the more."

Pamela remembered Wrenn sitting here at this table and unconsciously her fingers smoothed the edge of the table as his had done. She had known that day that she didn't really love him. She had no right to sit here now, dry-eyed, remote, feeling unreal . . . as though they were on the Pioneer Day float acting a part.

Madame Guinard sighed. "Nodder woman beating her head against a post," she muttered. "Always same thing over again. All womens made for, to get hurt. You done good, Pamela Lacey, if you don't love no man." Her black eyes bored into Pamela's; her face was a yellowish white, and her mouth worked as she spoke. She got up from her chair. "Don't listen to me; I talk like an old fool," she said.

"Madame Guinard, you go up and get a little sleep. I'll lie down on the couch in Wrenn's study, and then I'll get breakfast before I go," Pamela said in a dry voice that was hardly her own. "Please let me do that much."

Madame Guinard was so tired she tottered as she went toward the door. "Don't stay, then, Pamela. Rose won't want to see . . . anyone."

"No, I won't. I'll go on home," Pamela promised.

CHAPTER 9

January, 1941

Rose sat in the turret end of the bedroom, in the dark, watching the cars come down Prospect Avenue. Sometimes the lights made a chain as far as she could see; they were coming slower tonight because of the snow. Streets were slippery underneath;

maybe there would be a smashup right here at the corner. She almost hoped there would be.

When you looked at the car lights through the screen, they lost their round shape and became crosses, twin crosses. It must be the mesh of the screen that did it. She hadn't bothered to take down the screens this year or put up the storm windows; they had been away so much in October and November, and after that she hadn't cared whether the storm windows were on or not.

Just at the corner where the cars had to slow down, the lights flashed in the room and shone across the picture of Wrenn in the big silver frame, the one he had taken for the election campaign. Sometimes she just sat here and watched the lights touch his picture.

Now there were no car lights for a few minutes, only the street lights at dim intervals down the avenue. It must be terribly cold tonight. It was twenty-two below at five o'clock. There had been that to talk about. She and Mama had discussed it for fifteen minutes, and then Mama had said, "I'm glad I don't have to go out in weather like this; it's very pleasant for me to be living here with you, Rose." But Mama only lived here because she didn't want her to be alone. Mama liked her own little place best.

Lights were sliding down the street again. When she leaned back in her chair, they seemed detached, floating by themselves, coming toward her faster and faster. But they weren't detached; they belonged to a car full of people going some place together; maybe, someone like Wrenn, with his wife beside him, on the way to the station, going down to California for the cold months. She had gone off like that once, leaving this house standing here on its lonely corner. She had never thought that she would sit here in the dark, alone.

The pause, the lights flashed into the room, caught on the silver frame, swept across Wrenn's face, bringing it to life, and left it in darkness again. Let them go; she didn't want anyone stopping here. She couldn't stand people saying, "My, that was a terrible thing! You have my sympathy!" She didn't want anyone but Wrenn. She dug her elbows into her lap and buried her face in her hands. The weak, senseless tears of self-pity ran down her face.

"Wrenn, Wrenn," she whispered. "I can't stand it without you."

Mama kept telling her she should "be brave" and "keep busy" and remember how much happiness she had had with Wrenn, as though that didn't make it all the harder now! Yesterday Mama had been angry and shouted at her, "You think you're the only one who ever lost her husband? What you think about me? Did I get mad at the whole world and shut myself up?"

But Mama hadn't sent Papa to his death as she had sent Wrenn. She had urged Wrenn to go with that fool of a Hagen to make a speech so he would get more votes! How did you ever forget that? If she had only gone with him and been killed too! After a while she wiped her eyes with her arm. She didn't bother to do her face any more. She didn't care how she looked.

Mama must have fallen asleep, the house was so still. She had been going to sew the lining in a hat for Mrs. Moore. It didn't matter; they had plenty of time. They hadn't had much business since Mama moved her millinery shop up here. Mama blamed her and said she was rude to people. Maybe she was, but she wouldn't have people pretending to come about a new hat but really to see how she was taking her loss! Saying to each other that it was a funny thing Wrenn Morley hadn't left his wife better off so she wouldn't have to have a millinery shop in her front parlor, and wouldn't Ned Morley turn over in his grave if he knew it! She had heard them. They didn't know what it cost to run for governor; to get to the place where you were *thought* of for governor. She didn't begrudge it. She didn't care how she had to live now.

Mama said she was rude to Mrs. Moore yesterday; that Mrs. Moore had lost her husband and knew what it meant, but she hadn't lost Wrenn. "You just take one day at a time; that's the way I did," Mrs. Moore had said cheerfully. Rose clasped her hands together so hard her fingers hurt. She couldn't live that way with nothing ahead, knowing she would never have him again. That wasn't living, only existing.

Stephen had written from his army camp, "I wouldn't feel good about you, Mother, if it weren't that Grandmother is with you. I know she'll keep you jolly." He should see them. They were very jolly.

Mama was in the living room in Wrenn's big armchair. She had fallen asleep with her glasses still on and the hat she was fixing in her lap. Rose stood in the doorway and looked at her. She looked so frail all of a sudden.

Rose glanced at the grandfather clock across the hall. It was only eight-thirty. Evenings crawled. She couldn't sleep when she did go to bed. She wished Ted Horning would drop by. He came sometimes about something in connection with the office, since he had taken over Wrenn's practice. Mama made a little face about him and said, "What does he want this time?"

Maybe he was a little ordinary, and he hadn't paid as much as he should have for things, but he did admire Wrenn. He hadn't called him Wrenn when he was living, but he meant all right. "I remember Wrenn telling me . . ." he would say, and it took her back to those days when Wrenn was alive, when she was, too.

Eight-thirty-five. The clock seemed to tick in an empty house, as though no one was in it. Rose hid her hands in her neck and then clasped her arms around herself. What did Pamela do with her evenings alone at the ranch? She read books, perhaps. She was always lending Wrenn some book to read or telling him about one. But she didn't have to stay off out there. She was as free as the air. Charlie was down here with a housekeeper to take care of him; she didn't need to bother about him. Pam made plenty of money; she could come and go as she wanted. Pretty soon she would go off on one of her trips to New York. Was it just last spring Wrenn and she herself were in New York together?

Rose went on out to the dining room, aimlessly, pushing in

a dining-room chair closer to the table (they never used the dining room any more), but knowing all the time where she was going.

The three cut-glass decanters that had been Wrenn's father's stood on the built-in sideboard. Stephen used to beg for the silver lockets on them that said, Bourbon, Sherry, Scotch, in elaborate engraved script. Rose liked the wine best. She and Mama always had a little glass of wine before dinner, sometimes two. "In winter, it is good for the blood," Mama used to say. Lately she said, "It doesn't agree with me. I don't believe I'll have any, Rose." She saw through that. Tonight she had told Mama, "I'm going to have a glass anyway, so you might as well have one, yourself."

But tonight she took one of the tall glasses she had often set out for Wrenn's friends. She had stood here just like this and set the Scotch and bourbon on the silver tray with the glasses around it, and the ice and soda, hearing the deep murmur of men's voices in the other room. Sometimes they were serious; sometimes there was laughter, so much pleasanter than women's laughter. Often Wrenn or some one of them would come out to help. And after they had gone, Wrenn would tell her about the talk. The minute they had gone, she would hear him calling, "Rose! Where are you, Rose?" There wouldn't be any more of that, ever again.

She poured the whisky into the glass and carried it out to the kitchen to add tap water. She didn't bother about ice. The stuff was raw-tasting and burned her throat, but it was sharp. She took her glass into the parlor and sat there in the dark watching the cars come down Prospect Avenue.

CHAPTER 10

March, 1941

"By golly, looks like it's going to chinook, Charlie!" Ed Cheavers said. "Chinook!" he repeated louder when Charlie didn't hear him.

" 'Bout time. Two straight months with the mercury below zero," Charlie answered.

The two men stood in the lobby of the Western putting on their coats. Charlie had come down in the morning expecting to stay all afternoon, as he usually did these cold days. The desk clerk sometimes pointed him out to folks. "No matter how cold it is, in comes Charlie Lacey. Usually sits over in that chair by the radiator . . . knows about everyone. Must be in his eighties and never sick a day. Oh, these old-timers, they're tough."

But today the opening and closing of the front doors let in to the smoke-filled lobby the warm breath of the chinook wind. Water dripped from the eaves of the hotel and slowly, steadily beat little holes in the thick ice that covered the sidewalk. The occupants of the barrel-backed chairs in the lobby smelled the change in the air and began to leave.

"Want a ride home, Charlie?" Ed Cheavers shouted in Charlie's direction.

Charlie nodded, panting from the exertion of getting on his overcoat.

They walked over to the corner; Ed Cheavers, at seventy, taking small steps, watching where he put his feet down, fearful of falling on the ice; Charlie, at eighty-one, stooped a little, but still head and shoulders taller, even with his lame knee, tramping along as he had used to do at the ranch.

"What about Pam? She must be froze up out there," Ed said in the car.

"She hasn't been down for a month. Wanted me to go back

with her then." Charlie shook his head. "Course I used to stay out there all winter long. Didn't think anything of it. You get a good fire going in the range, you can keep comfortable. And I was out most the day, feeding stock, but I like it down here now. Pam's like I used to be; rather stay up there."

Ed Cheavers drove slowly, as afraid of the ice for his car as for himself. As they came to the Morleys' house on the corner, he said, "May took some chicken broth down yesterday, and Rose took it in and thanked her but acted like she wished she wouldn't come any more. Shut the door as quick as she could."

"Yeah." Charlie gave a barely audible syllable of consent. He shook his head. "Same way when Pam tried to call on her."

"How'd you think she's fixed, Charlie? Wrenn got a big salary, I guess. Lived it up, though, May says."

They were silent, drawing their own conclusions. Charlie studied the house as they passed, remembering when Ned Morley built it. Did it up brown with that rounded window up there and the colored panes. Maybelle wanted a tower or a cupola or something on her house because of that. Maybelle always said Pam loved Wrenn Morley. He didn't think so. Well, Pam had done well enough, made more money than her father ever did; but it was a queer kind of life for a woman . . . lonely. He wished Ruby hadn't pulled up stakes, but he didn't blame her or Hank either. Those dudes were what got Ruby. Got him, too, if he stayed out there too long.

"Thanks, Ed." Charlie took his time getting out of the car, taking hold of the old hitching post so he wouldn't fall on the frozen snow.

"Take care of yourself, now," Ed Cheavers said, thinking Charlie was getting lamer than he used to be.

"Oh, I will. Going to live forever, I guess," Charlie said with a wide grin. He went up the walk to his own door.

April

At the ranch, the air was warm with spring. For a week now it had been thawing. There were places in the river where the free-flowing water ran and ice rafts floated on the sluggish current, piling up there where the river narrowed, like a woman's thoughts, until the moment when their very weight would force a way out.

The bark of the willows was so bright a yellow you could warm yourself at its flame, and the branches of dogwood were red, and the aspens laid crooked purple shadows on the snow in the late afternoon. In the alders, the silly black-and-white chickadees broke the winter silence, darting in and out like notes on a score of music. Blue sky stretched from behind the mountains to the butte and out over the flat snowy fields. The deer tracks engraved in the snow crust were blurring as the snow softened in the sun.

Pamela drove back to town, bareheaded. On the seat beside her were two boxes filled with camp brochures, all addressed to mail. Plenty of time on winter nights up here.

She was like a child today, a child when school is out, or a woman after a long, lonely winter. A small drop of satisfaction rolled about her mind, like a lemon drop in the mouth. She had lived through it, waking in the frightened night to hear a pack rat racing over the roof, or a banshee wind screaming against the base of the hills, or her own stealthy breathing. It had been so cold some nights, in spite of the wood range in the kitchen and the oil heater in the big room, that she had wakened in the morning lame from trying to hold onto some small kernel of warmth.

But in time, the cold was nothing, and the fear of the dark silence was possible to ignore; but there was no protection against her own thoughts. Luke was sometimes her salvation, bringing up the evening milk or the eggs, ice-cold from the henhouse. And she would delay him so he would talk a little while she fixed something hot for him to take down for his supper. Luke cooked his own meals at the bunkhouse.

"Is your radio working, Luke? You must get lonely down there."

"Oh, it ain't bad; one winter in Alaska I never see no one for three months." Then he would go and she would be alone for the evening. Eight-thirty to eleven was worst. After that, with luck, she might get sleepy.

She had time to think about herself until, sometimes, she seemed almost a complete stranger. Pamela Lacey, spinster, in mind and habit and spirit. If she had ever really married, a marriage of the spirit and body and mind, that reached to ecstasy even if it dropped down to anguish . . . Careful! she told herself; after all these years she was back to the old dream. But if she *had*, she would be different now: happier, less lonely . . . but then she thought of Rose.

To stop her thoughts, she made herself a pot of coffee. She had drunk enough coffee this winter to stock a store. There was comfort in holding a hot cup in your hand. It did more than warm the throat and stomach.

And she had smoked enough cigarettes, and never one of them without thinking of Ruby. Ruby would have liked it here this winter; she would have been proud of her for getting the skunk with one shot. But Ruby wouldn't have liked the long days, when she wrote letters from nine in the morning until twelve at night:

"Any serviceable riding clothes will do here; although in the West we usually wear the famous blue denim jeans. . . . We do have hot and cold running water in the bathhouses adjacent to the cabins, and two cabins have their own bathrooms. For these cabins the rate is naturally somewhat higher. The fishing is excellent; the streams are stocked with both rainbow and Eastern brook trout, as well as the native cutthroat. . . ." Over and over again. "Rattlesnakes are sometimes found in the area, but we have never had a case of rattlesnake bite at the ranch in the last fourteen years. . . ."

One day this winter, in the midst of writing dude letters, she had pulled a sheet of paper to her and begun a letter with:

"Dear Rose: I am sorry that you wouldn't come to the door the afternoon I called . . ." But she had crumpled it up and thrown it in the fire. Rose was too proud to let her do anything for her; she could understand that.

She slid a fresh sheet into her typewriter and began again:

"Dear Mrs. Fish: I feel sure you would find that a month at the N Lazy Y would give you one of the most rewarding vacations . . ." But she let the letter lie unfinished in the typewriter and went over to the big window that framed the butte. How was Rose managing? Madame Guinard would be a help, but she was getting old. Rose liked to go places, and she had always wanted people around; now she saw almost no one. "Don't you get lonely out there practically alone all winter? . . . Honestly, I'd think you'd go crazy," Rose had said that time. Did she remember that now? And had she learned by now the desperate little tricks of keeping busy so you didn't go crazy? The winter here at the ranch could never be as lonely as her winter must have been.

But Rose had had Wrenn all these years. She had had so much. Wrenn had loved her. Let her remember that. She had had Wrenn's children. Yet, maybe, Pamela thought slowly, that wouldn't help; maybe it would leave her more helpless to stand the present. Or could she keep the image of Wrenn alive?

She tried it herself, remembering Wrenn in the seventh grade, in high school. . . . It was easier to think of him when he was young. She could see him clearly: walking his bicycle beside her; on that float on Pioneer Day; lying on the bank watching the swallows. She remembered the first time she saw him after she came back home, when he was toastmaster at the Development League celebration. She could see him standing at the table, speaking so quietly after all that terrible oratory. He had said . . . she remembered even now . . . "However the future turns out" . . . oh, my God! Remembering hurt too much.

She had to build up the fire then and turn on the radio and listen to the war news to keep herself from remembering so many things.

She hadn't been lonely all the time, nor sad. There were good days, too. There was one day, in particular, when the world was crystal: so cold and clear and sharp-frozen that each blade of grass, each twig on the stilled aspen trees, each hair on the steers' hides seemed separate and distinct. There was no wind, only sun. She had bundled up in her warmest clothes and slid like a child down the bank to the frozen river that wound ahead, a long smooth snow-covered highway.

It had given her a sense of power to stride up the river, feeling it solid under the snow, knowing that no one else walked the river for miles and miles. She had met a deer around a bend of crystal-spined willow branches, and the deer seemed unafraid of her, not moving until after she had passed. The sky had been empty of flying birds, and the air was completely still.

A sense of exhilaration had possessed her that day. She had realized suddenly that she was happy . . . maybe content was the word . . . but not because of anybody, nor for any reason of herself or because of any happening. She had gone back to the house in a kind of humble amazement. The feeling hadn't lasted, but if she had had it once, it would come again. That was something you might never feel unless you were alone she told herself now as she drove into town.

There were lights in the Morleys' house, downstairs in the parlor. She drove past very slowly. Someone . . . oh, it was that lawyer who had moved into Wrenn's office, Mr. Horning . . . was talking to Rose on the porch.

And there was a light in their house, and Papa sat in the front window looking at the paper.

CHAPTER **11**

As soon as Rose followed Mr. Horning out on the porch to talk, Madame Guinard let her hands lie idle on the hat brim she was sewing. Today, when the phone rang and Rose closed the library door, she had known it was Mr. Horning. Ted Horning, Rose was calling him now.

Rose couldn't stand it without talking to someone, and she had shut herself off from everyone else, all the friends she had had before Wrenn's death, as though she dreaded their sympathy. She seemed almost to hate people because they hadn't suffered what she had. Everyone had tried to do things for her, to invite her out, but Rose refused them so sharply, they were tired of trying now. Maybe it was better she had someone. Madame Guinard's shrewd black eyes were thoughtful.

This Mr. Horning admired Rose, and that was good for her. She was a pretty woman still, or she would be if she took any care of herself. Her eyes were bigger because of the shadows under them, and she was so much thinner. Most of the time she went around in any old dress, and the heavy coil of hair, that still didn't show any gray, slipping down in her neck; but, if Mr. Horning was coming, Rose took pains with herself; and she would light the fire in the gas grate and bring out the decanter from the sideboard. "Will you have some sherry with us, Mama?" Rose would ask. She always went in and had a glass with them to make Mr. Horning seem a friend of the family instead of just Rose's, but it was hard to stomach him; he was so common.

How could Rose look at him after Wrenn? But she knew her Rose, and she knew better than to say anything against him in so many words. He was a bachelor and very pleased both with the clients he had taken over from Wrenn's practice and being the friend of Mrs. Wrenn Morley, who would never have looked at him in her right mind.

From where she sat, she could just see Mr. Horning's head. "Ted wants me to go for a little ride. He thinks it would be good for me," Rose had said, when she came out of the library.

She had made a face. "But won't you be bored with him?"

"Oh, I don't know. He's not so bad," Rose said.

Why didn't they go? They just stood out there talking. No, Rose wasn't going. He was leaving by himself. Madame Guinard picked up the hat in her lap.

Rose was talkative when she came in; some days she hardly

spoke a word. "I saw Pamela Lacey drive by. She must have been able to get down because of the thaw," Rose said.

"Aren't you going for a ride?"

"No," Rose said. "I told Ted I didn't feel like it tonight."

As she sewed the braid, Madame Guinard's mind was busy moving over Rose's words. Had she changed her mind because she saw Pamela Lacey going by? Maybe she didn't want Pamela to know she was going with Mr. Horning. One day, one of the terrible ones between them, when Rose's anger at what had happened to Wrenn drove her to hurt herself, she had said, "I suppose you think that if Pamela had married Wrenn, she would have been heroic when he was killed!" She had ached so for her Rose.

"You do all right, *cherie*," she had said to her. And then she had had to add, "Wrenn loved you, not Pamela, remember." Rose had come over and kissed her and knelt suddenly on the floor with her head in her lap, sobbing like a child. Yes, undoubtedly, Rose had not gone tonight because of Pamela, and that was good. At least Rose cared what Pamela Lacey thought of her, if she didn't anyone else.

If Rose would only let Pamela come down here, she would be so good for her. Pamela had tried; and she had sent a basket of fruit at Christmas and some wine. Rose had barely touched them, and she had asked her to write a note to thank her. But, of course, Christmas had been a terrible time for Rose. Stephen hadn't been able to come, and she and Rose had been here alone.

She worried about what would happen to Rose when she was gone. In her loneliness, or because she couldn't manage on the little money Wrenn had left, she might turn more and more to Mr. Horning, or someone like him. The millinery business here at home wasn't going to work. Rose would have to get something downtown to do, and it wouldn't be so easy for Rose at her age. Madame Guinard sighed. Being shut up in the house all day worrying about Rose, got on her nerves, too. "I think I'll just step outside on the porch for a bit and get a breath of air," Madame Guinard said.

[376]

The air was fresh, but winter wasn't gone, not yet. She pulled the collar of her coat closer around her throat and took little steps across the porch and back. She could see the Laceys' house from here. If she could just get down there while Pamela was home and tell her how worried she was about Rose, maybe Pamela could help some way. "Rose will try to push you off at first, but don't let her," she would tell Pamela. Yet why should she bother Pam about her? Rose had taken Wrenn away from her. She had even been proud that Rose could. . . . God forgive her! Anything Rose could get away from these well-to-do pioneer families she had thought was all right; they had seemed so sure of themselves and so superior when she first came here. She saw enough of them in the shop. No, there was no reason why Pam should go out of her way to help Rose, except that they had been friends when they were girls . . . and who else could help her? Maybe only Time could help, but Time took too long. It worried her to see Rose drinking, not just a glass of wine with her; she smelled the whisky on her breath some mornings. There was Charlie Lacey coming down the block, out for his constitutional.

"Good evening, Mr. Lacey." Madame Guinard was glad to see him. "Not much like spring, is it?" She leaned over the balustrade so he could hear her.

He took off his hat and stood there in the cold air . . . at his age! "You can't trust April in Montana!" He said it as though it were something to be proud of.

"I see that Pamela is home."

"Yes. She surprised me. It's good to see her." He was going on, and she wanted to ask him to ask Pamela . . .

"Tell Pamela, Mr. Lacey, that . . . that I've got a hat I think she might like to wear east. Maybe she could drop up and see it. . . ." Talking so loud made her breathless.

"I'll do that, Madame Guinard." Charlie nodded. "Well, this is about as far as I want to walk tonight." He started slowly back down the block.

She didn't have a hat, not a one that Pamela would like or

that she would sell her, but maybe she would come to see . . . maybe not.

When Madame Guinard went back in, Rose was sitting under the light at the table. "You sewed this braid on crooked!" she said without looking up. The stitches came away with quick, angry sounds as she ripped. Madame Guinard watched her a minute. She couldn't reach Rose or help her, even with the hats, any more.

CHAPTER 12

Charlie Lacey came back and told Pamela what Madame Guinard had said, but she was busy at the desk, working on her dude business, and didn't seem much interested. He sat down and picked up the newspaper that he had finished before dinner and studied it for some time. Then without looking up from the page he said, "As long as Madame Guinard gives you an excuse, you better go down and see her hats."

Pamela went on writing checks. "I've tried before. Rose simply doesn't want me to come. I'm sorry for her, but I'm not going to have her practically shut the door in my face again."

"Maybe she won't this time." Charlie laid down his newspaper. "She don't hardly know what she's doing. Ruby was a little that way after Slim died. Bit my head off every time I spoke to her for a couple of weeks there. It isn't easy, Pam, when you've lived with someone half your life."

"Rose and I haven't anything in common any more, except that we've known each other so long." Pamela folded a check and slipped it into an envelope.

"That counts for something. And Wrenn meant a lot to you. He'd count on you to do all you could to help her."

She didn't answer.

"It's going to get warm pretty soon, Pam. I was thinking you might ask Rose out to the ranch. It would be a change anyway. In the spring, I always want to get out there, myself."

"Oh, Papa, Rose never cared anything about the ranch! She and Wrenn could have come out when Stephen was working there, but they never did. She wouldn't go if I asked her, which I certainly don't intend to do."

Charlie was slow in answering. "Well now, maybe she would, Pam. It would depend on . . ."

"On what?" Her voice was a little sharp.

"On how you asked her. If you told her it'd be doing you a big favor, that you get so lonely off up there . . ."

"I don't though," Pamela said quickly. "I've made a good life for myself."

"Well then, you don't. I thought without Ruby you might."

"As far as that goes, Papa, I was alone most of the time when Ruby was there; except for meals and late at night. Ruby was busy with her job and I was busy with the correspondence and ranch business." It still bothered her to talk about Ruby.

Charlie took his time lighting a cigar. "Maybe you could find a job for Rose at the ranch."

"I don't see how I could," she said. Why would Papa suggest such a thing? The ranch meant more to her than it would to most people. She had had to make it take the place of other things. She had built it up by herself, and paid off the mortgages. It took dudes to do it, but two days after the season was over and the dude cabins closed, the place was hers again. Rose had that horrid way of taking everything she had anything to do with for her own, like the way she took her horse that time. Rose would say "my cabin" and take even the view from her cabin for her property after she had been there a day. Rose was the last person she would think of asking out to the ranch.

"Well, it's just an idea I had. You do what you think best. I guess I'll go on to bed," Charlie said.

✦

Pamela never slept well for the first week after she came in from the ranch. The quiet was too thin. She missed the night sounds of the ranch that gave the stillness a greater depth. And there was too much light in the room here, even with the shades drawn. Tonight, she lay wide awake thinking about Rose. Papa was so old he was softhearted. He wanted to fix everything up for everyone.

Of course, Rose probably would get along with the dudes. When she ran the Red Cross she seemed to get along pretty well with people. And she would love planning things for the evenings, getting someone to sing and someone to play cards . . . "I wondered why you don't have planned entertainment in the evening," Fitz had asked her. "The ranch where I went last summer had movies three times a week."

"People are usually so tired after riding and hiking and helping with the cattle they just want to sit by the fire or go to bed," she had told her. But more and more she had dudes who didn't do much but sit on the porch and wait to be entertained. They used to drive Ruby wild. "Why in hell don't they go to a hotel, then?" Ruby had asked. Rose wouldn't mind people like that.

Perhaps in the summer she could give her a job; try her out anyway, but it would have to be a strictly business proposition. Papa could suggest to Rose that she might ask about a job; she wouldn't offer one to her and then beg her to take it and be turned down flat.

She had long ago given up any resentment against Rose, but that didn't mean that now she cared for her. They were too many worlds apart. They had practically nothing in common, as she told Papa, except living all these years in this town, being aware of each other all that time. But that didn't mean a thing.

Charlie went downtown the next morning and stayed all day, so Pamela had nothing but her own thoughts for company until Mrs. Cheavers came over.

"It's pitiful to see Rose Morley. She used to be such a handsome woman, and now she looks so down at the heel. Mrs.

Marsten said she acted downright queer to her." Mrs. Cheavers leaned closer to Pamela and said in a hushed voice, "I guess she's drinking!"

For no reason at all, Pamela felt protective about Rose. "I should think she might," she heard herself saying. What an old gossip Mrs. Cheavers was, and Mrs. Marsten. No wonder Rose shut herself away.

It was late in the afternoon before Pamela walked down the street to the Morleys' house. She walked so slowly that she had time to look up at the turret window and remember Wrenn's mother waving to them there, with the red and blue panes of glass coloring her shirtwaist. And as she went up the steps to the porch she remembered Wrenn calling into the house that time, "Rose, here's Pam."

She hoped Madame Guinard would come to the door, but Rose opened it. Her surprise at seeing Pamela hardly showed in her closed face. Her eyes brushed quickly across Pamela's face and came to rest somewhere over her shoulder. Now that she was older she was beginning to look more like her mother, except that her eyes were not bright and curious like Madame Guinard's, and her face was somehow dulled, like that time she was sick with the flu.

"Hello, Rose." Pamela made her tone light and casual as though she ran in like this every day.

"Hello, Pamela." There was no invitation nor interest in the tone of Rose's voice, and she made no move to open the door wider.

"I . . . may I come in a minute?"

Rose seemed to hesitate, then she stepped back so Pamela could enter.

"Madame Guinard told Papa that she had a hat she thought I might like," Pamela said. She knew now, before Rose spoke, that Madame Guinard had only said that to bring her here.

"Mama's crazy; we haven't anything that you would like. We hardly have any hats at all." Rose didn't offer to take Pamela into the library where the wooden hat block stood and a few

[381]

hats lay on the table and bookcase. While she was speaking her eyes seemed to be on some point behind Pamela's head, now they came back to her face, but only briefly. One hand fingered the neck of her dress.

Pamela said quickly, "Oh, well, it doesn't really matter. I won't need a new hat until I go east next month. How is Madame Guinard?"

"She's not well. Mrs. Cheavers took her downtown this afternoon. I thought she must have forgotten her key when I heard the doorbell." Her manner said, "Or I wouldn't have answered it." She moved slightly toward the door.

The silence pushed against Pamela. It had been a mistake to come, just as she had known it would be. Rose didn't want her here. She resented her coming. Pamela turned to go and then she saw them both reflected in the hall mirror: two middle-aged women standing awkwardly there, not saying anything to each other, not able to.

How had they come to this place? She looked away quickly and moved toward the door that Rose was already opening, wanting her to go. But she couldn't just walk away and leave Rose like this. Rose's life was too mixed up with hers.

She glanced at Rose's face, closed tight over any feeling. She had never meant to admit it to anyone, least of all to Rose, but now she wanted to tell her.

"Rose," she said quietly, "I've been very lonely out at the ranch this winter . . ."

Rose turned toward her and there was no dullness in her face. It wasn't so difficult to go on from there.